The Wedding Shawl

The Wedding Shawl

A SEASIDE KNITTERS MYSTERY

Sally Goldenbaum

AN OBSIDIAN MYSTERY

OBSIDIAN
Published by New American Library,
a division of Penguin Group (USA) Inc.,
375 Hudson Street, New York, New York 10014, USA
Penguin Group (Canada), 90 Eglinton Avenue East, Suite 700, Toronto,
Ontario M4P 2Y3, Canada (a division of Pearson Penguin Canada Inc.)
Penguin Books Ltd., 80 Strand, London WC2R 0RL, England
Penguin Ireland, 25 St. Stephen's Green, Dublin 2,
Ireland (a division of Penguin Books Ltd.)
Penguin Group (Australia), 250 Camberwell Road, Camberwell,
Victoria 3124, Australia (a division of Pearson Australia Group Pty. Ltd.)
Penguin Books India Pvt. Ltd., 11 Community Centre,
Panchsheel Park, New Delhi - 110 017, India
Penguin Group (NZ), 67 Apollo Drive, Rosedale, North Shore 0632,
New Zealand (a division of Pearson New Zealand Ltd.)
Penguin Books (South Africa) (Pty.) Ltd., 24 Sturdee Avenue,
Rosebank, Johannesburg 2196, South Africa

Penguin Books Ltd., Registered Offices:
80 Strand, London WC2R 0RL, England

First published by Obsidian, an imprint of New American Library,
a division of Penguin Group (USA) Inc.

First Printing, May 2011
1   3   5   7   9   10   8   6   4   2

LIBRARY OF CONGRESS CATALOGING-IN-PUBLICATION DATA:

Goldenbaum, Sally.
The wedding shawl/Sally Goldenbaum.
p. cm.—(A seaside knitters mystery)
"An Obsidian mystery."
ISBN 978-0-451-23319-6
1. Knitters (Persons)—Fiction. I. Title.
PS3557.O35937W43 2011
813'. 54—dc22   2010053462

Set in Palatino   •   Designed by Elke Sigal

Printed in the United States of America

In memory of

Polly Egan Arango

Acknowledgments

Once again, enormous and heartfelt thanks to my Kansas City friends and family, who have supported book signings, provided moral support, and tolerated my deadlines with such good humor.

To Bethany Kok, the very talented designer of the shawl that inspired Izzy's wedding shawl—and who generously gave permission for its reprint.

To Mary Bednarowski—for support and friendship, without which this book, in this year, might not have been finished.

To Joey Ciaramitaro and his Good Morning Gloucester blog, Amy Pierson of the Toad Hall Bookstore in Rockport, Massachusetts, and the staff of I Love a Mystery in Kansas City—for their wonderful support.

To the savvy Gloucester moms—Aria, Muffy, Jenn, Kate, Sarah, and Lucy—who have generously offered support and ideas (and celebrations!).

To Cecelia and Doug McNair for turnkey Gloucester research tips.

To Mary Jane Van de Castle and the Bijin Salon & Spa team for giving me a behind-the-scenes look at the workings of a successful salon and the intricacies of turning hair pink.

And to Aria and John McElhenny, whose own wedding inspired Izzy's garden ceremony.

The Wedding Shawl

Chapter 1

It would be a night of murder, they'd been told. And there'd be lemon squares, too.

The group, mostly women, gathered in a half circle, some in the old leather chairs that book browsers coveted and others in the folding chairs the bookstore owner, Archie Brandley, had set up for the special event. At the other end of the cozy loft, narrow aisles separated wooden bookcases that rose nearly to the ceiling. One section was crammed with mysteries, the spines straight and proud—a perfect background for the night of crime.

Danny Brandley sat in the center of the open area, hunched forward with his elbows on his knees, his sea blue eyes greeting acquaintances and strangers as they claimed their chairs. A wrinkled denim shirt, the sleeves rolled up to his elbows, showed off an early-summer tan. On the floor, near scuffed boat shoes, a few notes on scattered yellow sheets indicated that Danny wasn't much for formal talks. Izzy had called it a "discussion," and he'd taken his friend at her word.

The loft in Archie and Harriet Brandley's bookstore was packed with a larger-than-usual group. People chatted familiarly, helping themselves to iced tea or wine, and cookies or smooth, luscious lemon bars from a large red platter. They shuffled chairs and pulled needles and yarn from fat cloth bags.

Henrietta O'Neal, balancing her squat body with one hand wrapped around a cane, told Danny that she'd read every mystery known to man and she was ready for a new author. "And that would be you," she said, her blue eyes twinkling. "It's nice to have a home-grown boy who understands the fine art of murder."

Her full-blown laugh caused Nell Endicott to look up from a second-row seat and laugh along with her. Sea Harbor's self-proclaimed eighty-plus-year-old suffragette was in fine form.

"It looks like the whole town is here," Nell said to Cass Halloran. She waved to M. J. Arcado, owner of M.J.'s Hair Salon, who was finding a seat on the opposite side of the half circle. Several of her young stylists were with her. "It must be Danny's mystery-author mystique."

"Not to mention his sex appeal," Cass whispered back.

"Well, that, too. Izzy was smart to invite him."

The knitting book club was a product of Izzy's customers' demands. It'd be perfect, they'd assured the store owner, and with Sea Harbor Bookstore just a narrow alley away from Izzy's yarn shop, it made even more sense. Knitting, lemon bars, and mysteries. Heaven didn't get much better.

So Izzy agreed and the idea became a reality that filled Archie's loft every third Tuesday. Tonight was Danny's night. Instead of discussing a mystery novel, the group had invited a writer of one—himself a knitter, which only increased his attraction—to discuss the mystery-writing process.

"Be sure to talk about where you get your ideas," Izzy had directed. "Everyone always wants to know that."

Danny complied. When everyone quieted down, he started right in.

"People watching," he said. "You know, like Mary Pisano does—sitting out there on Coffee's patio every day watching the world go by." He doffed an imaginary hat to Mary, the newspaper's "About Town" columnist, and the group laughed, knowing that plenty of Mary's chatty columns did, indeed, come from watching customers go in and out of the coffee shop—not to mention conversations overheard at the bed-and-breakfast she owned over on Ravenswood Road.

"When you're a fiction writer, eavesdropping becomes research," he said, and another chuckle rippled around the half circle.

"So ideas come from life, I guess you would say. Life fuels the imagination, and next thing you know, a story unfolds."

He took a drink from a water bottle and then went on. "For mystery writers, a good source of ideas can come from reading up on cold cases, like on the TV show." He looked around at the half-moon of expectant faces. "An example? Okay, here's what I mean. . . ."

Then the writer dropped his voice ominously and continued as if telling a ghost story.

Knitting needles paused in midair while people scooched forward on their chairs to listen.

"Here's a cold case some of you may remember. It happened some fifteen years ago, right here on Cape Ann, at a quarry. It was the night of high school graduation, and teenagers were out celebrating, as kids do. But before the night was over, a tragedy occurred that changed lives forever and tore families apart."

Brows lifted and silence as thick as harbor fog fell across the room.

"It had been one of those perfect Sea Harbor days, people said. A golden day with the hot sun refreshed by salty breezes. That night, a full moon reflected off the springwater that filled the old Markham Quarry. Its reflection was so precise and perfect that a person standing on the edge of the quarry couldn't be sure which was real—the moon above or the perfect white circle in the still water below."

"The Markham Quarry," Laura Danvers said softly, her brows pulling together as if remembering something. Nearby, Cass Halloran nodded, too, as if they both knew where Danny was headed.

"That much we know for sure. And we also know that on that night, Harmony Farrow, who had just graduated from Sea Harbor High—with honors, they say—went out to the quarry in her mother's car. And sometime that evening, we don't know exactly when, Harmony's young body was swallowed up by the deep quarry water. It brought an end to a life that was just beginning."

A sigh escaped Laura's lips. "I remember her. We just didn't notice her; you know how that is? I didn't talk to her much. Not in four years of high school . . ." Her voice dropped off.

A hand flapped in the air, waving away Laura's sad confession. Beatrice Scaglia, a city councilwoman, spoke up. "I remember it well. It frightened parents half to death that such a thing could happen right here on Cape Ann. A few days after the girl disappeared, a hiker—my neighbor's cousin—spotted a lacy shawl stuck on a conifer growing out of the quarry's wall. It was a privately owned quarry back then—trespassers were not treated kindly—but sometimes some brave soul wandered in."

Danny nodded. "So they brought in divers. And hours later they pulled her body out of its watery grave. It had been caught beneath the surface, tangled in a tough vine. Trapped."

Archie Brandley, who was Danny's father, had come up the stairs and sidled up to the group. A scattering of customers, lured by the story and the tangible excitement spreading through the room, left the book aisles in the back of the loft and filled in beside him.

Archie nodded his head gravely and spoke. "The girl's folks lived over near the highway, just on the edge of town. The girl had gotten a scholarship—people said she held lots of promise. An awful thing."

Harmony hadn't been alone on the quarry's edge, Danny told the group. But no one came forward with more information. None of her friends. Nobody. As silent as clams. She just disappeared into the night air and the quarry water.

A few days later the autopsy revealed that the death was suspicious. There wasn't much, but she had bruises on her fingers and arms, as if she'd tried to grab on to someone or something before losing her grip. But although they were sure from the muddied footprints that she hadn't been alone—and the man who lived across the road had heard two voices going down the path—there wasn't any real proof that someone had pushed her.

"No one was ever arrested," added Esther Gibson, Sea Harbor's longtime police dispatcher. "The poor family received no closure. The parents split up, as often happens. Moved away."

"And the tragedy was shelved as a cold case," Danny concluded.

Some of the older knitters who followed such things remembered that other teens were mentioned as people of interest.

"I remember now," Margaret Garozzo, the deli owner's wife, said, searching back through the years. "The whole affair was hard on families."

Archie nodded. "They were good kids, the whole bunch of them. It was a shame, a real shame when they had to be questioning innocent kids and messing with their families like that."

"But they were only doing their job, Archie," Beatrice Scaglia, stepping into her city-councilwoman mode, reminded him. "That's why we have a police force. That's why we pay taxes."

Nell hadn't remembered any of that. Weekenders—which was what she and Ben were back then—weren't privy to such gossip. But she knew, as Archie stated, that families could be torn apart by tragedy. What an awful ordeal it must have been—for Harmony's parents, especially, but also for her friends. And even for kids in the school who weren't her friends, such as Laura, who knew of Harmony but didn't really know her at all.

"Harmony was pretty," Merry Jackson said. The co-owner of the Artist's Palate Bar & Grill tugged on a strand of platinum hair that had escaped her ponytail. "I was in that class, too. She was really smart. I think she played on our basketball team at the community center. That and studying seemed to be all she did. We didn't know much about her . . . not until after. And then people remembered all sorts of things, and who knew if they were true or not."

Her voice fell off as if the conversation was getting too personal, too close to home.

There was a shifting of bodies on chairs, and shoulders rose and fell with a certain uncomfortableness. It was one thing to talk about a cold case, but bringing up people who might be very much alive was another matter.

Esther Gibson sat straight up in her chair and said with her usual frankness, "As the police report clearly stated, no one they questioned was guilty of anything. The rumors put one of the families through a terrible time, as rumors often do." The older woman's voice was unusually stern. She picked up her fat knitting needles and resumed work on a pale peach throw, as soft as a feather and perfect for a cool night sitting on the deck. *Enough talk about our neighbors, our friends,* her silence said.

Nell looked over at Izzy, who had also sensed the tension in the room.

The yarn shop owner stood up now, her voice traveling over the tops of heads to Danny. "Okay, Danny, so when you're coming up with ideas, how does a cold case really help?"

"I was wondering the same thing," Merry Jackson said, her silky ponytail moving between shapely bare shoulders. "You don't want to write about real people, so what's next? You take a case like that and then you make up what *could* have happened?"

Danny nodded. "Something like that. Cold cases can provide springboards. You keep some facts if you want, triangulate them. Anything goes. You end up not writing about the actual people or event, like you said, Merry, but instead what your imagination has done with it. It's fiction."

Nell half listened as the group pitched in with dozens of different roads the story line could travel, taking it from the neighborhood tragedy to one that could have happened anywhere, and involved a cast of characters pulled from imaginations that ran wild.

But Nell's imagination was tied to the piece of land that she loved—Cape Ann—and her mind toyed with the tragedy of the young girl who had died that night. It wasn't fiction for her family— but a horrible happening that must have changed their lives forever. She could only begin to imagine their pain.

Nell looked over at her niece. Izzy was nearly as close to Nell as any daughter could be. Nell loved her fiercely and could only imagine the pain that Harmony's parents must have experienced.

She pulled a ball of bright green cotton from her bag and pushed aside the disturbing thoughts. One more sleeve to the cropped sweater she was making for her sister Caroline's birthday and she'd be done.

Hopefully in time for the wedding.

Izzy's wedding.

Izzy and Sam's wedding.

Tiny goose bumps rose on Nell's arms, and she rubbed them briskly, her heart expanding as it did so easily these days. A smile lifted her lips and her eyes grew moist. Ben teased her about wearing her emotions on her sleeve. But he felt it, too. It was a special time in Izzy's life, the beginning of a new chapter, and the joy that surrounded it was almost palpable—and certainly better to think about than cold cases.

"Daydreaming?" Birdie Favazza looked at Nell. A web of tiny lines fanned out from the octogenarian's bright eyes and framed her small face. "I know that look, Nell dear. You're thinking of lives beginning, new chapters. Not ending. I'm with you, dear friend." She patted Nell on the arm. "We'd be much better off talking about weddings than cold cases."

Nell pulled her attention back to the animated conversation Merry Jackson had instigated with the group. Of course Birdie knew what she was thinking. Years of friendship allowed certain privileges, like crawling into one another's thoughts without an invitation.

"So, okay, we have someone at a quarry," Merry was saying. "Maybe meeting a lover, maybe, or let's say she was blackmailing someone and was meeting him that night for money. She needed money for college? Or maybe it was a guy out there instead."

Merry's ideas were pounced on by others as the quarry quickly turned into a wealthy industrialist's swimming pool on a dark and stormy night and a band of unruly teens crawled over fences to skinny-dip in a stranger's pool. Intrigue. Murder.

Danny sat back and smiled at imaginations that had run rampant.

By the time he had reined them back in, the crime was outlined in a dozen different ways, and Danny had made his point.

Real life can lead to fascinating fiction.

Chapter 2

It was an hour later, longer than the normal meeting time, when Danny finally wound up the discussion to a round of robust applause.

After Izzy reminded the group of the next book club meeting, people began to disperse, some heading back to the aisle with the MYSTERY sign posted on the end, and others making their way downstairs. Animated talk about the extravagant plot they'd fabricated filled the air.

"Interesting discussion, Danny," Izzy said, collapsing chairs as the group thinned out. "Thanks."

"It was fun. Maybe I should have dug up an older case, but it sure stimulated talk. I could build ten new plots from all those ideas."

Cass handed Danny a chocolate chip cookie. "Why'd you pick that case?"

Danny shrugged. "No real reason. It's interesting, that's all, and I remembered it without having to do much research. I was in grad school when that happened, but I remember Mom and Dad talking about it when I came home that summer."

"It was the talk of the town for a while," Cass said. "I was away at college, but I lifeguarded at the yacht club over the summer. The high school kids were all into it. The girl was quiet, like they said, and not many people seemed to know her—but that didn't stop the gossip. But then summer settled in. People moved on."

"I brought it up in a J-school class once. Investigative reporting, I think it was. Those kinds of cases grab the attention of would-be reporters. They always think they could have solved it, given a chance."

Esther Gibson was sitting in the back row, packing up her knitting bag, watching them. She caught the end of the conversation and grabbed her cane, pulling herself up off the chair. She picked up her bag and walked over, imposing herself firmly into the group. Her eyes locked onto Danny's, her gaze steady and compelling. "Well, the investigative reporters didn't solve the case, now, did they?" she said. "So it's over. Finished." Her white brows were pulled together, and her usual smile had disappeared.

Esther continued to look at Danny, letting her words settle in. Then without another word she turned and headed slowly to the stairs, one hand reaching out for the railing to balance herself. She hesitated there, as if she couldn't remember what to do next. Then she looked back and focused again on the group. Her look was stern.

"Sometimes it's best to let the dead stay buried, let the living live in peace," she said. Her tone was measured and louder than usual.

A few lingering knitters, getting ready to leave, stopped chatting. People standing in the narrow aisles, leafing through books, paused. They all looked in Esther's direction, surprised by the weight of her words.

"Forget about cold cases," she said finally. "Leave it alone, for goodness' sake."

Before anyone could reply, Esther turned again and, with an agility that defied her bad back, made her way down the bookstore steps.

Archie Brandley's eyebrows lifted as he looked after the disappearing police dispatcher. "Esther likes to have the last say, now, doesn't she? Seems we hit a sore spot."

A flash of memory pulled Birdie's brows together. "Of course—that's why she's upset," she murmured. Then she looked at the others and said simply, "Esther was a close friend of one of the families questioned in the case. She's just protecting her flock. It's what Esther does."

Birdie's words, said with comforting calmness, seemed to set people in motion once again. Sandals flopped down the wooden steps, and from below, the tinkling of the bell above the bookstore door rang cheerfully as people left.

Archie dismissed Izzy from folding the chairs—leave it to the cleaning crew, he said—and reminded them that his wife, Harriet, was downstairs at the cash register, only too happy to help anyone with a book purchase.

Nell held up several books she had pulled from the shelves—a book on sailing for Ben, another garden book. Archie nodded his approval.

Gradually the remaining book club members disappeared down the stairs and into the night. Archie straightened a stack of magazines on a table at the top of the stairs, scanned the loft area a final time, and then followed Nell and Birdie down the stairs.

Quiet filled the loft as Archie's heavy footsteps faded away.

It was then, when the only sound in the room was the steady ticktock of the old grandfather clock near the stairs, that the attractive middle-aged woman emerged from the shadows. She was oblivious of the book she held in her hand, unaware of the cheery good-byes coming from the floor beneath. For a moment she stood at the window, staring down at the night shadows falling across Harbor Road. But she wasn't seeing anything, not the gaslights or the laughing couples strolling along in the cool evening air. For a minute, all she saw was darkness.

She pressed one hand against her chest, calming a heart squeezed tightly in a body that suddenly seemed too small to hold it.

She hadn't intended to listen to the group's discussion. She'd come only to find a new book or two, something to pass the pleasant summer evenings in the makeshift apartment she was occupying. She'd been surprised when people began climbing the stairs with knitting bags in tow, and then had remembered the sign below. A KNITTING BOOK CLUB, she remembered reading.

Earlier, she had smiled at one or two people, strangers to her, before she'd wandered down the narrow book aisle, reading the spines studiously, straightening a book here and there, pulling two or three from the shelves and tucking them under her arm.

In the background, she'd heard the shuffling of chairs, people greeting one another, the clink of glasses and buzz of light conversation.

She'd leave shortly, before they began their meeting.

But in the next minute, before she could gather her things and leave the loft, the group had quieted down. A woman had begun speaking, welcoming people and mentioning cookies, lemon bars, and drinks on the table.

And then the deep timbre of a man's voice had taken over. Pleasant and friendly.

She had looked around for a back exit. But the only way out was to walk in front of the attentive group, disturbing the discussion flow. And drawing attention to herself, something she didn't do readily.

So she'd stayed hidden in the shadows, settling down on a wooden chair at the end of the aisle, a pile of books on her lap. She began leafing through pages, checking back covers. She had nowhere to be, and it was comfortable and cool here with a large ceiling fan purring above. The voices in the distance were comfortable, too, and she half listened, half read.

She thought she had recognized a few faces earlier that were once a remote backdrop in her life. Margaret, the deli owner's wife. Esther Gibson. Nice people, she remembered.

Perhaps she'd made a good decision after all. She smiled into the musty-smelling air of old books and began to relax.

Relaxed.

Until the sounds that provided the pleasant background hum suddenly turned into real words—the way a baby's cry became urgent when it was *your* baby—one that would register with startling, heart-jogging clarity.

The Markham Quarry, someone said.

The chill that traveled through her body nearly stopped her heart.

It happened around here. Fifteen years ago.

A familiar anguish rose inside her. The rope tightening around her chest, the difficulty breathing. The desire to flee.

But she couldn't flee, not without running across a stage. So she stayed there in the hard wooden chair, frozen in place, until the eternal discussion ended, and finally, the last footsteps faded away.

Slowly the blood came back into her face and her mind began to clear.

Air. The night air would help. She walked slowly down the staircase, one hand gripping the polished railing.

On the first floor, Archie was lowering the blinds on the front door. Birdie Favazza stood at the checkout counter, listening patiently to Harriet Brandley's review of Lily King's new book, which she was attempting to purchase. Birdie saw a pretty woman walk down the stairs and absently looked over, smiled, then forced her attention back to Harriet's comments.

The woman looked down and saw that she still clutched a book in her hand.

She quickly set it down on a table near the window, then straightened up and took a deep breath, forcing composure into her body.

Pushing a smile to her lips, she walked toward the door, nodding to Archie as she approached him.

Archie looked up, surprised. Where had the woman come from? He thought the loft was empty. He could have locked her in. But he pushed away his surprise and offered a smile instead.

But his smile went unnoticed as the woman, her head down again, hurried past him and through the open door. He looked out, but she was swallowed up by the night.

"Birdie, you know that lady?" Archie asked. His wide forehead wrinkled in a deep frown.

Birdie handed Harriet her credit card and looked up. "I don't believe so, Archie."

"She was upstairs, at the book meeting. Least that's where she came from, though I didn't see her up there. Damndest thing—I might have locked her in."

"She's probably vacationing up here. I hope she enjoyed the discussion. Your Danny did a fine job."

"Sure he did. But you wouldn't know it from the look on that woman's face. Pale as a sheet, as if she'd seen a ghost."

Chapter 3

$\mathcal{N}$ell had asked them to come early Wednesday morning, while Izzy had a few hours off from the yarn shop and before Cass left to check her lobster traps or Birdie went off to the retirement home to teach her tap-dancing class.

Before the day got away from all of them.

She wanted their input on the backyard before she made any more decisions. It was looking perfect in her mind, but she wasn't the one getting married, after all.

Birdie arrived first, carrying a white box of beignets. She walked onto the Endicott deck, set the pastries on the table, and joined Nell at the railing, her eyes scanning the yard.

"I think you missed your calling," she said finally. "I've always loved this yard, even when your in-laws only used this place as a summer home. It welcomed people, whether it was for one of the senior Endicotts' parties, or simply for kids to cut through on their way to the beach. It was everyone's backyard. But this, what you've done, Nell—well, this is fit for a bride."

Nell smiled, clearly pleased, and rested her hand on her friend's smaller one.

Birdie's eyes, still clear and bright after eighty or so years of good living, followed the curve of the old flagstone path as it wound its way back, past the small guest cottage, then around a granite boulder left stranded by the last ice age. The whole yard, shaded by pines and old oak trees, sloped down toward the woods and the sea beyond.

But it looked different today, and that was what Nell wanted them to see. The flagstone path had been given new life—the cracks filled in and patches of crabgrass tugged out. And the towering trees were shorn of branches broken by nor'easters. Nestled into shaded plots were flowering hydrangeas and red twig dogwoods, the carefully mulched areas around them dark and damp.

Nell smiled. "It's beautiful, isn't it? Still casual—like Izzy and Sam—but lush and lovely. I find myself wandering down the path, smelling the pines. Being happy."

Birdie nodded. "Full of life. It's a perfect spot in which to get married."

"Who's getting married?" Izzy breezed through the deck door and across to the two women. She hugged them both, then stood between them, her hands flat on the deck railing. "Oh, my," she said, her voice hushed. "Oh, Aunt Nell . . ."

"What do you think?" Nell said.

"I think it's just perfect," she whispered.

Nell and Birdie both smiled at the catch in Izzy's voice. Her emotions lived right on the surface these days. Once she and Sam had finally opened up to each other and made a commitment, something had shifted inside Izzy, obvious to all those around her. The guarded look she'd held in place through adolescence, college, and a brief law career evaporated, and Izzy gave full rein to her happiness. She wore it on her sleeve for the world to see. It wasn't getting married that made the difference, she had told Nell. It was simply Sam. Sam and her. Suddenly, her world was different. *She* was different, essentially, deep down inside herself. She'd loved before, and been loved before, but not like this. Never like this.

Nell understood. She had felt the same way when she and Ben had decided to spend the rest of their lives together. She'd never been able to put it into words, but now she saw it written across her niece's radiant face, and words didn't seem necessary.

Nell pointed to a spot near the woods where thick, gnarled vines of an old grape arbor harbored a bench in a small clearing. "Claire suggested weaving some flowers into that old arbor. And big pots of yellow hydrangeas on the deck."

The banging of the deck door announced Cass' arrival. A few long strides and she stood next to Birdie. A lineup of women gazing out at the yard.

"I think you're damn good at this gardening stuff, Nell. It's great."

Nell laughed. "I just take orders from my gardener."

"Gardener? Sounds uptown."

"I told you about her. Claire Russell, the amazing woman I met at the nursery and stole right from under poor Fred Euclid's nose." Nell's head went back and she laughed as she remembered the surprised look, then the sweet acquiescence as the nursery owner agreed to her request to borrow Claire, but only if it was part-time and only if she'd give him her mother's bouillabaisse recipe. "In two weeks she's done all this. And we're not finished yet. She can talk a plant back to life faster than Cass can catch a lobster."

"Do I know this wonder woman?" Cass lifted her Sox cap, shoved a handful of black hair through the band, and pushed it back on her head.

"I don't know if you've met. She's been working at the nursery since spring. And you don't exactly hang around green plants, Cass. Your paths might not have crossed."

"The name isn't familiar to me, either," Birdie added.

"Then she's not real," Izzy said. "Birdie knows everyone."

"Maybe she's a garden elf," Cass offered. "No one can see her but Nell. Kind of like those elves that old shoemaker had. I always hoped they'd come out at night and clean my messy room when I was a kid."

"Well, whoever she is, I love her," Izzy said, her eyes misting over again. "And I love your backyard. And I—"

"Need a doughnut," Cass finished. "This love stuff is getting to me."

Izzy picked up the box of pastries before Cass got to them. "The lady doth protest too much."

Cass grabbed the box back and teased back at her friend. "None of these for you, bride. Aren't you supposed to be watching your weight? That's what I see on TV. Brides are cranky, nervous, demanding—and skinny."

"Not our Izzy," Birdie said, settling the argument by taking the box herself and placing it back on the table. She opened it and took out the powdery beignets, placing them on a platter while Nell poured mugs of coffee. "The thought of Izzy dieting is ludicrous. She'll be as willowy as sea grass, just like always. But she'll never stop eating."

"True," Cass said. "Sam claims you eat more than he does, Iz."

The others laughed but didn't dispute it. Izzy Chambers loved to eat—and it would take more than a wedding to disrupt her appetite. She was sometimes cranky—Nell would give her that—like when a shipment of new needles was lost in transit or a nor'easter knocked out her electricity in the shop. But the wedding planning wouldn't make her cranky. All that mattered was that Sam was there at the end of the day.

"Speaking of demanding," Izzy said, looking over at Nell, "I talked to M.J. at her salon about hair appointments for the wedding."

"Hair?" Cass wrinkled her forehead.

"For my mom. And some relatives. You can wear yours in that dirty Sox cap if you want. But that won't work for some of the Chambers clan."

"Nor me," Birdie piped up, patting her short crop of white hair. Her eyes sparkled. "I'd like to look my finest on Izzy's special day. Count me in for a fix."

"M.J. now has a wedding coordinator—Tiffany Ciccolo, that tall, quiet girl who used to work the desk. She even has her own office, M.J. says. She'll do all the arranging and make sure it's all perfect.

She suggested we go by later today to talk to her. Does that work for you, Aunt Nell?"

Before Nell could respond, the sound of squeaky wagon wheels coming around the side of the house diverted her attention. Nell swallowed a bite of beignet and grinned. "My gardening goddess is here." She wiped off her hands and waved as a woman in a bright green tank top came into view. A blue sweater was tied around her shoulders. "You see, you naysayers? She's as real as I am."

The gardener waved back, then pointed down toward a mound of mulch in the wheelbarrow. "All organic, Fred promised," she called out.

The woman's jeans were rolled up, her shoulders bare, tan, and freckled. A floppy straw hat and large sunglasses shaded her face.

"Come, have coffee, meet everyone," Nell called, and motioned toward the deck. "These skeptics don't believe you're real."

Claire tugged off her gardening gloves and walked up the steps to the deck, greeting the women with a smile.

"Meet my gardening goddess," Nell said proudly. "Claire—these are the people you've been hearing about every day. They are amazed at our paradise."

"It's beautiful," Izzy said. "Thanks so much for helping Aunt Nell with this."

Cass echoed Izzy's praise.

Nell looked over at Birdie, who was eyeing Claire Russell with a curious frown on her face. "Birdie?" she said.

Birdie shook her head, as if scattering a fog. She took Claire's tan hand in her own. "I don't mean to be rude, Claire; I was simply trying to place you in my life. I don't like it when my memory slips. A curse on senior moments."

Claire's smile was guarded as she shook Birdie's hand. "I don't think we've met. I lived around here years ago but didn't spend much time in town. But it's lovely to meet you. Nell has told me wonderful things about you. About all of you."

Birdie nodded absently, but her frown stayed in place. "Sometimes this happens to me. I can't remember where I saw someone, and then I realize it was the person in front of me in the checkout line at Shaw's."

Claire loosened the sweater from her shoulders and slipped it over the back of a chair.

Izzy was on it in a second. "This sweater is beautiful." She fingered the blue-gray yarn. The sweater was light and airy, with front edges that dipped lower than the back. "Cotton and cashmere, right? Did someone knit this for you? I love it. What beautiful yarn."

Claire was clearly pleased. "I made it. It's old. Knitting and gardening are my two passions. I've looked at your store from a distance, Izzy, not quite trusting myself to go inside until I've worked a bit longer, saved a little. But I'll get there."

"I hope so. We would love to have you. And you don't need to buy anything. Come sit. Talk knitting. I can tell from your gorgeous sweater that there are plenty of things we could learn from you. My coffee is atrocious, but the music, company, and vibes are amazing."

Claire handed the sweater to Izzy to look at more closely and took off her floppy hat, pushing her sunglasses up into her hair.

Birdie's frown disappeared. "That's it. I remember now." She smiled triumphantly, the irritation of a fading memory disappearing instantly. "You're right. We haven't met, not officially. But I at least know where I've seen you, and it's nice to put a name to such a lovely face. We *almost* met last evening."

Claire's smile fell away. "Last night?" She took a step backward, one hand resting on the table behind her.

"Yes. In the Sea Harbor Bookstore—after the discussion of that cold-case mystery that we all tried to solve. You're Archie Brandley's mystery woman."

Chapter 4

*N*ell admitted later that her timing was bad in handing Claire the mug of coffee just then. She hadn't had Birdie's vantage point, so she missed seeing Claire's ashen face, her gardener's tan disappearing right there in front of them.

The mug was filled to the brim when she put it in Claire's hands.

And though the gardener tried to grasp it, it slipped through her fingers as if freshly greased, and fell to the deck floor, spraying a rich French roast in all directions.

Claire's hands flew to her face.

"Not a problem. We do this all the time," Birdie assured her, checking to be sure Claire's sweater had escaped the spray.

"Except it's usually me," Izzy said, then followed up her words with a laugh and headed inside for paper towels.

Nell pulled out a chair and suggested Claire sit down, then filled another mug and set it down in front of her. She looked at her to be sure she was all right. Something had upset her, but Nell couldn't imagine what it might have been. The bookstore? But that didn't make sense—Archie's bookstore was the most welcoming place in town. Sometimes he stayed open late just because people had settled into his comfortable chairs and he hated to disturb them.

"One of these doughnuts will add a little boost to your blood sugar," Birdie said, finding an easy way to change the subject. "I find they're a grand way to start the day. Better than multivitamins."

"These aren't doughnuts," Cass said. "Doughnuts have *dunkin'* in front of them."

Birdie laughed. "They're *fancy* doughnuts, Catherine. Now, behave in front of our guest."

Claire pulled a small smile to her face. "Oh, Birdie, I'm not a guest; I'm a . . ."

"Friend," Nell finished for her. "I would never have spent all these hours on my knees without you."

And that was the absolute truth, she'd confessed to Ben a few days before. There was something about Claire Russell that was easy and comfortable, as if she and Nell had known each other a long time.

Perhaps they'd known each other in another life, Claire had suggested. It wasn't likely this one, since she'd only recently moved to Sea Harbor—and *moved* was not quite the right word. Claire was living in a small back room at Fred Euclid's nursery for a couple of weeks until an apartment became available.

With a bit of prodding as they knelt side by side, spreading mulch around newly planted red twig dogwoods, Nell had learned that Claire had been thinking of coming back east for a while. Now and then she'd check the Internet for jobs. When she saw the nursery position advertised, it seemed like fate. Gardening was the love of her life, working with the earth, with plants and shrubs. So she'd moved from California where she'd lived for more than a dozen years. On a commune, she confessed to Nell as they loosened the soil in a garden bed one day. "I was due for a change."

When Nell told Ben where Claire was staying, he had responded exactly as she knew he would. "That's foolishness. Staying in Fred's nursery? It's a storage barn. If it's only a couple weeks, why doesn't she stay in our guest cottage?"

Which was exactly what Nell was going to propose, once she had a few minutes alone with Claire.

Izzy finished wiping up the coffee and took another beignet. "The backyard looks wonderful, Claire. I've always loved every inch of Aunt Nell and Uncle Ben's yard. I didn't think a single solitary thing needed to be done to it for the wedding. But somehow—I don't know—somehow you've enhanced it without taking away any of what I love about it."

"That's what your aunt and I hoped to do. It will be a wonderful wedding, Izzy. This is a perfect setting." Claire wiped the sugar from her hands and stood up. "And now my soil is calling. I've a daisy bed to mulch."

"And I've a lobster trap to feed," Cass said, swallowing the last bite of her third beignet and grabbing the keys to her truck. She looked at Izzy. "Want a ride?"

Izzy nodded, then reminded Nell she'd meet her at M.J.'s to talk hair later that day.

"And for the record," she added as she picked up her bag to follow Cass, "you and Claire don't need anyone's input on what to do with the yard and the gardens. What you're doing is perfect.

"Absolutely perfect," Izzy whispered, hugging her aunt tightly.

When everyone but Birdie had left, Nell gathered the coffee mugs onto a tray and carried them into the house, with Birdie following close behind. They stood at the kitchen sink, Birdie's white head barely reaching Nell's shoulder. Through the window, they watched Claire Russell settle down in a dark bed beneath a tall maple tree. She sat back on her legs, looking up at the leafy branches that shaded her body.

Then she picked up her trowel and began to work the soil.

"If I sat back like that, my knees would pop so loud, people would hear them over in Gloucester," Birdie said. She picked up a towel and wiped the mug Nell handed her.

Nell laughed. "She's in good shape—strong as an ox. I guess it's all the gardening. Such a lovely lady, and she truly loves what she does," Nell said. "Working the soil seems to put her in another place. Sometimes when I look at her, I see a kind of sadness. But then she digs her fingers into the earth and I'm reminded of Buddhists, of people praying. I feel calm working next to her."

"She wasn't calm last night when I saw her in the bookstore. She had no color in her face, and she looked like a trapped animal trying to escape."

Nell frowned. "That doesn't sound like Claire."

"It certainly seemed to upset the poor dear when I mentioned it today. Her reaction was odd; didn't you think so?"

Nell looked out the window, then back at Birdie. "Are you sure it was Claire you saw last night? I got the feeling she thought you'd mistaken her for someone else."

"But she didn't really say that, did she? No, these old eyes see remarkably well, and I looked at her carefully because both Archie and I were surprised to see her walk down the steps."

"Steps?"

"She was in the loft. She must have been up there the whole time we were meeting, though I didn't see her."

"I didn't see her, either. That's strange. I would have noticed her immediately. Unless she was back in the stacks and once Danny started talking, she didn't want to cause a disturbance so she just stayed put."

Birdie nodded. "That may be. But it doesn't explain the look on her face."

"Maybe not." Nell looked out the window again. Claire was adding compost to the area, working it in. She moved her fingers with the same purposefulness the knitters used when working on a fine scarf or sweater. And with the same look of utter contentment. "Well, if anything was bothering her yesterday, I think she's working it out right down there in the soil."

Birdie followed Nell's gaze down to the back edge of the yard. "Let's hope so, dear Nell. We'll see." Birdie turned away from the window and slid her arms through the straps of her backpack.

Nell wiped her hands on a dish towel, watching a pensive expression play across Birdie's lined face. Then she walked over and hugged her friend, backpack and all. She knew Birdie so well. Her tone of voice and body language told Nell clearly that she didn't believe a word of it.

Birdie believed something was burdening Claire Russell. And it was something that digging a new garden plot wasn't about to resolve.

$\mathcal{N}$ell sat on a bench just outside Sea Harbor Bookstore, her cell phone pressed to her ear. When the call finally ended, Nell looked at the phone, sighed, and slipped it into her bag. Nearly five o'clock. The day had disappeared in a blink of an eye, her list of to-dos so long that she hadn't even had a chance to talk to Claire about moving into the guest cottage.

Tomorrow, she thought. Which would give her a minute to be sure everything in the cottage was in working order.

She had come down to Harbor Road early, hoping to pick up a book Archie had ordered for her before meeting Izzy for their five o'clock meeting at M.J.'s salon, but then her sister Caroline had called and used up most of that time. The book would have to wait.

Izzy's mother called constantly these days, gushing thanks to Nell for filling in for her with Izzy. She always asked a million questions about the wedding plans, and today she read off a list of things to do. Nell knew it pained her sister not to be there herself, but the art gallery she managed was shorthanded, and Caroline was invested in it, financially and emotionally. But she felt so far away, she told Nell.

Of course she did. Nell understood. It was her only daughter's wedding. And she was being heroic about it, in Nell's opinion. Not once did she complain to Izzy about not coming back to Kansas City to get married. Nell gave her great credit for that. The thought was always there, though, Nell knew, always at the edge of Caroline's thoughts. But she would never mention it to Izzy. She understood that this was Izzy's dream—getting married by the sea.

Which was true, Nell thought, but she also knew it was Izzy's only chance of having what she desperately wanted—a *simple* wedding, one she'd have little chance of having in Kansas City with her well-intentioned—and well-connected—mother in charge.

Today Caroline had called because she was concerned with a gathering Izzy had suggested having at the Artist's Palate, a casual bar and grill in the center of the Canary Cove Art Colony. Ben would plan a sailing trip for relatives who would arrive early for the wedding. Danny Brandley and Sam would help; then they'd all gather for beers at Hank's bar and grill.

But Caroline had thought the bar sounded a bit "rough." Perhaps the yacht club instead? But Izzy and Sam wanted it at Hank's, Nell told her sister. His wife, Merry, was a friend. Besides, next to the Gull Tavern, Hank had the largest selection of beers in town.

Caroline had sighed and hung up.

Nell slipped her phone into her bag and stood just as Izzy walked up.

"My mother again?" Izzy said.

"You can tell?"

Izzy laughed. Then she hooked her arm through Nell's and they walked down the block and across the street to M.J's salon.

M.J.'s shop had begun its life as a four-chair salon in her home. It reminded Birdie of Dolly Parton's back room in *Steel Magnolias*, and Margo Jeanne Arcado's clientele loved it—and her.

But four chairs weren't nearly enough to satisfy M.J.'s growing list of clients—young professionals trying to squeeze a cut in between meetings, retirees who lived in an enclave of elegant homes near the point, Bostonians who snapped up the luxurious vacation condominiums north of town, and teenagers who demanded edgier styles.

Expanding meant moving, and when the old Sullivan place on Harbor Road finally went on the market, M.J. bought it and moved in. She added a spa with massage beds in a darkened room, facials in comfortable white chairs, clean walls filled with art from the Canary Cove artists, and a cozy waiting area with soft music, coffee, and tall glasses of water with slices of lemon or lime. After five, M.J. offered wine. The quaint storage cellar below the building would slowly be renovated into offices and perhaps more spa areas.

Along with the move, M.J. had tried to change the salon name to Pleasure, but it never stuck. Nell thought it had its merits, though. Pleasure was exactly what she felt when one of M.J.'s young staff gently massaged her neck and her temples until she felt all the cares of the world replaced with the intoxicating fragrance of lemon balm.

But today was business, not pleasure, with no time to put one's head back and sip a cup of herbal tea while Norah Jones sang to you softly in the background. Today was for wedding planning.

When Nell and Izzy walked through the door, the receptionist motioned them directly back to the salon office. "M.J.'s waiting for you," she said.

The office was around the corner at the end of a long, meandering hallway at the back of the salon.

The door was open.

M.J. stood near a love seat tucked into a bay of open windows on the east side of the room. "Sit in the breeze, lovies," she said. "It's going to be exactly like this on your wedding day, Izzy—blue skies, gentle breezes. I promise."

"A full-service salon," Nell said. "You even handle the weather."

"Of course. Nothing but the best." M.J. smiled and pointed to a bottle of wine on the coffee table.

"A celebration?" Nell asked.

"All wedding planning should take place over a glass of fine wine," M.J. said. "Tiffany will be here in a minute. She'll be the coordinator extraordinaire on your special day, Izzy. She must be finishing up with a client."

"Not a problem," said Izzy. She looked out the window and breathed in the salty air. "It's supposed to be a perfect summer evening. I hope it brings out a crowd for the Fractured Fish's gig tonight.

Pete, Merry, and Andy have been practicing up a storm, Cass said. Her brother's band is getting quite a name for itself."

M.J. waved one hand in the air and tossed her head back. "How silly of me. I nearly forgot." She glanced at the clock on her desk. "I hope this wasn't a bad time to meet."

"No. It's perfect," Izzy said. "This leaves Ben and Sam with the sweaty job—helping Pete haul his equipment over to the Artist's Palate. We'll show up when they're all finished—and we'll smell nice."

M.J. laughed. "The girls in the salon have been talking about it all week. The Fractured Fish are becoming minor celebs around here. Tiffany never misses a performance. Pete and Andy will be fighting off their groupies before they know it." She handed them each a glass of wine.

Nell took a drink, then set her glass down. "I noticed you at the book club last night, M.J. What did you think? Did you like the discussion?"

The salon owner paused, then answered carefully. "It was interesting. But I think I'm in Esther Gibson's camp. I think Danny might have picked a cold case that happened in California or Oregon or Canada—somewhere far away from Sea Harbor. Fifteen years seems a lifetime to someone your age, Iz, but to some of us, it wasn't so long ago."

"But Danny's intention wasn't to talk about real people. He was just showing how real life can be a springboard for fiction."

"I suppose. And for people who didn't live here then—like Danny, like both of you—it probably seems more remote. But having it brought up like that brings back memories to some of us, and not necessarily good ones. People start talking about it again. Like Margaret Garozzo, for example. She was in here today getting her hair done, and you'd think it happened yesterday the way she was going on—not in a gossipy way. Just reliving it. Their son was just out of high school at the time. It scared parents half to death." She waved one hand in the air, as if scattering her words. "But enough talk about that. We have happier things to talk about." She checked the desk clock again and frowned. "Tiffany must have been waylaid. She's usually very prompt. I'll check with the desk—"

M.J. headed for the phone on her desk when a voice in the doorway stopped her.

"She left, M.J. Gone."

Tanya Gordon stood in the doorframe with her hands on her hips and an "I told you so" look on her face.

"What do you mean, 'gone'? Maybe she's in the basement, in her office."

"Yeah, you'd think. She spends a lot of time down there. But nope, not this time. I checked. Soon as her four o'clock was done, she split, like she had a plane to catch or something. Out of here. Vroom."

M.J. frowned. "Did she say when she'd be back?"

Tanya's thin shoulders lifted and fell. She ran her fingers through her hair. "You never know with her. She's, like, secretive. Especially lately. Doesn't tell me much. She must be PMSing or something."

"Well, thanks, Tanya." M.J. turned back toward Izzy and Nell.

Tanya took a step into the office. "Well, I could stay, if you want. I mean, I could easily handle the appointments and stuff for Izzy's wedding." Her red-lipped smile was directed toward Izzy, the words at M.J.

"We'll take care of it, Tanya. Thanks. You can go now."

The sound of Tanya's heels tapping angrily on the tiled hallway floor told them she had left.

M.J. shook her head. "She's still upset with me because I promoted Tiffany to our special events coordinator. Then, when I started renovating that old storeroom in the cellar and turned one of the rooms into an office for Tiff, Tanya went through the roof. She thought she should have gotten the job—and the office—because she's been here longer. The girl is short on manners but high on ambition."

M.J. laughed at the expression that flitted across Izzy's face. "That look tells me you know Tanya."

"No, not really. She comes into the yarn shop sometimes. She's fine, really, just a little loud and . . . well, gossipy, I guess you'd say.

And frankly, I can't imagine her dealing with Great-grandmother Chambers. She'll be quite particular about how she looks that day."

Nell laughed at the thought of the matriarch of the Chambers clan dealing with a flighty, not-so-capable stylist. Izzy's words were an understatement. Adelaide Chambers—not to mention some of Izzy's dad's sisters—was commanding and demanding. They would make mincemeat of Tanya in the time it took to heat a curling iron.

"Tanya will mature. Hopefully, anyway. And she might even get over being mad at me—and Tiffany, too. But the fact is, Tiff is a good stylist; she's nice to people and doesn't talk too much. And she's patient. Tanya has a way to go." She looked at the clock. "I know Tiffany's absence today isn't great verification of her competence, but if she left, she had a good reason. In the meantime, I apologize for wasting your time."

"It's not wasted," Nell assured the salon owner. She held up her glass and smiled. "This is a fine glass of wine."

"And we've plenty of time before the wedding," Izzy added. "Just have her call me tomorrow morning, and we'll figure out another time."

M.J. walked with them to the front of the salon, assuring them once more that it wouldn't happen again. Tiffany had looked pale that morning. M.J. suspected maybe she'd gone home sick. A reasonable excuse.

But Tiffany Ciccolo didn't look ill two hours later when Nell, Birdie, and Izzy climbed the steps to the Artist's Palate deck for the Fractured Fish's evening performance.

Izzy nudged Nell and pointed to a picnic table near the railing of the old deck. Tiffany sat alone, large sunglasses covering most of her face and her sandals tapping the wooden floor. At first the tapping seemed to be accompanying the plucking of Pete's guitar as he tuned the strings. But soon it turned into a nervous staccato, and Tiffany's gaze, as best they could tell, seemed focused on Andy Risso, not on Pete at all.

Andy sat on a stool, his ponytail hanging over one shoulder, and his long torso leaning forward. His eyes were on the drumhead as he fiddled with the lugs. The clicking sounds made by his key were picked up by Pete's mic.

Tiffany watched, as if the process of tuning a snare drum was the most important thing in her life at that precise moment.

She finally pulled her gaze from Andy and looked around the deck, as if noticing the gathering crowd for the first time. She stopped suddenly, her eyes on Izzy and Nell. Her hand flew to her mouth and she started to get up from the bench. "I'm so sorry," she mouthed.

For a moment Nell thought she was about to cry.

"No problem," Izzy mouthed back, and held up her phone. "Call me."

They followed Birdie to a table in the middle of the deck and quickly claimed it, piling sweaters and bags on the benches to make sure Ben, Sam, Cass—and whoever else might show up—would have a place to sit.

Izzy looked back at Tiffany. "She looks embarrassed, poor thing. It's not a big deal. People forget things."

Nell nodded. Tiffany was back to watching the band, but the look Nell had seen in her eyes was more than embarrassment. There was a touch of that, but something else. Worry? But missing an appointment didn't merit that, unless she thought her job was at stake.

Whatever the cause, something seemed not right.

Tiffany Ciccolo had been working at M.J.'s salon longer than Nell had been a client there. Nell remembered her as so shy, one barely noticed her as she swept the floors and straightened products and magazines. She was tall, slightly awkward, as if she weren't completely comfortable in her own body. Then, with encouragement from M.J., Tiffany became a receptionist and some of her shyness faded. Finally, she'd gone to beauty school and returned with more confidence and a new hair color—a deep shade of red as smooth and shiny as copper tile. She was still quiet, but after beauty school, she seemed competent, more assured, and M.J. had rewarded her efforts with another promotion and even an office of her own.

Nell liked the young woman—the little she knew of her, anyway. But that was the crux of it. She didn't know her well, not really. So why did she think something was wrong? Perhaps it was the details for Izzy's wedding crowding her head and her life, making her see problems where none existed.

"Yoo-hoo, Nell, are you with us?" Jane Brewster sat down on the picnic bench next to Nell, her long patterned skirt billowing in the breeze.

Jane's husband, Ham, was right behind her, one hand touching her shoulder. Ben followed close behind, balancing a tray of icy beer mugs, baskets of fried calamari, and bowls of dipping sauces.

Nell hugged her friend and motioned to Ham. "Come sit, all of you. Ben, you're all sweaty." She grimaced.

Ben leaned over her shoulder and kissed her soundly. He straightened up and walked around the table. "Salty kisses are good omens."

"You're full of it, Ben," Jane said. "But as long as you bring food and drink, we'll put up with you."

"Little Merry Jackson is rarin' to go," Ham said. The watercolor artist—and one of Nell and Ben's oldest friends—looked over the tops of heads toward the stage. "She's itching to start moving."

They all looked over at the diminutive blonde, whose husband, Hank, owned the Artist's Palate and the valuable strip of shore upon which it sat. She was snapping her fingers, gyrating her body to the sound of Andy's drums as he teased her with a few beats. Merry was clearly enjoying performing on her own turf.

When Pete had formed his band a few years ago, it was more for fun than for public entertaining. He and Andy Risso would get together, Pete strumming the guitar and singing and Andy on drums. Merry Jackson had heard about the jam sessions. Always looking for an excuse to get out of restaurant duty, she showed up one night at Andy's place with an old keyboard under her arm and enough energy in her tiny body to power their amps. Soon after that, the Fractured Fish was born. Now, no prominent Sea Harbor festivity was complete without the band livening it up a notch.

"Pete says he's doing more vocals with Merry now. They're thinking of adding another guitarist."

"We should get autographs while they're still speaking to us," Izzy said, dipping her fingers into the basket of calamari.

Cass and Danny wandered over with Willow Adams, a young fiber artist, and soon the picnic table was shoulder-to-shoulder bodies with conversations crisscrossing one another as news and food were shared in equal proportions.

As Pete began his first number, bodies began swaying with the beat, humming along with an old Beatles tune. Waiters, mostly college kids home for summer vacation, wove their way through the crowd, balancing burgers and fries, fish sandwiches, and hefty jugs of beer.

A gull swooped down beside Nell, then flew off with a piece of bun in his beak. She laughed and soaked in the salty night air. It was definitely summertime when you shared your meal with birds.

"What do you think of my girl?" Hank Jackson asked, leaning over Birdie's shoulder and acknowledging the others with a welcoming smile.

"A bundle of talent," Birdie said.

"Yep." Hank's head moved up and down as his eyes took in her every move. "She's amazing, isn't she? How'd I get so lucky?"

Nell watched Hank watch Merry, and smiled to herself. They were an interesting couple, odd in some ways, but marriage seemed to work for them. Although fifteen years older than Merry, Hank's looks were a striking complement to his young wife's—his darkly handsome face and over-six-foot frame a contrast to Merry's delicate blond beauty. It was a surprise to many Sea Harbor people when the cheerleader married the handsome community-center coach.

Ben had told her that Hank Jackson was a hard worker. After graduating from UMass, he'd come to a town he'd once known only in the summer, visiting a relative with a place near the sea. He'd loved Sea Harbor and, together with the energetic Merry, he accomplished his dream—a bar and grill that the Sea Harbor artists' community couldn't do without. Hank loved it, loved being his own boss with the woman he loved at his side.

The place was comfortable, with a wooden deck that swung out over the water on one side and hugged the small restaurant on another. When weather allowed, the Artist's Palate deck was never empty.

Like tonight. Festive and filled with happy customers, it hummed with the sounds of summer.

A bartender waved a white rag to get Hank's attention, and the owner hurried off, surveying the crowd as he went, his body swinging slightly to the beat.

"Will you be that sexy when you're his age?" Cass asked Danny Brandley. She bit into a strip of calamari, her eyes following Hank as he made his way around the crowded tables toward the bar, greeting customers along the way.

Danny followed her gaze, furrowing his brow in thought. "No," he said finally.

Cass' laugh floated into the darkening night air as the music pulsed and pounded around them. Her hand on his leg told him she thought otherwise.

Soon the crowd joined in, clapping and singing. Over near the bar, a small clearing allowed a group to get up and dance to the pounding beat.

When Pete announced the end of the first set and stepped down from the makeshift stage, the crowd cheered and hands waved to waiters, demanding more beer and burgers.

Pete made his way over to his friends and squeezed down next to Willow, helping himself to a long swig of her beer.

She took it back and elbowed him in the side. "You rock star, you," she whispered. "Are you trying to have your way with me?"

"With your beer, anyway." Pete reached for it again, this time sloshing a stream of pale ale along the table and onto Willow's lap.

"Ugh," Willow complained, leaning back from the table.

They were just friends, she and Pete—at least that was what

Willow claimed—but the glances and gestures told Nell that it was a friendship growing deeper by the day, something that they'd all cheer for if that happened. When Willow had come to Sea Harbor several years before, looking for her father, she was a lost soul, a "waif," Birdie had called her. She fit the description perfectly. But in time she came to grips with who she was—and with her father's death. Now Willow Adams was a vital part of the artist community, her reputation as a fiber artist growing each year. And she'd turned her father's Fishtail Gallery into something he'd be very proud of.

Nell got up and headed for the bar. She grabbed a pile of napkins and began weaving her way back through the growing crowd.

She glanced at Tiffany's table as she passed. Andy Risso was there, straddling the bench. One elbow was on the table, his shoulder lifted in an uncomfortable pose. He was listening intently.

Tiffany's eyes were intense, her face alive with urgency. She held out one hand toward him, her palm raised, as if presenting him with something that would change his life forever.

Nell moved an inch closer just as Tiffany stopped talking. She sat back, her face now expectant, waiting for a response.

Nell looked at Andy.

His mouth had dropped open, his eyes wide as he stared at the woman in front of him. Whatever Tiffany had presented him with was jarring—and disturbing, from what Nell could see. His brows were pulled together, his jaw set.

Beside him, Tiffany started talking again, her eyes large and her hands moving frantically in the air as if to wipe away his response.

Andy continued to listen, but his posture was rigid, his expression disbelieving. He forked one hand through his long hair and pulled himself up from the bench.

Nell turned away, but the harshness in Andy's voice stopped her, and she looked back once more to see Andy leaning forward, his palm flat on the table. "Blackmail?" she heard him say. "Is that what this is?"

Tiffany tore off her sunglasses, and Nell saw the tears gather, then quickly begin to roll down her cheeks. She reached out and touched Andy's arm.

He pulled back with a jerk as sudden as if she'd pressed a lighted cigarette into his arm.

Nell looked around. All around her people were laughing and talking, table hopping to greet friends; waiters scurried to replace pitchers and platters and baskets of fries. No one seemed aware of the drama playing out at the small table near the railing.

Just then a young waitress carrying an enormous tray attempted to move around Nell, and only then did she realize she was standing still, blocking traffic. Quickly, she headed back to her own table, looking back only when she'd handed off the napkins to Willow.

Andy was gone. She spotted him at the outdoor bar, grabbing a beer that the bartender slid across the counter.

Tiffany's eyes were on Andy's back, and the look of longing on her face was so intense that Nell quickly turned away. It was an awful, sad longing.

"You okay, Nell?" Pete stood next to her at the end of the table, wiping calamari from his hands.

She managed a smile, then looked across the deck, where Andy was heading back to the stage. "I'm fine. But is your friend Andy okay?"

Pete followed her look. Then he glanced over at Tiffany. "I hope so. I see she's here. No surprise. We can always count on an audience of one." He laughed, but his eyes were serious.

"You mean Tiffany?"

He nodded. "She's okay, I guess. Kinda quiet. At first I thought she was just a groupie, fawning all over Andy. It bugged him. But after a while he warmed up to her. They knew each other when they were teenagers, he said. So they started hanging out, mostly at Tiffany's instigation, I think. But Willow says, what's wrong with that? Men can pursue women and no one thinks anything of it. She has a point, I guess. Anyway, they were together a lot these last months. But lately, I don't know.

"The last couple weeks it seemed to get to Andy. He'd get this trapped look on his face. She came over early today, when we were setting up, offering to help. Andy tried to ignore her, but she wouldn't let him. She said they needed to talk about things. It was important, she said. I thought I heard her say something about . . ." Pete stopped. He frowned, then laughed, scattering his words as if he shouldn't have spoken them in the first place. He looked toward the stage. "Looks like we're ready for another set. Gotta go." He gave Nell a pat on the shoulder and melted into the crowd.

Nell watched him walk away, an uncomfortable feeling growing inside her. Across the room, Tiffany Ciccolo sat alone, her glasses back on and her face turned toward the stage. Her expression was unreadable.

By the time Pete had tapped the microphone to life, people had moved to their crowded tables and settled down, ready for another go-round.

The music grew in volume as the night darkened and the crowd thinned out, some settling in for the last few songs, others moving off toward home. Sam and Izzy left to take Birdie home, and by the time Pete stretched and Merry began belting out "Scarlet Begonias," Nell's lids were drooping. Beside her, she felt Ben's head nod once or twice.

"You're waking up just in time to help us tear down," Pete said, coming up alongside Ben and clapping him on the back. "Good man."

Hank followed him over and thrust a beer in his hand. "Good job, Pete. Here's one for the road." He looked around, spotted his wife across the deck, and waved her over.

But Merry ignored him. Instead, she walked over to the table where Tiffany sat alone, her elbows on the table, her head resting on her hands. She was staring off toward the water as if she'd lost something there.

Tiffany looked up as Merry approached. A neutral look, neither welcoming nor unwelcoming.

Merry sat down and put one arm around Tiffany's shoulders.

From the stage, Andy seemed not to notice. He wrapped up the thick cords and began to pack up his equipment.

Nell finished a cup of coffee that Hank had thoughtfully brought over and suggested to Ben that they leave.

"You folks go on," Hank said. "I'll help the band get their stuff together."

But before they could get up, Merry made her way over to the table and grabbed Hank's arm. "Go talk to Tiffany, Hank," she said. Her voice was firm.

Hank frowned and followed the point of her finger.

"Tiffany Ciccolo. You know, Hank. The shooting guard. Go. She needs to talk."

"To me?" Hank's frown deepened. "Is there a problem?"

"Just go. Now." Merry placed both hands on his back. Her head barely reached his shoulder blades. She gave him a shove.

Hank hesitated, but Merry stood resolutely behind him.

Finally he walked over to the table.

Tiffany looked up, her expression still sad, but she welcomed the bar owner with a smile. Then she reached up and hugged him.

"I guess it's weird to have a wife throw her husband at other women," Merry said to Nell, her eyes making sure Hank didn't abandon Tiffany Ciccolo. Out of habit, she began cleaning up the table, using a rag Hank had left behind. "He doesn't necessarily like it when I offer his shoulder like that, but Hank's easy to talk to, you know? When he coached our team a lifetime ago, we'd dump on him. This big lug of a guy. But he'd listen. He always listened." She stopped and laughed. "Maybe that's why he's such a great bartender."

The sound of car keys broke into Merry's chuckles, and Nell looked up. Ben stood nearby, a key ring dangling from his fingers.

"My chauffeur," she said, looking back to Merry.

But Merry was already off, hugging some friends at the next table, wiping surfaces, her smile selling a few more beers. She was beginning to believe Cass, Izzy, and Willow when they suggested that Merry Jackson was the real force behind the Artist's Palate.

Ben wrapped an arm around her and led her over to the steps. "I know what you're thinking. 'If only I had a tenth of that energy.'" He looked over at Merry, then pulled Nell close. "But you have all the energy I need, my dear."

Nell laughed. "For once in your life, you've crawled inside my head and come out with the wrong thought. I was trying to imagine Merry's elfin body on a basketball court; that's what I was thinking." And she was also thinking that beneath her bubbly exterior, Merry Jackson was a compassionate young woman—and one whose husband very nicely allowed himself to be pulled into that compassion, whether he was comfortable there or not.

Chapter 6

The next day Tiffany showed up exactly when and where she told Izzy she would. Eleven a.m. sharp. Twenty-two Sandswept Lane.

Nell opened her front door to an apology.

"I'm so terribly sorry, Mrs. Endicott," Tiffany began. She stood on the stone steps, a large bag slung over one broad shoulder and a notebook binder in the other hand. She wore a short-sleeved knit shrug, a single button holding it in place, with a tank top underneath, a silky summer skirt, and red sandals with clunky heels that lifted her to Nell's height. In her hand she held a bouquet of fresh flowers. The same huge sunglasses covered her eyes and half her face. "For you," she said.

Nell waved the apology away and suggested that Tiffany call her Nell. "I'll answer more quickly," she laughed, lowering her head to smell the daisies. "These are lovely. Thank you. Now, come on in. Izzy's pulling some scones from the oven. Let's talk wedding."

Tiffany had called early that morning, and Izzy suggested that they meet at Nell's house. It made more sense. Tiffany could get the lay of the land, determine what equipment she'd need to bring, how many stylists they needed.

Izzy waved at Tiffany from the island. "The blueberries are from the market. The rest is all Nell. You'll be happy you came."

"You're great, both of you. I might have fired me if I'd been you."

Izzy laughed. "You may wish we had when you get through

with my great-grandmother Chambers, not to mention Great-aunt Florence—she's ninety and has beetle-black hair."

Tiffany smiled and her shoulders relaxed. She pushed her hair back behind one ear and sat on a stool, opening up the three-ring binder and slipping on black-rimmed glasses. She leafed through the book, asking Izzy questions and scribbling down notes.

She was the kind of young woman people might easily forget. Plain and pleasant. But her coppery hair now added some signature to her, Nell supposed. People would remember the beautiful hair, if not the person. Whatever had bothered her the night before was hidden there behind the glasses, and Nell suspected that was where it would stay. Tiffany Ciccolo was keeping her distance.

Her movements were purposeful. Efficient and businesslike. Perhaps to erase any lingering images of how she might have looked the night before.

After scones and coffee, they did a quick tour of the bedrooms where the women in the bridal party would dress the day of the wedding. They'd use Nell and Ben's bedroom, dressing room, and bath, as well as the guest rooms. It would be more than enough room, Tiffany said, satisfied. She'd carefully written down the names of the wedding party and Izzy's relatives who needing styling services that day, and assured her it could all be done in an hour or two. Easy. Tiffany would bring champagne, orange juice, bottled water, and nibbles, along with her stylists. She suggested Izzy have some favorite CDs or an iPod loaded and ready to go. This would be another fun part of the day, she promised.

Tiffany took off her glasses and rubbed her eyes. It was then that Nell noticed how tired she looked. A sleepless night, her eyes said.

As if sensing Nell's look, Tiffany turned away and looked around Nell's kitchen. "This is a dream room," she said, admiring the six-burner stove, the inviting island, and the hanging rack of copper pots and pans. Sunlight poured through the open windows, flooding the breakfast area and highlighting the bamboo floors.

Nell's cooking area spilled directly into the family room, where wide couches and comfortable chairs sat on sisal rugs. At the far end the stone fireplace was surrounded by bookshelves crammed with books, small pieces of art, and family photos.

"I've always loved this house," Tiffany said. "It's even more beautiful on the inside. Someday . . . someday this is exactly the kind of house I want for my family. When I was in grade school I had a friend who lived around here, and we'd cut through your backyard on our way to the beach sometimes. My friend said all the neighborhood kids did it, but I was pretty sure we'd be arrested."

"Not a chance. There was an open invitation. So you grew up here, Tiffany?"

She nodded, her eyes still scanning the comforts of the homey living area. "Not around here, though. We lived out near the highway. But I went to Sea Harbor High, so I knew some kids who lived in town. Not many. There were cliques. You know how high school can be. Popular kids. Smart kids. Nerds. Geeks. All that awful branding." She fingered the edge of her sweater.

She half smiled, almost apologetically, Nell thought. As if it were her fault that there were cliques, or that she wasn't in the right one.

"Did you knit your sweater? It's lovely."

"Me?" Tiffany looked surprised, and then she laughed. "No. I'm still on scarves. But I keep trying. I've spent several paychecks in Izzy's store. When I was in high school, my friend's mother tried to teach us both how to knit once. She was such a cool knitter." Tiffany paused, a wistful look following her words. She looked down at her cotton shrug. "But this? My sister knit this. She's a fantastic knitter. She sends me sweaters and hats and socks all the time. Sheila's, like, amazing. You two should meet, Izzy."

"Does she come to visit you in Sea Harbor?"

"No. Never. She lives in Nebraska. But I keep trying to get her back. Who knows? Maybe someday." Tiffany slipped off the stool and walked over to the window above the sink. She looked out at the yard.

"This is a perfect place for a wedding. It's so beautiful, it should be in a magazine." She pointed toward the back of the yard and to a circle of fruit trees and shoulder-high rosebushes that nearly hid a small frame house. "I remember that little guest cottage back there, right near the woods. We peeked in the windows once. It had the highest bed I'd ever seen. I wanted to hide away in it and never leave."

Izzy laughed. "That's exactly what I used to do. It was my special place when I'd come here to spend summers with my aunt and uncle. I thought the backyard—woods, trees, hammock, cottage—all belonged to me. I loved it here. And now—well, now it seems the perfect place to get married. Come see." She headed for the French doors. "Aunt Nell and a friend have turned the yard into a wedding forest, green and soft and peaceful. It's a paradise."

Nell followed the two women outside. She noticed Claire at the far end of the yard, almost invisible in a green T-shirt that blended in with the bushes and trees. The gardener was hunkered down beneath the tall pines, mulching a border of brilliant green and yellow hostas.

Izzy gestured to the deck steps and the flagstone path. "My aisle," she said. Then she pointed out the grassy area where they'd set up chairs, where she and Sam would stand side by side and promise to be together the rest of their lives.

Tiffany looked over the whole yard as if watching a movie. "It's just perfect." Her voice caught, and for a minute Nell thought she might need a tissue. But then she seemed to catch herself, and she coughed lightly as if clearing away a frog in her throat. "Weddings make me emotional," she said, and then asked Izzy if they could check upstairs one more time. She wanted to be sure there were enough outlets for curling irons and dryers.

But Nell suspected she needed a change of view before her emotions got the better of her. She watched them disappear into the house. In her salon encounters with Tiffany, she'd not seen that emotional side of her, but the thought of Izzy's wedding gave her a catch in her throat. She certainly understood.

In the back of the yard, she watched Claire uncurl her body and stand tall, her hands on her narrow hips, admiring her work.

Claire had shown up to work early that morning, while Ben was just pouring his first cup of coffee. He had seen her through the window and urged her up to the kitchen to share a cup. While Nell was still getting dressed upstairs, Ben suggested to the gardener that she move into the guesthouse until her apartment opened up.

Nell heard the end of his sentence as she came down the back steps and added her encouragement, insisting that Claire say yes.

It took less than a cup of coffee for Claire to accept their offer with promises to somehow pay them back.

They promised to check out the cottage to be sure everything worked, and Claire could move in later that day. To seal the deal, Ben took a key from a hook on the wall and slipped it into her slightly shaking hand.

Nell added that using the key was optional. They rarely locked things up on Sandswept Lane.

Nell waved at Claire now to get her attention. "I feel like I've abandoned you," she called out.

"No, of course not." Claire looked up to the deck. "I love it here—and you must have a million wedding details to work out. That's your job. I can handle this." She dropped her trowel in the wheelbarrow and began walking up the path toward the deck. "This has become my meditation garden, Nell. I don't know what I'll do when the wedding is over."

"You'll come over often and simply *sit* in the yard for a change. Enjoy what you've nurtured here. That's what you'll do."

"You and Ben . . . you're unusual, you know? Your generosity—"

Nell cut her off. "No, no, we're not. This just makes sense. We have a nice guesthouse with the most comfortable bed in Sea Harbor, and it's not being used right now. It would be silly not to offer it to someone who needs a good place to sleep. I'm glad you said yes. And somehow it makes me feel more secure about all this wedding planning. I don't know why. It just does. Having you close will be nice."

Claire looked at Nell for a moment, as if she wanted to say more. Instead, she smiled a quiet, grateful smile that started in her eyes and spread quickly to her lips.

Her lips quivered slightly, but then she took a deep breath, peeled off her gloves, and spoke evenly, her composure intact.

"Do you have a minute? There are a few more things we should tackle before the wedding. I want to be sure we're on the same page."

Nell nodded, and Claire walked up the steps, pulling a rumpled yellow sheet of paper from her jeans pocket. She handed it to Nell. "See what you think."

Claire walked over to an Adirondack chair at the side of the deck and sat while Nell began to read through the list. Two blooming hibiscuses towered over the chair, brilliant peach blossoms as big as grapefruits opening up to the sun. It created a private nook on the open deck, a lovely place to curl up and read. Or take a nap. Claire reached up absently and deadheaded a shriveled bloom.

Nell stood apart, giving the list her full attention. Claire was so organized. Each item was treated as a task with a timetable attached.

She should really have her own business, Nell thought as she went from item to item. She had at least a dozen friends who would love to work side by side with Claire, learning from her as they tilled the soil, prepared compost piles, rid their yards of chemicals. Maybe Claire would consider a community-center class in gardening. Or a community garden. Nell suspected she'd be as good with vegetables as she was with hostas and gerbera daisies. Perhaps once this wedding was over she'd talk to her about it.

Izzy stuck her head out the door, squinting into the sunlight and scattering Nell's thoughts.

"I'm leaving, Aunt Nell. Headed back to the shop."

Tiffany was a step behind her. "Me, too. And thanks for understanding about yesterday. No more missed appointments, I promise. I had . . . I had some things on my mind, but I think I've taken care of them." She hesitated for a minute as if wanting to say more. But instead, she took a few steps toward Nell and hugged her awkwardly. Then she spun around on her clunky red shoes and walked back into the house.

The sound of their footsteps echoed through the hallway.

Nell stood there for a moment, looking into the empty room. Tiffany was certainly shy, slightly reserved even. Not a hugger. Not with someone she barely knew. The gesture had touched Nell. Perhaps it was a result of the magic that seemed to fill the Endicott home these days. And if not magic, certainly happy vibes.

Nell turned back to the list, and then remembered Claire, sitting in the shadows. "The list looks great. . . ."

Her sentence dropped off.

Claire was sitting in the deck chair, staring at the house, her mouth slightly open and her face twisted into a grimace.

An awful look. Pain? Anger? Nell couldn't be sure.

She hurried to Claire's side. "Are you all right? What is it?"

There was no answer.

Claire's chest rose and fell as she inhaled huge gulps of air. She bit down on her bottom lip and waved away Nell's ministrations. "I'll be fine. Please. But I need to leave. I'm sorry, Nell. I'm just not feeling too well. I didn't eat this morning; that's probably all it is."

"Well, then sit for a minute. I'll get you a glass of water."

But when Nell returned just seconds later with the water, Claire was down the steps and around the side of the deck. Nell glimpsed a flap of her green shirt as she rounded the corner of the house.

The only sign that she'd been there at all was a pair of flowered garden gloves, dropped to the floor as she had fled.

Nell picked them up and stared at the corner of the house. For two weeks she and Claire had worked side by side, digging in the dirt, sharing views, and talking about life. She found in Claire a kindred spirit.

"A gentle gardener" was how she described her to Ben one night.

But it wasn't gentleness she had read on Claire's face minutes ago.

The mixture of emotions on her face were ones Nell couldn't readily pull apart and describe. But the strength of them made her wonder if she really knew this woman who would soon be staying in their guesthouse. A gentle gardener? Or a mystery woman, someone she didn't know at all.

Chapter 7

"It was as if she'd seen a ghost," Nell said to Izzy that night. "A rather awful ghost." She stood next to the wooden table in the Seaside Knitting Studio's back room, pulling containers of food from her cloth bag.

"I saw the same thing," Izzy said. "She was standing at the corner of the garage as I started to back out of the driveway, staring at me, at my car."

"Staring at you? Did she say anything?"

"Not a word. I smiled at her, gave a small wave. But she didn't respond. It gave me goose bumps. Like in a movie. If looks could have caused my car to crash directly into your giant maple tree, I might not have made it back to work."

"That's not like Claire. She's usually so soft and gentle."

"I suppose I'm exaggerating a little. But it wasn't pleasant, Aunt Nell."

"What did Tiffany say?"

"Nothing. But she didn't have her glasses on. Which, by the way, we need to make sure she does when she's working on Nana Chambers' hair. She can't see without them. All she could see of Claire was a fuzzy figure." Izzy scooped up stray knitting needles and rulers as she talked and tossed them into a wicker basket in the middle of the table.

Birdie settled down near the fireplace next to Purl, the yarn studio's resident cat. Purl immediately hopped onto her lap, curled herself into a ball, and began purring. "Claire seems to be a lovely person," Birdie said, her fingers trailing up and down Purl's back. "But she does seem to have some quirks. It bothered her when I mentioned seeing her at the book club that day, which was a bit odd. Now this."

Cass pried the lid off one of Nell's glass bowls, listening, but her senses tuned in to Nell's delights. She breathed in the scent of garlic and mint and sighed dramatically.

Nell laughed and handed her a fork. She looked back at Birdie. "She came back a few hours later with a battered suitcase and cardboard box. I think Claire's life has had some rough moments."

"A suitcase?" Birdie's brows lifted.

"She's taken us up on our invitation to use the cottage for a few days."

Izzy looked up, surprised. "Your guest cottage?"

Nell nodded. "She's been staying over at the nursery in that back building. I think Fred used it as a storage room before he expanded. He lets workers stay there now and then. But it can't be very nice."

"Did she explain why she left so abruptly?" Izzy asked.

"She hadn't eaten anything before coming to work that day. Low blood sugar." Nell hadn't asked any more questions. Claire made it clear that she'd put the episode behind her and that was where she wanted it to stay.

"Blood sugar seems to cover a lot of sins these days." Birdie leaned forward and poured four glasses of wine. She settled back into the leather chair, her fingers still playing with Purl's fine coat. "I am not sure that's what it was at all. I think she's complicated. Something is going on with Claire Russell. First there was the eavesdropping on the book-club discussion. Now this."

"She wasn't eavesdropping." Nell wasn't sure where it came from, but she had a sudden compulsion to defend Claire in her absence. "As you just said, it was an open discussion."

"I think there's more to your gardener than meets the eye."

Nell laughed. "That sounds downright mysterious, Birdie. I think you're itching for a mystery."

"Maybe the book club did it to you. Danny's cold case." Izzy set a pitcher of water and some glasses on the table.

"It certainly created some controversy. A few people weren't happy Danny brought that up," Birdie said.

"He felt bad about it later," Cass said. She picked up the salad tongs and began piling the basil, mint, and cilantro salad into bowls. "He hadn't expected it to stir up memories the way it did. He was gone during that time, just like a lot of us. I was in college, and I only remember it because my mom was religious about sending local news clippings to me, no matter what the topic. It was her way of making sure we didn't forget from whence we came."

Nell laughed and took the bowls Cass handed her, spooning grilled scallops on top of the greens.

"It will die down soon," Birdie said. "The past has passed. Now, let's enjoy this meal so we can move on to the pièce de résistance. I've finished twenty more rows on Izzy's wedding shawl but will not allow it in this room until every bit of tomato sauce has disappeared, hands have been washed, and soft music is heralding this week's unveiling."

Izzy had opened the bay windows to catch the breeze, and evening harbor sounds drifted in, coating their conversation—the screech of gulls mixed with voices of tired fishermen hollering to shore.

The Thursday night ritual brought comfort into each of their lives. A chance encounter several years before—shortly after Izzy had abandoned her Boston law firm and followed a lifelong dream of owning a yarn shop—had resulted in a Thursday night knitting club that celebrated knitting and friendship over Nell's seafood pastas and Birdie's pinot gris.

"It was a miracle," Cass often said. And they'd all laugh, because for Cass, it was exactly that. She was a lobsterwoman by trade, and her knowledge of knitting back then had rivaled her ability to fly.

But none of them contested her sense of smell for food, nor her utter enjoyment in eating it. When she'd walked by Izzy's knitting shop that night, the combined aromas of Nell's wine and garlic fettuccine had wrapped around her and refused to let go, she'd said. She was in heaven, and if being privy to this group meant she had to learn how to hold a pair of bamboo needles in the same hands that hours before had dragged a lobster trap onto the dock, she'd do it. Oh so happily.

Birdie had stopped in for new knitting needles that night, and when Nell insisted she stay for a taste, she'd folded her nearly eighty-year-old body into one of Izzy's chairs and declared herself a charter member of the Thursday night knitting group.

And that was the auspicious beginning of the Seaside Knitters, as they'd tell anyone who asked them. Their ages spanned several decades, which fueled their amazing friendship—that, they'd say with a laugh, and Birdie's finest pinot grigio.

That was how it all began.

Yarn, food, wine, and friendship.

Tonight, the food disappeared before the sky completely darkened. A faint moon fought for its rightful place against the lingering light. Food was cleared, hands washed in anticipation.

Twenty more lacy waves of the most luxurious yarn that they could find.

Birdie brought the shawl into the room with great ceremony. It had been worked on for months, carrying the Seaside Knitters through a snowy winter and sensational spring. Together they'd knit—carefully, lovingly, with the attention friendship wrought.

And now, with the wedding just weeks away, they were working their way to the fine scalloped ends and the tiny beads that they'd stitch on last.

They worried at first that three women knitting the same piece would create a mismatch of tensions, uneven loops, and errors in the lacy design.

But it hadn't been so—Birdie, Nell, and Cass were proving

age-old wisdom wrong: six hands *can* work on the same piece and produce a beautiful, perfectly measured garment.

In recent weeks the pattern had emerged—an exquisite circle design that moved and curved with the grace of seaweed in a breeze, shimmering like sunlight on sand.

"Damn, but we're good," Cass said.

"Yes, we are. It's beautiful." Birdie draped the shawl over the back of the couch so it would be in place when Izzy returned from rinsing off their plates.

Nell picked up an edge and fingered the rippling design. A familiar flutter stirred deep down inside of her.

"This is exactly the way every summer should begin," Birdie said.

"With a wedding?" Cass frowned. She grasped a handful of thick black hair and slipped a band around it. Her face was flushed from a day on the water checking her traps. "Well, just don't be looking at me. I don't plan on getting married, maybe never."

Nell looked up and started to say something, but Cass filled in the words before she had a chance. "*Never say never. But I can say maybe never*, right?" Then she laughed, a slightly too-loud laugh that made the others laugh, too. She looked again at the shawl. "But I must admit, if there'd be a shawl like that in my future, I might be forced to reconsider."

Izzy took the three steps down into the room as one, then came to a sudden stop. She stood in front of the table, hand covering her mouth. Tears sprang to her eyes.

"Oh, my," she whispered.

"You will look so lovely, Izzy," Birdie said. She rested one small hand on Izzy's arm.

Izzy's eyes traveled over the intricately stitched rows. She had watched the shawl grow as it passed from Birdie to Nell to Cass and then began its round again.

It was a sacred ritual, passing from hand to hand.

But each week it was a surprise. Each week the rippling effect was more real and the lacy design more lovely. Each week it brought the ocean to life.

Birdie sat down on the couch with the end of the shawl stretched across her knees.

Nell brought her bag over and pulled out a bright green sweater, but her eyes shifted between Izzy and the wedding shawl.

Izzy was sitting in silence, her eyes following Birdie's fingers as they knit, slipped stitches, performed yarn overs, all with ease and expertise.

And they were all imagining her in her simple white dress, the shawl loose around her shoulders.

The ceremony would be simple. No bridesmaids, Izzy had decided after much distress. But blessings from friends. Her circle of friends. They'd each pick out a simple black summer dress—and Izzy would provide them each with a touch of color. A surprise, she said.

Cass reached over and fingered the soft, silky yarn, then settled back with a much smaller project, her annual hat collection that she doled out to her fellow fishermen every fall. She'd advanced to cables this year and worked carefully on a thick, wooly blend of black and gold.

No one noticed the time until Birdie complained that if she didn't get up soon, she'd be permanently anchored to the well-worn leather couch.

"Me, too," Nell said. "I should check on Claire and make sure she has what she needs."

"Aunt Nell, you're not running a hotel," Izzy said.

Nell brushed away the teasing. Izzy was right. Claire was a grown woman and could make herself at home just fine. And if she needed anything, she'd ask. She rummaged in her purse, looking for keys.

"Voilà," she said, dangling them in the air. "Come, Birdie, your chariot awaits."

Although Birdie had several cars at her disposal, including the gas-guzzling Lincoln Town Car, Ben Endicott's private campaign to keep their lively friend off the road at night had met with some success. That and several speeding tickets had convinced Birdie that sometimes having someone cater to your every whim was lovely. So she graciously took over the passenger seat, issuing directives on the most pleasant way to get from here to there.

All along Harbor Road, people walked beneath tall black gaslights, in and out of restaurants, the ice cream shop. In the distance, music blared from the open door of Jake Risso's Gull Tavern.

Next door to Izzy's knitting studio, Archie Brandley waved at them as he turned his sign around to CLOSED, pulled down the blinds, and locked the bookstore's door. Other shops along the block had closed earlier, but Archie never kept to the hours printed on his sign. "Who am I to stop someone in the middle of some fine line of text," he'd say.

"Look, Nell." Birdie pointed across the street. "Isn't that Claire Russell?"

Nell looked over and saw Auggie McClucken first. He was pulling down the blinds on the hardware store's front window.

And then she spotted Claire, directly beneath a gaslight. Her shadow fell out into the street, long and wavy. She wore a pair of jeans and the same green T-shirt she had worn that morning. Her brown hair was pulled back from her face and fastened at her neck. She walked slowly, looking at the doors of the shops along the way.

Auggie nodded at her as she passed, his thick white beard moving up and down against his chins.

Claire didn't seem to notice him, and Auggie lifted his beefy shoulders in a shrug and walked back inside.

Nell waved, then called out to her, but Claire didn't look over. Instead, her footsteps quickened.

A group of teenagers piled out of the ice cream store, nearly knocking Claire over, then gathering like a gaggle of birds beneath the lamplight. When they moved again, Claire was a shadow floating down the road.

"I guess she didn't hear you," Birdie said.

"I guess not." Nell continued to look down the street, straining to see beyond the young teen bodies now filling the sidewalk. Claire hadn't looked back, but Nell glimpsed her green shirt, and then she disappeared from sight.

Maybe Birdie was right. Maybe she hadn't heard her. Or maybe she didn't want to hear her.

Late that night, she and Ben sat together in the darkness of their deck, looking out over the world and sharing their day. It was a ritual as old as their marriage. "Settling the night," Ben called it.

Claire had installed tiny solar lights in the backyard that shined now in the blackness, casting narrow beams of light up into the pine trees and lighting the leaves of the hostas.

Ben handed her a cup of tea, then sat down beside her on the double chaise and stretched his legs out. "You like her, don't you?" he said, looking out over the yard.

"I do." And then she told him about seeing her alone, walking along Harbor Road.

"Lots of people do that. Me included." Ben chuckled softly, his way of easing away the worried tone that crept into Nell's voice. He rubbed the back of her hand.

"I know. It's silly. But I swear when I called out her name, she heard me. I could tell by the movement of her head. And then she hurried on, as if I were going to stop her."

Ben leaned his head against the back of the chair. "Sometimes, you find the damndest things to worry about."

"I'm not worried."

"You're *something*. I can hear it in your voice."

Nell sipped her tea and closed her eyes. *Something*. Yes. And then she told Ben about the day. About the look that twisted Claire's attractive face when Izzy walked out onto the deck. She'd been sitting off to the side, behind that huge hibiscus, so Izzy didn't even know she was there, Nell said.

"Do you think she was looking at Izzy?"

"No," Nell said, surprising herself with her sudden certainty. Claire had been hearing about Izzy for weeks as they worked on the yard and had met her just a couple of days earlier. There would be no way that seeing Izzy would cause such emotion on the gardener's face.

"So who?"

Nell grew silent then. *Who?*

There was only one other person within sight.

Tiffany Ciccolo, the shy hairstylist.

Chapter 8

If Birdie Favazza's hair hadn't turned pink that June morning, it might have been days before they found the body—the storage cellar wasn't an everyday trip. At least that was the thought of those who worked at the salon. But as sometimes happens, certain things fall into place so perfectly that one small move—like taking the wrong conditioning agent from a shelf—can transform an ordinary day into another kind altogether.

Normally Birdie left her gleaming cap of white hair alone. A shake of her head and a quick brush and she was set for the day. And that was just the way she liked it.

But this Friday, Lynn Holmes, M.J.'s energetic assistant, suggested a new conditioner. "Perfect for your hair, Mrs. Favazza," the young woman said.

She spoke with such enthusiasm that Birdie smiled into the muted light of the shampoo room. She was stretched out in the reclining chair, her sneakers barely touching the end. A towel cushioned her neck, and she was utterly comfortable. "Cushioned and coddled," she told Lynn. A lovely way to begin the weekend. New Age music and Lynn's hands caused her body to relax into weightlessness.

"Your hair will shine," Lynn whispered into her ear.

Birdie had no desire to shine, but she didn't want to hurt Lynn's feelings, and if a conditioner would prolong the amazing neck massage another few minutes, that would be fine.

It wasn't until she was seated back in the light of M.J.'s station that she looked into the mirror.

Nell was sitting in the chair next to her, waiting her turn. She looked over.

"Good lord, Birdie," she said, one hand flying to her own head as if whatever Birdie had might be catching.

Birdie's hands flew to her face. She leaned forward.

"A flamingo," she whispered into the mirror. "I look like a flamingo."

"You're not tall enough, dearie," Esther Gibson said, getting up in the middle of her own cut and ambling over to Birdie's chair. Her black smock flapped around her hips.

A shocked M.J. raced into the shampoo room to find Lynn. She was back in a minute, with the assistant trailing behind her looking like she'd lost her best friend.

M.J. held up the offending bottle in one hand and the new conditioner in the other. "The numbers are nearly the same," she said. "Oh, Birdie, I'm so sorry."

Behind her, Lynn stood in silence, tears welling up in her huge brown eyes.

Birdie turned toward the young girl. "Now, stop that, Lynn. It could be aubergine—not a good color for me at all. Or worse, kelly green. My Sonny would haunt me for the rest of my life if I turned up with Irish hair." She coaxed a smile out of Lynn.

"I've had blue hair once or twice," Esther offered.

"And M.J. often has red," Nell said.

"Colors are in," Birdie agreed.

"Well, this one is coming out," M.J. declared, stifling their optimistic overtures. "We have a solution that will clean this up in no time. Don't go anywhere."

Birdie smiled into the mirror. "I don't believe I will, dear." She patted the soft pink cap of hair framing her lined face.

Nell followed M.J. out of the room, offering to help.

"We keep all our extra solutions in the basement. It's out back." M.J. rummaged around on the front desk, mumbling about finding a key.

Tanya handed her one and called out as M.J. disappeared down the hallway to the back door, "Just FYI, your golden girl is MIA again. Third time this week."

The expression on M.J.'s face as she opened the back door told Nell exactly what she thought of Tanya's keeping a tally of other staff members' time—it didn't sit nicely with the salon owner.

They stepped out into the gravel alley that ran behind the shops, and M.J. turned toward the heavy storm cellar door beside the back steps.

"I know what you're thinking, Nell. Don't say it. It's foolish to have to go outside to get down here. But the cellar is always cool. It's a perfect place for the hair chemicals. Or wine," she added with a laugh. She leaned over and started to unlock the heavy metal lock, then frowned.

"Something wrong?" Nell stood just behind her.

"It's not locked. It's Tanya's job to lock things up." M.J.'s voice was clipped, disapproving. Two strikes against Tanya.

M.J. lifted the heavy lid and braced it back against the building. She walked down the stone steps, flipping on a light at the bottom. "You don't need to come down, Nell. I'm doing great things to the front of the basement, but, unfortunately, this part is still a dungeon."

But Nell was already on the bottom step. "Ben's family had one of those bulkhead doors on their house that led to the basement. We kept it, but during the remodeling we built an inside staircase."

M.J. laughed. "Yes. Yes. I get your message. It's on my list of redos. I've actually finished off one room down here in the back for Tiff to use as an office. It's pretty nice. She loves it. I just haven't gotten around to giving her an inside entrance. I think I might eventually make this whole area a spa. So much to do, so little time. Soon, soon." One hand fluttered in the air. "Now, where's that toner? Tiffany keeps things in order down here, but sometimes Tanya likes to change things around. I think just on principle."

She pushed a short step stool over to a tall metal shelf and climbed up, peering down a row of numbered bottles on a shadowy shelf. "Would you grab that flashlight on the counter over there, Nell? I may need the tall ladder, too. I need to get these lights fixed so a person can see farther than two feet in front of her. Tiffany keeps reminding me of that."

Nell stepped over a ladder lying on the floor, then found the flashlight on a counter that ran along the wall. She pressed the button to be sure it worked. Instantly a beam of light sliced across the stone floor and the fallen ladder. Then it seemed to stop—at least in Nell's mind's eye—blocked by something on the floor.

It was the shoe that she saw first. A bright candy red shoe with a chunky heel.

A familiar shoe.

She moved the flashlight over the shoe, across the concrete floor to a bare foot. Then up the leg to a wrinkled cotton dress.

Nell's cry bounced off the damp cellar wall and brought M.J. to her side in seconds.

They fell to the floor beside Tiffany Ciccolo, her black-rimmed glasses smashed at her side, her long, curved body as still as the air in the damp cellar room.

Chapter 9

Hours later, Nell stood at the kitchen sink, looking out into the fading sunlight. Through the open windows, she could hear Ben and Sam talking on the deck. The talk was quieter than the usual Friday night chatter when friends gathered on the Endicott deck to end their week, to let go of tension, or to share triumphs and good news.

The gravelly sound of ice being shaken in Ben's martini shaker was there, as always. A perfect martini was Ben's prescription to separate them from the stress of the week—or simply a mellow way of welcoming the weekend.

And she could hear Izzy shuffling through the stack of CDs over near the fireplace, picking her favorites. Cass and Danny had just driven up in Cass' noisy pickup, and she heard Willow's voice in the distance, talking about Canary Cove's next art showing. Through the kitchen window she watched Ham and Jane Brewster walking slowly along the far edge of the yard, exploring Claire's handiwork. They paused beneath the pines, their bodies gently leaning into each other with the familiarity forty years can nurture. Somewhere in the distance Pete strummed an old guitar of Ben's, humming softly.

Harold Sampson, Birdie's groundsman—or estate manager, as he liked to be called—had driven her over early. She was rummaging around in the back pantry now, looking for cracker bread to go with the spicy crab dip she'd picked up at the fish market.

The scene was familiar and calming in its routine. Normal. Ordinary.

But there was an undertone tonight.

Nell never knew how many friends and neighbors would show up on Friday nights, but she knew one thing from experience—bad news and good news, in equal measure, were sure to bring a sizable group together. They'd nurse Ben's martinis and find comfort in friendship and the familiar sizzle of fish being seared on the grill. They'd sit, sometimes in silence, listening to the music and watching the day disappear beneath the night sky.

Tonight they'd all come, saddened by the death of a woman who had died too early, though most of Ben and Nell's friends didn't know her well—some not at all. But the web that encircled small towns held a collective grief and passed it along from one person to the next.

Nell had walked down to the guest cottage earlier to see if Claire wanted to join them. When no one answered the door, she was almost relieved. She didn't want Claire to sit in the cottage alone while the sounds and smells of a party rolled down the lawn and through her open windows. But it seemed less than a perfect night to bring someone new into the mix.

She surmised Claire was working at the nursery, since Fred kept it open late on Fridays. If that was the case, it eased a bit of Nell's guilt, too, since she had been using Claire so much these past days. She certainly had to be the best employee Fred had on staff, and he was being gracious about the time she spent at Nell's.

"Will this platter do?" Birdie asked, coming in from the pantry. She set the crackers and large platter on the island.

Nell nodded, then looked at her friend for a minute. She took off her glasses and pushed them to the top of her head. "Your hair looks fine, Birdie," she said.

Birdie smiled, her hand absently patting her smooth, once-again silvery cap of hair.

Lynn had quickly redeemed herself that morning. M.J. had

insisted on getting the neutralizing solution upstairs to her so she could apply it to Birdie's hair as soon as possible. Time was of the essence, she'd said. The toner did its work, and M.J. had calmed Lynn down with a reminder that the bottles were distinguishable only by numbers, the mistake was one anyone could have made, and she would definitely get the lights downstairs fixed.

Nell stayed out in the alley to meet the ambulance. It appeared in minutes, its wheels spraying gravel in all directions as it screeched to a stop beside the salon's back door. Nell directed them to where Tiffany lay. A police car arrived minutes later and parked behind the ambulance. Nell and M.J. were asked to wait upstairs and to keep the news from the customers in the salon, something M.J. was only too happy to do.

"It was just hours ago," Birdie said now, breaking the thin cracker bread into pieces. "Time gets so distorted when things unnatural are thrown into a day. That poor young girl."

The paramedics had not even applied CPR. Tiffany had been dead for a while, Nell heard one of them say. And that fit with what M.J. said. No one had seen her at all that morning, even though she was scheduled to work.

From all appearances, she had climbed a ladder in the dimly lit room and toppled off, her head hitting the concrete floor. A hard, awful fall for anyone.

Izzy walked into the kitchen and pulled herself up on an island stool. Cass and Willow trailed close behind her.

"How unreal is this?" Izzy said. Her brown eyes filled her face. She brushed a sun-streaked strand of hair from her cheek. "We were with her yesterday. Just yesterday. And now she's dead."

Tears welled up in Izzy's eyes.

Nell knew what she was thinking. Even though they didn't know Tiffany, not really, somehow her connection to Sam and Izzy's wedding made her death more personal, more intimate, than it would have been a few weeks ago.

Pete carried a tray of martinis into the kitchen and set them on the counter. "Ben says you should have the first batch."

"Ben's absolutely right." Willow picked up an icy glass and handed it to Nell. "Did the police tell you anything?" The young fiber artist washed her hands and helped herself to a colander of cleaned, crisped lettuce and began tearing it into small pieces.

Nell shook her head. "It was Tommy Porter and his partner. He sent us inside, and they stayed with the paramedics. We were glad to disappear. M.J. said her customers weren't even aware of the commotion."

"I don't believe they were. They were more interested in my pink hair. I provided comic relief. Laura Danvers, shame on her, even took a photo of it with her cell phone." Birdie added the pot of clam sauce to the cracker bread and handed the platter to Pete as he walked by. "For the outsiders," she explained.

"M.J. liked Tiffany. This will be hard on her. She was kind of a surrogate mother to her." Nell pulled a tray of lobster tails from the refrigerator while she talked.

"I think I saw her mother once—the real one. She lives around here, doesn't she?" Jane Brewster asked as she began slicing an avocado for Willow's salad. "She came into the salon one day when I was there, but it was a couple of years ago."

"They used to live in a trailer on the edge of town," Birdie said. "I heard the father drank himself to death a few years ago, or so the rumor went, and I think Mrs. Ciccolo had a difficult time of it all, probably her whole life, then started having trouble remembering things. She's in that home over in Rockport now with severe dementia."

Pete listened silently to the conversation around him as he circled the kitchen, eyeing the lobster tails, then moving around the island to the stove and the pan of simmering butter sauce. Floppy hair the color of beach sand fell over his forehead as he leaned into the simmering scents of butter and lemon, orange zest and ginger, rising into the air. He straightened up and grinned. "I love you, Nell."

Everyone laughed. Like his sister, Pete was a pushover for food. He began topping off glasses, draining the pitcher of martinis. "Ben hates this, you know. Each drink should be shaken separately, have its own icy layer floating on top."

"Which means he never gets to enjoy them with us. Ignore him, Pete. Sometimes he needs to give a little, not demand perfect martinis."

"Yeah," Pete said. "That's what I told him. Though the perfect ones are pretty good."

"Speaking of telling things, Pete, does Andy know about Tiffany Ciccolo?" Izzy asked.

Pete shrugged. "I dunno, Iz. I called his cell when I heard about it, but he didn't pick up. It seemed like a lame thing to leave on voice mail, so I just hung up. He'll know it was me. He's had the weight of the world on his shoulders the past few days; at least that's how it looked to me. He never showed up for our jam session last night, and that's not like him." He took a sip of Willow's martini, then handed it back. "Merry and I couldn't figure out if Tiffany was good for Andy or bad. For a while there in the spring, they were tight. She was always around, and Andy seemed to fall into it, going off with her after jam sessions or shows. But I don't know—there was something weird. It was almost like they had gone through something that continued to hold them together. You know, like people who survive a catastrophe, like a car crash or something."

Nell listened at the sink as she snipped through the membrane on the undersides of the tails. Pete's interpretation of their relationship bond was an interesting one—and she understood, at least in a general way, what he meant. He'd also said that they were close—at least for a while. But they had seemed anything but close on Hank and Merry's deck a few nights ago.

"Grill's ready," Ben called in from the deck. "Bring on the Hallorans' gorgeous crustaceans."

Cass lifted her martini glass in agreement. "As always, we saved the best of our catch for the Endicott grill." Earlier in the day she and

Pete had dropped off a huge lumpy sack of scrambling lobsters. "A terrific morning on the water," Cass told Ben. "Hardly a throwaway in the bunch. My traps are magical this month. Good karma. I think it's because it's Izzy and Sam's wedding month."

Ben had cut off the tails for tonight's dinner. Nell would use the rest of the meat for a new casserole she wanted to try.

A giant maple tree growing beside the deck hung over the long teak table like a canopy. Birdie and Jane had already brought out place mats and flatware, pitchers of water, and a ceramic pot of pansies from Jane's garden. The others followed, bustling back and forth in a familiar rhythm, and in a few minutes they'd filled the table with baskets of French bread, a platter of sweet potato fries, and Willow's pear salad, complete with homemade croutons and sugared pecans. A heaping bowl of quinoa with bright green slivers of basil, mint, and parsley graced the center of the table.

The rest was up to Ben, who stood by the grill, brushing each lobster tail with the orange-flavored butter sauce. The group fell silent as they relaxed into the evening and the sounds of Dave Brubeck's quartet filling the night air. They passed around a platter of cheese and sipped their drinks, watching Ben, his body silhouetted against the darkening sky. Dribbles of butter sauce fell on the hot coals as he basted, and a magnificent sizzle filled the air.

In the distance, waves crashed against the shore and peace fell over the group. Ben's martinis had done their magic; the tension eased away like a receding tide.

The toast before dinner was the same as it always was—"To family, to friends. To peace . . ."—followed by a resounding "Hear, hear" as raised glasses clinked together.

Izzy sat next to Sam, her thigh pressed tight against his. He picked her hand up from the table and ran a blunt photographer's finger over the floating sapphire in her engagement ring.

She smiled, and the flush in her cheeks deepened.

"Hey, you two," Cass said, waving across the table. "None of that. Lobsters are getting cold."

"Oh? You don't like that lovey-dovey stuff?" Danny teased, and proved her wrong with a sound, silencing kiss.

In the laughter that followed, the ringing phone almost went unheard. Willow, sitting closest to the French doors, started to stand. "Nell, it's your landline. Do you want me to get it?"

"It's probably Mom, Aunt Nell," Izzy said. "Maybe you can call her back later?"

Nell looked down the table toward Ben.

He met her look and shrugged—he wasn't expecting any calls, his shoulders said. Nell felt uncomfortable, a feeling she immediately dismissed as being totally irrational. Most of the Sea Harbor people close to her were sitting around this table. And Nell knew it wasn't her sister Caroline. She'd talked to her a few hours before. It was probably a sales call or donation request for the firemen's ball—but she'd answer it anyway, then dismiss it wholly. Nell knew she'd never adopt the ease with which Izzy and Cass ignored cell phone calls.

"I'll get it, dear," she said to Willow, and walked inside.

Ben followed her, having noticed that the wine was disappearing as fast as the lobster and the water glasses needed to be topped off. Sam took over at the grill, filling another platter with stray chunks of lobster meat for the hearty eaters among them.

As Birdie began passing the quinoa around for second helpings, Ham Brewster took center stage with a lively rendition of the sailing class they'd taught that afternoon. His beard moved with the vigor of his story as he described the new batch of kids who had signed on for a summer of adventure. They were all from low-income families, and Ben, Sam, and Ham had patched together a program with the community center that kept the youths busy every season of the year—sailing and baseball in good weather, and for cold-weather months, they'd gotten Hank Jackson to help coach a basketball league.

Today it was Hank who stole the show, Ham explained. They'd recruited Hank—in spite of his protests—to help with the class because a couple of the college helpers couldn't make it. They quickly found out why Hank had not come on board willingly. Just out of the yacht-club harbor, the bar owner fell overboard while they were demonstrating a jibe to the neophyte student crew. He'd flown off the side to the enthusiastic cheering of the kids, who'd thought it was a great act.

"Poor Hank," Ham told his audience. "He hadn't told any of us his long-held secret—he doesn't know how to swim.

"He had tried his best to hide his fear, his life jacket buoying him up, but Sam realized what was going on—" Here Ham acknowledged Sam with a bow. "He told the kids to watch carefully, and jumped in after our floundering crew member as if it had all been planned."

And only the two men left to control the sail knew Hank hadn't done it intentionally to teach them to be wary. They all make mistakes, Sam and Hank told the boys as they climbed back up on deck. Then they warned them sternly, "But be always watchful of a sail changing directions."

Sam chuckled. "Afterward we were merciless with Hank. Teased him bloody. And he admitted after his second beer that he was much more comfortable on a basketball court than a boat. He'd not lived near water until he was out of college—and then was embarrassed to learn to swim."

A good sport, they all agreed. "And a waterlogged one," Ham added.

They'd gone on then, with sailing sagas, until Birdie's wineglass went dry and she realized Ben was still gone. She frowned, about to call for him when the door to the deck opened.

Nell stepped out with Ben beside her, his arm looped around her shoulders. She had slipped a sweater over her linen top, and a large slouchy bag hung over one shoulder.

A step or two behind them, standing in the shadows of the living area, was Tommy Porter in full police uniform.

The group grew silent and stared at the odd threesome.

"Have you two been arrested?" Ham joked to break the silence. "I knew it was just a matter of time."

Tommy's sober look stilled the laughter. "No. No way," he said. He spoke in staccato, each word punctuating the air with conviction.

Nell calmed him with a smile. "It's all right, Tommy. Everyone understands."

"That was Chief Thompson on the phone," Ben began. "Tommy was patrolling nearby, so he sent him over in case we needed a ride."

"Which we do," Nell said. "Or *I* do. Ben will stay here, and I'll be back as soon as I can. The chief would like to talk to me. M.J.'s already down there. It won't take long. But he felt it was better not to wait until tomorrow. I'll be back in time for Jane's key lime pie."

"Back from where?" Consternation flooded Ham's face. "What the hell's going on?"

"Ham is right, dears," Birdie said gently. "You're not making much sense. I think there's a premise missing in your little proposition. A missing middle, perhaps?"

Nell's face had lost a little of its color, and her fingers played with the straps of her purse. "Of course, you're right. Sorry for the ambiguity. It's difficult, that's all. It appears that Tiffany didn't fall off the ladder, as we first thought."

"And M. J. Ar-Arc-Arcado and Nell here were—were the f-first guys there," Tommy said.

Which everyone listening was well aware of.

And then Ben said what they were all dreading to hear—the reason why Nell's face was pale and Tommy's stuttering had returned.

"There are signs that indicate Tiffany Ciccolo was murdered."

Chapter 10

Izzy emerged from the Endicott woods and ran along the back pathway to the house, her running shoes sound and swift on the flagstone path.

Nell heard her before she saw her, and then a blur of long, lean body flew up the deck steps and into the house.

Nell sat at the kitchen island in a pair of capris and a loose cotton blouse. The Sea Harbor paper was spread out in front of her. Cups of cold coffee sat abandoned at the sink.

Izzy eyed the cups. "Three cups. Who beat me here?" She wiped her damp forehead with a wristband and peeled her tank top loose from her damp skin, then let it settle back in a slow bubble against her freckled chest.

"Birdie has come and gone. She stopped at Coffee's on her way and brought some gossip tidbits, then headed off to teach her dance class."

"What are people saying?"

"Birdie said most of the talk was about tighter security on Harbor Road. More security guards, brighter lights, that sort of thing. And there was some unfair criticism of M.J. for not building an inside access to her basement. That bulkhead 'was just begging a burglar to stop in and say hello,' Beatrice Scaglia said."

"I'd think a window would provide easier access for a burglar,"

Izzy said. "And there were plenty of those." She poured herself a cup of coffee and sat down next to Nell. "Is Ben off with Sam?"

"Yes. Another sailing class for the kids."

"They're obsessed with the kids winning the regatta again. I saw Ham peddling over from Canary Cove on his bike, headed toward the club."

"Keep the day as normal as you can. That's Ben's motto. I suppose it's a good one."

They had all waited for Nell to come home the night before. They'd cleaned the grill and washed up the dishes, but saved dessert.

As Nell had predicted, it hadn't taken long at the station. Unfortunately, they didn't have much to say to Jerry Thompson. Nothing very helpful. So after going over the story twice, Chief Thompson had called it a night and told Tommy to drive them home.

"I can't get my arms around this. And you, Aunt Nell—you were right there in the salon."

"Not when she was killed. They think it was the night before."

"While we were knitting in my shop?" Izzy said. "We're just down the street. Geesh."

"Maybe it was later. Around eleven or so."

"How could this have happened? Why Tiffany Ciccolo? She's such a quiet kind of person. Who would have anything against her?"

Chief Thompson had avoided that question the night before, dancing around it, but now Nell pointed at the paper. Izzy read the large headline out loud.

ROBBERY GONE BAD. YOUNG STYLIST KILLED.

"A robbery?" Izzy's voice was coated in disbelief. "What would a thief possibly steal from M.J.'s? Hair color? Scissors? Combs and brushes? That's odd."

"The police found some things missing. A laptop computer that Tiffany used, for one. There was a small office down there that she used for her event planning. Her cell phone. But Ben thinks it's being reported as a robbery for now to stop wild rumors from circulating. Maybe it was a robbery—but maybe it wasn't. They'll know soon."

Izzy put her hands on her hips and stared at the paper. "Well, I for one don't believe it was a robbery."

"But the alternative is equally hard to believe. Who would want to kill sweet Tiffany Ciccolo?"

Izzy nodded. Her bare shoulders and legs were glistening from her run along the beach, but Nell suspected the flush on her cheeks was as much from confusion as from exertion. It didn't make sense to Nell, either, though she had no grounds for her disbelief. Just common sense, she supposed. There were plenty of shops along Harbor Road that would have provided more of a cache.

Murdering someone for a laptop and a few dollars?

Izzy looked over at the clock on the stove, then back to Nell. "I need to go." She slipped off the stool and grabbed her cell phone from the counter. "Mae's nieces filled the store window with the most gorgeous butter-soft summer yarn you've ever seen in your entire life. I suspect the shop will be packed today. Summer projects." She took a few steps, then stopped short and looked back. "I almost forgot. I ran into Pete at the beach. He said he found Andy last night after he left here."

"Where?"

"He was sitting at the end of the pier, over near Gracie Santos' lobster shack, a bottle of whiskey beside him."

Nell frowned. That was unlike Andy. He was often teased because his family owned a bar—and he disliked the taste of alcohol. A beer every now and then seemed to be Andy's sole indulgence.

"He wasn't wrecked, Pete said, but had had a few. Pete assumed he knew about Tiffany, but he didn't; at least that was Pete's impression. And when Pete told him what had happened, Andy reacted strangely. Not at all what Pete expected—though he admitted he wasn't sure what to expect."

"What do you mean?"

"Andy looked at him and said, 'Harmony's dead?'"

"Harmony?"

"Well, Pete thought that's what he said, but he wasn't sure. Harmony, like in their music. Merry and Pete had been having some trouble harmonizing on some new lyrics, and Andy had teased them about it last week. At first Pete thought Andy was making another joke about it. Then he just sat still for a few minutes, staring at nothing and kind of rocking back and forth, looking sad. After a while he held up the bottle and offered Pete a drink. 'To old times,' he said."

"And that was it?"

"Then Pete took him home. They drove by Dunkin' Donuts for coffee on the way. He said Andy was quiet. A sad kind of quiet, like he was thinking about Tiffany—about her death. Pete offered to stay a while, to talk about things, but Andy brushed him off. Said it was late, that he was tired."

Izzy checked her watch again. "And speaking of late . . ." She walked over and planted a kiss on Nell's cheek.

"I love you," she murmured, more to herself than to her aunt.

But it didn't escape Nell's ears, and she watched through the open doors as Izzy sailed down the flagstone path and into the back woods, disappearing as quickly as she'd come, a lovely blur against the summer day.

When Ben returned home much later that day, he found Nell not far from where he had left her, sitting at the kitchen island. But the kitchen was cleaned up, the house smelled fresh, and the newspaper had been replaced by her laptop. She proudly announced that not only had she updated Izzy's wedding to-do list and returned a dozen phone calls, but she had taken a shower, been to the post office and the market, and written two proposals for the arts commission that had been hanging over her head. The day was disappearing—but it had been a full one.

The commitments Nell made because of her inability to say no in her retirement, Ben often said, rivaled the time she used to put in as a full-time director of the Boston nonprofit.

"You smell like the sea," Nell observed, taking off her glasses. "Nice."

"Which is why I'm off to take a shower before the Brewsters show up."

Nell raised her eyebrows.

"Movie night, remember? That new theater in Gloucester?"

She hadn't remembered.

"No problem. You've a lot going on. But eating might help your memory—here's a snack, if you skipped lunch. Leftovers. We took the boys over to Harry's after sailing." Ben dropped a bag of Harry Garozzo's Saturday hoagie specials on the counter. He took one out and peeled off the white paper, then set it on a plate. "A thing of beauty. Enjoy, my love."

The kiss he planted on Nell's lips was salty and delicious. She considered a second shower, then reluctantly turned her attention back to sending two final e-mails. Finally, satisfied her sent box was healthy and happy, she closed her laptop and turned her full attention to Harry's hoagie. It wasn't really a late-afternoon snack—it was a feast.

The crisp, homemade bun was so stuffed, she wondered how anyone could get a mouth around it. Layers of provolone, roasted peppers, purple eggplant, sweet gherkins, thinly sliced tomato, and sautéed onion were piled high and topped with Harry's thick pink sauce, which dribbled down the sides. Nell caught it with her fingertip and licked it clean. She cut the sandwich into small wedges.

Ben's gesture was sweet, especially since he was right. She'd become immersed in getting things done and had only snacked lightly. She walked over to the sink and stood there for a minute, absently washing her hands, her eyes scanning the yard.

Her favorite view. The yard painted in a dozen shades of green, the sea just barely visible though the tops of leafy trees, the sun casting long shadows across the yard as it made its way down the western horizon.

She had loved this yard from the first time Ben brought her to his family's vacation home. It was filled with memories—noisy picnics in the back with his brothers and various girlfriends, volleyball games. Clambakes and lazy afternoons in the rope hammock. Madeline and Jim Endicott made everyone feel at home at 22 Sandswept Lane, and Nell felt a certain pride in knowing she and Ben had carried on his parents' legacy.

Today the lawn looked especially welcoming. Was the grass greener since Claire came into its life? The flowers brighter? A movement out of the corner of her eye shifted her attention to the guesthouse, nearly hidden behind a thick row of rugosa roses. Claire was walking around the side of the cottage. She picked up a hose coiled near the corner of the house, turned on the faucet knob, and began spraying the roses.

Nell had almost forgotten that Claire had moved into the guesthouse. Ben had been more hospitable than she. Before leaving that morning, he'd gone down with the newspaper and a cup of coffee, which Claire had gratefully accepted. She was still in a robe, Ben said, and looked like she'd just gotten up, so he left her alone to begin her day in peace and quiet.

Nell watched for a minute, then, feeling like a voyeur, turned from the window. She found Claire fascinating. She was beautiful in a classic kind of way—long face and nose, high, round cheekbones. But her face held a kind of mystery, too, and had lines that Nell suspected had stories behind them. She often felt Claire's reticence to talk about herself when they worked together in the garden, though she asked dozens of questions about the town, about Izzy's wedding. It was like a dance. Some days Nell would feel she was on the cusp of getting to know what Claire was all about, and then there'd be graceful—but definite—steps back.

She looked at the sandwich wedges on the counter. Then she impulsively slipped them onto a plate with some raw veggies, grabbed napkins and two bottles of water, and headed toward the back of the yard.

Claire spun around at the sound of her footsteps. The hose flew up in the air, the arc of the water creating a rainbow in the sunshine.

"Nell, I'm sorry. I didn't hear you."

"You were deep in thought."

"Deep in watering, anyway." Claire got the hose under control and continued her watering, moving from the roses to a border of hostas, then on to the thirsty hydrangea bushes. Water beaded up on the deep green leaves.

"I don't know if I've even thanked you, Nell," Claire began, her eyes on the watering. "Your guesthouse is wonderful. I'm surprised you can pry people out of it once they spend one night in that magnificent bed—that and the sea air coming in the window. It's quite amazing. It clears your head."

"It's magic. The magic of the sea. And you're welcome to stay as long as you like." Nell put the plate down on a low wrought-iron table and motioned for Claire to join her. "Watering can wait, but this snack can't. A taste of Italy, compliments of Ben—and our friend Harry Garozzo." She sat on the curved garden bench. "Or save it for dinner, if you'd like. But, anyway, taking a break to admire your amazing green thumb is always a good thing."

Claire hesitated, but only for a moment. She turned off the faucet and took the plate Nell handed her. "Room and board, too. I am one lucky woman."

Nell laughed. "How is the painting coming on your apartment?"

"Fine. A week or two, they said." She chewed a bite of sandwich, then set it back on her plate. "But . . . well, I'm rethinking my plans."

"You've found something you like better?"

Claire looked over toward the gerbera daisies, brilliant splashes of pink, coral, and peach. She concentrated on them as if offering them a say in the conversation. Finally she turned back. "I don't know if I'll be here long."

Nell stopped in midbite. "You're welcome to stay, Claire—"

"No, I don't mean *here*, Nell. I mean in Sea Harbor. I thought it would be good to come back east, good for me . . . but I may have made a mistake. I have a sister in Texas, and she's always asking me to come down there."

"Texas . . ."

She nodded. "She has a place in the foothills. Plenty of room. And they always need gardeners down there."

"Not as much as we need them here."

"You're sweet. And you and Ben have been so gracious, quite wonderful, really. Opening your home this way. Working on the yard for Izzy has been the best thing that's happened to me in a long time. I'd always dreamed of preparing for a wedding this way."

"And you've done a wonderful job, but—"

Claire spoke in a rush. "Don't think for one minute I'd leave in the middle of this, Nell. I'd never do that. I'll make sure everything is perfect for the wedding."

"I'm not concerned about that. I'm just surprised. I thought you were settling in and liking it here. And selfishly speaking, I'm enjoying getting to know you. And I had hoped that would continue."

Claire was quiet for a minute, her eyes taking in the yard, the plants, the wooded path that led to the sea. She took a drink of water. "I meant it when I said you and Ben have been a bright light in my life. Probably the brightest in years, if truth be told. But you don't know me, Nell, not really. My life's been different, not a straight, nice road at all. It's been—"

Her words dropped off, interrupted by a sound coming from the deck. The two women looked up and saw Ham Brewster and Ben moving two Adirondack chairs into the shade. They settled down in the chairs, each holding a glass of Scotch in his hand. A minute later, Jane joined them and sat on a chaise.

Ben held up his glass and called down to them, "It's relaxing time. Join us?"

Nell looked at Claire, but she was already shaking her head and rising from the bench. "I have some things I want to do out here before it gets too dark," she said to Nell. She motioned toward a newly mulched area, filled now with snowy white impatiens. "And later, there's a stack of books waiting for me inside." A slight smile lifted her lips as if to reassure Nell that she was fine. "It's fine. *I'm* fine. It's my favorite way to spend a summer night," she said. Then she moved away and turned the faucet until the spray came out full and strong, and she aimed it at the thick stand of roses along the side of the guest cottage.

Nell covered the plate of food with a napkin, reminded Claire that it was there for her, and walked slowly toward the deck. She looked back at the slender woman, now moving in and around the planted beds as if she were among friends. *Curious,* she thought. She wondered briefly if the plants in her garden knew more about Claire Russell than she did. She suspected they did.

Claire turned around then, almost as if she knew Nell would be standing there, watching her.

Their eyes met, and Claire waved, a graceful, slow-motion movement in the darkening sky.

A sudden, discomforting feeling passed through Nell. Finally, she lifted her hand and waved back.

And she hoped it didn't mean good-bye.

Chapter 11

First she had forgotten the movie date with Ham and Jane.

The next day, Nell stood in front of the kitchen calendar, fresh from her shower, frowning. It had happened again—this time she'd almost forgotten an event that had been on her calendar for weeks.

She knew what the distraction was—it was Tiffany Ciccolo's death, of course. It was finding her body on the cold floor of M.J.'s cellar. Her heart mourned for the young girl, and her heart yearned for normalcy. The robbery and death had thrown the town into disarray. Things weren't normal, weren't what they should be.

That was what was causing Nell to go to the store twice in a day for milk and to leave her debit card in the machine's slot.

But today's forgetfulness bothered Nell exceedingly.

She had almost forgotten about the Danvers' party for Izzy and Sam, scheduled for that night. But there it was on the calendar, as big as life, printed in oversized letters. She stared at the calendar, scolding herself out loud.

"But you didn't forget," Ben said, coming up behind her. He wrapped his arms around her.

"Almost."

"Not even almost. It wouldn't have happened. That's why we put things on calendars. What you're upset about is that there's a shadow over everything right now. A young girl is dead. We're not sure why. People are concerned, worried. And you want it all to go away."

Nell nodded, still looking at the calendar.

"But we won't let any of this overshadow Izzy and Sam's time. We won't. It's just too fresh right now. Just a few days."

Nell knew Ben was right. It was all too recent. Too fresh.

Ben nuzzled her neck. "You smell good. And so does the coffee. And that's all we need to remember right now."

Nell turned and leaned into his body. Together they walked over to the island to coffee and juice and the comfort of each other.

Ben was right. They wouldn't have forgotten the party, and it was just what they all needed. And for all Izzy's protestations, the party would be a good thing for everyone.

Izzy had told them all months ago that she didn't want a bridal shower. They'd be living in Sam's place, which was small, and they didn't need much anyway, she insisted. Each of them had had their own place for a long time, complete with toasters and microwaves. Their wants were few.

Want what you have, she'd quoted to Nell.

But Laura Danvers would have none of it. She was having a shower for Izzy and Sam whether the bride- and groom-to-be came or not.

In the end, it had been a compromise. Laura had agreed to call it a party—a celebration, the invitation said—the beginning of a glorious life together. And at the bottom, a discreet note, much to Laura's chagrin and Izzy's insistence: *No gifts, please.*

The Danvers lived in a newer Sea Harbor neighborhood, north of the downtown area. Laura and her banker husband, Elliott, had married right after their Duke University graduations, and he'd built the house for his bride soon after. It was spacious and sprawling, a perfect entertainment house, and the Danvers used it often for just that, giving equal time to parties and to playdates and birthday parties for their two young daughters. The home was up a long, winding road of equally fine residences, but the Danvers' home was at the very top of the hill, at the end of the road.

"The pinnacle," Birdie said, climbing the wide granite steps to the house with one hand on Ben's arm. "A beautiful home. But why would anyone need so many rooms? They only have those two lovely little girls—" She looked up at the dozens of large windows in the contemporary styled home.

Ben simply smiled, and Nell did the same, refraining from reminding Birdie that she lived alone in the magnificent eight-bedroom house her first husband, Sonny Favazza, had built for his bride many years before.

The night held a soft breeze, and the large front door was open wide to welcome it.

"The guests of honor are out on the deck; there's a bar in the great room; make yourselves at home," Laura said, welcoming them with hugs. "It's a perfect night. And we all need a celebration, don't you think?"

"And you're the perfect person to make that happen," Nell said. She meant it sincerely. Though younger than Izzy, Laura Danvers was following in her mother's footsteps as a hostess with impeccable taste and the uncanny ability to make even the stuffiest corporate gathering fun.

But tonight's party wouldn't be peopled by bankers and CEOs. Tonight was reserved for all the people who had touched Izzy's life since she had moved to Sea Harbor and opened the Seaside Knitting Studio—from artists and shopkeepers to bar owners, knitting customers, and band members. A hodgepodge of earthy people. All of whom loved Izzy Chambers and Sam Perry.

Jerry Thompson was near the bar, surrounded by a group of women pummeling him with conversation, with a bit of flirtation peppering their talk. A widower for two years now, Chief Thompson had risen to the top of the list of Sea Harbor's eligible bachelors over the age of fifty. He threw Ben a "rescue me" look, and he and Birdie headed the chief's way.

Nell looked beyond the open living space that included a bar and sparkling granite and stainless-steel kitchen. A great fireplace and soft, cushy furniture. A wall of doors opened up to a back stone patio, where she spotted Jake Risso talking with the Brewsters—Jane was wearing a long, flowing skirt. Nell suspected Jane had brought the skirt with her when she and Ham happened upon Sea Harbor in the '70s. They'd fallen in love with the seaside town and never returned to their more bohemian life in Berkeley, California. Ham's beard was neatly trimmed, his jeans clean, and the sleeves of a crisp white shirt rolled partway up his arms. They stood near the edge of the patio looking down the hill, over treetops and houses and children's play equipment, to a panoramic view of an endless sea.

Nell looked around at chatting, happy groups of friends, hoping she'd spot Andy Risso. He'd been on her mind all day, and she was concerned about him. She wondered if he had come with his dad. Pete Halloran was there—and Merry and Hank Jackson. Lots of his friends. Surely he'd show.

"I don't think anyone knows if there'll be a funeral," she heard M.J. telling Merry and Hank Jackson. M.J.'s husband, Alex, stood next to her, just outside the patio doors.

"They haven't been able to find her sister yet," Alex explained.

"Tiffany had a sister?" Nell asked, coming up behind them.

M.J. nodded. "Sheila was older than Tiff. Tiffany told me her sister ran away from home when she was in her teens, but she called Tiffany often. They kept in close touch."

"She mentioned Sheila to me once or twice," Merry said. "She said her sister had a great job somewhere. Tiffany was proud of her."

"Did she say where she lived?" M.J. asked.

Merry shook her head.

"They're still looking for contact information," M.J. said. "The police thought I'd have it, but we don't ask for that kind of information from our staff. Maybe we should. The phone number would have been on Tiffany's phone, but it's missing."

Father Lawrence Northcutt was standing next to Merry, his gray head leaning in to hear the conversation. The pastor of Our Lady of the Seas had lived in Sea Harbor longer than anyone could remember. He knew everyone in town, regardless of their spiritual beliefs, and his presence almost always brought a comforting hug with it. "Tiffany's life was sometimes lonely after Sheila went off," he said. "She'd come see me sometimes. Things weren't easy at home. But you, M.J., you added good things to her life when you gave her that job. Working for you meant something to her. It made her think better of herself."

He smiled at M.J. and patted Alex Arcado on the back. "You've a fine life partner, Alex."

"M.J.'s a gem, Father; don't I know it." The fire chief's shoulders were as broad as a Patriots offensive tackle, but his smile was as soft as a puppy dog. He and M.J. had been married twenty years, and Alex Arcado still looked like he'd just proposed to her and been surprised beyond belief when M.J. had said yes.

"It's all so enormously sad," Merry said. Hank wrapped his arm around her, nearly burying her in the curve of his large frame, as if to protect her from the sadness. She pulled away. "So sad," she repeated.

Nell watched them, sensing the comfort Hank wanted to bring to Merry. And then she remembered back to that night at the Palate. That night Hank and Merry both had tried to comfort to Tiffany. She'd been upset. And they had tried to help her.

It was the day Tiffany had missed the meeting with Izzy about wedding day plans.

It was the day before she died.

Nell's thoughts were tangled, jumping from one thing to the next. Then settling back into the simple, sad fact that Tiffany Ciccolo was dead now, and whatever was bothering her that night was no longer relevant. The randomness of life had stepped in and taken it away.

The tinkling of a fork on crystal called for silence, and a hush fell over the patio. Those inside gravitated toward the open patio doors while Laura and Elliott Danvers moved to an open space near several blooming hibiscus plants, as tall as Laura herself. She motioned for Sam and Izzy to join them. Nell could feel the blush creeping up

Izzy's neck to her face. She'd given many presentations in law school and had been in the limelight during her days in the courtroom, but it had all been in the line of duty; being singled out this way was difficult for Izzy.

But that was just fine, Nell thought. She needed to know how loved she was, and that was why all these people were here. Even if Laura's speech might be longer than Izzy would like it to be.

But Laura surprised them. She asked everyone to lift a glass and said simply and sincerely, "To Izzy and Sam. Two people whose lives matter greatly to us. Two people who have touched each one of us in many ways. We love you both."

And that was it.

People cheered and clapped, and some whistles pierced the air from back corners. It was perfect.

To Izzy and Sam.

To Sam and Izzy.

We love you.

Nell's eyes were moist, even without the more sentimental toast she'd expected. It was as it should be. Laura Danvers got it right.

Izzy was at her side before she could pull a tissue from her bag. She looped one arm through Nell's and the other through Ben's. "Hey, you two. I love you, you know," she said softly. A squeeze to their arms accompanied her words. "Now, come with me. You need to join Sam and me in leading this hungry mob to the gorgeous buffet that Laura has spread out. She says we have to go first. I won't go without you."

Tables were set up on the patio and wide lawn, casual and low-key, just as Laura had promised and just what Izzy loved. No fancy silver or delicate plates that might break.

Wildflowers in clay vases and hurricane lamps kept the brightly colored tablecloths from flapping in the evening breeze, and the food was deliciously simple. Fresh garden and pasta salads, piles of crab and shrimp with spicy dipping sauces. Lobster rolls from Gracie Santos' Lazy Lobster and Soup Café. Ice-cold beer and mojitos. And a thick, moist chocolate cake for dessert. Hidden speakers sent a mix of vocals and instrumentals out across the air, coaxing bodies to sway and easing everyone into a celebratory evening.

"It's a perfect party," Nell said to Laura, walking up beside her.

The hostess was standing with Birdie near a teak table, sipping wine, people watching, and basking in the high, happy energy that filled her home. Behind them, the sound of the tide was musical, a perfect background for the evening.

Laura picked up a glass of wine from a passing server and handed it to Nell. "I'm so glad Izzy let me do this for her and Sam. I give parties for strangers all the time—all those people who bring business Elliott's way. The president of this or that. Or the charity galas, which I love to do. But this—" She opened her arms wide, gesturing toward Pete and Willow, who were pulling Izzy and Sam up to dance, to Archie and Harriet Brandley, joining them in the next beat and quickly showing them up with some drastic twists and turns. And over near the bar, Chief Jerry Thompson, Gracie Santos, Jane and Ham Brewster, all laughing at a story that Harry Garozzo was embellishing with wild gestures. Laughter rose into the evening air like flames from the tiki candles that lined the yard. "This is just plain, happy fun with people I like so much. This is exactly what we all needed."

"You're absolutely right, Laura."

"Tiffany Ciccolo's death is awful. I don't mean to belittle her at all—she was a sweet girl—but I hope that we can put this behind us soon."

"Did you know her?" Birdie asked.

"I used to see her in the salon. And we were in the same high school class a thousand years ago. I didn't know her much from school things, but we played basketball on a community-center team. But she was so shy that it almost doesn't count."

"You were in the same class?"

Laura nodded. "But it was a big class. I didn't really know her."

Ben came over and wrapped an arm around Nell's shoulder. He

pulled her close and swayed with her as Billy Joel crooned from the speakers. "My very own uptown gal," he whispered into her hair.

Laura laughed. "You two. You should loan yourselves out to prewedding parties. Show people what it'll be like in years to come."

Ben's deep chuckle joined Nell's light one, but they held inside the words that ran through their heads. What it was like "in years to come" was an enormous bouillabaisse of things. One that needed continuous seasoning so it didn't go flat. It was wading together through sometimes difficult times on your way to wherever. And rejoicing when you got there, then starting out again. *The journey.* It was all about the journey.

"Is Andy Risso here?" Nell asked, feeling in that instant that this might be the beginning of one of those difficult journeys. And she hoped the stream they'd be wading through would not be too deep—or too muddy.

Laura looked toward the dancing bodies near the bar, then beyond them to a quieter crowd. "I haven't seen Andy. I left a message on his phone, but he didn't call back. I was hoping he'd come. . . . I thought it'd be good for him, you know, because . . ."

Her husband, Elliott, caught her eye then, and Laura excused herself to say good-bye to some guests who had to leave early.

"Andy's not coming." The voice near Nell's elbow was deep, gravelly, and familiar.

Jake Risso, Andy's dad, moved closer, filling in Laura's vacated spot. He set his beer down on the railing.

"I didn't recognize you without your Gull Tavern T-shirt, Jake," Nell said. "You're looking good, all cleaned up like this."

Jake's laugh was tinged with years of breathing in tavern smoke—deep and rough. He looked down at his khaki slacks and knit shirt and shrugged. "Anything for our girl Izzy."

"Is Andy minding the bar?" Ben said.

"Yeah. His choice. There were plenty of guys to do it. I thought he should come, you know, for Izzy and Sam. And I knew Pete and all would be here. I thought it'd be a good thing. Even that nice Laura Danvers. She called. She knows. . . ."

"Knows?"

"Oh, you know—how hard this is. All the cra—All the things it dredges up. I wish his mother were still alive. Marie'd know how to handle it better than a crusty old geezer like me."

"You understand a lot, Jake. You've raised a fine young man."

Jake rubbed his chin. He was younger than Nell by a few years, but losing his wife to illness when Andy was in college—that, and the hard work of running a bar—had taken a toll on the tavern owner. The lines in his face bore testimony to the more difficult years. *Fishing,* he told anyone who would listen; fishing was his salvation. Get him out in a boat by himself, with line and rod, some fresh bait, and a school of cod or striped bass nearby, and he was a happy man.

But tonight Jake Risso looked anything but happy.

"It's tough, this girl dying like that."

"Tiffany," Birdie said.

He nodded. "Tiffany. Andy's having trouble with it. It was different than it used to be with them. But now, this. Two of them, can you believe it?"

"Two of them?"

"Two girls. Women. When Andy was in high school a girl he cared about died."

"Andy?" Birdie said. The lines in her face deepened as she peeled back the pages of her memory.

"The Markham Quarry," Jake said, as if that was all the explanation it needed. An infamous place because of one awful night. "She drowned in the Markham Quarry. Pushed, maybe? But she couldn't swim a stroke."

A collective intake of air followed Jake's words. Then, slowly, released.

A loose strand of yarn woven into place.

"Harmony Farrow," Birdie said. Her voice was hushed, not reaching beyond their group. And it held surprise, though when they looked back on it later, it shouldn't have. Only recently they'd talked about Harmony. And a boyfriend. Talked about a family that had suffered. But they all were involved in other things, such as knitting a wedding shawl. And sad thoughts of long-ago deaths were easily pushed aside.

"Yeah, that was her name," Jake said. "She was Andy's first real girlfriend. He loved that girl in a god-awful way. And then she was gone. Dead, just like that. It was graduation night—a big party at the school. But Andy didn't come home that night, and Marie and I were worried sick. When he finally dragged in the next morning, he looked like death warmed over. He'd been out all night looking for Harmony, he told us." He paused and took a swig of his beer.

When he continued, his voice had picked up some momentum as the memories flooded back, and the words were now pushed out on a wave of emotion. "They were always hanging out at our house, studying or fooling around. Marie liked it. Her terrific trio; that's what she used to call 'em. She'd bake cookies, make lasagna and her special fried chicken for them. They were together a lot, except when Andy was at band practice or the others playing basketball. Harmony and Andy were so smart. Top of their class, those two. They studied a lot, marched to their own drummer. They liked who they were for the most part; at least those two did."

"Marie called them a trio?" Ben said.

Nell pulled her light sweater closer against the sudden chill in the air.

"Yeah. There were the lovebirds, Andy and Harmony. And Harmony's friend. She was always around; Harmony's shadow, we called her. The two girls; they were joined at the hip, Marie used to say. Joined at the hip. The beautiful Harmony and her quiet friend."

Jake looked down at the flagstone patio floor. His words were muttered.

"Tiffany. Tiffany Ciccolo. And now she's dead, too."

Chapter 12

Tiffany and Harmony. Best friends.

Nell sat at a table on Coffee's patio the next morning with a large latte in front of her, turning the words around in her head. She picked at her still-warm cinnamon roll. "It's big enough for a family of four," she'd told the young man behind the inside counter.

She had walked down to Coffee's early to snag a table, knowing it would be packed. Summertime doubled Coffee's devoted clientele, and on a breezy, sun-drenched Monday, everyone would be elbowing their way to the outside tables on the flagstone patio.

Nell checked her watch. Birdie would be there soon—as soon as Harold pumped up her bike tires and declared her safe to pedal down the hill. And hopefully before the cappuccino Nell had ordered for her had cooled off.

They had left the party the night before when the music went up a notch and Ben could no longer stifle his yawns. He and Birdie provided a united front and whisked Nell away from a spirited conversation with Mary Pisano, Izzy, and Sam.

"It's time," they said.

Chief Jerry Thompson followed them out, claiming his week was going to begin in a matter of hours and sleep was a necessity. It would be a long week for him, they all agreed, and the chief's long face suggested not a pleasant one.

After Jerry had climbed into his car, Ben leaned in the open window and told him about the conversation they'd had with Jake.

Tiffany was Harmony Farrow's best friend. . . . Did the chief know that?

Jerry had shrugged and admitted he hadn't known that connection, though it would probably surface. He wasn't chief back when the Farrow case was in the news.

"Heard about it some, but that's about all," he said. And then he agreed that it was certainly an irony—two young friends, both dying tragically. An irony. But he had intentionally stopped with that, unwilling to add weight or meaning to a coincidence.

A coincidence. Two best friends killed fifteen years apart. The thought had lingered on the edge of Nell's consciousness all night, until Ben finally turned out the bedside light and convinced her that there were more interesting things to think about right then.

But when the sun came up, the thought was back, as if it had just taken a little rest and picked up some energy on the way. Now it presented itself as an annoying buzz that interfered with mundane pleasures—like enjoying Coffee's rich cinnamon roll.

Two young girls dead. Coincidence?

"It must be a coincidence. What else could it be?" Birdie asked now, pulling out a chair opposite Nell and sitting down. She set her bike helmet and backpack on the flagstone floor at her feet.

Nell managed a half smile. "There should be a law against you mining my thoughts the way you do."

Birdie reached across the table and patted Nell's hand. "Nonsense. That's what old friends do."

"Do you think it's a coincidence, Birdie?"

"Coincidence . . . or synchronicity. Is that what you're asking?"

"Yes. I'm not sure I believe in coincidences anymore."

"And that's because they don't exist," a clear voice beside Nell declared.

They looked up into the suntanned face of Mary Pisano. She

stood beside the table, trim and fit in plaid Bermuda shorts and a crisp white blouse, probably from the preteen department, which was where she bought most of her clothes. "Everything in life is connected," she said, more forcefully. "A web. At least that's how I see it."

"Mary, I didn't know you were so new age," Birdie said.

Mary laughed. "I don't like labels, but I do think we sometimes fail to see the synchronicity in events because we're just too busy all the time; we move too fast without stopping to think—or maybe, for some reason, we don't want to see the connection in the events that make up our lives." She put down her coffee cup.

"Here's a perfect example," Mary went on. "When I saw you two over here, I knew it wasn't a coincidence that I was sitting just a few feet away. You'd be talking about what I was thinking about. So, I said to myself, we'll just do it together." Mary reached back and pulled over a chair from her own table—her unofficial reserved seat. Everyone knew the table beneath the leafy maple tree to be hers, a place she occupied nearly every morning in decent weather. Her computer on her lap, she sat there and composed her "About Town" column for the *Sea Harbor Gazette*, the contents of which were sometimes gleaned from the conversations spinning around her on the crowded patio.

"Here," Nell said, pushing the plate with her giant cinnamon roll to the center of the table. "Pick away."

Mary seemed to have an agenda, but Nell wasn't sure exactly what it was. They'd find out in good time, she supposed. Mary didn't hold back.

But sometimes it took some chitchat to get her where she wanted to be.

Birdie pulled off a piece of the flaky roll and set it on a napkin. "How's your bed-and-breakfast doing?" she asked. A rhetorical question at best, since everyone in town knew the answer. Ravenswood-by-the-Sea was booked solid. Thriving. Birdie herself lived in the coveted Ravenswood neighborhood, just across the street from the old Pisano estate, which Mary had transformed into a lavish B and

B. Though its doors had been open less than a year, its reputation was already bringing return guests from Boston and New York. *The most comfortable beds on the Atlantic Coast,* a recent travel magazine had written alongside photographs of the magnificent home. *With breakfasts that Emeril Lagasse would die for. Exquisite lawns, woods for hiking.*

"It's fine. My grandfather would approve of what I've done with his home. And even my obstinate relatives are coming around. And it will shine when we put all the Chamberses up for Izzy's wedding."

Nell smiled. "Not to mention Izzy's glorious reception."

"Absolutely. It's going to be beyond belief. And that's one of the reasons we need to clear up this awful mess."

"Awful mess?" Birdie said.

"That's what's pressing on us this morning. Right? This awful business surrounding Tiffany Ciccolo's death. That sweet young woman. This is truly horrible."

Birdie and Nell sat back and sipped their coffee, listening, nodding. They knew Mary wasn't finished—she would go on for a while, and it wouldn't do any good to interrupt.

"It's summer, for heaven's sake. I told Jerry Thompson that he'd better have something for me today, some news to put people's minds at rest. I want to know that they've caught the thief and put him away somewhere far from here; that's what the town needs. The thought of robbers roaming Harbor Road is distasteful. And frightening.

"There, I've said my piece." Mary took off her sunglasses and picked up a large mug of coffee. Her fingers wrapped around it, and her blue eyes peered over the rim, waiting for their response.

"If it was a robbery, Mary, I would think the person would be long gone from Cape Ann."

"That's what Tommy Porter said when he stopped in here earlier this morning—that the guy might be long gone. Maybe as far away as Florida, he said. Not a very bright robber if he'd head for Florida at this time of year, I told him.

"But I knew that was just the police party line, and I told Tommy as much. He didn't need to play coy with me. He could trust me with the truth. Is there a suspect? Who? Why? We need some answers here." She set her mug down on the table.

Nell held back a smile. As if anything Mary Pisano was told would stay confidential. She was as well-intentioned as anyone on earth, but to Mary, secrets were meant to be printed in her column.

Nell looked around the patio. People were busy reading the paper, talking, some men and women in business attire, teenagers in shorts and tank tops headed for the beach. She wondered if she was imagining that the heads leaning close together, the lowered voices, were wondering about Harbor Road's robber, too. Today's paper gave an update that was really a rehash, nothing new added, except that Tiffany Ciccolo was a wonderful young woman who would be terribly missed by all the clients of M.J.'s salon.

Nell knew that no news was Jerry's way of handling these things. Even if there was something new, the chief would keep it under wraps, unless putting it out for public scrutiny would help catch the person who had broken into M.J.'s cellar—and left a young woman dead.

Beside her, Mary rolled a pencil between her hands, then stopped and started tapping it on the table. Finally she sighed and pushed back her chair, looking over at another table where the front page of the paper held the word ROBBERY in ninety-two-point Helvetica font. "*A robbery*; that's what they're saying."

"Do you think it was something other than a robbery, Mary?"

Nell and Birdie both looked at the younger woman, keeping their opinions to themselves. Experience had taught them how easily one's words could make it into Mary Pisano's chatty column.

Mary hesitated as if the question caught her by surprise. "Do I think it was a robbery . . ." she repeated slowly. Finally she answered in the definitive tone they were used to hearing from her. "Of course I do. Of course it was a robbery."

She paused, just long enough for her voice to lose some of its robust confidence, and when she spoke again, a note of wishfulness crept into her tone. "It had to have been a robbery. . . ."

Because. The unspoken word dangled in the air, as loud and clear as if it'd been spoken aloud.

Abruptly, Mary picked up her paper cup, turned around, and walked over to the shade of the old maple tree. She sat down on the bench, her back straight, her feet just touching the ground. Before her fingers ever reached the keyboard, her latest column began to take shape.

Birdie and Nell gathered their things and walked out onto the sidewalk. They collected Birdie's bike and walked it down the street to the yarn studio and a class they'd agreed to help Izzy teach.

"*Because,*" Nell repeated aloud.

Birdie nodded as the thought that was impossible to digest sur- faced and stood its ground, planting itself directly in their path.

Because . . . because if it wasn't a robbery, then someone had wanted to kill Tiffany Ciccolo.

Chapter 13

Izzy's yarn shop window was everything she had said it was—mountains of buttery-soft summer yarn. Mae's teenage nieces, Jillian and Rose, had done a wonderful job creating a beach scene, complete with sand castles, to provide a backdrop for the yarn. Piled in sand buckets and picnic baskets were balls of amazing cotton and cotton blends in the colors of summer: cotton candy and mint leaf, lemonade, peaches and cream, and sweet orchid. Sky and summer sea. And sitting in the corner of the window, right in the middle of several skeins of limeade-colored cotton, was Purl, the knitting shop's cherished cat, happy in her yarn paradise.

Birdie and Nell stood at the window, only the glass preventing them from digging their fingers into the soft yarn.

I'll get some for Claire, Nell thought. She was a beautiful knitter. She would create something extraordinary from Izzy's new yarn.

Nell had sat on the chilly deck in the early-morning hours, watching for some sign that Claire was still staying in the guesthouse. Finally Ben lured her inside, telling her that he'd seen a light when he went to exercise at the crack of dawn. She was there, and she was responsible. And she wasn't the kind of woman who would sneak out in the night without saying good-bye.

Of course she wouldn't, Nell had agreed. What was she thinking?

"How is Claire doing?" Birdie asked beside her.

"She may move to Texas."

Birdie was silent, her eyes still lingering on the magical colors in front of them. Finally she nodded. "I think she carries a burden, Nell. I hope she doesn't think it will be lifted by running away from it."

Nell was silent. She thought Claire trusted her, but her comments yesterday were troubling. Her reasons for leaving were vague, undefined. Birdie didn't know Claire as well, and perhaps seeing it with some detachment provided more clarity. She'd talk to Claire again. If there was a problem, she and Ben would help. Certainly. But Birdie was right. Running away wouldn't help.

They would have stayed there indefinitely, the two friends, letting the vivid summer colors soothe their spirits, had Izzy not stepped outside to put a rubber doorstopper beneath the front entrance.

She laughed at the sight. "I told you. Luscious, right? You want to eat it—ice cream, popsicles, peaches. Dip your fingers in, then lick them clean."

"Luscious only begins to describe it."

"I don't think I can afford to come inside," Birdie said, her eyes lighting on one color after another. "I want six skeins of each. Maybe seven."

Izzy hugged them both. "We can manage that. But come inside now. We've a crowd. They're all ready to tackle that lacy beach bag I made last summer."

Izzy's summer classes were always packed. Vacationers couldn't pass her store without stopping in, and the array of classes offered made it impossible for even nonknitters to go away empty-handed. At the least, they'd leave Cape Ann that summer with a scarf filled with memories and the smell of the sea.

Willow Adams was there to help, too, the elfin artist standing near Izzy's "soapbox"—a small wooden platform Ben had made to lift his niece above chatty crowds as she quieted them down, gave instructions, and answered questions.

Willow waved at Birdie and Nell and joined them near the cookie table. "Izzy said this is for advanced knitters. Don't know what I'm doing here." She chuckled, rearranging her thick black hair with her fingers.

"It's because you're famous. Imagine coming in to knit a bag and having the well-known fiber artist Willow Adams be your guide."

"Hah," Willow spurted out in denial, the sound surprisingly large considering its source. "But this is fun, things like this—and Laura's party. That was cool. Keeps people on the right track and assured that the summer will still go on, the ocean will still be here, in spite of the sad thing that happened in M.J.'s salon."

"Has Pete seen much of Andy?" Nell asked.

Willow nodded. "After Laura's party we went looking for him. He was at the Gull, like his dad said, not working, though. He was just sitting on a stool looking at nothing. So Pete pulled him out and we took him over to the Palate. It's not open on Sundays, but Merry and Hank were there, so they brought out a few beers and joined us. We had the place to ourselves. It pays to be buddies with a bar owner or two."

"Did Andy talk about Tiffany?"

"Not much. But the rest of us did. I guess we knew Tiffany as well as anyone, because she came to all the gigs, always doing nice things for the band, bringing water bottles and treats and offering to help set up. I was sometimes around, too, because Pete can't sing worth a darn without me staring up at him, all moonstruck." Willow laughed again, her face and eyes lighting up. Then just as quickly, the smile left her small face and she pulled her brows together, looking from Nell to Birdie and back again. "Here's what I think, if you want to know. Tiffany Ciccolo had fallen in love with Andy. And in a big way."

"And Andy knew it?"

Willow thought for a moment. "I'm not sure—sometimes guys are dumb about things like that—but somehow I think he did know. Just a feeling. At first, when she started coming around, he wasn't so friendly to her. All he told us was that he'd known her in high school.

"Pete thought Tiff was a groupie—she didn't seem to have many friends around town, but she knew Andy. And soon Andy started talking to her more. The two of them seemed to understand each other on some weird level. After a while, Andy almost expected her there, and they'd leave together, sometimes coming out with all of us—Andy, Merry and Hank, Pete and me." She nodded over at Merry Jackson, who was sitting in the front row, her long platinum hair making her as easy to spot as the sun. "But sometimes they'd go off just the two of them. And you could see that Tiffany was feeling more familiar with Andy, touching him, holding hands, cuddling up to him—that kind of thing.

"Andy clammed up when we'd say anything. He said not to read anything into it because there was nothing to read. But there was. I could tell—at least for Tiffany. There was that feeling that comes when . . . Well, you know—when two people are more than friends."

The tinkling of Izzy's bell filtered through the room, burying the questions that filled Nell's head. Like a wave, conversations softened across the room until there was silence.

Willow leaned toward Nell and Birdie and whispered the end of her thought. "But it's just a crappy ending; that's what it comes down to. Groupie or not, girlfriend or not, we'll miss her. It's a bummer."

Then Izzy's voice took over, first giving her usual lay-of-the-land instructions: the bathroom is off the Magic Room—Izzy's name for the children's playroom just opposite the galley kitchen—and there's lemonade and iced tea on the bookcase. "And cookies—but only when we're finished, so your yarn stays clean."

And then she began to describe the perfect summer project—a lacy, colorful beach bag. "It doesn't look it, but it'll hold your shorts, shirt, towel, and beach read, and even has a pouch for a cell phone and change," she said, holding up a sample that Esther Gibson had worked up for Izzy during a slow day at the police station. There were oohs and aahs, though most had seen the soft drawstring bag before when they'd picked out their yarn—a blend of silk and cotton, linen and nylon. The color choices were perfect for the beach—bright greens and lazulite, abalone and mushroom, and a shimmering gold.

Izzy had indeed picked a perfect project.

Nell wandered around, weaving her way between bodies sitting cross-legged on floor cushions or around the big table. She stopped at Harriet Brandley's side, helping her untwist her stitches as she joined a round. Some knitters sat on the steps and others in the comfortable fireplace area where the Thursday night group gathered. The beginning of the pattern was fairly simple, and except for some uncertainty about knitting in the round, the group seemed to be catching on quickly. Before long the chatter picked up again and spurts of laughter punctuated the air.

Laura Danvers was in and out of the room, checking on her two little girls, who were in the Magic Room under Jillian's watchful eye. But even with the interruptions, her bag was growing quickly beneath her nimble fingers.

Time passed quickly, and when no hands were left waving in the air, Nell wound her way to the back windows where Cass sat, her jeans, sneakers, and T-shirt a sign that she'd be heading out in the *Lady Lobster* to check traps soon. Purl had decided to leave her window perch and sat beside her, avoiding the crowd.

The kitten had wandered into Izzy's shop a few years before and never left. Soon she was as much a part of the Seaside Knitting Studio as Izzy or Mae or any of the knitters who considered it a second home. Today Purl sat as still as a statue on the wide sill, looking out over a harbor filled with white sails and fishing boats. Her back was a gentle curve, her expression one of perfect peace.

"In my next life, I want to be Purl." Cass ran a finger lightly down the cat's back.

Nell chuckled and impulsively wrapped an arm around Cass. She squeezed lightly and let go. For all her toughness and the long hours she put in on the water, beneath it all, Cass Halloran was as soft and cushy as the ball of fur she gently stroked.

Merry Jackson walked over, a floppy bag hanging from her shoulder and bouncing off a narrow hip. "Please tell Izzy thanks for me. She's busy." Merry nodded her head toward a frustrated Beatrice

Scaglia. Beside her, Izzy sat cross-legged on the floor, holding Beatrice's needles in her hands. A row of unraveled yarn lay curled in her lap. "Seems a bit of frogging is taking place."

"If anyone can calm Beatrice, it's Izzy," Cass said. "Frankly, Beatrice drives me bananas. So dramatic."

"Speaking of drama," Merry said, glancing over her shoulder to see if anyone was listening. She looked back and leaned in. "A reporter came by the Palate last night."

"To drink?"

"Nope. Asking questions about Tiffany Ciccolo. Hank said I shouldn't talk to him, shouldn't encourage that kind of thing. Let Chief Thompson take care of it, he said."

"Hank's a wise man," Nell said.

"Well, he knew I wasn't liking the guy being there. I don't mind talking to reporters when it will bring business to the bar and grill or promote the Fractured Fish, but not when he wanted to talk about someone who was dead. Besides which, I was trying to write up the menus for the week."

"What did he think you'd be able to tell him?" Cass asked.

"Well, that's the curious thing. I didn't know Tiffany well. She'd been hanging out with us some because of Andy and was always around the band. She was sweet, I guess. But that's about what I know. Knew. I didn't even know her from the salon. I usually take care of my own hair, as you can probably tell." She flipped a long platinum ponytail over one shoulder. "But here's the thing. The guy didn't seem interested in her work at the salon, only in what she was like in high school. In *high school*; can you believe that? High school was fifteen years ago—that's almost half my life ago. Besides, no one should be held accountable for what they were like in high school—and that's exactly what I told him."

"I almost forgot that you went to high school with Tiffany."

Merry nodded. "A long time ago. And I can barely remember what she looked like back then, though I think she had lost weight recently. We didn't hang out. Can you remember people from your high school? It's, like . . . like, a lifetime ago. And why does anyone care about high school, anyway? They should be caring about the here and now. And what's going on now is that poor Tiffany is dead. And that's what he should be asking about. Who broke into M.J.'s salon? Who killed her?"

Merry shifted her bag on her shoulder. "But I think that's the end of it. The guy finally apologized for bothering me. He said I was right. He didn't care much about high school, either. He gulped down a beer Hank offered him and then left. Hardly took any notes at all. Poor guy—no inches for him in tomorrow's paper."

Chapter 14

B ut Merry Jackson couldn't have been more wrong. It had taken the reporter two days, though—not one—to collect his information. By Wednesday morning, he had plenty of inches on the front page of the *Sea Harbor Gazette*.

TWO FRIENDS—TWO DEATHS—TWO TRAGEDIES

"So much for ignoring coincidences," Nell murmured.

"I guess Chief Thompson had a change of mind," Birdie said.

"Maybe not. This might be that young reporter's attempt to sell newspapers and make a name for himself."

Below the headline were two photographs, side by side, from a high school yearbook. The pictures were familiar in the way of high school photos—the freshness of youth, hair brushed and shining, smiles intact. One of the girls wore glasses. She had brown hair and a slightly self-conscious smile. The other photograph held a quiet loveliness that came through the photographer's lens and onto the page. The girl's hair was a deep blond, long and wavy, with a natural glean. Harmony, with a name that fit the face, the straight nose and interesting eyes, lips that were slightly asymmetrical, yet all fitting together perfectly to form a lovely whole. A harmonious whole.

Harmony Farrow—and her best friend, Tiffany Ciccolo.

It was the first time Nell had seen a photo of Harmony. She wasn't smiling in the typical yearbook way. Instead, there was a gentle lift to her lips. But there was something arresting about her, too, that made Nell want to look beyond the photo, to see other photos. To sit down and have a conversation with Harmony Farrow. She looked like someone Nell would like to know.

In a box off to the side, the reporter recapped Harmony's death fifteen years before. It was a sketchy story, worn with age, even though the writer had tried to bring new life to it. Not much more detail than had been reported at the book club when Danny Brandley spoke. Graduation night. A party. Harmony left early. And then she wasn't seen again until a delicate, leafy knit shawl—clinging to a branch that jutted from the side of a quarry—urged someone to look for her there. To pull her from her watery grave.

"Best Friends Forever," the subhead read.

The reporter went on to talk about the two young women and how they were inseparable in high school.

"Those words sound like they came directly out of Jake Risso's mouth. I wonder if he talked to the reporter," Nell said.

Birdie frowned and took off her glasses. "I hope not. Harmony's death was hard on that family. I knew Jake's wife, Marie. After fifteen years, I'd nearly forgotten about it. But now that it's all come to light again, I remember how much Marie liked that young girl—almost like a daughter, Esther said. And then when the rumors started—" Birdie paused, then took a sudden breath and put her glasses back on in a rush. She ran one crooked finger beneath the lines of type, line after line, scanning the columns. "Oh, for heaven's sake," she said, her words dripping in displeasure.

Nell followed the point of her finger.

The reporter may not have gotten much from Merry Jackson, but someone had been more than willing to talk about a young Andy Risso, who was "a drummer in the high school band, class of 1996, and now a popular member of Sea Harbor's own Fractured Fish band." It went on to talk about the coincidence—how Andy was friends with both of the young women whose lives had ended so abruptly.

There were two smaller photos, one faded and barely distinguishable, a newspaper shot of a long-haired guy and a young girl who had both won academic scholarships to Boston University. They each had on a gray T-shirt with BOSTON UNIVERSITY printed across the front in tall crimson letters. The other photo was more recent, a clear, digital shot. It was taken after a recent Fractured Fish performance, shot down at the pier just three weeks before. It was unposed, a snapshot of band members eating hot dogs and laughing, and standing close beside the band's drummer, her eyes focused on his face, was Tiffany Ciccolo.

"Awful, just awful. Well, at least Marie isn't here to be hurt by this all over again."

"What do you mean? It's just a photo."

"I ran into Esther Gibson yesterday and she revisited all of this with me. She reminded me that when Harmony died, they questioned everyone that had been seen with her that night, as you'd expect. She'd been at the graduation party for a while, with Andy, people reported. So the poor kid was questioned over and over by some overly diligent young policeman. It nearly broke Marie's heart. And shortly after that she got sick. So Andy gave up his scholarship and stayed around here, doing odd jobs and going to a community college so he could help take care of his mother. I think he partly blamed the rumors and stress of it all for making her sick, probably blamed himself, too, is what I think. Of course it wasn't him at all. It was the cancer. But it was a hard time."

"Well, Jerry won't let an overzealous reporter dictate his investigation," Ben said, walking into the last part of the conversation. He grabbed a sports jacket from the back of a chair and shrugged into it, making sure his shirt collar was straight. "I'll be seeing the chief shortly at a city planning meeting. He's showing up to give us some information on crime areas. Maybe I'll find out what's behind this."

He kissed Nell on the cheek, gave Birdie a hug, and headed toward the door.

"Ben," Nell called after him. "Do you have the morning paper? This is Birdie's. I thought I'd take it down to Claire with some coffee."

Ben turned back with a smile in his eyes. "I know you, Nell. You want to indoctrinate her into the fine living available here in Sea Harbor. I beat you to it. I left it on the cottage steps with coffee and a copy of a book I picked up at Archie's store—*Beautiful New England*."

Of course he did. Nell smiled to herself. He understood that a place like Sea Harbor was a good place to find oneself, if that was Claire's goal. He liked her, too.

Birdie continued reading through the article. "Well, this doesn't really say much," she said. "But you can bet it'll generate talk. Poor Andy."

Nell picked up the coffeepot to refill their mugs, but Birdie waved her off. "I've got a list of things a mile long to do today, including working on Izzy's wedding shawl. I picked it up from Cass. I guess I felt the need to bury my fingers in that lovely cashmere yarn and think of what an extraordinary bride she will be. It calms me down. Puts things into perspective and rids my palate of less-pleasing tastes."

Nell knew exactly what she meant. But before she could share her agreement, Birdie was gone, her exit an art she had mastered fully. No lingering good-byes, no standing at the doorway in awkward half silences. When it was time to leave, Birdie left.

Nell poured herself another cup of coffee, then picked up Birdie's newspaper and wandered out to the deck. She slipped on her glasses and looked down the front page again. It was a hodgepodge of comments and a rehashing of events. There was nothing new regarding Tiffany's death or why someone would have chosen that particular shop to vandalize.

Nell set the paper in her lap and thought about the shop, the robbery. With her brows pulled together in deep concentration, she tried to slide the pieces in place.

The basement of the salon hadn't been vandalized, not really, at least not what she had seen. Wouldn't a robber have looked for more equipment or valuables? Even Tiffany's office, M.J. said, with files and bookcases and desk drawers, was neat and clean. A light had been left on near her desk, but nothing seemed amiss. A Bose player was still there, and it was still on when the police checked the room. An iPod and speakers were in full sight. A flat-screen television and DVD player that M.J. had used for training classes. The laptop Tiffany used was gone, M.J. had said. And no one could find her cell phone.

Nell thought about that now. The cell phone would have told them whom she had talked to that day. Her murderer, perhaps? The thought sent a cold shiver of fear up her back.

She read through the reporter's description of the crime scene. It was short, fairly accurate, revealing nothing new. It was clear that the facts of the case didn't interest the writer. He was far more interested in exploring Tiffany's childhood, just as Merry had said. And he seemed to be trying to make a sensation out of best friends dying in tragic ways, fifteen years apart.

A story made for a Hollywood movie.

Nell leaned her head back against the chair and looked out over the woods, the newspaper flapping in the breeze on her knees. Such a peaceful day to be reading about such dire happenings.

The breeze coming up off the ocean intensified, rustling treetops and slicing through branches, scattering the morning quiet. In the distance, gulls cried out. Their noisy cawing grew louder as the wind lifted them in flight. Nell closed her eyes, the sounds melding together into a plaintive cry of nature.

And then the wind died down again, the sun warmed her face, and her body began to sink into the soft cushions of the chaise.

But the plaintive wail continued.

Nell's eyes flew open. She stood and looked down toward the woods. An injured animal? A fox, maybe. Ben had spotted one recently near the new community center.

She stood still, her palms flat on the deck railing, listening.

The sound, mixed with the wind and incoming tide, continued. An agonizing sound.

Nell rubbed her arms against a sudden chill that traveled through her. She walked down the steps toward the woods, tentative at first, then more hurried.

As she neared the guesthouse, she stopped.

The cry was louder now, a keening that pierced the air and sliced through Nell.

She walked around the side of the cottage. The door facing the woods was open, the coffee carafe Ben had brought down earlier untouched on the step.

Sitting on the floor just inside the door, her head in her hands and her anguished cry filling the small room, was Claire Russell.

She was dressed in cotton pajamas, and spread out in front of her, rumpled and darkened with tears, was the morning *Sea Harbor Gazette*.

Chapter 15

*N*ell fell to her knees and wrapped her arms around Claire's shaking body.

They stayed that way, the two women, rocking back and forth on the braided rug.

Finally the rocking movement slowed, and the keening softened to a moan.

Nell shifted on her knees but stayed beside Claire, her body offering support.

Claire didn't look up, nor did she resist Nell's presence or her touch. Her eyes stayed glued to the soggy newsprint.

"She was my daughter," she said finally.

Nell forced herself to breathe evenly, in and out, listening.

"Harmony. Harmony Grace."

With one hand, Nell reached up and lifted a box of tissues from an end table. She pulled one out and pressed it into Claire's hand.

"I'm sorry," Claire managed to say. "I don't . . . I don't lose control of myself. At least not in front of anyone."

"You haven't lost control, Claire. You're grieving—all over again." Nell wasn't sure if Claire heard her, but it didn't matter. Her grief was ripe and filled the room.

"Sweet Ben's been bringing me coffee, leaving it on the step." Her voice was strained as she sought control. "Today the paper was with it. I opened it, and there she was, my beautiful girl, looking at me."

"Ben didn't know. . . . We . . . we had no idea."

Claire blew her nose, her head moving from side to side. "No, of course you didn't. And it shouldn't have been a shock to me. When that girl . . . When I read that the Ciccolo girl had been killed, I knew it was just a matter of time before someone pieced this together. No reporter could pass it up. The coincidence. Tiffany was Harmony's best friend. It was bound to get dragged through the papers again, through the town. All of it, all the heartbreaking horror." She reached for another tissue and took a deep breath. Finally, she looked at Nell, her face a study in sadness. "I wasn't prepared, though, even though I should have been. Even after all these years have gone by, the wound can be ripped open in an instant, as raw and bleeding as the first time."

"Is that why you are thinking of leaving? Because Tiffany's death will bring up Harmony's again? People will be talking about it?"

Claire wiped the tears from her cheek. "Yes. Somehow, somehow I thought that enough time had gone by. And I needed to come back here. After Harmony . . . after she died, things were awful between my husband and me, even worse than before, and he left me. He didn't even want me keeping his name. That was fine with me— except that it was Harmony's name. But I did as he asked. I became Claire Russell again, and I left Cape Ann. I couldn't live here. I couldn't live with myself. So I went away and became someone else in whose body I could exist. I was a nomad. Living in communes with strangers. Finding some solace in working the earth. But I was always running. Finally I had to stop. I thought I was ready to come back to Cape Ann and face that awful chapter in my life. I wanted to put my demons to rest once and for all.

"When Harmony died, I died, too. But I couldn't just go to sleep, forever, like she did. I had to wake up every day. I had to get up and shower, make my coffee and sit at a table by myself. I had to walk through the day, step after step after step. Day after day. I had to pretend to people that I was alive. That I was a normal person." Claire's fingers played with the tissue in her lap.

"I thought if I came back here to face the reality of her death, and somehow, I don't know, somehow release her spirit, let it fill me, I might find peace again—I might feel Harmony close to me. And for a few weeks, I thought I had made a good decision. Your garden, the beauty here on Cape Ann—it was good."

Claire got up from the floor and moved over to a small table near an open window. The breeze moved the gauzy curtains, and sunlight rippled through, painting wavy stripes across the surface.

Nell pulled out the other chair and sat down.

"And then one night . . ."

Nell knew what Claire was going to say next. Of course. "You were at the bookstore that night, and you heard the cold-case discussion."

She nodded. "I didn't go there for that. I was browsing for books, but I lost track of time, and suddenly people were talking out in the open area. I stayed in the back because I didn't want to walk in front of everyone."

"It must have been painful for you."

"No one intended it to be. No one even knew I was there."

Nell heard her cell phone ring but pressed it to OFF. Across from her, Claire traced a band of sunlight along the tabletop with her fingertip.

Nell got up and came back with two glasses of water. "What happened to Harmony's father? Were he and Harmony close?"

The silence that followed was so long that Nell regretted asking the question. Finally Claire began talking again.

"Richard Farrow—Harmony's father—was very strict with her. She was a wonderful, amazing daughter, so smart and so beautiful. She was . . . she was perfect. But it never seemed enough. Richard wanted more . . . more piety, I'd guess you'd say. More devotion. He wanted church to be more important in her life."

"Father Northcutt's church?"

The tears had stopped, and while the pain was still deeply visible in the lines of Claire's face and the inordinate sadness in her eyes, she seemed to want to talk. "No. Shortly after Harmony was born, Richard 'found religion,' as he put it. Some little group up in Maine, near his parents' home. He had gone on a retreat up there and drank a kind of destructive Kool-Aid. At least destructive to our family. He wasn't the same after that. When we moved to Cape Ann, he started his own little group, following the same strict principles. No dating, no parties. No drinking—or music or books that weren't religious. No boys. Women shouldn't cut their hair or dress a certain way. Somehow he allowed me my transgressions, but not Harmony. He wanted to raise her to be one of them, he said. He wanted her to go to a small church college instead of using her BU scholarship. He wanted so many things. . . ."

Nell was silent. She thought of Izzy and how she'd been raised. Her family had loved her unconditionally and allowed her the freedom to be herself. Even when she'd tossed aside a promising law career, her father had swallowed his disappointment and replaced it with pride when the yarn studio in Sea Harbor prospered.

"I tried to work around Richard's rants and to give Harmony what I thought she needed. I was so young when I had her—nearly a child myself. But I threw myself into being her mother with every ounce of energy I had. I gave her lots of love. Support. Understanding. I was so proud of her." Claire's words caught in her throat. "I'd make up excuses of where she was so she could be with friends. Never, of course, at our house."

Nell thought about Marie Risso and how she'd opened her doors to Harmony, and all because her mother bravely made it possible. That explained her having a boyfriend. A life apart from the one behind the closed doors of the Farrow home.

Nell could see exhaustion settling into the contours of Claire's face. The lines in her forehead were deeper, and her eyes were red and swollen. But leaving her alone, suggesting she rest, didn't seem a wise option.

"The new grasses are coming today, right, Claire?" she asked.

Claire nodded.

"How about if I give you time to shower and dress, get something to eat. A little time for yourself. Then I'll meet you in back with our garden tools this afternoon? I think we both need some time in the sun, time with the earth. What do you say?"

Claire managed a tentative smile and pushed back her chair. Her hair was pulled back in a ponytail, she wore no makeup, and in spite of the burden weighing on her shoulders, she looked young. In fact, she looked very much like the young graduate peering out from this morning's *Sea Harbor Gazette*.

Nell walked toward the door, then turned back to be sure Claire was all right. There were lots more things to be said, but there'd be time.

Claire had headed to the bathroom. She turned, her hand on the knob, and looked at Nell. The semblance of a smile was still there, but beneath it was the raw pain Nell had seen earlier. "You're being kind, Nell."

"We're friends, Claire. It's what friends do."

"But you don't know everything, and right now, that seems unfair. If you're my friend, you need to know the truth. Richard knew it—and that's why he left me." She paused, choosing her words carefully.

"You need to know what really happened that night," she said. "I did it. I'm the reason my daughter died."

Nell walked slowly up to the house, her heart heavy.

Claire hadn't finished her last thought. Hadn't explained it to Nell. She had simply stopped talking, as if no explanation were necessary. And then she had turned the other way and walked into the bathroom, and Nell had heard the sound of the shower spray beating against the tile. Beating against a woman who felt she needed to be punished.

Nell's mind was fuzzy; parts of the conversation with Claire were disjointed. By the time she reached the deck she had chosen to abandon Claire's last words entirely. They didn't make sense. Until

Claire explained more fully what she meant, Nell would ignore them and concentrate instead on a mother coming back to Cape Ann to heal herself. To somehow find her daughter's spirit. To find peace.

She thought about Claire's journey. About her former husband. Her daughter. A family ripped apart in the cruelest way.

When she walked into the kitchen, the ringing of the phone pulled her from her thoughts.

Ben wondered if she was there. He said he'd be home shortly for lunch.

He'd had an interesting morning, and there were some things he needed to talk to her about.

Chapter 16

"Although the robbery motive is still out there, the police are looking seriously at other possibilities. It's going to affect people we know."

Ben leaned against the counter in the kitchen, watching Nell cut an avocado into thin strips. Izzy straddled a stool on the other side of the island, checking messages on her phone.

A morning meeting at the courthouse had ended in a long conversation with Ben's good friend Jerry Thompson. Often Ben and Jerry used each other as sounding boards, playing on each other's strengths. They also knew the other's word was good. Things that should remain private, would. This turn of events, Ben said, was probably already on blogs and the local talk show or running along the bottom of the soap operas like school closings in the winter—a mini news flash. People would know that the police were trying to find someone who wanted Tiffany dead.

"Why the sudden change in thinking, Uncle Ben?" Izzy looked up from her phone. She'd stopped in for lunch, too. She was starving, she said, and though the yarn shop was busy, Mae insisted she leave and find food somewhere—her growling stomach wasn't good for business. "Go to your aunt's," she'd commanded, pointing at the door. "She'll have food." And Izzy had happily complied, sprinting up the hill to Ben and Nell's home.

"It's different things," Ben said. "Though I think the robbery idea was put out there without much logic to it. It was a motive for people to latch onto until the police had time to do some more investigating. Robberies aren't that uncommon, which makes them easier to live with, I guess. It's awful if it ends in murder, but it seems more accidental, less frightening, and people see it on TV all the time.

"But then the investigators started asking the obvious questions. Why would someone take a cell phone but leave a television or fancy CD player? And why the salon and not a bar or McClucken's Hardware? Things we were all thinking. A few conversations with staff at M.J.'s led them to consider Tiffany more closely, and that she might have been the target, not the few items stolen. They'll look at everything, of course."

"Tiffany was sweet. Ordinary. It's awful to think that someone might have wanted her dead," Izzy said. "I hate that thought."

"I wonder what talk at the salon turned the police in this direction," Nell said. She set a platter of tomatoes, watercress, avocado, pickles, and slices of chicken and provolone on the island. A small bowl of spicy yogurt-dill-mayo sauce sat beside three plates. "This is a help-yourself lunch."

"I suppose whatever was said was more than gossip?" Izzy offered, taking one of the plates.

Nell glanced at her, having had the same thought. Tanya wasn't one to hold back, and she didn't much like Tiffany; that was clear to everyone.

Ben poured them each a glass of iced tea. "It seems Tiffany was upset that week about something—and that wasn't normal for her. She was usually on an even keel. But recently she was forgetting appointments and not her usual efficient self. That was one thing."

Nell and Izzy looked at each other. That certainly matched their experience with Tiffany.

"There's not much information, not yet, but they'll be talking to other people, too. Tiffany and Andy Risso had some kind of a relationship. And we know they had an angry exchange that night at the Palate."

Another episode they'd personally experienced. Nell flashed back to the look on Tiffany's face that night. Something was bothering her. But the exchange had seemed angry only on Andy's part. At least from a distance. Tiffany had seemed earnest, at first, then distraught at Andy's reaction to whatever she'd said.

And in love.

"So . . . do they have any theories?" Izzy piled her roll high with chicken, cheese, and greens, then slathered it with the sauce.

Nell glanced out the window, waiting for Ben's answer. She hadn't seen any movement in the cottage. She assumed Claire would prefer to be alone for a while, rather than join them for lunch. She'd go down soon, as planned. They could garden or talk or take a walk. Whatever Claire needed. And then later, she'd let Claire tell Ben her story herself. It was hers to tell, not Nell's.

Ben was silent, chewing thoughtfully on his sandwich. He wiped a stray sprout from his mouth and finally shook his head. "No theories that I'm aware of. The police don't exactly know where to go with the two girls' friendship—but it's an odd coincidence, everyone agrees. They'll have to explore it. But the Farrows haven't lived around here for years. Tiffany Ciccolo has no family here, just her mom, who is pretty far along with dementia, Jerry said. There are more dead ends there than anything else."

Nell's breath caught in her chest. Claire's name wasn't the same as her daughter's. Fifteen years had passed. No one would automatically connect her to Harmony Farrow. But the police needed to know, at least. Although at that moment, Nell wasn't sure why. Claire had been through her hell. Why put her through it again?

Nell looked over at Ben. He was scooping up the crumbs around his place, then walked over to the sink. "Sorry to eat and run," he said over his shoulder. "I have another meeting, this one about the boys' club program. This retiring is going to be the death of me."

"I need to run, too. I promised Mae I'd be back in a jiff. A ride, Uncle Ben?" Izzy slid off the stool and put her plate in the sink.

They each gave Nell a quick kiss and disappeared out the door to Ben's car, honking another good-bye as they backed down the drive.

Nell stood at the door, watching them disappear down the road. She suddenly felt disloyal, as if she were keeping a secret from Ben. But he had rushed out, and tossing after him the news that Claire Russell, their houseguest, was Harmony Farrow's mother, didn't seem quite right. She would tell him at dinner, when they would have time to talk about it.

But deep down a part of her was relieved she hadn't told him. Nor Izzy. This was Claire's information to tell. Not hers.

Claire. A mother who had suffered the greatest loss a mother could experience.

Claire . . .

Nell frowned, her mind playing with the shadows splashed across the driveway, moving this way and that as the breeze played with the branches. Claire.

She had barely mentioned Tiffany this morning. *That girl*, she'd called her once.

And then Nell remembered the look on Claire's face as she'd sat in the Adirondack chair, staring at the deck door.

It wasn't Izzy she was looking at. Nor a few minutes later when she stared at Izzy's car.

It was Tiffany. Now it made sense.

And the look was one Nell would like to forget.

Nell cleaned up the kitchen, returned a few phone calls, and went upstairs to slip into jeans and a T-shirt. Claire wasn't outside yet, either, so she took her time. The time alone was probably a good thing.

Things certainly hadn't turned out as Claire had planned. She had come back to Cape Ann to put a life back together. Not to have an old life pulled apart all over again.

It occurred to Nell then that Claire hadn't referred to Harmony's dying as a murder. Nor made any reference to who might have done this to her daughter. Maybe that made it even more awful, more difficult to accept. Or maybe it was something else.

She grabbed two bottles of water from the refrigerator, then headed to the garage for her gardening gloves and a trowel. It was nearly two. Claire would be ready to work. There were so many things Nell wanted to ask, but she'd hold her silence and let Claire decide.

There was time.

Nell walked out the back door of the garage and into the afternoon sunshine.

It was a perfect day for gardening. Bright sunlight and a cool breeze.

The wheelbarrow was parked where she'd seen it that morning, just at the edge of the cottage. Claire's gloves and tools were lined up neatly inside it. A sack of mulch was leaning against a tree.

Nell frowned. She glanced over at the door. It was closed, and the window they'd been sitting in front of a few hours earlier was shut. Claire's gardening clogs were lined up neatly beside the door.

Nell walked up the step and along the narrow porch below the windows. She peered through a window, her chest tightening.

The water glasses they'd used earlier were put away; the bed in the alcove was neatly made up.

Nell rapped on the door, but she knew before the sound echoed through the cottage that no one would answer.

Claire Russell was gone.

Chapter 17

"She'll be back," Ben assured her as they drove along Harbor Road on their way to the store. The sky was a deepening blue, with brilliant rose bands painted across it as the sun slipped down behind the western edges of the town.

Nell had spent an hour working in the garden alone, somehow sure that if Claire knew she was messing with her plantings, she would show up in an instant.

But when Ben returned from his meeting and Claire still wasn't back, he suggested a quick trip to the new cheese store on Oak Street. "You know what they say about a watched pot," Ben said. "Besides, I need a bite of manchego tonight. Just a small sliver."

So Nell had gone with him to the Cheese Closet, and they'd walked the narrow aisles of the charming new shop, filling a basket with cheeses, crackers and olives, jars of pickled onions and sweet gherkins, black olive tapenade and homemade salsa. Ben looked longingly at the smoked salmon and applewood ham. Nell laughed and dropped them into the basket next.

And in between paying for far more than a hunk of manchego cheese and climbing back into Ben's car, Nell quietly told Ben the story of Claire Farrow Russell.

Claire wouldn't mind. Nell was suddenly sure of that. But even if she did, the news would come out.

Ben had listened carefully, as he usually did. Asked a question here and there. Before he turned the ignition to head back home, he'd hugged her close. "That's a sad story," he said. "A broken life. Hopefully it can be mended."

They had each lapsed into their own thoughts then, knowing that mending a heartache as great as Claire's might take a lifetime to do.

"This will teach us to leave our house unlocked," Ben joked when they walked into their house.

Pete, Willow, and Merry sat at the island, Sam and Izzy were piling beer into the refrigerator, and Cass was washing her hands at the sink. Standing outside, alone on the deck, was Andy Risso.

"Hi," Izzy said, her head poking around the refrigerator door.

"Hi back," Nell said. "What's up?"

Merry looked up, a blush traveling across her cheeks and forehead. "This isn't too cool, is it? Barging in like this." She looked around at Izzy, then Pete and Cass. "They said you wouldn't mind."

Nell laughed. Merry's enormous eyes filled her face, and she looked like a child caught with her hands in the cookie jar. She hadn't spent as much time at the Endicott home as some of the others. The open-door policy was foreign to her. "We don't mind at all, sweetie."

"We had a late-afternoon band practice, and then Andy got that outrageous phone call," Merry began, glancing out to the porch.

"What call?" Nell turned and saw Andy standing at the railing by himself, his fingers wrapped around the neck of a beer bottle.

Merry rushed on. "And we usually go out somewhere after practice. Izzy and Sam were going to join us tonight."

Pete filled in. "But after the call, well, we didn't feel much like the Gull—"

"The Edge was packed," Izzy added.

"And Wednesdays at the Artist's Palate are crazy busy. Hank would be waving at me every other minute to help," Merry said.

"No excuses necessary," Nell said. It flattered her, if truth be known, that Izzy felt so comfortable bringing her friends to the house unannounced. Nell suspected that once Izzy sold her little cottage and moved into Sam's wonderful seaside home, that would change. So she'd relish it while she had it, and she was happy to have it, tonight especially. Claire's VW was still missing from the side of the drive where she'd been parking it, and Nell would have spent the evening worrying. Company was good.

She looked over at Sam. He was helping Ben unload the cheese shop treasures, most of which would be spread out on the center island and promptly eaten, she suspected. She took some platters from the cupboard and handed them to him for the ham and salmon.

"You're nice to let us barge in like this," he said. "Pete's band was bummed out, so Dr. Izzy suggested coming over here. A place to talk without crowds and noise. So we picked up some beer, thought we'd order a couple pizzas." He looked at the spread that was magically appearing from the thick Cheese Closet bags and laughed. "Looks like we lucked out. Sure beats pizza."

"You wanted to talk?" Ben asked. "About anything in particular?"

Before anyone had a chance to answer, Andy walked in from the deck, his bottle empty. He set it on the island and managed a lopsided smile. "Hope you don't mind the invasion of the Fractured Fish and friends."

"Nope," Ben said. "Not in the slightest. Glad to have you, Andy." Ben clapped him on the back.

"Good folks, these guys," Andy said, looking around the room. Cass was turning on the CD player and Izzy was heating up some bread she'd brought along.

No one even noticed when Birdie appeared, her light step carrying her across the room. "A party without me? Shame on all of you," she said, then chuckled and began slicing the applewood ham. "Andy, dear, I've just been to the police station."

"You, too?" Andy said.

Ben frowned. "What's going on?"

"The police are shifting gears on Tiffany's murder," Birdie said. "Old Angus McPherran fished her computer out of the ocean when he was hoping for carp this afternoon. Now, why would any robber worth his salt throw the one valuable thing he took away? Her phone is probably down there somewhere, too, swimming with the fishes."

"So they're thinking someone wanted Tiff dead. They're looking at people who knew her," Andy said.

"That would be everyone who had their hair done at M.J.'s," Nell said, uncomfortable with the direction in which they were going.

"But we'd known each other a long time, Tiff and me. Much longer than the folks who get their hair done. Harmony Farrow was my friend, too, as anyone who reads the *Sea Harbor Gazette* now knows. And she was Tiff's best friend. So some people think that a tight trio like that has to mean something, especially when two out of the three are dead." Andy tried to keep his voice neutral, calm, but his words were coated with sadness.

And fear, Nell thought. A sliver of fear.

"Birdie, why were you at the police station?" Ben asked.

"Harold got another speeding ticket—not me, Ben. I was talking it over with that sweet Judge Simpson. For a man who moves with the interminable slowness of a turtle, Harold is a regular Dario Franchitti behind the wheel of my Lincoln. I suspect there may be a driver's ed course in his future." She shook her head at the thought and went on. "I visited with Tommy Porter while I was there. He told me that they had invited you down to talk, Andy, and I told him exactly what I thought of that."

Andy managed a smile. "Thanks, Miz Birdie."

"You're too old for that now. Call me Birdie. When you were a tot, your mother, bless her soul, liked for you to be formal. But 'Birdie' will do nicely now."

"My mom liked you a lot."

Birdie nodded. "And I liked her. She was a lovely woman. I also know that no son of Marie Risso would ever be connected to a murder."

Nell thought she saw tears collecting in Andy's eyes, but just as quickly he clenched his jaw and looked each of them straight in the eye. His voice was as firm as the manchego cheese Izzy was slicing. "No, he couldn't. Not then. Not now."

"It was a new guy on the force who called. Tommy Porter would know not to interrupt band practice," Pete said, attempting to lighten the mood.

"What did he say?" Ben asked.

"Just that they wanted to talk to me," Andy answered. "He wanted me to come down to the station right then, but when I hesitated, he backed off and said tomorrow morning would be okay."

Nell issued a sigh of relief. "Well, that doesn't mean anything, Andy. They will talk to everyone. Merry, Pete. Everyone who knew Tiffany. M.J. and I have already been to the station once. I wouldn't be surprised if we were called back."

Andy nodded, though he wasn't convinced, Nell knew. Maybe the hardest part of this for him was that he'd been through it all before. He knew what it would be like. It was a remembered pain that had never really gone away, and now it was an anticipated one.

As if by magic, plates and napkins appeared, and platters of bread, cheese, ham, and salmon crowded the island. Nell's dill sandwich sauce and Ben's array of French mustards filled a lazy Susan, and Ben busied himself with martinis for those with that bent. It had become a bit of a drama, Ben and his silver bullets, and he used it now to entertain, to push thoughts of murder to the edges of their lives so they could enjoy cheese and smoked salmon.

"I've never had a martini," Andy confessed.

Ben laughed and told him that then this would be a night for learning. He didn't need to drink it, but he needed to appreciate it. "Now, I'm a guy who likes mine very dry," Ben began with great pomp. "The vermouth just wants the gin to know he's thinking about him. It's the gin's show, after all."

Nell watched for a minute, smiling at Ben's antics, then stepped out onto the deck. What she wanted to see was a guest cabin filled with lights. To see movement behind the thin curtains.

But it was dark. And nothing had moved. Not the wheelbarrow, the rake beneath the tree. The pile of mulch she'd left there earlier, knowing Claire wouldn't want it left out and would move it the minute she saw it. Though the sky still held light, the sun had disappeared and shadows fell heavily across the yard. It looked suddenly sad to her.

And that couldn't happen. She wouldn't allow it to happen. This was Izzy's wedding site—and it would be filled with great joy. No matter what.

Birdie appeared beside her with a martini. "Ben's about done with Martini 101." She followed Nell's gaze toward the back of the yard and frowned.

Nell felt Birdie's look before she saw it. "Birdie, I get the feeling that there is more on your mind than martinis," Nell said. "What really brought you over here tonight?"

Birdie looked around. Izzy, Cass, and a few others had followed them out into the twilight. Andy stood at the door, talking with Pete about music.

Birdie hesitated briefly.

"It's all right, Birdie; we'll talk later."

"No, it's fine. This is no longer private information. Tommy Porter told me tonight that another person they want to talk to is Claire Farrow, Harmony's mother. Chief Thompson tracked down Harmony's father. He lives in Maine now with a wife and half dozen kids. He's some kind of a preacher. Richard Farrow told Jerry that Harmony's mother no longer had a right to the Farrow name and he had insisted she legally change it."

"Claire Russell," Izzy whispered as the pieces fell into place.

"Yes." Birdie looked at Nell.

"What did he mean, that she no longer had a right to the name?" Cass asked.

"I'm not sure, but they divorced after Harmony died."

"What did you say to the police?" Nell asked.

"Nothing. But I think we need to pass this information along to your houseguest." She looked back toward the guesthouse. "I think it'd be easier on her to at least be prepared."

Nell sighed. "She's gone, Birdie," she said.

Twilight slid into evening, and a huge moon filled the sky and lit the Endicotts' backyard. Everyone agreed to call it an early night. Sam, Izzy, and Cass were meeting up with Danny and some old friends for a prewedding toast at the Franklin in Gloucester, and Merry had asked Pete and Willow to drop her off at the Artist's Palate. Hank had called a couple of times, suggesting she come and help him close up.

Ben said he needed to fill up his gas tank, so he'd take Birdie home. Maybe have a talk with Harold while he was there.

Birdie wholeheartedly agreed. Keeping Harold out of traffic school—or jail—was beginning to wear on her.

Andy had his own car, he said. He followed the others through the house, then stopped at the door and looked back.

"Your keys?" Nell asked from the family room. "Keys or phone. That's what Pete Halloran always has to come back for."

"No. It's not that. It's—" He looked back out the front door, then took a deep breath and walked back into the family room. "I heard you talking about Claire, Harmony's mom."

"I didn't know until today that she was Harmony's mom. She's been staying here, helping me get the yard ready for Izzy's wedding."

His lips lifted in a half smile. "I remember. She was really good with flowers. Harmony used to say she had a bright green thumb."

"Did you ever see her garden?"

He shook his head. "I never even saw the inside of their house. It was out on the edge of town. We never went over there because of her dad. He didn't want guys around. We went to my house instead."

"Your mom liked Harmony, didn't she?"

"Yeah. Harmony was like a daughter to her. It was sad, because Harmony loved her own mom more than anything, but I barely knew her. I only met her a couple times. Once I was at Shaw's and I saw Harmony there with her mom. Another time it was at an awards ceremony at school. And then . . . then there was the service."

"Where was that, Andy?"

"The school did a memorial. The funeral was somewhere else, up in Maine, I think. No one went to the house, not even Tiffany. I guess we were afraid of what her dad would do. But Harmony's mom came to the school service. No one talked to her, though. I don't know why. We just didn't. Dumb kids."

He shifted from one large foot to the other, his gentle face mirroring his memories. Finally he looked back at Nell. He pulled his keys out of his pocket and rotated his shoulders like an athlete, as if preparing himself for some feat.

"But here's the thing. I heard you say that Claire was gone. I don't mean to interfere. But I think I might know where she is."

They took Andy's truck, a well-cared-for Toyota Tacoma, perfect for hauling drums and amps, he told Nell. His dad had given it to him a couple years before. A birthday present.

"It's my baby," he said proudly.

"It's beautiful, Andy," Nell said. She fastened her seat belt, sitting up high beside him. "Is it far, wherever we're going?"

"Not far. A few miles."

They drove in silence, through the winding neighborhood streets, and soon the lights of Sea Harbor were behind them. "I can't promise we'll find her, Nell," Andy said, his eyes following the curve of the road. "But I know she's been out here."

"Out where, Andy?"

An oncoming car took their attention for a minute, and then they were alone again, with just the beams of Andy's headlights lighting the narrow road. He drove smoothly, with the assurance born of familiarity. It was clear to Nell he'd traveled this route before.

"Just over this hill," he said. He drove over the hill, then turned onto another road that skirted a thick woods. He glanced over at Nell, then back to the road. "The Markham Quarry."

Nell's breath caught in her chest. "The quarry?"

He nodded. "I come out here sometimes. I talk to Harmony. Tell her what's going on. It's so quiet here. Peaceful, even. Is it awful that I do that? I mean, this is where she died."

Nell was silent. What was awful or not awful? It was the last place that Harmony stood, the last place she breathed. If Andy felt her presence here, was that bad?

"I was out here a couple weeks ago," Andy said. "Tiffany and I—we were having some problems, and I came out here to talk to Harmony about it. Harmony knew Tiff inside and out."

He made a sound, then—a kind of self-deprecating laugh. "I sound crazy, don't I? I'm a grown man, and acting like a kid."

Nell looked at him. "Why? It's not foolish to want to be close to someone you cared about. And if you can accomplish that, good for you. It's not crazy at all."

Ahead of them, the moon seemed to sink low in the sky, nearly touching the treetops. The forest was lit from above, a black silhouette against a giant yellow ball.

"That day, I was hiking in to the edge of the quarry, like I always do. It's a well-marked path now that the county owns it, but back when we were in high school this place was privately owned. Some kids got caught skinny-dipping out here once, and the lady actually had them arrested. Word spread and this place was avoided like the plague. She was crazy, kids thought. Now hikers are welcome, though." He slowed slightly, glancing over at the woods bordering the road.

"That day I'd almost gotten to the clearing when I saw that someone was already there. There's a pile of granite boulders at the edge of the water, big ones to climb and sit on. She was there, this lady. I didn't know who it was, but I could see from the back, from the way her shoulders were shaking, that she was upset. I figured she needed her privacy. So I turned around and walked back through the woods to my truck.

"But then I started wondering about it—about who the person was and why she was out there, in my spot. That's the way I thought about it. *My spot.* So I sat in my truck and waited. A little while later, she came down the path, and there she was. It nearly knocked the wind out of me. The sun was at her back so her features were blurred, fuzzy, like in a movie. She looked almost ethereal. But mostly, she looked just like Harmony. Like it was Harmony walking toward me in slow motion.

"Finally my head cleared, and I saw a lady climb into a little blue Volkswagen bug and drive off. I knew right away it was her mom. I didn't know she was back in Sea Harbor, but I knew for certain that's who it was."

Andy pulled his truck over to the side of the road and parked. "There's the trail." He pointed across the road. Then he looked around and pointed again, this time to a gravel strip just deep enough for cars to park and not obstruct traffic. "And there's her car."

Andy didn't want Nell to walk through the woods to the quarry by herself. "It's tricky, lots of ruts in the path, and there's only the moonlight to light the way." He led the way, through the thick stands of maples and sumac.

Nell was glad to have his company. They walked slowly through the trees, around bends, through thick patches of wild berries crowding the trail. Several times Nell nearly tripped on gnarled roots that crawled across the path. The night sounds were eerie and deep—a sudden rustling of invisible animals skittering out of their way, the gulls above, and the wind whistling through the high, unseen tops of the trees. She had seen many Cape Ann quarries, but not this one. It was off the beaten path, tucked away near some berry orchards. It was a small quarry, and mostly forgotten.

He would lead Nell to the quarry, Andy said, but he wouldn't stay. It didn't seem right for him to meet Harmony's mother in this place. It would be awkward, hard for her. And she'd be able to give Nell a lift home, though he'd wait in his truck if she wanted him to. He stopped in the path and turned toward Nell. "Do you know what I mean?"

She did. She didn't completely understand the emotions filling the space between Claire Russell and Harmony's friends. But whatever it was, forcing an uncomfortable encounter in such a private, emotionally charged place didn't seem wise.

At the edge of the clearing, they stopped. Nell pulled some thistles from her jeans and looked into the open space. In the distance was the quarry, and next to it a large mound of granite boulders, just as Andy had described.

He pointed in that direction.

The still silhouette of a woman sat at the top of a granite pile.

It was unmistakably Claire. Her head was held back to the sky, and her arms were wrapped around her knees, holding her steady on the boulder. Moonlight bathed the contours of her face.

Andy looked at Nell, his expression an amalgam of regret and sadness. He lifted one hand, a silent wave, then turned and walked back into the woods.

Nell waited a minute, then took a few steps closer, quietly calling out Claire's name.

Claire turned toward the voice and smiled. She didn't seem surprised to see Nell. She gripped the craggy boulder and edged herself down from the pile of rocks. Shivering, she rubbed her arms. "It's chilly. It was warm when I came out."

Nell smiled. "It was daylight. Sunny."

"Yes." She walked slowly to the edge of the quarry, and Nell followed. Together they stood on the high bluff and looked down into the bottomless quarry. It was breathtaking. A pristine, bottomless sea surrounded by slabs of granite, magnificently carved by the joined forces of nature and man. Catbrier, bayberry, and shadbush grew in patches along the ledges, and here and there a tiny pine tree sprouted, clinging for survival. The center of the quarry held the moon's perfect reflection, a white globe suspended, as if by an invisible hand, in the still water.

The pure water that had swallowed up the body of a beautiful young girl.

Nell took off her sweater and wrapped it around Claire's shoulders.

Together, without the intrusion of words, they turned and walked away from the Markham Quarry.

They rode together in Claire's small VW, back along the narrow road and into town. Claire didn't ask Nell how she'd gotten to the quarry or why she'd come. It didn't seem to matter, and the quiet that filled the car was comfortable.

Ben was waiting at the door when they pulled into the driveway. The lights were on, giving a soft glow to the house, warm and welcoming.

"Time for a nightcap?" Ben said, holding open the screen door and peering into the darkness.

Nell could see that Claire was tired. She was beginning to understand the kind of emotional retreat that the gardener had subjected herself to that day.

But Claire surprised her.

"Yes," she said to Ben. "I'd like that. A glass of wine . . . and the company of friends. A good combination."

The raw grief that had defined the features of her face that morning was softer now, tucked inside and replaced with the haunting beauty that Nell had been drawn to the first time she saw Claire at the nursery. Her brown hair hung loose to her shoulders, and her slender body, in slim jeans and a light cotton blouse, appeared far younger than her fifty years.

Ben had turned on lights near the fireplace, and they cast soft shadows across the cherry floor and sisal rugs. It was a lived-in area with comfortable green and beige upholstered furniture, soft lights, and built-in bookcases around the smooth stone fireplace. It was a room that beckoned people to come in and stay a while. To be with friends. To be safe.

Claire took the glass of wine Ben offered and sat beside Nell, looking around. "This room reflects you both," she said. "It's warm and lovely at once. And if a room can be kind, well, then that, too."

Ben chuckled and set a bowl of nuts down on the table. He sat across from the two women and leaned forward, his elbows on his knees. "You've had a hell of a day, Claire. I wouldn't have set that newspaper on the step if I'd known. You know that."

"Of course I know that—you were being kind and hospitable." She managed a smile and turned to Nell. "I didn't mean to worry you. I know you were expecting me in the garden."

"I worried, I suppose. I tend to do that."

"An understatement, Claire. Nell has perfected that art."

Nell shushed him with a look. "It's the circumstances that worried me. I didn't know what to do to help."

"I'll be fine," Claire said. "But thank you for caring. I came back to Cape Ann to somehow make myself whole again, but I didn't expect this. Tiffany's death, having things brought up again. It's thrown me a bit."

"That's certainly understandable," Ben said. "The timing is unfortunate. But the police would like to talk to you. They're trying to cover all the bases, that's all. Chief Thompson's a good man. He'd avoid this if he could."

Claire nodded. "When I read the newspaper this morning, I could see that the investigation was taking a different direction. So I supposed this might happen. It would only take a few phone calls to find out that I had changed my name—and probably not long at all to find me." She rolled the wine stem between long fingers. "But I wasn't trying to hide from anyone. The name change, that was something . . . Well, it wasn't to keep secrets."

"We have good men on the police force. It's just routine," Nell said. But she had no idea if it was routine—or what Jerry Thompson and his crew were thinking. Ben supposed it was the coincidence itself, and then the further coincidence of Claire being in town. They just want more information, he had assured Nell.

"I haven't spoken to Tiffany Ciccolo since before my daughter died. I don't know what I could possibly say to them about her death. But I'll go to the station anyway. And I'll tell them anything I can."

"Did you know Tiffany well?"

The question seemed to confuse Claire. She took another drink of wine before offering a guarded answer.

"No. Not all that well. There was one time, when Harmony first met Tiffany, that I tried to teach them both to knit." Her face softened with the memory. "We spent some time together then."

"But they were good friends?"

Claire nodded. "Yes. I think it started when Tiffany didn't have anyone to eat lunch with at school. She was shy. And Harmony—she was more of a free spirit. She was always rescuing birds and rabbits and little critters. I suppose it began like that. But a teenage friendship all those years ago . . . It seems to me that the police are grasping at straws."

"You're convinced there's no connection?" Ben asked.

"What could it be? For a while—and I know it's a terrible thought, but I was grasping at anything that might make sense of it all—I thought that somehow Tiffany might be connected to Harmony's death. I don't know how or why, but she never came to see me afterward, never offered me any comfort by telling me about Harmony's last night. And I was desperate for information. Anything at all. Who did Harmony talk to at the party? Did she have a good time? Did she eat anything? Did she dance?

"Tiffany and Andy Risso were the last people I know who saw my daughter alive, and neither of them ever came to me or told me any of the things I needed to know. I called Tiffany's house once, but she told me she had to work and couldn't talk to me. All I wanted was another glimpse of my daughter. Something beyond the look on her face when she left home that night."

"It was a graduation party at the school, I understand," Nell said.

Claire nodded. "When she left that night, Harmony hugged me so hard it almost hurt. She told me she loved me and that everything was going to be all right. Then she slipped out the kitchen door and walked off."

"Everything was going to be all right?"

"I thought at first it was an odd thing to say, but I think she meant that she'd be sure her father wouldn't find out she had gone to the party. That there wouldn't be a horrible scene in the house. Her eyes were so bright when she looked at me—full of promise and life. I don't think I've ever seen her look so beautiful. There was a special look about her. And then she went off into the darkness."

"She went to the party alone?"

"No. She had my car. She was picking Tiffany up and dropping her overnight bag there—they were going to spend the night together. Richard had forbidden her to go out that night, but she was desperate. She'd graduated with honors, and it seemed so unfair of him to forbid her to go. She wanted to go so badly and wouldn't back down. She was going, 'or else,' she said. She was determined in a way I hadn't seen her be before. She had missed so much over the years because of her father, but this night seemed especially important to her. Her father was unrelenting, so she begged me to make it happen."

Nell watched a shadow fall across Claire's face as she reached back into her memory to that night. And in that moment, she knew what a horrible burden Claire had lived with all these years. She'd met the demon Claire had come home to exorcise.

Claire finished her wine in a single swallow and set the glass down on the table. Her voice had flattened to a monotone.

"You have to make it happen, Mom, she begged me. And so I did. I lied to her father. I made up a story about where she was going that night. A fake babysitting job. Then I bought her a new dress, although she asked me not to. And I sent her on her way. I made it all happen, just as she asked me to.

"I made it possible for her to walk out of our house that night—to her death.

"I'm her mother. And that's what I did."

Chapter 18

$\mathcal{N}$ell's morning meeting was at the Sea Harbor Historical Society, the monthly board meeting. A short meeting, she hoped.

As she pulled out of the driveway, she noticed that Claire's car was already gone. It didn't surprise Nell. For all the secrets and pain she harbored inside herself, Claire Russell seemed honest, and Nell suspected she was already at the police station, just as she had said she'd be.

They were all drained the night before, and Claire went out to the guest cottage soon after finishing her wine. She took some aspirin Nell offered her but said talking had helped, and she thought sleep might come more easily that night. She'd go to the police first thing in the morning, answer as many questions as they put before her, then go out to the nursery and pick up some root stimulator for the plants she planned to transfer.

Don't worry, she said as she headed toward the guesthouse. *I'll be fine.* And the yard and gardens would be fine for Izzy's wedding, too, she promised. No worries. None. But the tone in her voice reflected far less certainty than the words themselves.

I certainly hope everything will be fine, Nell thought now as she pulled onto Harbor Road. She wasn't worried about the yard—it was already perfect, in her mind—lush and green and beautiful. Anything more that Claire did would be icing on the cake.

But the promise that everything *else* would be fine registered with a discomforting hollowness. A murder had occurred. And whether it was fair or not, Claire Russell's history connected her to it.

Nell stopped at a stop sign and waved at Merry Jackson as she jogged by, her small, shapely legs rotating faster than bicycle wheels, her ponytail flying behind her. Nell smiled at the fleeting figure, so compact and cheerful. She was an advertisement for positive thinking. *A dose of Merry is a good thing for all of us,* Nell thought.

She pulled into the parking lot, a narrow gravel strip that ran alongside the historical museum. The redbrick building was on the historic registry, and over the years, the century-old ship captain's home had been turned into a wonderful library and museum that showcased the town's history. She hoped the meeting would be a short one and that the coffee would be strong.

Birdie's long Lincoln Town Car was parked at the curb with Harold at the wheel when Nell reached the steps. She waved at Birdie's groundsman and opened the door for Birdie.

"Kismet," Birdie said, slipping out of the car with the spryness of someone twenty years her junior. She waved Harold on and looped her arm through Nell's. The top of her head barely reached Nell's shoulder, and she tilted it to one side now, looking up at her friend.

"I just ran into Jake Risso," she said without preamble. "We shared a table at Coffee's, not my usual way to start the day—nor his, I suspect. But there he was, looking a bit bedraggled, as if he'd had a night he wanted to forget. I hadn't planned on stopping at Coffee's, but I spotted him on the patio and his slumped shoulders beckoned to me."

Nell entertained the image in her mind. The gruff, unshaven bartender, sitting across from a neatly dressed Birdie Favazza, her large sunglasses nearly covering her face. An unlikely duo.

"He hadn't slept, he told me, so he might as well be drinking Coffee's poison, as he calls it."

Nell followed Birdie up the steps and into the museum lobby. The meeting room, just to the left, was already buzzing with board members when they walked in. Birdie pulled Nell into a corner. "Jake said the police called Andy back in this morning, and Jake is ready to kill someone. It's the same thing all over again. Just like fifteen years ago. Putting his boy on the hot seat because of some damn girl. Those were his words, not mine."

Birdie and Nell knew Jake Risso had a short fuse. They'd seen it first-hand when a homeowner had tried to keep him from taking his fishing boat down to the cove on their access road. He'd single-handedly—with the help of a backhoe—forcefully pulled out the cement barricade. Jake was not easily deterred.

"It's tough to see him reliving those days," Birdie said.

"I wonder what they think Andy might know."

"Jake says Tiffany was in the bar a lot when Andy was working. And he knew they were seeing each other. Once he called Andy's place and she answered the phone. Jake thought she was a bit obsessive about the relationship—but then, he said he thought she'd always been kind of obsessed with Andy. Even back when they were teenagers. She was Harmony's best friend, but Jake thought she also had a crush on Andy."

Nell lifted her eyebrows, but before she could pursue it further, Laura Danvers walked into the room with a platter of warm, cheese-filled Danish.

"Straight out of the oven," she announced. She set them on the side table next to a pot of fresh coffee, took out her notes, and began tapping on a water glass. "Let's get started, ladies," she urged.

Nell sat down at the end of the table, and Birdie took the chair beside her. The meeting began, and Nell tried hard to focus, but the word "obsessed" crowded out the discussion on repairing the steps and funding new exhibits for the front hall. When she closed her eyes briefly, images of sweet Andy Risso filled her head. Tiffany was crazy about Andy; that was as clear to her as the Danish Birdie had just set in front of her. But obsessive? From all accounts, he'd reciprocated her affection, at least for a while.

The meeting ended in record time, thanks to Laura's expert

handling of the issues. Nell marveled at the young woman's ability to keep women twice her age in line and on target, and she told her so as the women packed up their things to leave.

Laura accepted the compliment graciously. "I owe it all to Sea Harbor High."

"Class president would be my guess," Birdie said.

Laura laughed. "And we had lots of issues that year. So I learned how to keep people in line."

"Andy Risso was in your class, right?" Nell asked, though she knew it to be true. Laura. Tiffany. Harmony. Andy. Merry.

"Sure. Andy was smart, kind of shy. We were in honors classes together. I didn't know him well back then—he was a band kid, and I wasn't very musical. But he was one of those kids that people liked. Sweet, I guess you'd say. Just like he is today. Andy's great."

Laura smiled over at one of the museum guides who was waiting to talk to her. "Gotta go. But thanks for coming to the meeting. Sometimes in summer it's hard to get people here." She disappeared through the door, her shiny brown hair waving in the breeze.

"Shall we?" Birdie began walking to the door, and Nell followed.

Outside, Harold stood patiently at the side of the Lincoln, holding the back door open.

"Harold, stop that," Birdie scolded as she and Nell walked down the steps. She wagged a finger in the air. "People will think I have a chauffeur."

"You do, ma'am," Harold said, his eyes twinkling.

"Nonsense," she said, and closed the door, then opened the front door and climbed inside. She rolled down the window and told Nell she would see her tonight. She'd already put the pinot in the wine cooler.

Tonight. The thought sent Nell scurrying to her car. It was Thursday, knitting night. Good. Cooking always cleared her thoughts.

Nell was the last to arrive that evening, but she knew they wouldn't start without her. She had the food, after all.

"Smells great," Izzy said, holding open the shop door as Nell walked through with an armload of bulging bags.

"Lord in heaven." Mae stepped from behind the counter and took some of the load from Nell's arms. "You cooking for an army tonight? Sometimes I wonder why every sweater you gals make doesn't come with permanent food stains on it."

"We separate our passions, Mae," Izzy said, taking the bags from Mae. "Eating, *then* knitting."

Mae laughed and stepped back behind the counter as a customer approached. She shifted into store-manager mode, smiling at the customer and approving her choice of yarn. "Well, go on, then," she said to Nell and Izzy, peering at them over her rimless glasses as she tallied the purchase. "As long as you keep our gorgeous yarns pristine, I'm happy. And by the way, Izzy, I may be here a bit longer tonight, so don't call the police if you hear noise. Got some new yarn books I want to check in."

"Thanks, Mae. Come back if you get hungry." She followed Nell down the steps.

Cass and Birdie were already deep in conversation near the fireplace. Purl had settled between the two of them, her soft tail moving rhythmically against Birdie's thigh while Cass scratched her head.

The windows were open wide, and Birdie's wine was uncorked, with the glasses lined up, waiting. A pitcher of water was beside them. Beyond the windows, an orchestra of boat horns announced the end of a glorious day of sightseeing or whale watching, of sportfishing or filling a sturdy boat with lobster and crabs for area restaurants.

They pulled themselves out of the conversation to greet the others. Some unwritten pact established in the early days of the Thursday night knitting group dictated pleasurable conversation before the foursome got down to the more serious issues of solving their friends' and neighbors' problems, or the difficulties in knitting an I-cord or picking up dropped stitches in a lace pattern.

"The shawl?" Izzy asked, eyeing the large bag on the big library table in the middle of the room. She looked expectantly at Birdie.

In the beginning they planned to surprise Izzy with the wedding shawl. But very quickly they decided that someone with Izzy's taste would need to be in on the design. And so she had been. But Birdie, especially, was determined that Izzy could have weekly peeks—and even offer suggestions as the shawl took shape—but she would never see it completed until her wedding day.

And Izzy had finally agreed.

Birdie pushed herself up from the deep cushions and walked to the end of the table. "I'm turning the shawl over to Nell this week. She does such a fine job on the circle design. But it's looking grand, Izzy dear. Suitable for a beautiful bride." She opened the bag, tugged out a small sheet, and spread it across the end of the table. "Now we're ready. Not that your table is dirty, but caution never hurts." Then, carefully, with a kind of reverence, she pulled out the folds of exquisite cashmere, waves of knitted lace rippling across the fabric she set it on.

They gathered close and looked down at the exquisitely detailed shawl. The shawl of friendship.

Izzy stood in silence as she had each week when she was allowed her glimpse of the shawl. Nell saw her eyes mist over. A lump appeared in her own chest, just as it did each week.

"That's your treat for this week. A peek is all you get, Isabel," Birdie said.

Cass awkwardly wrapped an arm around Izzy. "It gives me goose bumps, Iz," she said. "I think it's all of us here together, watching it grow, the wedding coming closer, the whole kit and caboodle, as my mother says."

"Yes. It's all a work in progress," Birdie said. "Just like our friendship. Always meandering this way and that, whatever comes its way." She folded the shawl as she spoke and slipped it back into the bag.

Izzy handed the towel to Birdie. "Well, a glimpse is all I need to know that it couldn't be more beautiful. It simply couldn't."

"Oh, but it could," Birdie said, pushing away the emotion and drawing smiles. "And it will, you'll see. It's not finished yet. Now, what's for dinner?"

Nell took out the plastic containers, then a wooden salad bowl. She pulled the foil off the bowl and stepped aside to make room for Cass, hovering at her elbow.

Cass eyed the tossed watercress, walnut, and peach salad. Nell had made a vinaigrette dressing with a touch of crushed strawberry and added fresh croutons. She handed Izzy the salad tongs and moved over to the other container as Nell removed the top. A plume of odors rose over the table.

Cass leaned into the smells and closed her eyes. "Hmm. Lemon zest. Wild mushrooms and roasted zucchini? A touch of sherry, I think. Some snips of dill? Ricotta cheese?"

"You're amazing, Cass." Nell looked at her dubiously as she set down the lid. The long container was filled with warm, flaky galettes—each stuffed with a mixture of mushrooms, red peppers, and zucchini, tossed in a lemony ricotta and sherry mixture. "How in heaven's name did you do that?"

"She saw your scribbled recipe on the kitchen counter the other day," Izzy said.

Cass' laugh was her confession. "But I'm getting better at it—I'll soon be the most discerning gourmand fisherwoman on Cape Ann. Wait and see."

Cass not only loved food; she loved the thought of food, and ever since Nell had introduced the lobster fisherwoman to a world beyond canned beans and hot dogs, she was obsessed with new recipes, lured to them as greedily as her lobsters to salted mackerel. And after she clipped the recipes out of newspapers and magazines, she dutifully passed them over to Nell, "to a good home," she'd say, hoping that the recipes would return to her someday in finished form.

"But how did you do that, dear?" Birdie asked, her brows lifting into a maze of tiny forehead lines. She gestured toward the galettes and the salad. The quichelike pastries were perfectly formed round bowls with scalloped golden-brown edges. Picture perfect. "This is fancy—and time-consuming. We don't expect this, Nell."

"It was therapy. I opened the windows, put on a little Joni Mitchell"—she ignored Izzy's and Cass' grins at her musical choice—"and put my mind and energy to cooking . . . and to thinking. It was time well spent. At least I think it was."

She slid a spatula beneath each pastry and placed them on plates, then motioned toward the salad bowl. Birdie took care of the wine, and in minutes they were curled up in their favorite chairs, Izzy's iPod filling the air with a medley of old cover songs. At first the only other sounds were sighs of satisfaction and the clink of forks against stone plates.

But once the initial edge of hunger disappeared, Nell looked over at Cass and Birdie. "You two have something on your minds. And I do, too. Let's get it out there in the open, and maybe there's something we can do about it."

Cass picked up Nell's thread without a pause. "Pete and I were out in the boat today and had a long time to talk. Andy's falling apart. We need to do something, throw him a line. Help him."

"Jake says the same," Birdie reported. She repeated the conversation she'd had with him that morning.

"Tiffany was crazy about Andy. We all could see that. But she was sweet, harmless—"

"And for a while, anyway, she and Andy were together," Izzy added.

"But he certainly had nothing to do with her death," Cass said.

"I keep thinking back to that night, the night she died. It was just like tonight; we were all sitting here knitting, a normal night," Izzy said.

"But not so normal across the street," Birdie added solemnly. She leaned forward and poured herself a glass of water.

"The Fractured Fish had band practice scheduled that night, the night she was killed." She paused, then said carefully, "But Pete mentioned that Andy didn't show that night."

They were silent for a minute.

Nell felt the familiar knot in her stomach. She cared about these people—Andy. And Claire, too. M.J. and her staff. And whoever else in this town was affected by Tiffany Ciccolo's death.

And she cared about her niece's marriage.

She wanted to make all the unhappy things go away.

"Has Andy said where he was that night?" Izzy asked. She looked at Cass.

"He told Pete he went looking for Tiffany, over at the boarding-house where she lived. He needed to apologize for something, he said. But she wasn't there. No one had seen her that night."

"Where did he go after that?"

"He went off, alone. He said he had some things he needed to think about."

"That wouldn't be a very satisfactory explanation for the police," Birdie said.

But they all believed him—because they knew him. Knew his family. Cared about them. Nell played with the thought, then asked rhetorically, "But would we be so quick to believe him if he were a stranger in town, or a worker on a boat whom we'd never met?"

"But that's the point," Cass insisted. "We *do* know him. And we know without a doubt that he could no more murder anyone than speak in tongues. It's just not Andy."

"But it won't go away until we figure out who did it," Birdie agreed. "And it's not right that Andy go through this again. We need to put our heads together and make this whole thing go away."

They were all thinking the same thing, but no one would say it out loud. Just short weeks ago they were moving into a glorious Sea Harbor summer, to be capped off with the joyous celebration of Izzy and Sam's wedding.

Now, suddenly, their lives were caught up in a murder.

And they all wanted the glory days back in a desperate, urgent way.

"Dessert," Nell said, gathering up the empty plates and pulling a pan of blueberry cobbler from a bag. "No butter, skim milk. And it's delicious," she said, spooning small mounds onto dessert plates.

In the distance they could hear Mae whistling as she shuffled boxes and papers. Occasionally they'd hear voices and presumed Mae was listening to *Prairie Home Companion* on the iPod—or talking to herself, something she often did when alone in a room.

"I think I'll take Mae some cobbler," Izzy said. "She's been here all day."

A new voice joined Mae's, one louder and more present than Garrison Keillor's or Guy Noir's. Izzy checked her watch. The store closed at seven on Thursday nights. "Mae must have left the door unlocked," she said and walked over to the steps. "She's like Archie at the bookstore—she can't turn a potential customer away."

Izzy took the plate of cobbler and walked up the steps to the front of the shop. "Sweets for the sweet," she said, laughing.

Mae met her at the archway. "Maybe. But first, there's a gal out front—she's been here for a while, just wandering around. Doesn't say much. Kind of a 'yes' and 'no' sort of person, if you know what I mean. I thought maybe she was lost or about to rob the store or something, but so far no guns have been pulled. She doesn't seem to want to talk to me. Never saw her before in my life."

Their interest piqued, the others followed Izzy up the stairs.

Though there was no need, Mae pointed to a woman dressed in expensive-looking slacks and a sweater walking slowly around the yarn displays. She examined the yarn cubbies and the racks of needles, then looked at the table displays with great interest and longing, the way knitters did, her hands scrunched into balls to keep from touching the skeins of cashmere on the center table, the summery cotton and silk next to it. Her sweater spoke of a knitter, too—a cashmere blend in a brilliant shade of red, worked up with a ruffled edge and beautifully put together.

She looked familiar to Nell—a tall woman, brown hair and freckles. A firm jawline. Determined.

And sad.

"May I help you?" Izzy asked.

Nell, Cass, and Birdie were close behind.

The woman looked up. "How long has this yarn shop been here?"

"Just a few years," Izzy said.

"That explains it." She looked around again. "I haven't been here for a while, in town, I mean." She slipped a plastic bag of walnut needles from a hook and examined them.

"Do you have family in Sea Harbor, dear?" Birdie asked.

The woman looked at Birdie curiously, as if the question was odd or out of place.

"No," she said. The word had an abruptness to it that said, "Don't mess with me." She placed the needles back on the hook and looked back at the small white-haired woman who was looking at her kindly.

But it was kindness mixed with Birdie's soft intensity and relentlessness.

Nell could see the woman's thin coat of armor begin to fall away.

"Well, I suppose I do have family here," she said, then added, "But not really."

Birdie nodded and smiled, as if the answer made perfect sense. "Well, then," she said, "let us show you around Izzy's shop. It's one of the loveliest yarn shops in this hemisphere."

That drew a smile, and Mae stepped forward. "Do you need some yarn?"

The woman shook her head. "I have a closet filled with yarn, and a knitting bag with three projects in it back in my room at the bed-and-breakfast. I knit when I need to calm down. Or to help me through things that are difficult. Knitting is my therapist."

"And this is difficult for you?" Again it was Birdie, the "this" going undefined.

"Oh, not this." The woman spread her hands, taking in the shop. "This is . . . this is a bit of heaven."

"Then . . . what?"

Again the woman's eyes found Birdie's. "Being back in Sea Harbor. That's difficult for me. I never thought I'd come back. But now I have. I've come back." She looked around again, then back to Birdie.

"I always said coming back here would be over my dead body. I never in a million years thought it would be over my sister's."

Chapter 19

Sheila Ciccolo was thirty-seven years old, five years older than her sister, Tiffany. She had run away from an alcoholic father and spineless mother when she was sixteen, she said, and she'd never come back. Not once. Not until today.

"But if I had known about the Seaside Knitting Studio years ago, I might never have left," she said, but the grave sadness in her eyes said otherwise.

Purl had welcomed Sheila immediately, curling up on her lap.

Mae locked up and went home, carrying her cobbler in a plastic container, and the others settled in the knitting room, Sheila in Ben's old leather chair with a warmed-over galette in front of her and a cup of coffee next to it. It had taken little encouragement to suggest she sit for a while. She'd left home at dawn, then had a delayed flight and two plane changes. Her drive from Logan Airport got her in town just in time for her appointment with the Sea Harbor Police. It had been a grueling day.

The galette was gobbled down quickly, followed by a second. And finally an ample helping of Nell's cobbler. The food had relaxed Sheila, and they sat around the coffee table and talked comfortably about ordinary things—Sheila's early life in Omaha with a kind Aunt June who'd taken in an unruly teen. Her scholarship to the university there. Her job in a bank, where she'd recently been promoted to ATM manager.

Jobs, the Midwest, the condo Sheila had just purchased.

But nothing was said about a younger sister who had been murdered in a basement, a hundred yards from where they sat.

It was the elephant in the room, waiting to trumpet its presence.

"I'd almost forgotten how intoxicating this place could be—the sea and boats and all. We don't have much of that in Nebraska." Sheila looked out the windows. The sky was dark now, but the sound of waves lapping against the stone wall behind Izzy's shop was a familiar one. Beyond the wall, the harbor was dotted with moored boats, lights blinking in the blackness. "It's beautiful. It was my life that wasn't beautiful, I guess. And that's what matters when you're sixteen—not sea and sailboats."

"But Tiffany stayed here, didn't move on." Birdie spoke the words carefully, like dropping an egg into boiling water.

At the mention of her sister's name, Sheila's voice changed tone, but she took a deep breath, as if steeling herself, keeping the emotion at bay.

"Tiffany's life was awful, too. Our father was either drunk and screaming at us or gone out on some fishing boat. And our mother was either cowering or in her room with the door closed. No one ever cared where we were or what we did. We could stay out as late as we wanted. It's a miracle that Tiffany didn't turn out bad, or pregnant, or a runaway, like me. But we . . . we were different birds, she and I."

"She was a sweet girl."

"Sweet and shy and always trying to please. Tiff was chubby as a kid, big boned, and unsure of herself. She thought she was ugly. And there wasn't anyone to tell her differently. I tried. But who was I? The troublemaker in the family."

"You never saw each other, all these years after you left?"

"Just once. We met in Boston. I sent her some money and she took the train down. I flew in, and we stayed at a great hotel on the waterfront. She didn't tell Ma. No one knew about it, except probably her friend Harmony. It was right before she graduated from high school.

We had a great time. It was almost like we'd never been away from each other."

"It must be difficult for you to be back here. But it's good you came," Nell said. "Apparently your mother isn't able. . . ."

"No, she isn't. She doesn't know anyone anymore. I hear she just sits and stares at nothing all day long. My father's lovely legacy, I suppose. Living with a mean alcoholic was a living death for our mother. Tiff used to visit her all the time, but recently she stopped. It was all too sad, she said."

"It sounds like you and Tiffany stayed close," Izzy said.

"Close from afar, I guess you'd say. We talked on the phone all the time. When I couldn't reach her last week, I was scared. I knew"—she touched her chest—"in here, you know? I knew something was wrong. I could feel it. You know things like that when you love someone."

"Did the police contact you? There was some concern about finding you."

Sheila nodded. "They found an old birthday card I had sent Tiff, and my address was on it. It was on her bulletin board, they said." She pulled a tissue from the box Izzy slid across the table and wiped away the tears that rolled down her cheeks. "Sorry. It was an awful call to get. Even if I felt something was wrong, I didn't think it could be this wrong."

Sheila wiped her nose and went on. "The police wanted to talk to me. They had a lot of questions, and there were papers to sign. Arrangements."

"M.J. said there wouldn't be a funeral?" Cass asked.

"No. Tiffany . . . She wanted to be cremated; we both did. We talked about all those kinds of things—because of my mother, I guess, and having to make arrangements for what would happen to her. The police want to talk again—and there's more paperwork. A lawyer. The cremation. So I guess I'll be here a day or two; then I'll collect her things and be gone."

"None of us are able to get our arms around this, no one."

Sheila shook her head. "It doesn't make sense. I'm the kind of person people would want to kill. Not Tiffany. If she had a fault, it was trying too hard to get people to like her."

"People did like her, though, whether she tried or not," Birdie said.

"The last few weeks we were a little out of touch. I was traveling some for my job. But we'd catch up when we could. She'd leave me messages. She was a little short with me, though—like something was on her mind. And . . . well, maybe I was a little harsh with her."

"Why?" Nell asked. It was hard to imagine someone being harsh with Tiffany.

"Tiffany was a dumbbell when it came to men." Sheila got up from the chair and looked around for her purse. "Maybe, like I told the police, that was a big part of the problem." She rubbed her eyes and held back a yawn. "I apologize for barging in on you like this. I can tell it's time for me to get some sleep before I say things I regret."

Nell carried her plate to the kitchen and returned with one of Izzy's business cards with all their cell numbers scribbled on it.

"Is there anything we can do to help you while you're here? We've all felt at a loss. When something like this happens, you usually go to the family to help. Take food. Run errands. Meet planes. But we haven't been able to do anything. It's a selfish thing, in a way. But now that you're here, Sheila, please let us help."

Sheila slipped the card into her purse and thought about Nell's offer.

At first Nell thought she'd say no. She suspected Sheila Ciccolo didn't accept favors easily.

But in the end, she said yes. "I have to go over to Tiffany's boardinghouse and clean out her things. I talked to the woman who runs it and she said I could come anytime. It . . . it would be nice not to go in there alone."

They settled on a time—Sheila said Saturday morning would

work best. She was seeing a lawyer on Friday and, frankly, needed some time to be alone and get her head on straight. It was difficult coming back, but from what she had seen of Ravenswood-by-the-Sea when she checked in, the bed-and-breakfast would be the perfect place to put her mind in order.

A rush of affirmation followed.

"It's the perfect place for soothing the soul," Birdie said. "You'll be in good hands—and Kevin, the cook, makes one of the best breakfasts known to man."

Sheila said she was grateful for their help. Having been gone as long as she had, she didn't even know where the boardinghouse was. "All I know from Tiffany," she said, "was that she hoped to be moving soon. She was ready to settle down, to get married, to have kids. It was time, she said. She had it well planned. She wanted four kids, and she needed to start now to have it all happen."

They walked to the door, and Sheila turned to say good-bye. Then she hesitated and looked at the women gathering around her like a protective cloak, women who hours ago had been complete strangers. She gave each of them an awkward hug. "You're good people, as my old aunt June used to say. Thank you."

Nell and Birdie followed her out onto the sidewalk, lured by the cool night breeze. The stores up and down Harbor Road were closed for the night, but lamplights flickered and music streamed from the open doors of bistros and bars and the porch of the Ocean's Edge restaurant. From above, the moon turned the street into a platinum river.

But even the moon couldn't dispel the clouds of murder, Nell thought. The lights were the same, the music and laughter. The waves against the shore and summer breeze. All the same.

And nothing was the same.

"Are the police any closer to a suspect?" she asked Sheila. "Were you able to help them?"

"How could I help?"

"It sounds like Tiffany talked to you more than anyone. Maybe she said something that would help the police? Something that seemed unimportant but might have a connection."

The quiet that filled the space between them was unsettling. Sheila seemed hesitant to speak, but Nell could feel emotion welling up inside her, pushing to get out.

"Sometimes Tiffany would get secretive, even with me, especially if she thought I'd be judgmental about it. And I felt that recently. But the only concrete thing I could tell the police was what I felt—what I *feel*—deep down inside me." She brushed fresh tears from her cheek with the back of her hand. "I told them whose fault it was. I told them that there is only one man who could be responsible for this."

They stared at her.

"It's his fault that my sister is dead. If not for Andy Risso, she'd be alive today."

Chapter 20

"They can't arrest Andy just because Sheila Ciccolo doesn't like him. As much as all of us—including the chief—want this case behind us, that's not the way anyone will go about doing it." Ben carried the coffee carafe and mugs out to the deck, the morning paper stuck beneath one arm.

Nell followed with heaping bowls of her homemade granola topped with the leftover blueberries from the cobbler. "Of course not. But it doesn't help to have Tiffany's sister accusing him. The poor fellow is being punished for simply having women like him—the teenager Harmony and the grown-up Tiffany."

"Did Sheila explain the basis for her accusations?"

"No."

As soon as Sheila had dropped her comment at their feet, she had turned, missing the distress on their faces, and hurried across the street to her rental car.

"She was exhausted and emotionally drained, and I don't think she's aware that Andy is a friend of ours. Frankly, I don't think she even knows who he is. She had run away from home before Tiffany was in high school, and that's where she met Andy."

"So it has to be something that her sister told her?"

Nell nodded. It had to be. But what that could have been was a total mystery. Surely Tiffany wouldn't say bad things about Andy. Nell couldn't have misread her that severely. Maybe a visit to Merry would help clarify Sheila's strong reaction. Merry was astute, she'd been with Andy and Tiffany, and, most of all, Merry loved to talk.

Ben scanned the headlines as he spooned up Nell's milk-soaked granola. "Damn good," he murmured.

Nell watched him with a smile, enjoying the fact that he found pleasure in ingredients he'd probably avoid if he knew what they were—flaxseed and coconut flakes, oats and figs and prunes. She lifted her coffee mug, the strong aroma awakening sleepy senses. Through the steam she looked down toward the guesthouse, her thoughts wandering easily from Andy to cereal to Claire Russell.

The windows were open, and the pleasant sounds of NPR's *Morning Edition* floated up from a radio. She hadn't had a chance to talk to Claire the day before, and wondered now about her talk with the police. Hopefully it was short and unemotional for Claire.

"I saw Claire yesterday while you were at Izzy's place," Ben said, looking up from the paper and stepping into her thoughts. They sat at the table, looking out over the lawn. "She's quite a gardener. It's an art form for her. Like a landscape in which the colors have to be perfectly blended, the shades of green contrasting with the rest of the painting. We walked around, and she showed me a whole plot of grasses that she's going to replant somewhere else because the balance and contrast aren't quite right."

Nell chuckled. What her diplomatic Ben was *not* saying was that her own gardening prowess was definitely in contrast to Claire's. She loved it, the feel of the earth, the smell of rich, loamy soil. But once something was in and surviving, it was there to stay. And she often buried a handful of unknown bulbs in a worked bed in the fall to see what surprises would pop up in the spring. The survival of the fittest was a fair garden mantra for Nell.

"Speaking of balance, did she mention her visit to the police?"

A flash of sunlight on a shiny spade drew their attention to the back of the yard. Claire, dressed in her usual jeans and T-shirt and floppy hat, waved up to the deck.

Nell stood and called down to her. "Coffee?"

Claire hesitated for just a second, then pulled off her gloves, tossed them into the wheelbarrow, and joined them on the deck.

"I feel like a broken record, but it looks amazing, Claire," Nell said, handing her a cup of coffee.

Claire surveyed her work, then pulled her brows together critically. "It will. Not quite there yet. It has to be perfect for Izzy."

"I apologize for not being much help these days. It's been a busy time. And somehow, the aftermath of Tiffany's murder seems to eat up chunks of time, though I couldn't tell you how or why. It's a disturbing distraction, at the least."

Claire sipped her coffee, any emotion hidden beneath her calm exterior.

"I don't suppose the police shed any light on it when you talked to them?"

"No. My meeting was short. They brought up Tiffany and Harmony's friendship, as we supposed they would. And I told them what little I could. They were teenage friends. And along with Andy Risso, they were a threesome. I explained that Andy was Harmony's boyfriend, though we kept it secret from her father." Her voice dropped to nearly a whisper. "What secrets. What lies . . ."

"You were doing what you thought was best for your daughter."

"We've all done a little of that in our lifetimes," Ben said. He took a drink of coffee and sat back in his chair. "You were protecting her. That's what good parents do."

Claire poured another stream of half-and-half into her coffee. "Yes, that's what we do, I suppose, for better or for worse. There are plenty of days I wonder why I didn't leave him and raise Harmony alone."

"Did you consider that?"

"Now and then. But I was afraid, I suppose. Where would I go? I had no family except for my sister in Texas. Richard paid the bills; we had a house, an income. I had the garden to work in. But the real truth, I suppose, was that I wasn't strong enough back then."

But strength seemed to have come to Claire Russell over the

years. Strength and a determination to not let her life slip by. Nell could see it in the set of her jaw, the steely look that sometimes lit her eyes, even as they fell into sadness when difficult times were brought to mind.

"So at least the time with the police went smoothly?" Nell said. "That was probably all they needed from you, affirming the relationships. Covering all their bases, I suppose."

"I suppose. But they asked me to stay around for a few days in case they had more questions. I told them where I was staying, which brought a nice smile from Chief Thompson. He told me I was lucky to have such friends. I said I was completely and totally aware of that."

"He's a good man," Ben said. "He has kids, grown now. But he understands how hard reliving this must be for you."

"He said as much. He concentrated more on Tiffany, what she was like as a teen. I told them what I knew, though much of my information was through Harmony's eyes, the things she used to tell me about her friend. She wasn't the kind of teenager other kids would notice much. Plain. Always trying to please. She was good at basketball; I remember that—the kids played over at the old community center. I was glad she had something she was good at. She needed that. Oh, and Harmony told me once that she had a crush on Andy Risso—and I told that to the police, too."

"Did it bother Harmony that Tiffany liked her boyfriend?"

"Bother her? Oh, no. For all the dysfunction surrounding her growing-up years, Harmony was self-confident. If I fostered that, maybe I did something right." She stirred her coffee. "She knew Andy was crazy about her and that he put up with Tiffany because they were friends. Tiffany idolized Harmony."

Nell watched the emotions play across Claire's face as she pulled things from memory. Now that it was all out in the open, she seemed better able to deal with these unexpected forays back to a terrible time in her life. Claire Russell was a complicated woman, something Nell hadn't fully realized in those early days of gardening, back when Claire kept her past tightly protected from outside eyes. She loved her daughter fiercely. And the image Nell had of this young woman she had never met was ever changing, like a slide show, gathering color and definition as it played on.

A smart, self-confident daughter. With an adoring boyfriend and girlfriend on either side of her.

And now two of the threesome were dead.

"I also told them that even though the three teenagers seemed inseparable, the allegiances died with Harmony, almost instantly, because after she died, I never saw either of them again. Nor heard a word from them." The feeling of betrayal crept back into Claire's voice, and she tried to cover it over. "I know that sounds childish. I need to let go of it, and I'm trying. It was hurtful—but they were just kids; that's what I keep telling myself." Claire took a last drink of her coffee and stood up. "Again, what would I do without you two?"

"Have less dirt beneath your nails?" Nell laughed.

"I love that dirt. It's a badge of honor. Now I need to get back to it," she said, and with a wave, she walked purposefully back to her tools and a waiting pile of mulch.

"Me, too," Ben said, getting up. "I'm helping Auggie McClucken with some business things today. He's thinking of expanding the hardware store and needs some advice."

Nell followed him into the kitchen and piled the dishes in the sink.

"Don't forget the deck is being power washed today. And Sam insists it's his big chance to have Friday-night dinner at his place. A kind of thank-you, he said, for all the wedding preparations—though that's totally unnecessary."

Ben nodded, half listening, as he headed to his den.

Nell watched him walk off, already thinking ahead to her own day. So many of the to-dos involved Izzy's wedding—candles, cameras, some painting touch-ups to the porch stairs she'd hired a teenager to do. RSVPs. But over it all hung a cloud so thick and heavy that if it fell, it might suffocate them.

Suddenly, making that cloud evaporate rose to the top of her list. There were still so many questions floating around, and Sheila's unexpected appearance the night before had taken away their opportunity to come up with answers to some of them.

Nell rinsed the bowls and slipped them into the dishwasher. It was Friday. She might be able to catch Cass. She and Pete were hiring a few extra guys to help with their small lobster business, and it sometimes freed her up a little. And Birdie would drop most things—even her tap-dancing class—for an adventure. Izzy probably couldn't get away. She headed to the kitchen island and her phone.

"Danny might be over at the Palate, too," Cass said, pulling on her seat belt as she leaned forward in Nell's car to talk to the two women in the front seat. "He spends a lot of time on the deck. I think Hank may make him honorary resident writer one of these days. Maybe put up a plaque when he's famous."

"Or a statue, like that Fitz Hugh Lane statue over in Gloucester."

They laughed at the image of a bronze Danny, his laptop on his knees, staring out over the Palate deck.

"I imagine it's a perfect place to write on days like this," Birdie said. She looked out the open window, admiring the wildflowers that lined the narrow road to the Canary Cove Art Colony. "I would need more quiet, myself, were I to somehow find myself with the gift of spinning intriguing tales."

"I know for sure you have a million tantalizing stories to tell, but I can't imagine you secluding yourself to write, Birdie," Nell said. "You'd shrivel up."

She laughed. "That I would. Perhaps that's why I was never blessed with that talent. I need the sounds of life and laughter around me. That's what fuels my soul."

"And it looks like that's what you shall get," Nell said, pulling into the parking lot adjacent to the Artist's Palate deck. At the back end of the lot, just at the edge of the deck, a group of shirtless guys shot baskets in the hoop Hank had set up.

Although it was too early for lunch, the deck was also bustling with activity, artists taking a break from the galleries that surrounded the bar and grill, a few tourists here and there, some summer students with computers balanced on their legs. Danny sat at a table beneath a tall oak tree, its branches a canopy over the table and corner of the deck.

Nell liked the Artist's Palate best in the earlier part of the day, before the bands, twenty-seven kinds of beer, and stomping feet took over.

Danny didn't look up as they walked by, his fingers moving rapidly over the keys, so they left him in the grips of his creativity and found another shaded table not far away.

Merry Jackson appeared at the table in an instant, wiping her hands on a white apron tied around her tiny waist. Without a word, she pulled out a chair and sat down. "I'm so glad to see you guys."

Nell had called her earlier on her cell, wondering if she'd have a few minutes to talk.

"Are you working, dear?" Birdie asked. "We wouldn't want to get you in trouble."

Merry's laugh was light and sparkling, just like the person she was. "Now, Birdie, I ask you. What's the boss man going to do, fire me?"

"Not a chance of that," Birdie said, looking over at Hank Jackson. He stood wiping glasses at the outdoor bar, his eyes focused on his young wife.

"He couldn't do this without me," Merry said, waving the tips of her fingers at her husband. "I'm the real force behind this place, you know."

"It wouldn't surprise me one bit," Nell said.

"But before we get deep in talk, I should bring you something. My treat." She sprung up and disappeared inside.

In the time it took them to put bags beneath the table and for Birdie to pull out the cashmere sweater she was working on, Merry had returned with a tray of iced tea, a bowl of fresh grapes and strawberries, and a basket of warm bran muffins. "I'm trying to get people around here to eat better. At least in the morning. Some of these artists, they'd eat Fritos for breakfast if I let them."

"You won't abandon the fried calamari, though, will you?" Cass asked, her voice dripping with feigned anguish.

"Not in your wildest nightmares." Merry laughed. "There's definitely a limit to this healthy stuff. Now, where were we?" She put her elbows on the table and cupped her chin in her hands. "Pete was over here a minute ago to drop off some music, and he says that Tiffany's sister is in town. I didn't even know she had a sister. What's that about? Why do the police want to talk to her?"

"I think it's just routine. And she's the only family Tiffany had. Someone had to gather her things."

"But Pete says she's defaming Andy. This has to stop, Nell." Her brows drew together and her voice rose over the tops of customers until Hank looked over, concerned.

He strode over and began massaging her shoulders with his large, sure hands. "You okay, babe?"

Nell looked up at Hank and smiled. Thick, dark hair fell over his forehead as he looked down on Merry.

"I'm fine, Hank," Merry said, wiggling out of his massage. "Just upset about this whole thing. I want Andy back like he was before, safe and sound, a drummer without stress."

"New developments?" Hank looked over at Birdie, then Nell and Cass. His eyes mirrored his voice—concern for Merry. If she was worried about something, he'd take it on as well.

"Not really, not about solving the crime, anyway. Tiffany's sister, Sheila, is in town," Nell said. "The police contacted her and suggested she come to gather Tiffany's belongings."

"I didn't know there was a sister," he said, and then his face slowly registered recognition. "Oh, sure. I remember. She ran away when she was just a kid. Tall, like her sister."

"And now she's back spewing out bad things about Andy," Merry said.

"What would she know about Andy? She hasn't lived here in ages," Hank said. "Does she even know him?"

Merry shrugged. "Who knows?"

"She won't be here long," Nell said. "We're going to help her box up Tiff's things at the boardinghouse tomorrow. There's also some paperwork she has to take care of. But she's anxious to leave. This is difficult for her."

Hank nodded, then looked up as a waiter whistled at him through his fingers, waving him over to solve a leaky-keg problem. He said a reluctant good-bye, then was gone across the deck, the answer to his question going by the wayside.

"He'd rather stay with us and listen to gossip," Merry said.

"He's one handsome dude," Cass said. "I always forget that, because he's, well . . ."

"Old?" Merry giggled. "Well, not that much older than you, Cass. You're getting up there."

"He's *way* older," Cass insisted.

"Yeah, I guess," Merry said, looking over at Hank. "He's maybe forty-five. I don't much keep track of things like that. I liked that he was older when I married him, but I'd like to put a lid on it now. The older he gets, the more he seems to worry about things." She glanced over at her husband again, and then brought her attention back to the group. "Enough about that. It's Andy we need to talk about."

"That's why we came by," Cass said. "Well, that and these muffins." She took a bite out of one. "They're actually good."

"Another convert." Merry clapped her hands.

"Pete's talked a little about Andy and Tiffany and their relationship," Nell said, easing into the topic they wanted to talk about. "But sometimes women see things men don't."

"And sometimes see things differently," Merry added. "I get it. Pete and I have talked until we're goofy about the last couple weeks, trying to figure out what went on."

"Tiffany had been hanging around for a while, right?" Cass said.

Merry nodded. "Like I said, at first we thought she was just a groupie. She started coming to our gigs when she came back from that beauty school, all spiffed up. That was a while ago. She looked different, prettier, had a little more confidence than when she was in high school. Next thing we knew, she was hanging around *after* the gigs, that kind of thing. She'd make us brownies and cupcakes, brought pizza, offered to help carry things. She was *too* nice, if you know what I mean? But how can you accuse someone of being too nice?

"So we tried to shrug it off. Just let it be. If we were performing in a place that served food, like the Gull, she'd sometimes order a sandwich for Andy, then invite him over to her table at the break to eat it. To be nice, you know?"

"What did Andy do?"

Merry shrugged. "At first, not much. She kept playing up the high school thing, but Andy said they only hung out back then because of Harmony. Tiffany was nice enough, but Harmony was the reason they even knew each other. I don't remember much about that. Andy was in the band; I was a cheerleader. According to high school social rules, we didn't mix much. They were kind of their own little clique, I guess. I didn't really know Andy until we got the band together." Her brow furrowed for a minute as if she was realizing something important for the first time. "What a shame. Maybe he could have been *my* boyfriend instead of that quarterback I dated. He would have been a better choice."

Cass laughed. "But you said Tiffany sometimes went out with you afterward, right?" She slathered another muffin with honey butter.

"Sometimes. We'd go out after a gig just to unwind. And sometimes she'd just be there, where we were going, like the Gull or the Franklin. Like it was a coincidence. She'd act surprised to see us."

"Do you think she followed you?"

"I don't know. But it seemed odd, especially because she was usually alone. Would you do that, Cass? Go to a bar all alone?"

"Guys do it all the time."

Merry fluttered a hand in her face to shush her. "The answer is,

'No, you probably wouldn't.' Whether it's fair or not, we just don't usually do that. But shy Tiffany did. Anyway, if what she was after was Andy, it worked. After a while they'd actually make plans together, and he'd go off with her alone. But then, well, the last few weeks, I don't know, Andy started to pull back. Didn't go with us if she was there, always politely, but he told Pete he didn't want Tiffany to get the wrong idea. He'd maybe given her conflicting messages. I think the poor guy felt a little smothered. She was too available; you know what I mean?"

"Do you think Tiffany had built more into the relationship than was really there?" Nell asked.

"I think so. At least that's my take on it. But the more Andy pulled back, the more she seemed to press him. It was uncomfortable for Andy. Hank thinks I overreact. He says Tiffany was just a shy girl with a crush."

"You and Hank both talked to her that night the Fractured Fish played here at the Palate. Did she say what was wrong? She was distraught," Birdie said.

Merry's eyes got big. "That was strange. She was upset; you're right. I don't know exactly what she said to Andy, but it made him mad—something he rarely got. When we got ready to play again, Pete and I could see how upset he was. He muttered something about underestimating Tiffany."

"Do you know what he meant?"

"No. But he's such a nice guy that I don't think he realized Tiffany's expectations. They were having a good time together; at least I think that was his take on it. Maybe, when she laid it on him, he realized that she saw it as a serious relationship."

"So what did Tiffany say to him to make him mad? She looked so sad." Nell remembered the tears—and the look of yearning.

"She didn't tell me much, just that she knew Andy must have feelings for her and she didn't understand his anger. They had a bond, she said, that no one else could possibly understand. A secret that they shared. And then she started to cry."

"And that's it?" Birdie said.

"Just about. Except for something Tanya told me—you know that gossipy girl from the salon? She told me later that night—I think maybe she'd had too much to drink—that she asked Tiffany why she left work early that day. Tanya was mad because it meant extra work for her. As she walked over, she saw Andy standing there, so she waited a minute for him to leave. She heard Tiffany say something about a secret, which I suppose made Tanya step closer. And then she heard the word 'baby.' That was enough for her, she said, so she took off."

"Baby . . ." Cass repeated the word slowly, as if it were about to explode. "Geesh."

Nell frowned, and Merry stepped in. "Like I said, Tanya was tipsy. And who knows what she really heard."

But it could certainly upset Andy. Nell pushed the thought away. Gossip like that could cause serious problems. But there would have been an autopsy report. . . . Her thoughts bounced around as she tried to find significance in Merry's comment. She asked, "So you think Tiffany was simply sad that Andy was pulling away?"

Merry thought about the question, then sat up straight, her small breasts straining against a well-fitted T-shirt. "You want my honest opinion? I think she was lovesick. Plain old lovesick. She wanted Andy, plain and simple. Wanted him to be her husband."

"What did Hank say?" Birdie asked. "He seemed to have calmed her down."

"Hank's good at that. I give him lots of practice." Merry laughed. "But that's why I sent him over. I thought Tiffany would talk to him. He talked to her for a while, but when I asked him about it later, he said she was just PMSing or something. Emotional, he said. She needed someone to nod and tell her everything would be okay, so that's what he did."

"I guess we all need a bit of that now and then," Birdie said.

"Well, I sure do," Merry said with a grin. "And now I'd better get back to work before the handsome beast bellows at me."

"Excellent alliteration," Birdie said as Merry sailed away.

Beside her, Cass half stood, waving a muffin in the air at a tall figure coming their way. Danny Brandley walked up, his computer backpack slung over one shoulder, and a five o'clock shadow darkening his chin.

"How's the book coming?" Cass asked, then grimaced and ducked, waiting for Danny's groan.

"Not a good question to ask a writer pushing a deadline," he explained to Nell and Birdie. "And the vixen knows it, which is why she asked." He took the muffin from Cass' fingers and bit into it. "This is good," he said. He stared at it. "It's not fried. Hank is losing his touch."

Nell laughed. "You and Ben. If it's good for him, he's always a tad suspicious."

"So what brings you amazing women to my turf?"

"Last I heard, this was a public restaurant, Brandley," Cass said.

He took off her baseball hat and mussed her hair, then straddled the bench next to her. "I saw you talking to Merry. It looked too serious for the Palate deck, so I stayed away. What's up?"

"It's Tiffany Ciccolo's death," Birdie said.

Nell noticed how artfully they avoided the word "murder." It was too heavy. Too awful when said aloud.

"We're just trying to make sense out of some things. Andy is on the hot seat, and we'd like to remove him from that uncomfortable position as soon as possible." Cass leaned into his chest.

"Yeah, it's tough. Andy is a good guy." Danny reached over and fingered the rich caramel-colored sweater Birdie was working on. It would be a thank-you to Mary Pisano for her kindnesses in taking care of the Chambers wedding party. "Soon as I master the purl stitch, will you show me how to make one of these, Birdie? I mean a little bigger maybe. Different style. But I'm ready to move on, I think."

Birdie laughed and gave his hand a pat. "That can be arranged."

A sudden thought came to Nell, far removed from sweaters and Danny's challenge with the purl stitch. She dove in.

"Danny, when you were preparing your talk for the knitting book club, did you come across any references to Harmony's life, things other than the usual? Were there any 'human interest' kinds of stories that might shed some light on who she was and her connection to Andy and Tiffany?"

"Before the talk, I just did a cursory scan of the articles. I wanted a framework of a cold case, that was all. But I went back to my notes after that article showed up about Harmony and Tiffany. Lots of teenagers were interviewed back then, and many of the comments were the same—'I didn't hang out with her,' 'didn't know her,' that sort of thing. But Tiffany was interviewed several times, as you'd suppose.

"Harmony's mother wasn't very accessible, I don't think, and the father all but pulled out a shotgun when people tried to get close. His only comments seemed to be condemning the mother. It was all her fault, in his mind."

"She has her own demons to deal with," Nell said. "She allowed Harmony to go to the party that night. It's something she's still dealing with, all these years later. But Harmony was her own agent. And you can't stop a seventeen-year-old from living her life, no matter how hard her father tried to do that."

"At least Harmony had a mother who loved her dearly," Birdie said. "And maybe her father did, too, in his own way. Tiffany's home life was the opposite. She was pretty much on her own."

Danny leaned forward, his elbows on the table. "Which may have explained her relationship with Harmony. It was probably the one solid thing in her life. And like I said, she was quoted a lot. One reporter, in particular, got to know her a little. He probably made Tiffany feel secure. When he asked her about her friendship with Harmony, she talked about it at length, about how inseparable they were. And then she said something I found a little curious." Danny took a drink of Cass' iced tea, then went on.

"Tiffany said that she was the only person Harmony shared everything with. The way the reporter wrote it, she was saying it as a matter of great pride. She told the guy that she was the only one who really knew Harmony's secrets."

"Secrets?"

Danny nodded. "And when the reporter asked her what the secrets were, that maybe it was something that would help people understand her friend's tragic death, Tiffany was clear in her answer—and she said she'd tell the police the same thing if they asked."

"It sounds like a dramatic teenager getting attention she sorely lacked in her life," Birdie said.

"Could be," Danny said.

"What was it she said? What was her answer?" Cass asked with some impatience.

"She said, 'You'll never know. I'll take Harmony's secret with me to my grave.'"

Chapter 21

They all left shortly after, Cass and Danny wandering down Canary Cove Road to look at Willow Adams' new fiber arts display and perhaps come across the perfect wedding gift for Sam and Izzy. A formidable task, they both admitted.

Nell and Birdie drove in the opposite direction, toward Harbor Road and their homes.

They drove in silence for a while, each sifting and sorting through the conversations that had pummeled them in the past few days. When Nell finally spoke, it was with a heaviness that they'd both carried away from the Artist's Palate.

"So much of what we've heard lately paints Andy in a terrible light," Nell said. "A part of me wants to put a halt to all conversation. And then have a nor'easter come and blow it all away."

Birdie agreed. "But the other part wants to talk to everyone who ever had any contact with Tiffany Ciccolo, so we can figure out what this woman was all about and why in heaven's name anyone would want to put an end to her life."

"Maybe that's exactly what we need to do, Birdie. Sheila's arrival last night cut our evening short. We need to gather up Cass and Izzy and peel apart the layers of Tiffany's life. Surely we'll find something there that will relieve Andy of this burden."

And Claire, too, Nell thought. Her distaste for Tiffany was

controlled when she talked to Ben and Nell about her daughter's best friend. And it had been with the police as well, she supposed.

But the expression on her face when she saw Tiffany standing in Nell's doorway the day before she was killed was not controlled in the slightest.

Nell turned left onto Harbor Road and slowed just in time to avoid two teenagers in beach gear, cell phones pressed against their ears, walking slowly across the street.

"Do you have a minute?" Nell asked, spotting a parking spot in front of McClucken's Hardware Store. "I'd like to check in on M.J. and see how she's doing."

Birdie gave a thumbs-up, and Nell backed into a spot between two small cars.

"It's odd that Tiffany didn't have more friends here," Nell said. She pulled the key out of the ignition and dropped it in her purse.

"Some people do fine with just a friend or two. Look at my Ella and Harold."

That was true enough. As far as anyone knew, Birdie's groundsman and housekeeper had Birdie as a friend. And that was it, except for a brief friendship Ella once had with a neighbor who had died. Their world was small, and they were utterly content to live within it. Perhaps that was Tiffany's choice, too. But somehow it seemed a sad choice for a sweet young person.

As usual on a Friday, M.J.'s salon was buzzing with activity. Animated chatter, bursts of laughter, and the soft hum of hair dryers filled the mint-scented air. Fit young bodies moved effortlessly, escorting clients from the waiting lounge to the softly lit hair-washing room, to the line of styling stations and swivel chairs.

Nell and Birdie waved to Margaret Garozzo, her wet hair combed out and waiting for a trim. In the next chair, her teenage granddaughter sat patiently waiting for strands of long brown hair to be wrapped in foil.

Tanya Gordon looked up from the desk. Her eyes widened in greeting. "Hey, you two. I mean, hello. Welcome. I bet you're looking for the boss. One sec." She disappeared down the back hallway and was back just as quickly. "M.J. said to go on back. She's in her office." Her smile was huge, and her step light.

Nell found herself looking back at the young woman as she walked down the hall, wondering about the sudden change. The last time she had seen Tanya, she was glum and spiritless. Today she was filled with sunlight.

They found M.J. at her desk and nearly hidden behind a pile of papers. A young man wearing a belt filled with carpenter tools stood nearby.

She stood and hurried around the desk, thrusting a stack of paint samples into his hand, then turned toward Birdie and Nell. "I'm so glad to see you both. Sanity. That's what you mean to me." Her eyes were sad but her greeting gracious. "It's been quite a week, you know?"

Birdie gave the salon owner a quick hug. "We know."

"This is Tim." She turned back to the young worker. "He works for D. J. Delaney's construction company. They're doing a little remodeling job for me. D. J. is even giving me a deal, if you can believe it."

"The basement," Nell guessed.

M.J. nodded. "An indoor staircase, for starters, paint, new walls."

Tim moved toward the door. "And I need to get back to it."

"Tanya will show you where everything is," M.J. said.

Tim tipped his ball cap toward them and disappeared.

Birdie looked at M.J. with the look they all knew meant "Let me have my say," and then said, "M.J., even if you'd had a staircase, this would have happened, dear. You cannot take the burden of this on yourself, none of it, not one iota."

M.J.'s semblance of a smile was appreciative. But whether she could believe in Birdie's words just yet was doubtful. It was her salon. Her employee. Her basement. "A part of me knows that, Birdie. The other part . . ."

"It will come, dear, once we find out who did this."

"A hair salon can be a hotbed for rumors," M.J. said. "I ignore it most of the time, but with Tiffany's death, any mention of her name puts me on alert. I keep thinking I'll hear something worthwhile, something that will make me say, 'Of course! That's what happened.'"

"And instead you're probably hearing things that make you cringe."

"Yes. Lots of innocent people get caught up in these things. . . ." She hesitated for a minute, then went on. "I had coffee with Auggie McClucken this morning. He said he saw Claire Russell that night. She was walking down Harbor Road. Headed toward the salon."

Birdie and Nell looked at each other. They remembered that night with startling clarity. Claire, her head down, walking down Harbor Road.

But she could have been going anywhere. To the Gull. Or the little café that stayed open late, which was what Nell had decided when she'd looked back on that evening with Ben. "She may have just been out for a walk," Nell said quietly. "It was a nice night, if I remember correctly. Birdie and I were on Harbor Road that night, too. And lots of other people."

"Of course," M.J. said. "But that's what I mean, stories spinning out of control all over the place. You want to get out the broom and sweep it all away. Bring order back into our lives."

"Hopefully the sweeping will be done soon," Birdie said. "But in the meantime, we wanted to check on you, dear. And to see if there's anything we can do."

"You're angels, both of you. It's been hard, keeping the salon team on track. I had one young girl quit. Her mother was afraid for her safety, she said."

Nell frowned. "I'm so sorry. That's silly, of course, but this whole thing has rekindled old fears, I think. Especially with the connection between Tiffany and Harmony."

M.J. nodded. "I know that rationally. And we're doing our best. The young women who work here are wonderful for the most part, but they've gotten caught up in it, too. None of them were close friends of Tiffany's, which in a way is bad. There's no one to be loyal to her memory. So instead, they dissect it all with a kind of detachment, wondering who did it, who didn't, but it seems disrespectful, somehow. They've pointed fingers all over the place—deliverymen, the Fractured Fish. . . . They've even accused Tanya."

"She wasn't crazy about Tiffany; I remember that from the day Izzy and I were here—"

"That's right, I forgot. You saw Tanya with her claws out. But good grief, she's not a murderer; she was simply jealous. Tiff had pulled her life together, gotten some sophistication, and Tanya was a ways off from that. But she's really trying. She drives me crazy sometimes, but I think the girl has potential."

M.J. glanced down at a notepad on the table, then frowned. "Another thing I need to take care of. I talked to Tiffany's sister yesterday. Have you met her?"

"We have. She's a knitter, and wandered into the shop last night."

"She seems nice enough. This must be difficult for her. I guess we all share a bit of guilt when it comes to Tiffany."

"I'm sure she has the bigger chunk."

"Maybe. I suggested she come by to pick up Tiffany's personal things. She said she'd try to find time but didn't sound happy about it. Maybe it's just too difficult for her. But Tim needs to get in that office soon, so I may have to have Tanya box up her things."

Somehow the thought of Tanya going through Tiffany's things seemed wrong. Nell looked at Birdie and read the same thought on her face.

"Why don't we do it for you?" she said.

Birdie glanced at her watch, then agreed. "Good idea, and if the work crew needs to get in there soon, we might be able to do it now. Nell?"

"Now would be perfect."

"We'll be seeing Sheila tomorrow and can take the things to her."

"You're amazing, both of you. That'd be a terrific help," M.J. said.

"I don't think there's too much, but I don't want the workers in there until her personal things are removed. And it's crazy up here in the salon or I'd do it myself. Tiffany kept things running so smoothly, and losing her is like losing five staff members, not one. You're lifesavers." M.J. walked to her desk and made a quick phone call to the front to tell her assistant, Lynn, where she was, then headed for the door.

Birdie and Nell collected their bags and followed her down the back hall.

Nell paused at the foot of the outside stairs, her hand still on the railing, her mind still on the rumors that M.J. was having to live with every day. "M.J., was Tiffany distracted by anything that last week? She had missed the appointment with us—were there other things that maybe the staff noticed?"

"Maybe a few. I think she was distracted. For a few weeks, actually. Relationship difficulties, I think."

"With Andy?"

"I think so. The girls up front said they were together, a couple, for a while, and that Tiffany was obsessed with him—they tend to exaggerate, though, so I hear everything with half an ear. 'The drummer,' they called him when they were teasing her. Frankly, I think they were jealous. Andy, Merry, and Pete have become rock stars around here.

"But to your question—Tiff didn't confide in me much, but she did talk about Andy some. She told me about their high school friendship and how nice it was to be together again. She talked about his music, going to the Fractured Fish concerts, that sort of thing. Her face definitely lit up when she said his name and I suspect it's a feeling she's harbored for a long time.

"Alex and I don't exactly hang out in the same places as the younger crowd does, so I didn't see them together, but Tanya brought in reports now and then, much to Tiffany's chagrin."

"Did Tiffany ever mention Harmony to you?"

"Yes. And that's why it unnerved me that night when Danny

brought up her murder at the book club. Tiffany always seemed a bit fragile. I didn't want this rocking her boat. And then all this happened and it was like a dam burst.

"I didn't know for a long time that Tiffany knew Harmony. But one night she stayed late to help me with something and she got to talking about it. She told me that her best friend had been murdered, how awful that night had been. I got the feeling it was the first time she had ever had anyone to talk to about it."

"So she told you about the night Harmony died?"

"Yes. A lot of it was in the paper, but she talked about the party, and that Harmony was supposed to spend the night at her house. They were going to exchange graduation presents, and she'd stocked up on 'sleepover' food—late-night frozen pizza, doughnuts for breakfast, that kind of thing. She thought Andy would come by for breakfast, too. It might have been a normal thing for some kids, but it was a big deal to her. A special event.

"There's something poignant about that," Nell said.

M.J. agreed. "The two girls met up with Andy at the school gym and did whatever kids do at those events. Apparently Tiffany was off talking to a chaperone, and when she went back to find them, they were standing near the door, arguing. They'd been doing that a lot, she said. But this night it seemed worse. They walked outside and she followed them. Harmony started walking fast across the parking lot, trying to get away from him, but he chased her to her car."

"While Tiffany watched."

M.J. nodded. "And that was it. That was the last time she saw Harmony."

"So she thought they went off together?"

"She *saw* them go off together, at least to the car." M.J. moved to the basement entrance.

Nell looked at the metal bulkhead. It was open, leaning against the building and exposing the stone steps leading below. She paused at the top, then took a quick breath and followed M.J. and Birdie down the steps.

Unlike the last time she was here, the basement was ablaze with lights. The workmen had strung them up everywhere. The shelves had been dismantled, and supplies were packed away in clearly marked boxes. In a far corner, Tim and a worker were cutting pieces of drywall with an electric saw while another man screwed joists in place along the wall. The air was thick with sawdust.

"You can see why I want to get Tiffany's things out," M.J. said, her voice straining over the noise of the saw.

They turned toward a door at the opposite side of the basement, and M.J. opened the door. "This was Tiffany's office."

A sudden movement in the center of the room sent the three women reeling backward.

M.J. let out a yelp.

The figure screamed.

"Tanya!" M.J. regained her composure and stared at the frightened young woman sitting behind the desk.

She stared at M.J., one hand still in the open desk drawer. Tape and scissors and notepads were scattered across the surface.

"What do you think you're doing down here, Tanya?"

Tanya immediately stood at attention, tipping back the chair. Her long brown ponytail whipped behind her. "I . . . I was making sure that—" Her voice faltered.

The expression on the young woman's face was so distressed that Nell felt a sudden impulse to wrap an arm around her and assure her it'd be all right.

But she had absolutely no idea if it would be.

"Making sure that what?" M.J. asked. Then, before Tanya burst into tears, she suggested she leave, go upstairs where she was needed at the desk, and they'd talk about this later.

Tanya bowed her head and scuttled by Nell and Birdie, trying unsuccessfully to smile their way.

M.J. looked at the desk and the open drawer. "I have no idea what this is about, but I'll definitely find out." She walked over behind the desk and looked into the deep side drawer that seemed to be of interest. She rummaged through it, then looked up and sighed. "For all her faults, she's not a bad person."

Nell smiled. And neither was M.J. Arcado. Calm and cool, and always looking at the half-full glass, even when her life had been turned upside down.

"You handled that well, M.J.," Birdie said. "I'm impressed."

"I suppose having preteens at home helps," she said with a wry smile. "Except Tanya isn't twelve. She should know better. Going through Harmony's personal things like this is inexcusable."

Nell looked around the room as M.J. checked again through the drawer. She had managed to make a cheery small space for Tiffany in this secluded basement spot. She imagined the young woman down here, sitting at the desk. Making calls and keeping records of her clients. Feeling accomplished. Feeling at home.

Colorful ocean-view prints hung on the walls, and a long wooden bookcase held magazines and books and framed photos. Some personal items—a small box for hair clips or jewelry, a stuffed animal perched on a shelf, a tray with water glasses and a pitcher next to it. In front of the desk, two chairs sat side by side. Several area rugs added color to the room, and in one corner, a small couch was piled with cushy pillows; an iPod dock sat on a table next to it. M.J.'s big television that they used with training CDs was on a cart in one corner.

"What a nice room—such a surprise in the middle of the basement. It's like a cozy den."

"Sometimes I think Tiffany liked it down here better than where she lived. She often stayed late if she didn't have anything else to do, rather than going back to the boardinghouse. She'd organize the storage room or just settle in here, reading the massive collection of wedding magazines she collected, listening to music. She's the one who made it so homey. She was at the house one night, and I let her rummage through my basement, picking out pillows, rugs; anything not in use was hers to bring over here. And she did."

She pointed to some boxes in the corner. "You can use those to put her things in. I've tagged what stays. The furniture and office supplies, TV. But most everything else belonged to Tiffany. The books, photos, mementoes—those are hers."

M.J. thanked them again, then excused herself and went out to give the workmen more instructions before hurrying upstairs to the salon.

"This is more than an office," Nell said, walking around the room.

"It reminds me of a college dorm room." Birdie pointed to a bulletin board filled with newspaper clippings, poems, articles, and ads cut from magazines.

A space in the corner of the bulletin board was empty. *The birthday card*, Nell thought. The one that led the police to Sheila. In the center of the board was a photo of the Fractured Fish along with an article about the band. A small refrigerator was just beneath the bulletin board.

"She could have entertained friends down here," Birdie said.

They looked around in silence, but their thoughts were twisting and turning together, pulling tight on the threads of Tiffany's life. *Maybe she did.*

It wouldn't have been odd at all for Tiffany to have invited people other than clients down here. It would have been a normal thing to do.

Nell rubbed her arms against the sudden chill brought on by memories of that night. Was Tiffany walking someone to the door that night? Was it someone she knew, someone she might have invited there herself? Had it been a planned meeting?

There were no prints, no real signs of robbery. No forced door.

Only a dead body to mark the horrible invasion of Tiffany's space.

Nell walked over to the bookcase and began filling a box with books. Mostly paperbacks—romances and sweet family sagas. Some hairstyling manuals. Lots of self-help books. She scooped them up and placed them in the box. If Sheila didn't mind, she'd look through them more carefully later. Perhaps they'd provide a peek into the woman who had chosen to fill her cozy office with them. In a closed cupboard beneath the bookcase she found a few more CDs, plastic plates and cups, a pair of sneakers and some socks, running shorts and shirt, and other assorted clothes, even some pieces of lingerie. She piled the personal items in another box beside the books. A raincoat and jacket hung on brass hooks near the door, and Nell took them off, along with an old backpack hanging beneath the jacket.

It took less than an hour and several cardboard boxes to pack up all of Tiffany Ciccolo's things.

Tiffany's life, neatly packed away in cardboard boxes.

Birdie and Nell carried the boxes out to the steps and went back for a quick final check. Behind them the hammering continued and a staircase began to take shape in the far corner.

Nell surveyed the room while Birdie emptied a wastebasket.

The space looked lonely now.

She put her finger on the light switch, and a sudden wave of sadness swept through her. The warmth was gone, and in its place was a sterile, cold office with a metal desk, empty shelves, and silence. She turned out the light.

Tiffany Ciccolo was gone.

Chapter 22

Outside, the sun was shining, and the bright, pleasant day defied the sadness they left behind in the salon basement. An ordinary day.

Life went on.

"I'll box sit while you get the car," Birdie said.

But when Nell drove down the alley a few minutes later, Birdie wasn't alone on her boxes. A frustrated Tanya Gordon stood over her, her hands on her hips.

She spun around at the sound of wheels on the gravel alleyway, then blurted out to neither of them in particular, "I know it looked bad."

"Well, it didn't look good," Nell said. She climbed out of the car and walked around to the back, lifting up the back door of the CRV.

"I was just looking for something, like pictures of Andy, maybe. Something cool. Something no one else would want. I don't steal."

Birdie frowned. "Tanya, you can take Andy's photo anytime you want. Just go to a concert with your cell phone."

Tanya stared at the ground. She kicked a stone with her shoe, and it skittered into the dirt. "She didn't like me."

"And you didn't like her, I suspect," Birdie said. "Sometimes that happens."

Tanya was silent for a moment. Then she said, "M.J. thought I made things up about Tiffany. That I gossiped. She thought Tiffany was perfect. But she wasn't."

"Few of us are," Birdie said.

Nell walked over to the boxes. "It sounds like you mean something specific."

Tanya seemed relieved that someone would listen to her. "We all knew she wanted to marry Andy Risso. And she'd have done anything to get him. *Anything.*" She gave Birdie and Nell a knowing look. *Read between the lines,* it said. *You know what I mean.*

"Tanya, what were you really doing in Tiffany's office? You weren't looking for pictures of Andy Risso, were you?"

Tanya sighed. "Okay. I was looking for a preggers test. Or something. There. That's it. I heard her, I swear. She said something about them having a baby between them. I thought . . . I thought if I found something, showed M.J. that I wasn't a gossip—"

"And maybe that Tiffany wasn't as perfect as M.J. thought she was?" Nell picked up a box and carried it to the back of the car.

"Yeah. I guess."

"So if Tiffany was less perfect, you looked better?" Birdie said. Her voice was kind, but her message was clear.

Tanya kicked another stone. Then she looked up and managed a half smile. "Dumb, huh?"

"Yes, dear." Birdie patted her hand. "Now, about what you think you heard that night? Sometimes too many beers can distort hearing. So I suggest you leave that alone. Instead, you might want to concentrate on proving to M.J. that she can trust you. Once you've done that, who knows what will happen? I suspect good things."

Tanya stood there for a minute longer. Then she looked down at the boxes. "You guys get in the car. I'll load these for you. I work out, you know."

Standing in the doorway at the top of the steps, M.J. smiled, then disappeared back inside.

Nell dropped Birdie at home a short while later, along with a reminder that Friday night dinner was at Sam's that night, not Sandswept Lane. The Endicott deck was being sprayed, and the house was a bit of a mess. Sam was giving Nell a nice gift.

He had insisted Nell not bring a thing for dinner, and in a surprise move, she had agreed. It would be a welcome relief to sit back on Sam's deck, look out over the ocean, and push away thoughts of M.J.'s basement and young women losing their lives before they'd barely begun to live. For a brief time she'd abandon all thoughts of the painting touch-ups that the upstairs bathrooms needed before the wedding, the small gift bags they needed to put together, and a dozen other things that Izzy had added to her wedding list.

The sun was sinking in the west by the time Nell and Ben drove up hilly Magnolia Street, through a lovely old neighborhood. The narrow streets were lined with trees and well-kept friendly homes, all just a stone's throw from the sea. Ben pulled into the gravel parking strip in front of Sam's house and waved to Cass, who drove in right beside them.

Izzy had found the small shingled house for Sam a few years before when he had come to Sea Harbor to teach a summer photography class and then decided to stay a while. A photojournalist could live anywhere. Being near Izzy and the sea wasn't a bad choice.

The house was small and airy, wood and glass, with open spaces disguising the size. All it needed was a woman's touch. And in a few short weeks, it would be getting plenty of that.

Cass opened the truck door for Birdie, and Danny Brandley unfolded himself from the small back space. "I'm declaring war on this truck," he announced, greeting Nell and Ben.

"Don't knock it, Brandley," Cass scolded. "Beggars can't be choosers, as Mary Halloran often used to tell her children."

"Well, dear," Birdie offered gently, "it does smell a little like your crustacean friends."

Cass laughed and helped Danny unload the beer and cooler of haddock from the truck bed. They had told Sam they'd stop at the dock and bring whatever looked the freshest. And the haddock had won—firm and white and ready for the grill.

Music streamed through the house, meeting them at the open front door. In the distance, through the wall of glass in the family room, they could see Sam on the deck, standing by the grill with Pete and Andy.

Ben held the door as they paraded through the clean white entrance. Off to the right, Izzy and Willow tossed a salad on the small kitchen butcher block, and Nell wandered in while the others took the fish out back.

After quick hugs, Nell nodded toward the deck. "I'm glad Andy's here."

Willow grinned. "It's Pete's doing. We stopped by Andy's apartment, and Pete told him if he didn't come with us, we'd camp out on his floor all night." She grimaced. "I was holding my breath on that one. Pete's place is a mess, but Andy's? Let's say I'd rather ride in Cass' truck."

Nell laughed. "But he came. That's good."

"He's taken up meditation, he told me. Maybe become a Buddhist. Who knows."

"If it helps him through this, it's a good thing."

Izzy nodded toward the stove. "How about you give that a stir, Aunt Nell. It's an experiment. Inspired by you."

Nell looked into a pot of simmering chunks of pineapple and cilantro. She took a wooden spoon from a jug and stirred, inhaling the sweet fragrance. "Smells great, Iz."

"Sauce for the fish."

Cass came in then and ordered them all out of the kitchen. "Sam says this is his party and he doesn't want you messing in his kitchen. Out on the deck. All of you. Now."

Izzy rolled her eyes. "The man is a tyrant." But she happily turned off the burners and followed the others through the family room to the deck.

Sam was busy outside, muddling the mint leaves and sugar as he made up a pitcher of mojitos. He set it down next to a platter of cheese and crackers and a container of iced tea. "Help yourself, ladies."

The deck stretched across the back of the house, corner to corner, with a few wide steps leading down to a narrow patch of yard.

Beyond the open green space was a meandering path that led down through white pine and mountain laurel to the beach.

It was the deck, Sam had told Nell, that sold him on the house, though Izzy was quick to extol its other virtues—the nice neighborhood, the clean white walls for his photographs, the windows and wood in the living area, the efficient kitchen. But the deck was nirvana to Sam, and he'd lined it with Adirondack chairs, a low table here and there, and a monster grill. He'd bring out his telescope on a clear night and visit Mars and Jupiter and the Big Dipper. Or settle down to watch a family of whales after a long day of photography. Birdie had generously given him a stack of Hudson's Bay blankets to extend the season, their wooly warmth an invitation to hunker down beneath a crisp fall sky.

Nell settled into a chair slightly apart from the others and leaned her head back, the chatter and light laughter around her as comforting as James Taylor singing in the distance about the moon. She felt suspended, the worries of the week relegated to some other life, some other planet. She sipped the mojito slowly, savoring the soothing scent of the mint, and watched the faint outline of the moon define the night.

Voices from inside announced the Brewsters' arrival, but Nell barely moved. She wondered if she'd ever move again.

Izzy walked by, patted her aunt's shoulder, then wandered over to the steps where Andy sat. He was leaning against the post, his long legs extending down to the bottom step. She sat beside him, bending her own legs, balancing her elbows on her knees. Loose golden and brown strands of hair fell over her face as she talked, and in minutes her husky laugh had coaxed a smile to his face. He leaned his head to one side, listening, nodding.

Andy was a nice-looking man, his slender body leaning slightly as he listened to Izzy. He looked like his mother, Birdie had told her—with prominent cheekbones and a strong chin. But it was his eyes that attracted Nell, and in them she read his keen intelligence and the thoughtful bent that had always drawn her to the tavern owner's son. He complemented his father's robust roughness with his own gentle strength. But it was that thoughtful bent that must be making his life hell right now. An evening with friends would be a good thing.

Willow was out in the yard, wandering around by herself, her small frame belying the strength that had helped her through hurdles in her life. Nell suspected her keen eye was examining the wildflowers that grew around the pathway and figuring out how to reflect the colors in a new piece of fiber art. Willow had made good use of the environment in which she now lived, pulling the sea and the sand and the flora, shellfish, and coastal colors into her amazing creations.

"Hey," Nell heard her call out now. One arm shot up in the air and waved down to a couple on the beach. She twisted around and looked up at Sam. "Got extra food, Sam? I see the Jacksons down there."

"Sure," Sam called back. "I've been trained by the master." He grinned at Nell.

Willow tore down the path, the wind whipping through her black hair, until she reached the couple at the bottom. They were walking along the sand carrying their shoes.

Willow chatted and pointed to the deck. In the next moment the couple happily followed her up the path.

"We are actually free of bar duty tonight, *a Friday night*. Can you believe it?" Merry said. "A new manager is finally getting up to speed, and I convinced the old man here to let him prove his mettle without Hank hovering over his shoulder."

Hank shook his head, but laugh lines deepened around his eyes. "What can I say? It's hard to give up control."

"But good in the long run," Birdie said, welcoming them each with a tall chilled mojito. "Balance. We all need balance."

Merry looked up at Hank. "See, that's what I told you. Wipe that stress and worry off your face."

Sam crouched down beside Nell's chair as the others moved in and out, filling drinks, and admiring the gallery of Sam's black-and-white photos.

Izzy had done it as a Christmas gift, knowing Sam would never do it himself. She'd picked her favorites and had Jane Brewster mat and frame them in simple black frames. They were beautiful, and as embarrassed as it made Sam to have people circling his house looking at his work, Izzy was adamant and gently reminded him that it was her house now, too. Or would be as soon as she could get her name on the mortgage papers.

"So, Nell, how are you doing?" Sam said quietly.

"I'm fine. A bit worried, perhaps. So many things going on."

He nodded. "Me, too. I worry about Izzy. She doesn't say much, but this mess is eating away at her. She likes Andy a lot. He's such a good kid."

Nell looked over at Izzy and Andy. Their heads leaned in toward each other in private conversation.

"But even more, maybe, I worry about the danger. No one talks much about the fact that a murderer may still be around here, roaming these streets. It happened so close to Izzy's shop. And at night—she's often there late."

"But they think it's an intentional murder, Sam. Someone wanted to kill Tiffany. So it really doesn't put those who might be in close proximity to that spot in danger."

"Maybe not. But what if the person thinks someone saw something or knows something? If you've murdered once, it seems to me it wouldn't be so hard to do it again."

"You're too serious, Sam," Pete said, leaning into the conversation. "But I'm with you on this one. Everyone's freaked. They may not be talking about it out loud, but it's there, that fear." He glanced over at Andy.

Sam followed his look.

Nell looked down. They were all thinking the same thing. Andy could not have murdered Tiffany Ciccolo. Not in a million years.

It didn't matter that he was seen arguing with her, that she seemed to be obsessed with him and wouldn't leave him alone. That someone heard them talking about a baby. And that he was the last person seen with her best friend before she suspiciously died in a quarry fifteen years before.

They knew Andy.

But buried deep down beneath their utter belief in their friend was a tiny, never-articulated thought: *What if he did?*

Sam insisted that since this might be his last party as a bachelor, he was going to put the men to work and give the women a break, logic that didn't entirely make sense to the women, but not one of them argued. The pine table inside was soon filled with plates and salads, a basket of foil-wrapped baked potatoes. Butter, bacon, and a pot of sour cream, along with Sam's token nonfat yogurt, waited nearby.

Outside, the grill was sizzling with fresh haddock fillets, dribbled with lime juice and basted with Izzy's pineapple and cilantro sauce.

"I think we have competition," Nell said to Ben as he and Izzy helped Sam slide the fish onto a platter. "This looks fantastic, Sam."

Sam thumped his chest. "Me do anything for my woman."

Izzy leaned in and kissed him on the cheek. "As it should be."

Sam grinned at her, then held up his grilling fork. "So, my friends, shall we eat? Never again will I be able to have such command in this house." He put down the fork and pulled Izzy close to him, kissing the top of her head. His eyes told those close enough to see that losing command might be the nicest thing that ever happened to him.

"Come," Sam said gruffly, a sudden catch in his voice, and ushered them all inside to fill their plates.

By the time the sky had darkened to black and everyone had taken a turn at Sam's prized Celestron telescope, the pie plates were put out and filled with huge pieces of Margaret Garozzo's gooseberry pie. When it was gone, the plates licked clean, Sam ordered the men into the kitchen.

"Cleanup time," he said.

"I could get used to this," Merry said, her head leaning back as she looked up at the star-studded sky. "If you change your mind, Izzy, let me know. I'll marry him."

Izzy laughed. "I'm sure Sam has pulled out a bottle of single malt Scotch to soften the blow in there. Check it out."

Nell leaned forward and looked through the open door, past the living area and into the kitchen. The dishes were piled in the sink, and the men stood in a huddle, holding flared-lip glasses and listening to Sam as if the most important play of the game were being called. "They look like they're up to no good."

"It's possible," Cass said, lifting herself out of the chair to peer inside.

"But we have these delicious moments alone with the stars," Birdie said. "Let them be."

They settled back beneath the blanket of stars, darkness folding in around them. Bodies disappeared in the night, and only the sound of their voices brought life to the peaceful deck.

Merry was the first to speak. "Sheila Ciccolo was over in the Cove today, walking around with Mary Pisano."

"Mary has been very hospitable to her," Nell said. "She's in good hands."

"They stopped by the Palate for a cold drink. She wanted to meet people who knew her sister, she said. So Hank and I sat with her a while. She wanted to know about the band, about that night, the night that she came to see Andy play." Merry looked back into the house where the men were still huddled, then back. "She says the police are paying more attention to a connection between Harmony's death and her sister's. And she feels sure, she said, that it somehow hinges on Andy Risso and for the life of her she doesn't know why he isn't behind bars."

"That's crazy. It isn't Andy's fault that Tiffany was infatuated with him," Cass said.

Nell listened, forcing her feelings to overpower logic. It seemed clear now that Andy had had a relationship with Tiffany. And he'd been angry with her the night of the concert. But Andy was a sweet, nonviolent man. . . .

"Hank says we need to stop messing with this, talking about it, let the police do their thing," Merry said. "He says someone could get hurt."

"Sam says the same," Izzy said. "But it's hard not to try to sort it out when things seem to be moving so slowly."

"It hasn't been very long," Birdie reminded them. "It only seems that way. The police haven't even released Tiffany's body yet."

Tiffany's body. Of course. Pregnancy test or not, the police would know if Tiffany had been pregnant.

Nell tucked the thought away and said aloud, "But it's been fifteen years since Harmony died. Maybe that's what has brought all of this into such a time warp. Each day seems like a year."

"And sometimes the opposite. Sometimes it seems that Hank and I opened up the Artist's Palate just yesterday." Merry looked into the house, and her eyes settled on Hank, standing at the kitchen door, his cell phone to his ear.

"I can remember coming up on weekends while you were working on it," Nell said. "Hank was so determined. It always impressed me. He wasn't a Sea Harbor native, but that land, that bar, was so important to him."

"He proved his father wrong, at least," Merry said.

"Not a happy relationship?" Cass asked.

"Nope. Hank grew up in the shadow of successful siblings. Me, too. My brother was so smart. I hated following in his footsteps. Hank was the ne'er-do-well in his family. When he dropped out of college, his dad pretty much disowned him."

"How'd he end up here?" A transplant herself, Willow loved stories of other people landing on "her turf," as she called it.

"Hank had a relative who let him stay up here if he shaped up. 'Tough love' was how he described his process. The relative yanked his chain. Made him stop partying and get a job."

"Sounds like my kind of person," Birdie said.

Merry smiled. "Sometimes it works, I guess. Hank got a job, worked hard, and even inherited the place when his relative died."

"And that's when the Artist's Palate was born," Jane Brewster said. "I remember the day that ramshackle bait shop was torn down. Ham and Willow's dad, Aidan, helped Hank tear it down. We all celebrated. The place had become a drug house or who knows what, but we were thrilled to see it go."

"Not to mention getting a restaurant right in your own neighborhood," Nell said.

"That was nice, too. It's a great place. You must be proud of it, Merry."

"I am."

And proud of Hank, too, Nell could see. Some people had to "survive" family situations—like Harmony and Tiffany. Hank. And others were nurtured and blossomed in the bosom of families. Life was unpredictable.

They lapsed into silence again, savoring the comfort of the night, of friends, until finally Jane Brewster stood and stretched, her figure looking ghostly on the moonlit deck. "Saturday is an early day for us. I'm going to collect my man and head home."

Merry echoed her sentiments, and Cass yawned agreement.

When the sounds of movement drifted through the open doors, the men disbanded, and soon a chorus of good-byes and the crunch of wheels on the gravel drive left the house half-empty.

"One more thing," Sam said, motioning for Izzy, Nell, Cass, and Birdie to stay put.

Ben and Pete stood behind in the doorway, smiles lighting their faces.

Birdie looked at each of them. "You men look like the proverbial cat and missing canary."

"They're up to no good," Izzy asked. "Sam, are you all right?"

Sam laughed. "Yes. And you will be, too. We have a surprise for the four of you."

Izzy's brows pulled together. "You know I don't much like surprises, Sam. . . ."

Sam ignored her. "We've cleared your schedules for tomorrow afternoon. Meet at Ben and Nell's at one o'clock."

Nell thought about the next day. "We're helping Sheila . . ." she began.

"In the morning," Ben said. "Afternoon is clear.

Cass looked at Pete.

"No problem, sis. Andy is going out with me on the *Lady Lobster* to set some traps. And those college kids we hired are doing a good job. You're not needed."

"Not needed?" Cass looked indignant; then she looked at Sam. "You don't have us going to some spa or a Chippendales show or some embarrassing prewedding thing, do you?"

"Spa?"

"Chippendales?"

"Prewedding thing?"

The men laughed.

Izzy glared at Sam.

"Marriage is built on trust," he said. He slipped a loose strand of hair behind her ear and leaned down, whispering, "Is this any way to begin our life together, Iz? Suspicion? Distrust?"

Izzy wiggled free and looked over at the others.

Nell chuckled.

And with that Ben offered Birdie a hand and helped her out of the chair. "Time to get the show on the road," he said, moving toward the front door. "This body needs a bed. Tomorrow's a new day."

A new day, indeed, Nell thought, following him out the door. She looked over at his face in the moonlight.

The sudden rush of emotion that swept through her had nothing to do with a new day. At that moment, the present was all Nell needed.

Chapter 23

$\mathcal{B}$en was ready to leave the house by the time Nell had showered and come down for coffee the next morning.

He had things to do, he told her with an enigmatic smile, then disappeared into the garage.

Nell waved him off. She was completely in Izzy's camp. She didn't much like surprises, especially right now when their peaceful life had been jarred by one too many. But she had no time to think about it now. She checked her watch. Time to go.

Nell skipped the coffee, found her purse, phone, and keys, and left the house. Claire was already in the yard, hose in hand, watering the gerbera daisies.

Nell waved, made a mental note to check in with Claire later, more to see what her mental state was than her garden state, then got in the car and headed down the hill.

She'd pick up Izzy, Cass, and Birdie along the way to the bed-and-breakfast.

Mae and her nieces had practically insisted Izzy not come in this morning. They'd handle the yarn studio just fine, thank you. Mae then reminded Izzy that she should be taking more time off and spending less time stocking yarn shelves. She should be getting ready for a wedding. *Her own*, Mae said with some emphasis.

Getting ready for a wedding. That was what they should all be doing, Nell thought as she stopped in front of Izzy's house. Thinking about the wedding. About picking up cocktail napkins and making sure the champagne had been ordered. Thinking about Izzy's wedding shawl. That was what this glorious June was to be about. And here they were, for the second day in a row, packing up a dead woman's belongings.

Izzy and Cass climbed into the car and in short order they pulled into Birdie's drive, just as she came out the side door carrying a stack of flattened boxes and tape. "We probably won't need these. Somehow I have a feeling we will be needed more for moral support than anything else. But maybe we'll learn something along the way."

Birdie was in her mover-and-shaker mode, Nell could tell. Things were moving too slowly for the octogenarian, even though she had tried to put it into perspective for all of them the night before. It had been a matter of only days, not months, since Tiffany was killed. And the police were doing a fine job. But they sometimes had restraints, Birdie said—like laws and rules that slowed them down.

Sometimes ordinary folks could speed things up a bit.

Sheila was waiting outside when they drove up the long Ravenswood-by-the-Sea drive, just across the street from Birdie's estate. Mary Pisano stood beside her as the car pulled up. She walked over to Nell's window and handed them each a travel mug of strong Colombian brew, while Sheila climbed in beside Izzy and Cass.

"Compliments of Ravenswood-by-the-Sea," Mary said, waving them off.

Nell sipped the coffee gratefully, urging life into her still-sleepy body, and drove back through town.

The boardinghouse where Tiffany had lived was on Bell Street in an older neighborhood that now housed many rentals.

Nell pulled up in front of a once-grand three-story Victorian home. A sign in the yard read SUITE FOR RENT.

They climbed out of the car and followed Sheila up the painted wooden steps.

A row of mismatched rocking chairs lined the porch, and pancake-sized flakes of gray paint fell from above the bay window.

It was an old-fashioned place with some rough edges, but it looked comfortable. The décor, however, made Nell suspect that Tiffany had been several decades younger than the other residents.

The landlady—"Just call me Mrs. Bridge," she told them—ushered them through the entry hall, muttering soft condolences to Sheila. "A lovely girl, a lovely girl," she said several times.

Mrs. Bridge pointed with a chubby index finger toward a back hall and the kitchen—a public space for all residents, she explained—and the winding staircase that led to the upper rooms. "We have a lovely place here. *Suites,* you understand, not just a room like some other boardinghouses."

Then she walked them through the parlor, a formal space with velvet chaises, lace doilies on gateleg tables, and a series of dusty porcelain angels gracing the mantel top. Heavy brocade drapes kept the room in semidarkness.

"Residents relax here or may entertain if they so choose," the buxom woman explained. "Tiffany was a good renter," she said, again lowering her voice. "She always paid her rent on time. I was sad that she was going to move out. Hoping to get married, she said. And then this horrible thing happened. Unbelievable. The residents were aghast."

"Tiffany told you she was getting married?" Sheila asked.

"Not in so many words, but I knew there was a man in her life. She said they had something special between them. Course, I didn't push her on that. None of my business. But I guessed she had some plans to settle down and start a family."

Sheila's expression didn't change.

"Except for my place, hers was the only first-floor suite," Mrs. Bridge went on. "It's a lovely space, with an outside entrance as well as the hall door. She liked that, being able to come and go as she wanted without walking through the house and disturbing anyone. Sometimes she'd work late at night or would be out late because she went to listen to the band. She loved music, you know. Never missed a performance of that fish group."

Sheila's shoulders grew rigid.

Nell noticed the shift and stepped in. "It sounds like you and Tiffany were friends, Mrs. Bridge."

"Friends? Friendly, maybe, I'd call it. Sweet girl. No trouble. And she'd bring me milk and bread when my bad hip kept me in on icy days."

"Did Tiffany have friends over?" Cass asked.

"Not that I saw. Like I said, she wasn't here much."

Sheila smiled at the landlady. "You've been kind, Mrs. Bridge. We'll make sure that the apartment is clean and everything removed."

Sheila was anxious to get this over with. To pack up Tiffany's things and move on. To put a sad, grueling week behind her. Nell could hardly blame her.

"Oh, there's no cleaning you'll be needing to do. Tiffany kept what few things she had here neat as a pin. I checked the place yesterday. Clean as a whistle. You would hardly know anyone lived there. It was always like that." She took out her key and unlocked the door. "I'll be in the kitchen if you need me," she said, and lumbered down the hallway.

They stepped back, letting Sheila go in first.

Sheila took a deep breath, then opened the door and took a step inside.

She stopped suddenly, the movement so unexpected that Nell bumped into her from behind.

Her purse dropped from her shoulder and fell heavily to the floor.

"Good lord," Birdie said, easing her body between Nell and Sheila.

They stood, frozen in place, staring in silence at the scene in front of them.

Tiffany's room was average size, with a couch and chairs, television stand and desk. A galley kitchen at one end held cupboards and miniature-sized kitchen appliances.

But from one end to the other, the long room looked like a nor'easter had blown in one end, rearranged the room's contents, and then flown out the other.

Couch cushions littered the floor, desk drawers were toppled from runners, and loose papers were tossed haphazardly everywhere. A floor lamp leaned precariously against the wall.

Through the archway at the other end of the room, they could see a bed, a dresser, and an open closet in similar disarray.

Cass was the first to pull her phone from her pocket.

"What are you doing?" Sheila asked.

"Calling the police."

"Why?"

"Sheila," Nell said softly, one hand on her arm, "someone has broken in here and ransacked your sister's room. Someone who may have killed her. Someone who may still be walking around this town. The police need to come."

"It won't bring her back. What's done is done."

And with that, the tears came, and Sheila Ciccolo folded up onto the floor and allowed herself to mourn for a life she had walked out on twenty-one years before.

Esther Gibson took Cass' call and said she'd have men there in minutes—or less.

Cass told her there was probably no rush. No one was hurt or dying.

That had already been done.

Next, Birdie went down the hall and came back with a distraught Mrs. Bridge. She stood in the doorway, her hands covering her open mouth, her massive chest heaving in and out.

"The police are on their way," Birdie said.

"We don't know if anything was taken," Nell said, "but someone was clearly looking for something."

"She didn't have much here," Mrs. Bridge said when she found her voice. "No pictures, nothing. No valuables. She told me so herself. She got rid of it, I suppose. And I double-checked yesterday, just in case there was something, you know, that might be valuable."

She had moved it all to her office, Nell thought. That was why the basement room in the salon was so cozy—and the rooms they stood in so sterile. Even amidst the mess, it was impersonal and cold. Only her clothes spoke of the woman who had once rented the space.

Nell walked into the bedroom where Izzy was standing, staring at the mess but careful not to touch anything.

Izzy looked up.

Nell wrapped an arm around Izzy's shoulders. She wished she could whisk her away from all this.

"I wish I had had the chance to know her," Izzy said, and walked out of her aunt's protective embrace.

Nell walked into the bathroom and looked at the pile of bottles in the sink. No drugs. A bottle of fish oil capsules. Vitamins C and E. That was it. She followed Izzy back into the living room just as the police arrived.

Tommy nodded familiarly at each of the women, then took time to talk with Sheila. This was an awful thing, he said. They'd find this person if it was the last thing they did. He knew how difficult it was for her.

Nell watched the young man she'd known since his paper route days. She remembered the teenage crush he revived each summer when Izzy came to visit. And then he had pulled it out in adulthood when Izzy moved to Sea Harbor permanently. But in recent times, Tommy had found a love of his own, a nursing student who reveled in Tommy's strengths. And each year Tommy became more of a gentleman, more at ease in his policeman's shoes, and more supportive and sensitive to the vulnerable people he sometimes had to deal with. Tommy Porter would be chief someday, was her silent prediction.

"Nell," he said, coming up beside her, "I guess you can all leave. We'll look around. See if we can pick up any prints. Sorry you had to come upon this. Geesh. One more thing, huh?"

Nell smiled.

"The intruder came through the back door. The lock's been jimmied, but even a kid could have done it. Mrs. Bridge here says the lawn service people have been out back for hours. And they worked yesterday until about eight."

"So it happened during the night?"

"Looks like it. We checked this place out thoroughly after Tiffany died. It was spotless, not much around. Nothing valuable. So I'm not sure anything was even taken during the break-in. The television is still here. An alarm clock in the other room. A flowerpot with some change in it. So what did he or she want?" He scratched his head.

"The big question," Izzy said.

"Yep. The big question. And whatever it was or is or has been, was it worth killing a nice person for? That's the real question, far's I can see."

They left quietly, leaving Mrs. Bridge on the phone with a locksmith.

Sheila had gratefully accepted Mrs. Bridge and Tommy's generous offer to pack up Tiffany's things once they were finished with their investigation. It was mostly clothes and makeup, as far as they could tell, but Mrs. Bridge would be on top of it, securing what was hers and treating Tiffany's things with care.

Sheila asked to be dropped off at the bed-and-breakfast. She had another meeting with the lawyer. More paperwork. And after that, she said with a touch of embarrassment, she was going over to the nursing home to see her mother.

"A little overdue. She won't know me."

"But you'll know her," Nell said.

"Yes, I will."

Father Northcutt was taking her. And they'd have a little dinner afterward. "I haven't talked to him since Davey Delaney and I stole the vigil lights from the Blessed Virgin Mary's altar in eighth grade. But I think this means he's forgiven me."

"I think it does," Nell agreed. She shifted the car into reverse.

They waited until Sheila was out of earshot before dissecting the morning, but opinions had already been formed and gushed forth.

"Tiffany was murdered because she had something that someone wanted," Izzy said.

"Or it was something incriminating. But incriminating to what?"

"Harmony Farrow's death. It has to be," Cass said.

"That would be the link. Tiffany knew something about what really happened to Harmony that night."

Nell idled the car once again in Birdie's driveway. "But why wouldn't she have told anyone? The police, Claire . . ."

"If she knew the killer, she certainly would have," Izzy insisted. "She couldn't have lived with that. Harmony was her best friend."

"But what if she thought it would have incriminated someone she cared about. And that maybe it was more of an accident. So she protected that person."

Cass bit down on her bottom lip. She stared out the window. Birdie played with the strap on her backpack, and Nell's fingers tapped rhythmically on the steering wheel.

Izzy sighed. "Our brains are on overload. I find myself looking for clues in wedding invitations, being suspicious of people who are sending regrets. As if not coming to my wedding makes them murder suspects. This is crazy."

That was exactly what it was. Crazy. Ridiculous. And the only way to sort it all out was to do what they did best. Get out their knitting, do some frogging to get rid of the dead ends, and begin to knit it all back together again. Weaving in loose ends. Filling in holes. And then they would know who killed Tiffany Ciccolo. Nell looked at Birdie, then turned and looked in the backseat at Izzy and Cass.

"I don't know if our 'surprise' today will have us in a bar or a salon, in a movie or on a train ride, but bring your knitting and comfortable clothes. Prepare for any alternatives, because we've some work to do."

Chapter 24

Sam and Ben did it up right, blindfolds and all. But the smell of the sea and the groaning wooden boards beneath their feet refused to be disguised.

They stood out on a pier, each of them gripping an arm of Ben's or Sam's, chins lifted into the salty air for balance.

"Be quiet for a minute and listen. Then the blinds come off," Sam said sternly.

"This was Sam's idea," Ben began. "It came to him last night between muddling mojitos, grilling the haddock, and feeling the stress of the week emanating from your lovely bodies. So all the guys put their heads together and came up with this plan. Here's the deal."

Izzy fidgeted next to Sam and touched the cloth covering her eyes. Sam took her hand away, then kept it wrapped in his own.

"We're crazy about the four of you," Sam said. "That's number one. And number two, we know you better than you know yourselves sometimes. Here's what we know up front and is not subject to debate: You're the damnedest, most stubborn women it has been our pleasure to meet. The only way you'll relax is if we take you away from civilization for a few hours with nothing to do but enjoy each other and be pampered a little. And make my bride-to-be think of the amazing life ahead of her instead of all the worries rolling up and down Harbor Road." He squeezed Izzy's hand.

"Drumroll," Ben said, and they slipped the folded scarves from each of the women's eyes.

Docked in front of them, at the deepest end of the pier, was a fifty-foot schooner, its three sails already hoisted and silhouetted against the blue sky.

Their surprised yelps collided midair.

"A schooner! Sam, are you crazy?" Izzy said, her face bright with excitement.

"Maybe a little. Think of it as your bachelorette party."

"Whose boat is this?" Cass was clearly in awe. "It's a beauty. Pure luxury."

"Hank Jackson knew a guy who knew a guy, wealthy frat brother, we think. He called him last night from Sam's, pulled in some favors, and voilà—"

"But . . ." Nell looked dubious. "Ben, none of us has ever sailed a schooner. . . ."

"And that's why the boat comes with a crew." They walked closer and watched a fit man with a tan face and laugh lines fanning from his eyes climb up out of the cabin. Behind him, a woman in shorts and a blue denim shirt waved. "We're all ready for you, ladies. All aboard?"

"We're going sailing," Birdie said. Her voice lifted along with her entire face. "How glorious. You are truly delightful men. We shall keep you. Now, if you'd be so kind as to gather our bags?" She walked over to the boat and accepted the broad flat hand that reached out to steady her. "My Sonny would be in his glory."

"Wait up, Birdie," Cass yelled, excitement dripping from her voice. "You're not going without me."

Nell turned to look up at Ben. She started to say something, but he pressed a finger against her lips. "Enjoy," he whispered, and slipped a set of car keys into her hand. "We'll leave your car in the parking lot for the return trip."

They looked at Izzy and Sam, arms wound around each other.

"It's a calm day," Sam said to her. "I ordered that, too. Didn't want to take any chances. Can't lose you now with all these people coming to town expecting a wedding."

"This is . . . it's . . ."

Sam looked over the top of her head. "Ben, could you video this with your iPhone? Izzy is at a loss for words."

Izzy wiped a tear away, kissed Sam soundly on the lips, and hurried after Nell.

"You know they just wanted to keep us from snooping around, don't you?" she said to Nell's back, her voice still thick with emotion.

Nell nodded. She knew.

On board, George Hanson introduced himself and his wife, Ellie. "Ellie's the best cook on the Atlantic, bar none," he bragged. "Everything fresh, wholesome, incredible."

"Food? We get food, too?" Cass said.

In minutes they were happily settled on the comfortable aft deck while George guided the schooner along the harbor and out to the open sea. "Won't be too exciting today with this low wind," he shouted back to them. Ellie passed out big floppy hats.

"And that is just dandy with me," Birdie said, tugging on her hat. "A gentle sail will suit this sailor just fine."

"Look," Cass said, pointing to the shore as they passed the banks of the Canary Cove Art Colony.

Merry Jackson stood waving wildly on the rocky strip of land below the Artist's Palate. Then she picked up a hand-lettered sign that read: AHOY, MATIES. HAVE FUN!

"It looks like this wasn't a secret to anyone but us," Izzy laughed. "Sneaky friends."

"We're usually booked up this time of year," Ellie told them. "But right before Hank called last night, our charter for today canceled. Karma. So settle back, enjoy yourselves, and nibbles will be ready shortly."

"Amazing," Izzy said. She pulled her bare legs up on the cushioned bench, wrapped her arms around them, and leaned her head back, her hair flying in the breeze. "Heavenly."

"Ben and Sam are as transparent as glass. This is their subtle way of keeping us out of trouble," Nell said. "Izzy's right."

"Works for me," Cass said.

"But instead, what they've given us is what we've desperately needed," Birdie said, pulling her nearly finished sweater from her bag. It was coming along nicely. Mary could wear it in the fall on Coffee's patio when the weather turned chilly. The rich caramel color would look wonderful on her. "They've given us this amazing together-time away from phones and customers and computers, from errands and lobster boats, meetings and cooking. Time away from Sea Harbor. It's deliciously perfect." Caught up in the drama of her monologue, Birdie waved her knitting needles in the air and went on.

"We need to look back on our town from a distance so we can see the whole forest. We're outside the box, my dear friends. And I think that being away from Sea Harbor and our daily lives will give us fresh perspective on why a young woman was murdered in our town. And her best friend died suspiciously nearly fifteen years before. We've a week to do it."

"A week?" Cass' head appeared in the cabin opening, where she'd been examining George's elaborate computer setup. She climbed up the steep steps and settled in next to Izzy. "Why a week?"

"Izzy and Sam get married in two weeks. *Two* weeks," Birdie said. "We have to bring some closure to this before we move into her wedding week. That gives us one week to bury all this." She tried to soften her demand with a smile at Izzy. "I don't want a distracted drummer playing at your reception, dear."

Izzy took a deep breath and expelled it slowly. "It's not just the wedding, though. It's the town, the heavy cloud that hangs over it. All the people who are affected by this—that's what I worry about."

"And that's what I mean, sweetie. Lots of people's lives have been disturbed; you're right."

"Birdie's right," Nell said. "And we can figure this out in a week if we put our heads together."

Birdie took the lead. "It's a mess. There are more dangling ends to this than in that first sweater we forced Cass to make for her mother.

"So let's agree on something before we start: There *is* a connection between Harmony's and Tiffany's deaths."

They all nodded, although running beneath their conviction was the police report that Ben had seen. It said no facts had been found linking the two deaths. In fact, while Tiffany's death was clearly intentional, no concrete facts indicated that Harmony's death was more than an accident. *Suspicions* were all the police had. And that was only because a neighbor saw two people going into the woods that night—and no one came forward to report her drowning.

"So maybe the same person killed both?" Izzy pulled out a silky lace-weight yarn in cobalt blue and squeezed it gently.

"That's a hypothesis we could work with," Nell said. "Although maybe we should say the same person is connected to both."

"What do you mean?" Cass looked at Izzy's yarn, then rummaged around in her own pack and pulled out a ball of soft wool. A mannish color—tweedy gray with flecks of black.

Perfect for Danny, Nell thought. A hat maybe, or gloves. Who would have thought that a man—a knitter, no less—would be the incentive they'd needed to make a more enthusiastic knitter out of Cass.

"I've been thinking a lot about Harmony's death—and I talked to Danny about it since he'd done a little research," Birdie said. "They never proved that it was a murder—we need to keep reminding ourselves of that. I think that's why it became a cold case so quickly. There were scratches on her body, but the police think it was from the fall down the side of the quarry. There were signs that someone else was there, but she wasn't choked or hit with anything. That quarry was steeper than some, and the sides have shrubs and branches sticking out from the sides. She tried to grab on to them, they think."

"But she could have been pushed."

"That's true. And that's unanswered. But she also could have accidentally fallen off the edge," Nell said.

Birdie frowned. "But if she wasn't alone, and it was an accident, then why . . ."

"Didn't the person with her save her?" Cass finished.

"Exactly," Birdie said. "Jump in after her."

"That's why it's suspicious, I suppose. Someone was with her. She died, and no one ever came forward with information. If it was a pure accident, why?"

Nell thought of Claire having to deal with the knowledge that someone had been with her daughter that night—and let her die. Why? Did Claire think that person was Andy Risso? Or . . . The thought came to her with a jolt—Tiffany Ciccolo? Could that explain her feelings about her daughter's best friend?

"Tiffany told the police that after Andy and Harmony disappeared, she left the party, too. She went home to an empty house, walking the three miles in new heels and crying the entire way," Nell said.

"A first fact, then—Andy was with Harmony that night," Cass said, pulling their thoughts together. "No one disputes that. People saw them together."

"At the party," Izzy said. She began casting on the soft blue yarn with the authority of one who sees the exactness of the stitch through the play of her fingers on the needles. "I asked Andy about that last night. He followed her across the parking lot, like people said. And he was angry. But that was it, the last time he ever saw her."

"So why was she leaving alone? He was her boyfriend, right?"

"He said they'd been having some problems for a while. He really loved her, I think. But he's sure she was meeting someone else that night. She'd been distracted most of the spring, he said. She wouldn't show up at his house to study when she said she would, that kind of thing. That night, she climbed in her mother's car, locked the door so he couldn't stop her, and drove away."

"Where did Andy go then?" Cass asked.

"He tried to find her. He drove all over town. Her house, Tiffany's place. He spent all night looking for her," Izzy said.

"Which leaves him without an alibi that night." Birdie frowned.

"But if we can figure out who was with Harmony, Andy might not need an alibi."

"I wonder if Tiffany suspected there was someone else in Harmony's life," Izzy murmured, her fingers counting the cast-on stitches.

"She said she knew all of Harmony's secrets."

The boat rocked gently as they played with their thoughts. The sun beat down on the deck, warm and relaxing. The wind was light and cool, the salty spray refreshing.

Cass leaned her head over the side, her eyes closed, letting the wind whip her hair back. "I think Tiffany really thought Andy was with Harmony that night, no matter what he said. If she was watching them from the gym entrance, she couldn't have seen what was happening out in the parking lot. She probably thought they got in the car together and drove off."

"That's what she told Sheila," Nell said. "I think Cass is right. Tiffany would have no reason to lie to her sister."

"So the secret, the one Tiffany said she'd take to her grave, had to be something else," Izzy concluded.

"I think when we find that out, we will be a lot closer to knowing why Harmony died. And maybe why Tiffany did, as well."

When we find out . . . Birdie's words echoed in Nell's head. Not if, but when. A commitment.

"Andy has no alibi for the night Tiffany was killed, either. He was walking around trying to get his head on straight, he said," Izzy said.

"Add to that the fact that plenty of people saw them at the Palate that night, arguing," Birdie added.

"And at least one person heard Tiffany say something about a baby," Cass said.

"The autopsy report will be available soon," Nell said. "That will put an end to any speculation."

"Even if she wasn't pregnant, maybe she wanted Andy to think she was? It's a ploy as old as Methuselah," Birdie said.

The thought wasn't a new one, but no one wanted to dwell on it. The one thing they didn't need was yet another motive for Andy to want Tiffany Ciccolo out of his life.

"Anyone hungry?" Ellie Hanson's cheerful voice preceded her as she climbed up from the galley carrying a tray.

Nell and Izzy scurried to make room for it, collecting sunglasses and tubes of lotion from the teak table fastened to the deck.

"What luxury," Nell said.

George appeared behind his wife carrying a pitcher of iced tea and a bottle of chilled wine.

"Our son is dropping anchor. The wind isn't going to allow much of a sail, so we're going to park out here for a while and just let you be. The swim ladder is ready to go if anyone wants to take a dip. Plenty of suits down below. Dinner at sunset."

The long, elegant schooner bobbed and rolled gently, its white sails bright against the blue sky. It was as if they were alone in the world, and all around them, nature sang, holding them fast and firm and safe. Nell could feel the beginning of saneness seep slowly back into her body. "This could be habit forming," she murmured.

Cass removed a linen cloth covering the tray. Fresh sushi, strawberries with yogurt and mint, lobster spring rolls with a spicy mustard sauce. Small bowls held almonds and dried cranberries.

"I'm in heaven," Birdie said.

Ellie and George chuckled, clearly enjoying their guests' pleasure, and disappeared below.

Cass filled a small plate and settled back. "I think we need more information from Andy. If there was someone else in Harmony's life, it's important."

"Okay. That's number one. Talk to Andy again," Izzy said.

"Birdie and I also have several boxes of Tiffany's things from her salon office that maybe we can go through if Sheila says it's okay. The police have been through it once, but who knows?"

"Number two," Birdie said.

"And maybe talk to Esther?" Izzy suggested. "She was Andy's

godmother, his mom's good friend. Maybe she remembers something from that night."

"Esther never forgets anything. Good idea," Cass said. "She still remembers every single one of your speeding tickets."

They laughed because it was true. Izzy had stacked up a few in her youth.

"Andy—Esther—the boxes from the salon office," Birdie noted, as if writing a to-do list on a blackboard. "And Claire?"

Nell sighed. "It's hard to know if this is simply too intrusive. She's been through so much. But so has Andy, I guess. I'll talk to her. See if she can remember anything from those weeks before Harmony died."

"Especially if there was another man in her life."

Nell nodded.

"And if there was more to the look she gave Tiffany than we think. From what we saw, Aunt Nell, she had strong, awful feelings about Tiffany."

That was true enough. Nell remembered the look with utmost clarity. But the thought of Claire doing anything to Tiffany was beyond what her imagination could handle. Unless Claire thought Tiffany had had something to do with Harmony's death.

"And we saw her headed toward the salon the night Tiff died," Birdie added.

They were right, both Birdie and Iz. And they all knew that liking someone didn't always mean a lot. Not when someone had been murdered.

"Moving forward, in time anyway," Cass said, "we think Tiff was in love with Andy, and upset about something."

"And shortly after a fight with Andy, she was dead."

"In her office," Nell said.

"Probably by someone she knew."

"A motive. We desperately need a motive. What did she know? Who was threatened by her?" Birdie slid back on the cushioned bench until her head rested against the cushions.

The questions hung in the sea air like gulls waiting to dip into the water for a snack.

They refilled plates and sipped their wine, their thoughts and questions finally fading beneath the magic of the sun and sea. Nell looked over at Birdie, her feet up on the bench, her hat covering her closed eyes.

Cass and Izzy followed her look and laughed softly at their sleeping friend. They uncurled themselves from the benches and went below to see if there were swimming suits that fit.

In minutes they were down the back ladder and after a quick swim climbed into the plump inner tubes Ellie had thrown overboard. Nell watched them, their lean bodies growing limp in the bright yellow floats.

She stood at the top of the ladder and snapped a few pictures, then reclined in the seat, enjoying the moment. It was perfect, and no matter that their conversation wasn't about weddings as Sam had hoped, their spirits were revived and the week's frustration was drifting away on the gentle sea. *Hope.* In addition to everything else, the day had instilled them with hope. *This, too, would pass.*

By the time Izzy and Cass had climbed back on board, showered, and dressed, Ellie was fussing around, setting the table for a sunset dinner, and the schooner was gently heeling as their son began a wide turn toward the setting sun.

True to George's word, Ellie's dinner was amazing—Swiss chard drizzled with a champagne balsamic vinegar dressing, crunchy coconut crab cake appetizers, grilled asparagus spears—and the most amazing chutney-glazed snapper Nell had ever eaten.

Stuffed and sleepy, they sat on the deck with Ellie, extolling the trip, the food, a day that had brought life to their lives.

George wandered back and forth along the roped side, helping his son and basking in the compliments.

"It was a perfect day," Nell said. "Thanks, George."

"It's what we do, me and Ellie—and Bart, when we can get him. Another son helps out, too. We're following a dream."

"Quite a nice one. Hank has nice friends. How do you two know each other?"

"Our families knew each other. But we became friends in college. We both had dreams—we were into proving things, I guess. We both wanted to build something of our own. Neither of us fit into the corporate lives our fathers lived. I grew up on these waters in the summertime, sailing. I wanted to see if I could make a living at it. I never really imagined doing anything else. Hank wanted a bar and grill, a place people liked to come to. We both got what we wanted."

"And I'd guess, as idyllic as this is, you work harder than you ever imagined." Nell thought about Gracie Santos, working so hard to open her little café. And Willow, taking over her father's gallery and proving to herself that she could make him proud. And her own niece, following her dream of owning a yarn shop, working day and night to make it happen. Hank and his friend George. So many strong, determined people following their dreams.

Ellie confirmed Nell's words. "Even when you're living a dream, it can be grueling work sometimes."

"Shore ahead," Bart bellowed from the bow.

Slowly, as they made their way into the harbor, the sun slipped soundlessly behind the inward edge of Cape Ann.

Reluctant to leave, they followed one another slowly onto the pier, lugging their bags and walking silently side by side toward shore. Above, the moon was bright, the stars blinking like tiny white Christmas lights across the sky.

It couldn't have been more perfect, they all agreed.

"Ben left the car on the far side of the parking lot, over near the park," Nell said, pulling her keys from her purse. The parking lot light near the SUV was out, but they found the car easily by the light of the moon, and Nell unlocked the back for their bags.

Cass dropped hers in first, then stepped back to make room for Izzy and Birdie. She looked at the car from a distance and frowned.

"What's wrong?" Nell said, looking back. The look on Cass' face was strange.

"I don't know. But something is." She walked around the side of the car and stared down at the cement.

"Damn."

The single word punctuated the night, slicing through the fragile peace they'd carried back to shore.

They all hurried around to where she stood, following the stare that led them to the bottom of the car, now perilously close to the concrete surface of the parking lot.

Every tire on Nell's car was completely and utterly flat.

Chapter 25

Sam and Ben arrived in minutes. They'd been next door at the Ocean's Edge, having a drink and catching up with some friends, when Nell called.

"Don't worry," Nell said. "The car is okay. It's just a flat. . . . Well, four flats, I suppose." Her voice was steady. *Call AAA and we'll be fine,* it said.

Sam walked around the car, poking at the wheels, tapping the hubcaps. Ben followed him with a flashlight.

Danny Brandley had been at the Edge with them, too. He stayed and paid the tab, then came down to the pier, arriving minutes later. He stood now with the huddled group of women, listening to the part of the day that had been untouched by flat tires. A memorable day, they told him. The kind you tuck away in a corner of your mind and pull out on a cold, windy winter day to make you warm all over again. Perfect.

Until now.

When Sam finally straightened up and walked to the back of the car, the expression on his face was grave. Ben stood beside him, his cell phone in his hand.

"Who are you calling?" Nell asked. AAA was the answer she hoped for, but she knew before he punched in the number that it wouldn't be his first call. The tires had been balanced less than a month before. They were in good shape, good condition.

"I'm calling the police. The tires have been slashed, every single one of them," he said.

For the second time in a single day, Tommy Porter found himself in the thick of petty crime, or so he described it. "First a messed-up room with nothing stolen, far's we can tell. And now some goofball has screwed your tires. I hate vandalism. No reason, just ornery kids."

"But it's not a petty crime, Tom," Ben said. "Neither of these events is petty, not if they're connected to a murder."

Tommy was silent.

Nell suspected those were Tommy's thoughts, too. But he knew protocol, knew not to alarm innocent bystanders.

He forked his fingers through a swath of thick hair, pushing it back off his forehead.

"You could use a haircut, Tommy," Birdie suggested, trying to ease his discomfort.

"Sure could, Miz Birdie." He pulled a dog-eared notebook from his pocket and looked around at the circle of faces.

And even though Nell was like an aunt to him and he'd known Birdie all his life and had been half in love with Izzy for a lot of those years, he was a good officer who played by the rules. He'd ask all the questions. He'd dot his i's and cross his t's and, in the end, write a report that would cover everything, even the things that made no difference.

"Now, where did you say you've been today?" He pulled out a stubby pencil and started scribbling on the spiral pad. Nell and Birdie dutifully filled him in while the others stood off to the side talking quietly. They knew that where they'd been or where they were going or who owned the schooner didn't make a whit of difference. But Tommy asked for the information, so they would give it to him. And at the end of it all, they would tell Tommy what they firmly believed to have happened in the harbor parking lot.

Someone wanted to send a message to Izzy and Cass, to Birdie and Nell, and that person wanted them to hear it loud and clear.

Mind your own business, the slashed tires said. The words roared around the parking lot as if shouted from the steeple of Our Lady of the Seas.

Mind your own business . . . or else.

They were tired and sunburned, but not ready to leave one another, so they gathered at the Ocean's Edge restaurant for a nightcap. The hostess led them through the dining room to the cozy lounge, filled with leather couches around low tables and a skylight that brought the moon inside. Open windows all along the back framed the harbor, lit now with the lights of boats bobbing in the black water. In the background, music played and occasional hoots of laughter pierced the air from Saturday night revelers. Cheers from the bar broke out at every Sox pitch replayed on the huge flat television screen.

Tommy had told them that they'd question people—but on a Saturday the park area next to the lot was always packed. Dogs, Frisbees, families and kids, tourists watching the parade of boats. And all day long people would be driving in and out of that lot, pulling picnic baskets and kites and bikes out of the backs of SUVs. Who would notice someone bending down near the side of a car?

"A needle-in-a-haystack kind of search," Tommy had said. "But we'll sure give it our all. You can bet on that."

Ben ordered drinks for everyone and a pot of ginger tea for Nell, who couldn't rid herself of a slight chill.

Ben's face was grim. "It's gotten serious; you all know that." He looked around at them. "You've been noticeably involved in all this— from discovering the body, the break-in at Tiffany's house, cleaning out her office. People talk. People know those things."

"But who knew my car would be in the lot today? We didn't even know that until you gave me the keys, Ben."

The silence was ominous. Filled with each of them searching

through the day, the party at Sam's. Finally Cass said, "It doesn't make any difference. We can make a list of people who knew the four of us were on the schooner today. But Nell's car is noticeable. She still has bumper stickers from the last presidential election on her car."

"And from last year's Save the Arts campaign," Izzy added.

It was true. People in Sea Harbor knew one another's cars, for better or worse. And ones with distinctive markings especially.

"So . . . the person who did this, the person who murdered Tiffany, is someone who knows us," Cass said. "Someone who knows the kind of car Nell drives. That's personal." She took a long drink of the beer Ben had ordered for her and sat back.

Nell watched her carefully. Sometimes she thought she knew Cass better than Cass knew herself. And what she read in her tan, lovely face was exactly what she'd expect. Cass was angry. Ben glanced over, and he saw it, too. Her dark eyes flashed, and her shoulders stiffened. Battling the whims of nature to build a successful lobster-fishing business had strengthened Cass in ways that transcended the muscles in her arms. Cass was a fighter.

Birdie was more difficult to read, but she wasn't afraid; Nell could see that. Birdie knew practically everyone in Sea Harbor, and the look in her eyes said that she dared a single one of them to hurt those dear to her. She would fight them tooth and nail. And she would win.

"So the facts are that someone who wasn't afraid to slice through your tires in the middle of town—maybe in the middle of the afternoon—probably isn't afraid of a lot of things."

The worry on Ben's face was planted deep in the furrows across his brow. They often teased Ben about the lack of gray in his hair, a contrast to his best friend Ham's salty beard. But today Nell thought she saw a few sprinkles, a few white hairs born of the women sitting around him.

Nell took his hand in hers and played with his fingers, but he didn't respond and his jaw remained set, along with the concern in his brown eyes.

"So what do we do about it?" he said flatly. He looked around at each of them.

Nell knew what he wanted from them, and what he knew he surely wouldn't get. He wanted each of them to give him her solemn word that they would let the police figure this case out. They'd back off and insulate themselves against any kind of danger, real or otherwise. That they would stay safe.

Birdie met Ben's eyes and smiled. She sipped her wine, biding her time, seeking acceptable words. Ones that might soften the look on her dear friend's face. She set the glass down on the table and leaned slightly forward. "I imagine," she said slowly, "that we'll do what we always do, only more carefully. We will live our lives, celebrate daily those we love—" She looked over at Izzy and Sam, their bodies pressed close together on the small love seat. "We'll listen carefully to what goes on around us, and we'll most certainly avoid danger. We'll not be foolish, Ben Endicott; you know that. But we—"

Her words fell off.

Birdie was right. They'd be careful and they would stay safe. They had every reason in the world, some of them sitting right there in front of them, to do exactly that. But in the silence of their minds, Nell, Izzy, and Cass finished Birdie's sentence—

We'll not be foolish . . . but we'll find this awful person who has disrupted our lives and the lives of those we love.

Safely, but surely. And then we will move on.

Chapter 26

$\mathcal{N}$ell and Ben lay side by side beneath the sheet, the windows open and white moonlight washing across the bed. They'd had a nightcap, at Ben's suggestion, but sleep still seemed miles away.

"It's a dangerous game," he said, his eyes focused on the ceiling fan.

Nell moved her head on the pillow, her body still. Yes. It was a dangerous game. Each of them had felt it keenly tonight, each in different ways. Sam's, Ben's, and Danny's anger was tied up in a fierce caveman need to protect the women they loved. Grab clubs and slay the invisible beast.

Nell knew from the expressions on Birdie's, Cass', and Izzy's faces that they felt the same anger, the same fear as she did. The four of them were the ones who'd been threatened. Someone—maybe someone who lived down the street or on Harbor Road, or someone they talked to in the supermarket—had images of the four of them in his head, knew who they were, knew Nell's car. Somebody had intentionally and effectively taken a knife and pushed it through the thick rubber of her tires, listening as the air slowly hissed out into the harbor air.

It was personal.

And it made them angry.

A day ago they were chasing bubbles in the air that popped as soon as they touched them. But today it was different. Today they knew that something they had done or asked or said was worrying someone, worrying them enough to ruin the ending of a beautiful day.

Beside her Ben stirred, his lids growing heavy. "Let it go, Nell," he murmured.

Nell rolled onto her side and wrapped one arm across his chest, wide and familiar and comforting. Through her palm, she felt the slow in and out of his breathing. She breathed in the lingering scent of Old Spice and rubbed her hand back and forth across his chest.

He pulled his eyes open and rolled his head on the pillow, his eyes holding her still.

"You are my life. My life."

Nell leaned up on one elbow and pressed her fingertips against his lips. Then she leaned down, kissing away the emotions of the night. She pulled away and looked into his eyes.

Ben was her life, too—her lover, her best friend, her eyes said.

And as the moon played over the curves of their bodies, she showed him without a doubt that her eyes spoke the truth.

Ben suggested that Claire join them for breakfast the next morning, and Nell delivered the message. She stood at the door of the guest cottage, urging Claire to come.

"It's Ben's big indulgence of the week, Annabelle Palazola's eggs. And if you haven't been to the Sweet Petunia, that's practically criminal. It's an institution."

Claire seemed in need of company, even though, at first, she protested the invitation. But it didn't take Nell long to convince her to meet them in the driveway in ten minutes. She realized early on that Claire initially protested any kindness. It made Nell wonder what living a nomadic life for nearly fifteen years did to one's sense of worth, not to mention one's ability to trust.

The Sweet Petunia was off the beaten path—up a narrow Canary Cove Road just beyond Willow Adams' Fishtail Gallery.

"It's been here less than ten years," Nell said as Ben maneuvered his Prius into a parking space beside the restaurant. "It was an old house, halfway up the hill, nearly hidden in the woods. Annabelle bought it after her husband drowned at sea. People pitched in to help—like the old barn raising, almost, wanting her to know she wasn't alone. Annabelle had four children to raise—and this restaurant enabled her to do it. She's done an amazing job—both as a mother and as a restaurant owner."

"And as a cook," Ben said. "She makes the best eggs you've ever tasted."

Annabelle herself met them at the door of the restaurant. She wiped her hands on her apron, pushed a stray strand of hair behind her ear, and shook Claire's hand. "You're the amazing gardener Nell's been telling me about. Welcome." She lifted a stack of menus from the hostess desk and motioned for them to follow her through the inside restaurant to the deck beyond.

"You're early today. You get your pick of places." She spread her arms wide. The narrow deck, just wide enough for a long line of tables, stretched around two sides of the restaurant and looked out over the tops of trees to the art colony below, and beyond that, the harbor waters.

"A true bird's-eye view," Nell said, picking a table for five in the corner. "Even without the eggs, you can see why we like it here."

Annabelle got them settled with menus, turned over their mugs and filled them with steaming coffee, then hurried back inside as voices announced more guests.

"We never know who might show up," Nell explained, seeing Claire glance at the empty places. "And the tables out here will all be snapped up as soon as church services are over and the first wave of runners have showered."

Claire laughed. "Small-town life. So predictable."

"Well, yes. That's good and bad, I suppose. But it's certainly a part of our lives."

Ben unfolded the Sunday *New York Times*, another Sunday morning ritual at Annabelle's, Nell explained. "And here's my ritual." She pulled out an arm of the sweater she was knitting for her sister Caroline. "It's all predictable," she said, "but predictability breeds comfort, I think."

"I suppose." Claire sipped her coffee. "We didn't experience the true small-town feeling when we lived here before. Being out on the edges of the town removed us a little. We didn't know everyone, like you do. In fact, we hardly knew anyone. I suppose some of that was Richard. But we were rather isolated in a strange way."

"Was that difficult for Harmony? Did she miss being more a part of the town? Having lots of friends living close by?"

"Well, she wasn't a part of the popular group, I guess you would say. But I think she was content with her life the way it was. She had a boyfriend, a girlfriend. She won academic awards. She played basketball—I guess that was where she mixed with a larger group."

"Did you go to her games?"

Claire paused. She poured some cream into her coffee and stirred it with her spoon. "Sometimes I went, but I couldn't always manage it. I know this sounds like we led a double life, Harmony and me, but her father didn't approve of girls playing sports. He never knew about it. There was a good program at the community center, and I encouraged her to do it. I thought she needed that experience, to be a part of a team."

"Did she like it?"

Claire smiled. "Yes. And she was a good player. She talked the coach into taking Tiffany, too. Tiffany was awkward, but she seemed to come into her own on the court. It was a rewarding experience for both the girls."

Nell smiled, remembering Izzy at that age. She played on a soccer team, and it was a terrific experience. It brought out the best in her, leadership qualities she didn't know she had, a sense of physical well-being, not to mention the genuine thrill of cheering teammates on and being a part of something bigger than yourself.

Izzy's dad was her coach back then, and if for no other reason, Nell knew then and there that her sister Caroline had chosen a fine man to marry. Craig's compassion and gentleness brought out the best in even the shy or awkward girls on the team, and his ear was the recipient of more teenage problems and angst than the school counselor's. She smiled at the memory and hoped that Harmony—and Tiffany, too—had had such experiences.

Claire was looking out over the woods and galleries below, and Nell could almost see Harmony there in the treetops, bringing pleasure to her mother through memories. When Claire turned back to Nell, a faint happiness lingered.

"Harmony wasn't unhappy in high school. She loved getting good grades, the honor society. And her small group of friends. And then, that last semester, there was a shift, not a bad one, but she seemed different somehow. She laughed at me when I mentioned it, but there was definitely a change. A mother can see those things. She acted as if things had come together for her in exactly the way she wanted them to. It was as if she knew what was ahead for her."

"College, I suppose? I remember Izzy going through that. Her mother would tell me how excited she was, but scared, too, all at the same time."

"I'm not sure. It wasn't so clear with Harmony. She had the scholarship to BU, but the closer graduation got, the less interested she seemed. Those last couple weeks I could hardly get her to talk about college. We'd accepted the scholarship and sent in the papers, but I couldn't get her to sign up for orientation. Think about a dorm room. None of it. She'd just smile happily and make excuses when I brought it up."

A young woman set a basket of miniature blueberry muffins on the table. "Straight from the oven, Miz Endicott," she said. "Delish."

"Thanks, Janie," Nell said as the waitress sailed off, traversing the narrow deck as if on roller skates.

Standing in her wake was Birdie, bright and smiley in a pair of neon green Bermuda shorts, knee socks, and a canary yellow T-shirt.

Ben looked at her over the top of his reading glasses. "Birdie, you look like a radioactive elf."

Birdie waved him to silence. "It keeps crazy drivers from running me down on my bike." She gave Nell a hug and greeted Claire warmly. "I picked this up at the newsstand." She dropped the Sunday *Sea Harbor Gazette* in the middle of the table. It was folded open to Mary Pisano's "About Town" column. She sat down next to Ben.

Nell slid on her glasses, took a deep breath, and read aloud:

"Summertime: When the Livin' Is Uneasy."

"Catchy," Ben said, but his voice registered wariness.

Nell went on:

It's June. The weather is splendid, the sea breeze soothing. The flowers are a riot of color and the beaches are beckoning. But all is not what it should be in our magnificent town. When a lovely boardinghouse is broken into and when the tires of one of our cherished residents' car are slashed in the middle of a public place, we need a call to action. We need the good citizens of Sea Harbor to sit up and take notice. We need to say "no!" to vandalism. To say "no" to mindless destruction. We need to be vigilant neighbors on the watch for one another.

And most important of all, we need to rid our town of those who do mortal harm to others. And we need to do it now.

Ben put down his coffee. "It could have been worse."

"She's following the police line. Vandalism. I suppose that's fine."

"Except for that last little line."

Claire looked puzzled, and Nell hurried to explain.

"Someone slashed the tires on my car yesterday while we were out sailing."

"I'm so sorry. How awful. Why would someone do something like that?"

Nell took a deep breath. "We think it was a warning to us from someone who didn't like us asking questions about Tiffany Ciccolo's death."

Claire's head shot up. "Why would someone target you?"

"Because sometimes Nell, Birdie, and company try too hard to help the police do their job," Ben said. His expression was grave.

Nell ignored him. "And though I know it's difficult for you to have this brought up again, we think this death is connected to Harmony's."

Claire sucked in a breath of air, then released it slowly. She took a drink of water and sat back in her chair. "I think so, too."

"You do?" Birdie was incredulous. "Somehow, I thought . . ."

"That I didn't care who did it? Or didn't want to know what really happened that night? I suppose I went through a stage like that when I was just numb. All that had any reality to me was that Harmony was gone and nothing would bring her back. Then I would switch over and lash out at the unknown person who had been with her. I would hate that person, rail at them in my dreams. Who were they? Why didn't anyone know what happened?

"But I've had years to think about it. And Tiffany's death brings a new dimension to it, too. I think she knew something, something important about Harmony. I can feel it in my bones, almost as if Harmony is telling me. I don't know why she kept it a secret, but I know she knew something."

"Maybe she didn't know back then that the secret would incriminate someone else." The thought had wandered around in Nell's head early that morning as she lay in bed, trying to piece the puzzle together. Maybe whatever it was had risen to the surface only in recent days. Or maybe there was a good reason for not revealing it. And then she'd let the thoughts go. There were too many "maybes" still clouding the picture.

"Claire, dear," Birdie said gently, "did the autopsy report show any injuries to Harmony that might have indicated force? Anything other than the scratches that may have come from sliding down the side of the quarry?"

She shook her head. "But the autopsy wasn't complete, you know."

Ben frowned. "What do you mean?"

"Autopsies were forbidden by Richard's church. It was desecrating the human body. And that body had to rise again."

"But the death was suspicious. Autopsies are usually done in such cases."

"Unless you have an angry church protesting. And a medical examiner who is about to retire and doesn't want to create a fuss. In the end, they did a cursory external examination that ascertained she drowned and didn't have unusual external injuries. And that was it."

Ben was quiet. He shrugged. "I suppose things like that happen. But autopsies can reveal all sorts of things."

Nell read his thoughts. Of course. If Harmony had been drugged, it would have indicated that. Or . . .

But Ben didn't pursue it. There was no reason to. It was over.

"Claire, the night that Tiffany Ciccolo was killed . . ." Birdie leaned her elbows on the table and looked at Claire with the gentle, unthreatening gaze that Cass often called her "mother-confessor look." The one that could squeeze the truth out of hardened criminals. "That night we saw you walking down Harbor Road, on your way somewhere."

"I saw you, too. I was headed exactly where you thought I was going, and my head was full of what I wanted to say to Tiffany. 'What did you and Harmony talk about that night?' 'Was she happy?' 'Were she and Andy dancing?' 'Was he gentle with her?' 'Was she having fun?' All the things I never knew, the things she and I used to talk about before . . . before she closed up on me. I needed to know how to picture her in my mind, carefree, beautiful, having a wonderful time on her graduation night."

It made absolute sense to Nell. Of course a mother would want to know that. Every single detail.

"Did Tiffany know you were coming?" Birdie asked.

"Yes. I called her. It was difficult, on the phone like that. I saw her at Nell's that day, and I was filled with the old awful feelings, that she had gone off with my daughter that night—and somehow she should have kept her safe. I know it was irrational, but seeing Tiffany so unexpectedly brought all those old feelings to the surface in a split second. I wanted to shake her. To hurt her.

"Instead, I went for a long walk and calmed myself down. I decided that I needed to talk to her, so I called the salon. She took the call, even seemed relieved to hear my voice. She said she wanted to talk to me, too. She wanted to share Harmony's secrets, things her mother should know, she said. She said the salon closed at seven that night, and I could come then. She'd be staying late. I think she was meeting someone later, maybe a late haircut or something."

"But it was later than seven when we saw you."

"At the last minute, I decided not to go. Why put her through that awful night? *Let it go,* I told myself. But, of course, I couldn't. I kept thinking about it. About Harmony. Wondering what she meant about Harmony's having a secret. So I walked down there, even though it was late."

"What happened?" Ben asked.

"The door was locked, and only a few security lights were on. I knocked for a while, but no one came."

Because Tiffany was downstairs, in her cozy office, with a murderer. Nell took a long drink of water.

The waitress returned with tall glasses of fresh-squeezed orange juice and four plates. She set one down in front of each of them— creamy baked eggs, perfectly cooked. Watercress and roasted peppers were scattered like confetti around the eggs, and a basil-and-cheese sauce was drizzled over the top. Chunks of banana, cantaloupe, and mango bordered the eggs like fresh flowers. "Our Sunday special. Annabelle said you'd adore it." She set a plate down in front of each of them, then stood back, beaming at the culinary masterpieces.

"And she was right," Birdie said. "Beautiful as a Monet painting."

Janie grinned, refilled their coffee mugs, and disappeared.

"Sometimes it happens like this, Claire," Ben explained, with a note of apology. "They forget to ask. But it's always exactly what you'd want—even if you had had an actual choice."

Claire laughed and picked up her fork. "It looks perfect. And so beautiful." She picked up a sprig of watercress decorating the side. "Nell, you should plant this next year. It's very good for you."

She was more relaxed than Nell had seen her in a while, and considering the conversation, it was a minor miracle. As the tension eased from her body, her face relaxed and the beauty hidden behind her sorrow began to emerge—inch by inch.

"This is wonderful," Claire said. "And here is what else is wonderful. For fifteen years I haven't talked about my daughter to anyone. She was trapped in my head and my heart every minute of every day for all those years, until some days I thought I would crack open and disintegrate into a pile of nothing. I didn't anticipate . . . I never thought that talking about her, letting her out of those locked rooms, would be a good thing for me, so I never even told people I had a daughter. At first—when her photo appeared in the paper alongside Tiffany's—it was awful. But now it's easier. It's almost like . . . like allowing her to have had a life. Acknowledging her. Letting her come back to me."

"Even talking about what happened to her that night?"

"Even that." She sprinkled some pepper on her eggs, a dash of Cholula sauce, and dug in, as if she hadn't eaten in a long, long time.

The deck was filled now, as Nell had predicted, and all along the railing, conversations rose and fell and platters of every imaginable egg combination were greeted with great anticipation. Nell waved to the Brandleys, who were halfway down the row of tables. Her gaze lingered on the table next to them as the occupants shoved back their chairs, getting ready to leave.

She turned to Claire.

"Have you seen Andy Risso since you've been back?"

She sighed. "I've harbored ill will for him for so long, just like I did with Tiffany. I didn't really expect either of them would still be around Sea Harbor. I thought most of the young people would be gone, off to big cities. But here they both are." She bit down on her lip. "I will see him. Baby steps, I guess."

"He's standing over there." Nell nodded toward the door that led inside.

Ben and Birdie turned and looked down the row. Claire's eyes followed theirs.

"He's with Esther Gibson, Father Northcutt, and his dad, Jake. Helluva nice guy," Ben said casually. "Jake would have known Harmony, too, since she spent time over there."

"Esther is his godmother," Birdie explained. "After Andy's mother died, she filled in as best she could."

Jake was holding the door for Esther and Father Northcutt and spotted them as he turned. He smiled and lifted his hand in a hello. Andy looked over then. He spotted Claire and, for a minute, his face froze. But in the next instant, his smile returned, and he waved, then followed his dad through the door.

"Andy's mother died?"

"She was officially diagnosed with cancer the summer after the kids graduated," Birdie said. "Andy gave up his scholarship and went to a community college instead. He wanted to be close."

Claire was silent as she processed this new fact, and Nell could tell it was shattering an image Claire had held over the years. *Andy going off to a fine school living the life that should have been Harmony's, too.* Certainly a reason to resent him, at least from a grieving mother's point of view.

"I think Andy loved Harmony very much," Nell said. She watched as the group walked through the door. Andy hesitated once, glanced back at them, then disappeared.

"I think he did. Harmony talked about it with me. She liked that he loved her so much. She loved him, too, in that way that teenagers do. I don't think it was as serious for her. He was her good friend— but that last semester it changed. She clammed up when I would bring up his name. I knew they still studied together, but something was different, at least for her."

"Could she have been seeing someone else?"

Claire paused. "I don't think so," she said finally, but her words were weak. "Maybe it's that I want to think, even now, that she'd have told me if she were seeing someone else. I was her protector. I didn't judge her. I loved her unconditionally. But she hadn't said anything to me. She wouldn't go there with me, even when I pointedly asked her what was going on. But it was clear that something was different. She had a look about her—"

"What kind of a look?" Nell asked.

"A blissful look. Especially graduation night. She was radiant. As if her life were suddenly about to begin. The look I've seen on Izzy Chambers' face when she wanders through your backyard, pausing beneath the pine trees when no one is looking. The look I imagine she has on her face when she glimpses the wedding shawl you are knitting her.

"That kind of look."

Chapter 27

It was a picture-perfect Sunday afternoon. Sunny sky, soft breeze. A light-sweater day. Though it was late afternoon, the longer days held the sun high enough to light treetops, sending splashes of gold across Sea Harbor.

Claire was working in the garden and had turned her iPod to soft breezy music that matched the day. Light jazz—rich, belly-feeling vibrations of trumpets and saxophones—floated across the backyard.

Sam, Ben, and Ham Brewster had taken Ham's new boat out for a test sail—the fourth in a week. "You can't be too careful," Ham had rationalized to Nell. "You have to be sure everything works perfectly and it doesn't capsize when we take all of you out."

Nell, Cass, and Birdie sat on Nell's deck with Izzy's wedding shawl spread out on the table in the middle of them. The knitted folds of yarn glistened, rippling weightlessly. It was almost finished. The lacy design, knit in a circle, was a true work of art. It would take the place of a train or a veil—the only thing she'd wear other than the wedding shawl was her elegant and simple dress. The Isabel gown, Birdie called it, because it seemed to be designed for Izzy and her alone—elegant, intricate, surprising. And beautiful.

Nell fingered the widening circle, the ripples expanding, like water when a stone fell in a still pond. She stared intently at the shawl.

"A mistake?" Birdie asked.

Nell shook her head. "No, no. It's perfect. I'm trying to find an answer in it. We started in the very center, right here—"

"You're talking about something other than the shawl," Cass said.

"Yes. But it's similar. We started this shawl, not knowing what the whole would look like, casting on a few stitches, then more and more until the circle expanded."

Birdie looked back at the shawl. "Then the pattern began to emerge—"

"Yes," Nell said, her voice lifting with Birdie's addition. "Exactly. The leaves and shells, clues to the design . . . and then it became simple again, the waves fanning out."

The banging of cabinet doors in the kitchen caused Nell to scoop up the folds of lace. She folded it carefully and slipped it into Birdie's protective cloth bag. "I know that bang. Izzy's here. And she's hungry." Nell held back her smile. Izzy was showing up frequently these days, often unexpectedly, for food or hugs or time alone with her and Ben. Or just to hang out. Trying to soak it all up because she thought marriage might change it somehow.

Nell and Ben had simply smiled, enjoying her presence, and knowing that she'd have to find out for herself that some things never changed. No matter what.

Voices accompanied the banging as the refrigerator door opened and shut. Minutes later, Izzy, Pete, and Andy appeared on the porch. Izzy carried a platter of cookies and Pete held several beers, their necks threaded through his fingers.

"Hi," he said. "Anyone want a beer?"

Andy followed slowly behind them. "These guys are like leeches, aren't they?" He offered a half smile.

"On good days," Birdie answered.

"We were supposed to rehearse today—we have this, ah, this wedding reception to get ready for"—Pete looked over at Izzy—"but Merry stood us up. Said Hank needed her at the restaurant."

"Humph," Birdie said. "Hank was shooting baskets when I bicycled by there this morning."

Andy flopped down on the chaise, his long, skinny feet dangling over the end. "Ah, Hank's a good guy. Besides, it'd be a cold day in hell when Merry Jackson lets anyone push her around. She scares me."

They all laughed. Andy did, too, which pleased Nell inordinately.

She wondered if he ever talked to anyone about all the events spinning around him. At the time of Harmony's murder, he was just learning his mother had a terminal illness. And she would have been the one to hold him close, make the bad go away. Maybe Esther was there for him now. She was older than Andy's mom was, but they had been close friends. Like she and Birdie were, she thought. Years were irrelevant when spirits touched.

"So, like I said, we were walking along, thinking a hike might be okay, maybe one of the quarries or Ravenswood, when Izzy comes out of her shop looking lost."

"Looking hungry," Izzy corrected.

"Yeah. Harry's Deli was packed. The Edge had too many ladies drinking tea."

"So here we are." Izzy smiled and grabbed for a cookie before Cass devoured them all. She spotted the familiar bag at Nell's feet, and her eyes widened.

"Don't touch," Nell said. "We're too close to finishing. You and your shawl are going to have to stay in separate rooms until your wedding day."

Izzy's brows lifted, and she pressed a hand into her chest. "Breathe, breathe," she told herself. "Geesh, a wedding day."

"And that demands more than cookies. At least let's get some protein into you." Nell disappeared and was back in minutes, her platter filled with a round of Camembert and hunks of aged Gouda, white cheddar, and a tangy goat cheese. A basket of bagel crisps and a bowl of grapes were on the side.

Pete eyed the tray. "This settles it. I'm moving in."

Andy sat up, his legs bending over the side of the chaise. His smiled disappeared. "Hey, we heard what happened yesterday."

"I suppose the world has, now that Mary has made us the lead in her 'About Town' column."

"I heard it in the bar," Andy said.

"When?"

"Last night. I was working for my dad so he could get a break. Some guys came in, vacationers, I think. I didn't know them. They'd had a few. They said someone was working over some tires at Pelican Pier. They thought it was a big joke. They'd never have even seen it except one of the guys' Frisbees flew in that direction. I couldn't leave the bar, but M.J. and Alex Arcado were there with the Brewsters, and they all ran down to the pier. They didn't see anything, though, and couldn't find the car the guys were talking about. It was packed. Kids playing everywhere. Kites all around."

"What time was it?"

"Around six, six thirty."

Six thirty. Someone knew they were gone for the day and that the parking lot was packed at that time on a Sunday. People having dinner at the Edge or Gracie's Lobster Café, picnicking on the wide green space adjacent to the pier. It was a favorite place to be on an early summer night.

And somebody, someone knew all those things.

It'd been planned so carefully. And done while it was still light, which was maybe the scariest part of all.

"It's about Tiffany's death, isn't it?" Andy's voice was low, his eyes looking at Nell in a way that demanded an honest answer.

"Yes, we think so."

"Someone is worried that we're asking too many questions," Izzy said.

"Maybe you should stop, then," Andy said. He looked down at his hands. One leg jiggled slightly as he talked. "The police . . ."

"Are doing a fine job," Birdie said. "But there are such things as neighborhood watch groups that do a fine job, too."

Pete laughed, a belly laugh that rolled around the deck and drew smiles. "So you're now a neighborhood watch team?" He gave Birdie a bear hug.

"Someone has to be, young man." She shook off his hug and lifted herself straight. Her eyes were on Andy.

Pete's smile fell away. "I think that's fine. But this is a dirty thing that's happening here. It's murder." He looked hard at his sister. "Cass, when did you learn how to catch murderers? You had a hard time catching me in tag."

But Pete wasn't joking. And it wasn't Cass' lack of skill at tag that bothered him. Nell understood. But what Pete didn't understand, what Ben and Sam and Danny didn't, was that women sensed danger, too. And once their antennae detected it, they'd do what they needed to do to be safe. Beside her, Birdie took Pete's big, guitar-strumming hand in her own and held it, two of hers to one of his. Her face was smiling but her words were dead serious.

"The thing is, Peter, the police have to go on facts. We can pepper those with intuition and emotions. Sometimes that works; sometimes it doesn't. But until proven otherwise, that's what's going on here."

"And the facts all point to me," Andy said. His voice was resigned but ragged.

"That's exactly right, Andy, dear," Birdie said with just a touch of humor. "You could use a dose of emotion and intuition; all of you could."

"There are facts," Cass said, looking at Andy. "But not a shred of proof."

"Right, no proof, nothing like that, but the chief is pretty up front with me. Tommy Porter is, too. I may act like life is a cakewalk, but I know what's going on, and I know my picture is probably sitting in front of some Sea Harbor cop right this minute, wondering what they've missed. They called me last night, soon as they started working on the tire slashing. 'Where were you at such and such a time?' I guess I was lucky I took over for Pop—I had a dozen witnesses who wouldn't have had a beer in their hand if I hadn't been there. But I might not have. I might have been home alone. No alibi. Again."

The wear on Andy's face grew more obvious as he talked. He had walked in with a smile in place that Nell suspected he worked hard at keeping there, probably for Jake's sake. But once the smile was stripped away, Andy was in pain.

"Andy, that night, the night she died," Nell began.

"Which one?" he said, and the sky seemed to darken with his words.

Not which night. *Which girl?* he was asking. Nell looked out toward the yard and the guest cottage. Claire had turned off the music, gathered her things, and gone on inside.

"The night Harmony died."

He nodded.

"Did something happen that night that you haven't told a hundred times?"

"I doubt it. It's kind of like you said, though. With the police, I told them every fact I could think of. But emotion wasn't part of it, not like talking to you guys, or to my dad."

"Could you tell us, then?" Birdie asked. Her question brought with it enough compassion to wrap Andy up on a winter night and keep him warm.

"Graduation. Somehow Harmony got her mother to sneak her out for the party that night, so we met up at school—Harmony, me, Tiff. But I was anxious that night. Things hadn't been right with Harmony and me for a couple months.

"We'd been best friends, inseparable since advanced algebra class. We were newbie freshmen and she was better at math than I was. She helped me get ready for a test." He looked up at the sky, as if saying, *Yah, you know you were, Harmony.* "I don't think we ever studied alone for a math test after that. She was . . . she was everything to me. My best friend, my girlfriend."

"But something happened?"

"It was about the time I noticed my mom getting so tired—so it was spring, senior year. I remember because my mom liked Harmony a lot—and Mom missed her when she stopped coming around. She'd say she was coming over, and then I'd see her drive off in another direction."

"Where'd she go?"

"She wouldn't tell me. But she was pulling away. We were both crazy busy studying that last semester. I had band practice; she was on a basketball team. But something between us was strained. It was a hard time. For me, anyway.

"Harmony and I had always told each other everything. I knew all about her crazy father, how hard her mom worked to make her life good, pushing her to study, to join the basketball team when she didn't want to—and then she loved it, just like her mom said she would. She told me it was the best thing that ever happened to her. I knew how her mom scraped to buy her the kind of clothes she wanted. And then the talk stopped. Days would go by without us getting together, and then I'd see her at school and it would be like nothing happened. She'd hug me. Maybe come over after school that day."

"Do you think she was seeing another boy?"

Andy was silent for so long, Nell thought he wasn't going to answer, and she stepped in to ease the moment. "That's probably hard to ans—"

"No, it's okay. For a long time I didn't think so. I'd watch her at school, see who she talked to. Crazy, huh? One day I noticed she didn't have her class ring on, and I asked about it. I thought maybe she'd left it at some guy's house. She looked at me with kind of a startled look, then walked away. It was strange. Tiffany didn't know what happened to it, either, but she still insisted that Harmony told her everything—they had absolutely no secrets and she'd be the first to know if there was someone else. And there wasn't, she said. Finally, though, I realized that Tiffany was saying what she wanted to be true—but she was wrong. This was one thing Harmony wasn't telling even her best friend."

"Why did you think that was?"

"That's a mystery. If she really liked another kid, her mom would probably have been okay with it, just like she was with me. And Tiffany would have been okay with it, too. She didn't care who Harmony's boyfriend was."

"But Harmony still came over to your house sometimes, even fooled Tiffany into thinking you were still together. You went with her to the dance that night."

"I think I was her front, her protection. And I couldn't see it because I didn't want to lose her. For whatever reason, she didn't want to tell her mother—and it was fine for her to be with me. So I was her excuse."

"And the night of the dance?"

"That's when I knew for sure. We were there together. The three of us, just like always. But Harmony kept looking at her watch. Tiffany had gone off somewhere, and I asked Harmony point-blank what was going on with her. I needed to know. I *had* to know.

"So she told me."

"She told you she had another boyfriend?" Birdie asked softly. Except for an occasional clink of a beer bottle against the table or the knife slicing through the cheese, the deck was silent.

"Not at first. She started walking away, out to the parking lot. I followed her. I was mad, tired of it all. I demanded that she tell me. Yelled it at her back. People were looking at us, so she hurried up, and then I hurried up, all the way to the far end of the parking lot, where she'd parked her car. I grabbed her shoulder and pulled her back. I told her I had to know the truth.

"She turned and looked at me like I was a stranger. She told me she was in love. It was for real, and if I loved her at all, I would turn and walk away. And then she jumped in her car, slammed the door, and locked it. I pulled on it—I don't know why, I guess to stop her from leaving me, as if it would have done any good—"

The fact that it might have saved her life was on everyone's mind, but Andy was deep in the moment, and he went on.

"She started up the car and tore out of the parking lot. She nearly backed over my foot."

"Did anyone see her racing out?"

"I don't think so. Some people were going into the gym and saw me chasing her to the car. And maybe someone saw the car tearing out of the lot. I took a shortcut through the bushes to my truck and went out after her, but I was too late. When I pulled out onto the street, she was gone. I drove all over the town all night. I was sure if I found her, I could make it all right."

"What about Tiffany?"

"We just left her stranded at the gym. Cool of me, huh? I wasn't thinking too clearly. Later that night I drove by her house to see if Harmony might have come back there. I saw Tiffany in the window, but Harmony's car wasn't there. She wasn't anywhere."

She wasn't anywhere. The words lingered as silence fell over the somber group.

Andy rested his elbows on his knees, leaning forward and looking at none of them. "It took me a long time to come to grips with all of it. I think I put everything on hold while my mom was sick. Then I reached a degree of acceptance of it all. It was a bad time in my life."

"Was the experience something you could share with Tiffany?"

The question seemed to startle Andy. "Tiffany?"

"You had this shared experience, this mutual friend," Birdie began, but Andy was shaking his head.

"Our link was Harmony, sure. But when Harmony was gone, there was no link."

"Maybe to you, man, but not to her." Pete's comment was thoughtful, not judgmental. "My take is that even back then, Tiff probably had the hots for you, Andy. And once she did all that beauty school stuff, she decided to go for it. To go for *you*, I think is what I'm saying."

Andy half smiled. "I don't seem to have the best luck with women, do I?" He looked up through a swatch of blond hair that had escaped his ponytail and fell in front of his eyes. "Yeah, I don't know. After Harmony died, she called a few times, but I never called back, and then she kind of disappeared. I didn't even know she was around Sea Harbor until a few months ago when she appeared at one of our gigs. She was more assertive than the quiet girl who hung around Harmony. She'd lost weight, colored her hair. She seemed to be everywhere I looked."

"So what was that about?" Izzy asked. "Seems she was star-struck."

"I don't know. I guess it's like Birdie said; she suddenly wanted there to be this link between us. It was uncomfortable at first, but then it was kind of nice. You know how that is. Sometimes you just don't want to be alone, and she took all the uneasiness out of 'dating.' So we started being together. It was good. For a while, anyway."

"And then?" Nell said.

"Then recently she started getting really possessive, like we were joined at the hip. Like she had some claim to me. She even mentioned marriage the other night at the Palate. It was probably partly my fault. I just went out with her for fun. To be with a woman. She was easy to be with. But she looked at it differently, and I didn't see that at first. I was dumb. But when I did, I tried to explain, to back off."

Nell was quiet. Andy had been so forthright. But they were all pushing him, and moving into areas that might be too private.

Pete took a swig of his beer. "Okay, there's an elephant in the room." He looked at Andy. "People heard her at the Palate that night, man. She was loud. And she said something about having a baby."

An awful silence fell on the group. Oppressive and uncomfortable.

Cass glared at Pete, but Andy just shook his head as if too tired to protest.

"It's okay. I figured someone heard her."

"Did Tiffany think she was pregnant?" Izzy asked.

The question seemed to catch Andy off guard, as if it didn't segue naturally into the conversation. He was quiet for a minute, as if processing Izzy's simple query and trying to figure out why she asked it. And then, as if a light went on, he shrugged and looked at her.

"I don't know if she was pregnant, but I suppose the autopsy report will tell us for sure." His lips lifted in a smile that wasn't happy or sad. He looked defeated. "But if she was pregnant," he said, "there's one thing I know for sure. It wasn't mine."

The words were said with the conviction of someone swearing on a loved one's grave. Nell found herself breathing a sigh of relief. She wasn't sure what difference this information made in the scheme of things, but it was one less thing to weigh down the scale against Andy Risso. And that made her happy.

Pete appeared with another cold beer and offered it to Andy, but he shook his head and stood up. "Nah. I need drums, not beer. Think Hank might let us steal Merry away for an hour?"

"If not, we'll fool around with some drum-guitar duos." He grinned at Izzy. "How about that for a processional? Nice little drumroll and some sweet strings?" He strummed an imaginary guitar and in a wobbly falsetto, sang, "Here comes the bride."

Pete managed to escape the deck just seconds before Izzy's plastic water bottle landed where his head had been.

Chapter 28

"Sheila is getting ready to leave town," Birdie said the next day. She called Nell early, right after her morning bike ride. "I stopped by Ravenswood-by-the-Sea to check on her, and she said the police have cut her free. The autopsy report will be out soon, which they'll mail to her if she wants it."

"What about the boxes of things at my house?" Nell asked.

"She doesn't want them. Not even the clothes and things from the boardinghouse. She's giving it all to Father Northcutt for the homeless shelter."

"But she doesn't even know what's in the boxes you and I packed."

"I gave her a brief description, though I said we hadn't looked through things carefully before stashing them in the boxes. She said no thanks. She doesn't want books or knickknacks or old newspaper clippings. She and Tiffany weren't savers, she said. Probably because there was nothing of their growing-up years worth hanging on to."

"That's sad."

"But true, I think. So I assured her we'd go through the boxes and give the padre whatever we thought he could use. And if there was anything that we thought she should have, we'd mail it to her."

"That's a good plan. Did you get her contact information?"

"We can get it tonight. I invited her out to dinner. Gracie's Lazy Lobster and Soup Café."

Nell chuckled. As always, Birdie picked the perfect place. Noisy and happy. Sheila would enjoy herself, and it might give her at least one good memory to take back to Nebraska with her.

It was a good night for it, too. Ben was in Boston for a board meeting at the Endicott family company. Her quiet night would now have company.

"Dinner is a nice idea. But, Birdie, I think we—" Nell began.

"I completely agree," Birdie said, breaking into Nell's sentence. "We should look through those boxes before we meet Sheila for dinner. Just in case . . ."

The "just in case" had all sorts of thoughts bundled around it. *Just in case* there was something special there, something Sheila should have, whether she wanted it or not. *Just in case* there was something there that brought more questions to mind to ask her before she left town. *Just in case* . . .

"I'll pick up some sandwiches at Harry's Deli and be there at noon," Birdie said. "That leaves you free for those endless meetings you seem to fill your Monday mornings with."

"Old habits die hard." Monday mornings *were* often busy. Some days her calendar was so full she thought she might as well be back at work in the Boston nonprofit she directed for years. *Meetings*. Followed by *meetings*. But then she'd remind herself that now on other days there were *no* meetings—nothing but a quiet beach to walk along, or a garden to tend, or an evening with Ben, looking up at the stars or sitting in front of a fire. And then she'd relish all over again their decision to retire to the roomy old Endicott home in Sea Harbor.

Today's meeting was with an arts group in Gloucester. It wouldn't last long. She went into the den, collected her papers and purse, and told Tiffany's boxes, stacked neatly in the corner, that she'd be back. She hadn't forgotten them.

Mondays were Cass' sacred days. She and Pete usually worked their lobster crew on Saturdays and then took Monday off. Cass liked having a free day that wasn't a weekend, she often told Nell. That way she could decide for herself how to use it and not be influenced by the city calendar or the newspaper lists of weekend events. Other people could go off to work on Monday and leave Cass alone to her own devices.

"So, come help us," Nell said into her cell phone. She was stopped at the railroad tracks on her way to Gloucester, waiting for the morning train to pass by.

Cass was sitting at Coffee's, her feet up, a coffee drink on the table in front of her and a book closed on the table.

"I might as well. I can't stop thinking about Andy," she said. "Danny and I went over to the Edge last night, and it was like he was there with us, he was on our minds so much. The guy looks whipped, don't you think?"

Nell agreed. Even though he had smiled, even joked, after he'd purged himself the day before, there was a trace of defeat in the smile. A look that said, *Just get it over with.*

"Jake came into the restaurant with Ham and Jane Brewster," Cass went on. "The Brewsters had gone by and picked Jake up, insisting he go to dinner with them. He's whipped, too. He said the police keep talking about circumstantial evidence, even though they can't find anything concrete to link Andy to the crime."

Circumstantial evidence. Nell nodded. She and Ben had had a quiet dinner at home last night, then settled on the deck to talk while she sewed tiny beads onto Izzy's wedding shawl. Ben brought up the same thing. The police couldn't ignore the awful argument that Andy had had those many years ago with Harmony. And then almost a repeat of the scene with Tiffany at the Palate. His anger. His accusing Tiffany of blackmail. His lack of alibis. A fling, if that was what it was, with Tiffany. And riding beneath it all, Tiffany's obsession with him.

But most of all, or so it seemed to Ben, the fact that there wasn't anyone else left that they could bring in to question made Andy stand out. Young Tanya at the salon hadn't liked Tiffany, had wanted her job, and they'd found her rummaging through Tiffany's drawers, but she was seen at the Gull the night Tiffany was killed. And even though no one was sure when she left, there was something so naive about Tanya Gordon that Nell had a difficult time placing anything more weighty than gossip on the young woman's shoulders. Claire didn't have an alibi, either, but her motive didn't hold much water. All that was left was Andy . . . or another cold case to file on a shelf in the dusty police archive room. The thought brought a shudder to Nell. The sight of her slashed tires was a reminder that there was someone *out there*, someone who had killed a young girl. Maybe two. And someone who quite possibly could kill again. There was nothing cold about that, not at all.

They all arrived within minutes of one another. Birdie with wrapped veggie paninis that Harry had grilled minutes before, Cass with Izzy in tow.

"The girl has to eat," Cass said. "I scooped her up from the shop. Mae was delighted. She said Izzy's getting entirely too bossy as the wedding gets close. And with everything on her mind, Mae's afraid she's going to forget to eat."

"Fat chance," Izzy said, unwrapping the sandwiches and pulling a bag of chips from Nell's cabinet. "Have you ever known me to pass up food?"

They all admitted that they hadn't, and of all the things that could happen before a wedding, Izzy starving was not one of them.

They grabbed Cokes and iced tea with mint and in minutes were sitting cross-legged on the floor of Ben's den. Birdie opted for the leather chair in the corner. "Just in case of fire," she explained. "Getting down there is easy, but it takes a while to get up." She settled into the chair, her feet barely touching the floor.

Nell passed around plates and napkins to catch the dripping cheese from the grilled sandwiches.

Cass licked her fingers. "Can't believe I like these as much as I do. A sandwich without a hint of cow or pig—and it's good." She peeled back the top crust and eyed the mushrooms, tomatoes, and thin slices of grilled red onion and zucchini. Harry had added sprigs of basil and oregano, slivers of pepperoncini, and a creamy sauce, the contents of which he refused to reveal, all topped with fresh melted mozzarella cheese.

Izzy put her half-finished sandwich down and pulled the first box over to the group. She tore off the tape and lifted the cardboard flaps. "Clothes?"

"She kept a bit of her life in that office. More than at Mrs. Bridge's boardinghouse, we think," Birdie said.

Izzy pulled out jackets and checked the pockets. "You never know," she said, looking up, but they were empty except for some loose change and a pair of sunglasses. She folded them neatly and took out a pair of nylon running shorts and several shirts. The rest of the box had more of the same—several underwear items, a baseball hat.

Nell took out a Magic Marker while Izzy refilled the box. *Father Northcutt*, she wrote across the side.

Cass opened another box and lifted the battered backpack out, setting it aside.

"The rest are all books," Cass said. She opened each one, then flipped the pages upside down to release any notes or receipts, or stray bits of paper. Anything that might add details to Tiffany Ciccolo's life. She checked the titles, but there was nothing out of the ordinary, and she packed them all up again.

Birdie leaned over and pulled the backpack to her lap. She unzipped the main compartment and looked inside. "This is interesting." She pulled a cotton nightshirt from the bag. Next was a red lightweight hoodie. Birdie held it up. SEA HARBOR RED HOTS was written across the back.

"That's the name of a community-center basketball team. I think I played on it one year. I was awful," Cass said.

"Tiffany played basketball," Nell said. "She must have saved it. Claire said she was a good player."

Birdie held the shirt up by the shoulders and scrutinized it more carefully. "It must have shrunk over the years if it was Tiffany's. It's not very big."

The nightshirt and shorts were small, too. She pulled out a

hairbrush and small bag holding creams and elastic bands. Deodorant and a toothbrush. A clean T-shirt and pair of jeans were folded together, along with underwear. Birdie set them aside and unzipped a side pocket. She found a pair of earrings and a black velvet pouch. Inside was a thin gold chain.

"What's that?" Izzy said.

Birdie dangled it in the air. A rectangular charm hung from it. It had a raised design on the gold-plated surface. "An amulet. It looks like an Egyptian cartouche."

Izzy took it and turned it over. She rubbed a finger over the design. "It's pretty." She squinted and looked at it more closely. "It's an odd design, two or three horizontal lines. The letters are rubbed down, hard to see, but there's something about the design that looks familiar."

Nell took it from her and looked at it. "Maybe we should show this to Sheila. It's jewelry, maybe something from their family?"

They all agreed, and Nell set it aside.

"This box is all picture frames, some with the original store picture still in them. And CDs. Father Northcutt?"

Nell nodded, and Cass closed the box and marked it.

Birdie pulled a pair of flip-flops and a bathing suit from another compartment in the backpack. "I guess this is it for the backpack."

Cass stared at the items. "These are odd things to carry in a backpack. It sure doesn't look like yours, Birdie. No yarn, needles. Not a single bottle of pinot grigio."

They laughed.

"Cass is right, though. It's odd. Where do you suppose Tiff was going?"

"It almost looks like she had packed for an overnight," Izzy said.

Nell looked at the pile of clothes on the floor near Birdie's feet. "That would be my guess. Claire said Tiffany mentioned meeting someone at the salon later that night. She assumed it was a client, but maybe not. Maybe it was someone she was going away with."

"What about that front pocket?" Cass said. She pointed to the bag. "It has a bulge."

Birdie unzipped the remaining compartment. She frowned, then pulled out a package. The wrapping paper was slightly torn and dirty, but the design on it was distinct. Caps and gowns. It was a wrapped present.

"A graduation present?"

"It's June. Maybe she knew a graduate and was giving them a gift."

"I wonder who." Birdie tore the paper off and stared down at the paperback sitting in her lap.

The title leaped off the cover. It was a perennial best seller, a book they'd all seen staring out at them from bookstore racks.

What to Expect When You're Expecting.

"Good lord," Nell said.

"So Tiffany . . . was pregnant?" Izzy said. "Tanya was right?"

Nell took the book from Birdie's lap and opened the cover. Across the inside, in the loops and swirls of teenage penmanship, was written:

Happy Graduation(!) to Harmony, my best friend in the whole world. I will always be with you, through thick (ha, ha!) and thin.
From your secret keeper, your soul sister.
BFF,
Aunt Tiffany

Nell stared at the inscription. *Aunt* Tiffany.

Izzy reached over for the jeans they'd pulled from the backpack. Size 2. "This isn't Tiffany's backpack," she said. "These aren't her clothes. These jeans are outdated, and much too small for Tiffany."

Cass said what they were all thinking. "It's Harmony's. All packed and ready to spend graduation night with her best friend, the keeper of her secrets."

"Tiffany had the present wrapped and ready to give to her friend when they got back from the party," Nell said.

"So it was Harmony who was pregnant."

A hush fell across the den. An eerie quiet, except for the silent thud of more puzzle pieces falling like bricks to the floor.

"So the baby that Tanya heard Tiffany mention . . ." Cass began.

"Was Harmony's baby," said Izzy, her voice hushed.

"That's what Tiffany must have been talking about that night at the Palate," Nell said. "But, why? Why all these years later?"

"Do you think Andy knew about the pregnancy before Tiff told him the other night?" Cass asked. "Maybe that's what she was telling him."

They all thought back over the days, the conversations.

"He knew last night when he was over here; that was clear. He was surprised when we assumed it was Tiffany who was pregnant," Birdie said.

Nell nodded. "He almost seemed amused by our mistake." She thought back to the night on the Palate deck, Tiffany needing to talk to Andy. It was urgent. Something she had to tell him.

"This was the secret Tiffany talked about," she said out loud, the words spilling out. "Harmony's secret that she had entrusted to Tiffany."

"And a secret she kept for fifteen years," Izzy said.

"She was desperate to get Andy's attention," Birdie said. "That would certainly be a way to do it."

"I wonder why Andy didn't say anything last night, correct our thinking." Izzy smoothed out the jeans and folded them absently.

And Nell wondered whether Claire Russell had known she was going to be a grandmother.

Izzy took the backpack and opened the zipper as far as it would go. She splayed the canvas apart on the floor. On the inside, shadowed in the faded material, was written in black marking pen: *Harmony Farrow. Phone #: 978-555-0982.*

Izzy massaged the bag, feeling for anything they'd missed. In an open pocket, folded in half, was an envelope. She pulled it out and read the words written across the outside:

Tiff, I may need this. Please keep in a safe place. Luv ya. Harmony.

Izzy tore it open. It was a lab report from a free clinic in New Hampshire. She scanned it quickly, then passed it around the group.

Patient ID: 972456555
Patient Name: H. Markham
PT Medications: multivitamins
D.O.B.: 4.6.78
Specimen collected: May . . .
Test: hCG
Result: Positive.
Blood type: AB positive
Comment: Patient request copy of lab report.

It was followed by a list of tests, with numbers following them, and signed at the bottom by a physician.

Harmony hadn't settled for an at-home pregnancy test, though Nell suspected she'd probably done that, too. And then she'd gone somewhere where no one would know her to have her pregnancy confirmed.

She'd been happy that graduation night, Claire had said. *Radiant. Radiant because she was pregnant?*

"Harmony Farrow *wanted* this baby," Birdie said out loud.

"I wonder if the father did." Nell looked again at the dates. Harmony was seventeen. Young for her class. Underage. She was probably sixteen when she got pregnant.

"If Andy's story is accurate, he's not the father."

"And if it's not accurate . . ."

But that thought was too hard to hold in their heads for long. The police might be able to do it, but Nell, Izzy, Birdie, and Cass refused to.

Nell looked at the sheet of paper once more. She frowned, then looked closer. "The false name she used." She showed them the lab report again. They hadn't noticed it before.

Markham.

The place where she was killed.

"Why would she use that?"

But none of them had any answers.

"Wouldn't the autopsy have shown that she was pregnant?" Cass asked.

Birdie explained what Claire had told them the day before. The incomplete autopsy. External. No one knew she was pregnant.

Probably not even Claire, Nell realized now. Unless Harmony had told her, and that seemed unlikely.

They pulled themselves up from the floor, more questions than answers cluttering their minds. But new facts required a shifting of things. And perhaps in the shifting, there'd be clarity at last.

They lined up the items that hadn't been put back in the boxes headed for Father Northcutt's shelter.

A book.

A pregnancy lab report.

A teenager's backpack, filled with all the things she'd need to spend the night at a friend's house.

"The pack needs to go to Claire," Nell said. "It's hers to do with as she wills."

They all agreed.

"And the necklace?" Izzy asked. "Could Harmony have been giving that to Tiffany for graduation?"

But it wasn't wrapped as a gift. And it was worn, not new, as you'd expect a graduation gift to be.

Izzy's brows pulled together. "I know I've seen those lines or letters somewhere before on something."

"I'll bring it to dinner tonight. Just in case Sheila can shed some light on it."

It wasn't until later, as Nell pulled out of the driveway to pick up Izzy and Cass for a night at Lazy Lobster and Soup Café, that Nell second-guessed her decision. Should she have shown the necklace to Claire first? But something inside her said that Claire would have no idea where the necklace had come from, even if it belonged to Harmony. She probably had never seen it before, which was why it was hidden away in a velvet pouch at the bottom of a backpack.

Chapter 29

$\mathcal{M}$usic streamed from the open door of the Lazy Lobster and Soup Café as the five women walked down the pier to Gracie Santos' restaurant.

"Sounds like a band playing," Izzy said.

"Sounds like *the* band," Cass said. "I forgot the Fractured Fish were playing here tonight."

Nell looked over at Sheila and wondered if she had put it together. Tiffany would probably have mentioned to her sister that Andy played in a band. But Sheila had been in town only a few days, and she might not realize that the drummer in the well-loved Sea Harbor band the Fractured Fish was Andy Risso.

Sheila's face showed no emotion, leaving Nell without an answer.

Gracie met them at the door. "We're rockin' tonight. Where would you like to sit?"

Nell looked over the room. The band was out on the deck at the far end of the small restaurant, squeezed up against the railing and surrounded by picnic tables, where broiled lobsters were greedily pulled apart and eaten off paper plates. She pointed to an empty table near the fireplace, far enough away from the band that they'd be able to hear one another. Gracie led them over and passed tall laminated menus to everyone. She gave Izzy a quick hug. "Hey, bride-to-be, I can't wait for the big day. And can't wait to see the 'secret' shawl— I've been hearing about it for weeks."

Izzy laughed. "The best thing about the secret shawl is that it will draw attention away from the bride, and I can be invisible and have a fantastic time."

"Oh, Iz, that'll never happen—but you'll have a fantastic time anyway. We all will. Joy. That's what we all need."

Nell introduced Gracie to Sheila, and Gracie murmured her condolences. "Tiffany used to come in here with Andy sometimes. She loved my lobster rolls."

Sheila smiled her thanks and showed no reaction to the mention of Tiffany's companion. Nell watched her settle in. She seemed more relaxed, more comfortable. Mary Pisano had worked her magic at the bed-and-breakfast, she guessed. Someone new to "mother" was Mary's cup of tea.

"I'm anxious to get back home," Sheila said, accepting a beer the waitress handed her. "But I didn't expect what I found in Sea Harbor. I came back here, knowing full well how awful it would be, facing a town I ran away from. The murder of a sister I loved—and deserted. A mother I hadn't seen in decades. But there's been some closure, some things set straight, and that's good."

"But not everything," Birdie said. "I wish we had more closure for you."

"That will come. I feel it right here." She pressed a hand against her heart.

And Nell felt it, too. They were close. Very close.

A basket of fried clams appeared magically on the table, along with a spicy red sauce and plenty of napkins. "Take your time, ladies," the young waitress said.

Through the open deck doors, Pete was singing a ditty about the walrus and the carpenter, much to the delight of a family of five seated at one of the picnic tables.

Sheila smiled at the clapping and laughter. "This is a great little place."

"Gracie, the owner, is a friend of ours," Cass said. "She built this café with blood, sweat, and tears—hers and ours—but it's been worth it. Everyone in town loves it, and you won't find better lobsters anywhere in Sea Harbor."

Izzy explained to Sheila, "Cass and Pete's company provides the lobsters. So yes, as Cass so humbly reports, the lobsters are the finest, bar none."

"Oh, quiet, you," Cass said, then snagged their waitress and suggested she bring them five specials. Steamed lobster with lemon butter, sweet potato fries, fresh corn on the cob, and coleslaw, with Gracie's crusty sourdough rolls on the side.

"What's the band?" Sheila asked, looking through the crowd of people.

For a second no one said anything; then Izzy said matter-of-factly, "The singer-guitarist is Cass' brother, Pete. I think you've met Merry Jackson, the singer-keyboardist. And the drummer is Andy Risso."

Sheila's smile dropped for a minute, but she collected herself quickly and took a quick drink of beer. "They're good."

"Sheila, if we're not being too bold here, could you tell us why you dislike Andy so much?" Birdie looked across the table with the peaceful, loving countenance of a confessor. "He's a lovely boy, and I know he and Tiffany had a long history together."

Sheila accepted the question thoughtfully. She nibbled on a fried clam while the waitress handed out Gracie's heavy silk-screened bibs.

"Maybe that's what I dislike, Birdie—that long history. The history I purposefully extricated myself from. Maybe I resented that? Or maybe it's because Tiffany was so head over heels in love with the guy. And then, when they finally got together after all those years, he treated her the way he did."

"What do you mean, all those years?"

"Tiffany loved Andy since high school. She used to call me about him and talk endlessly. But that was the kind of person she was. She had this teenage crush—but she'd never, ever let her friend Harmony know. In fact, there was a time before graduation when Harmony was pulling back from Andy and Tiffany was depressed about it because it made Andy sad. She wanted him to be happy—even if it meant she didn't have a chance with him."

"After Harmony died, what did she do?"

"Nothing. She was desolate over losing Harmony. I wanted her to come stay with me, but she couldn't be that far away, she said. Far away from our mother. So she got a waitress job up in New Hampshire. She told me once that she thought Harmony's death was really an accident. And she wished the police would leave it alone."

"But she came back to Sea Harbor?"

"When my mother had to go into a home, Tiff came back and took care of it. See? She was the good daughter. Always pleasing everyone. But when she came back, she discovered Andy was here, too, and it started all over again. She went away to that beauty school, lost a bunch of weight, fixed her hair, and it was all for him. She told me as much. Her time had finally come, she said. This was it.

"And I thought it was, for a while. They started going out. She'd call me, ecstatic. She was going to marry him, she told me. Then just like that, he pulled away. It was like he was playing with her, you know? But she wouldn't give up. She had more confidence this time around, and she told me she'd get him by hook or by crook. She had a few tricks up her sleeve, she said.

"And all I wanted was for the guy to tell her to go away. To let her loose."

"But maybe he tried."

Sheila nodded that it could certainly have been the case. "Tiff probably wouldn't have heard it. She was determined. I guess it's not Andy's fault. But when you've been blaming yourself for so many years, it's a relief to have someone else to lay the burden on for a while, unfair or not."

The waitress cheerfully announced that their feast was ready and began filling the table with baskets of warm rolls and honey butter and a bowl to hold shells. Next came the plates, steaming hot and piled with corn, baked potatoes, and a magnificent lobster sitting in the middle of each. "Careful. They're hot and they're heavy," she said. "Dig in."

And they did, as if they hadn't eaten in weeks. Cass instructed Sheila on the process, first by gently twisting off the legs.

Sheila dropped the skinny appendage into the bowl, and Cass immediately retrieved it. "Oh, no, no, no. Plenty of good meat in there." She put it back on Sheila's plate and continued with a lesson in using the nutcracker, showing her how to break off the tip of the claw, pushing out the meat with a forefinger, then all the way to what was arguably the pièce de résistance, the tail. Finally, with exaggerated drama, Cass pulled out the digestive tract and dumped it ceremoniously in the bowl.

Sheila's cheeks flushed with enjoyment. "I don't think I ever had lobster when I lived here. Not once. And once I left, I never wanted it. Nebraska pork chops helped me create new memories that were easier to live with."

The talk spun around them, cheerful and upbeat, and the earlier conversation drifted to the background. Not gone. But removed. When Gracie sent over a bottle of chardonnay to go with the lobster, no one objected. Birdie poured glasses all around. "Gracie refers to the Lazy Lobster as a shack. I've scolded her for that."

"Not a shack, no way," Izzy agreed, wiping a dribble of butter off her chin and pushing her chair back a few inches.

"Right," Cass said. "Shacks don't have fireplaces."

"The Lazy Lobster and Soup Café is the jewel of Pelican Pier, as I like to think of it," Birdie concluded.

"Speaking of jewelry . . ." Nell reached into her purse and pulled out the velvet pouch they had retrieved from the backpack. "Sheila, I almost forgot. We found this in Tiffany's things and thought it might be a family keepsake. We didn't want to give it away until we'd checked." She held the chain and amulet in the palm of her hand.

Sheila looked at it, puzzled. "I wonder where this came from. It's old, don't you think?" She looked at it closer, touching the worn letters.

"Would your father have been in some kind of club? The Elks club, maybe, or something like that?" Cass asked.

Sheila looked at Cass, startled at the question. She stared down at the necklace. And then she laughed, a sad laugh with a touch of pain. She took a drink of water and then apologized. "I'm sorry; the question surprised me, is all. My father was a drunk, plain and simple. I think maybe he started drinking when he was just a kid and never stopped. He barely finished high school. And the thought of him even knowing what a civic club was is as bizarre as wondering if he'd ever been president. But you didn't know all that. You must think me a little off balance."

"Not in the slightest," Birdie said. She reached over and patted her hand. "We're all a bit daft around here. And proud of it."

Sheila looked at the necklace again. "Are you sure this was Tiffany's? I can't imagine her having something like this, honestly. It's old, so it must have belonged to someone else first, and if anyone gave her something like this, she'd have told me. At least, I think she would."

Nell slipped it back in the sack and into her purse. "Maybe it was someone else's," she agreed.

"And maybe we'll regret it terribly if we leave here without a piece of dear Gracie's amazing key lime pie," Birdie said. "What do you say?"

A short while later, filled to the brim with lobster and key lime pie, the five women pushed back their chairs and agreed to call it a night.

Birdie and Sheila were the first to leave. Sheila volunteered to drop Birdie off on her way back to Ravenswood-by-the-Sea—and her last night in the most fantastic bed she had ever met.

But first she hugged each of them as if they were lifelong friends. She passed around business cards with her phone number and address scribbled on the back and brushed away the moisture that collected in her eyes. "I suspect we haven't seen the last of each other," she said. "At least I hope not."

"The welcome sign is always out," Nell said.

Nell, Cass, and Izzy stayed a few more minutes, standing near the fireplace and listening to the Fractured Fish close out the evening with a rousing rendition of "Twist and Shout." The Lazy Lobster, its diners, and the empty plates of key lime pie vibrated in appreciation.

"You're wonderful," Nell said, hugging a perspiring Pete as he came over to say hello.

"Yeah, aren't we great?" Merry said, an inch behind Pete. She was still jiggling her tiny body. Hank stood right behind her, his eyes confirming their greatness.

Andy was across the room. He'd stopped at Esther and Richard Gibson's table to say hello. Nell noticed Esther's face soften as Andy leaned over and kissed her cheek. She could almost feel what the police dispatcher was feeling, the urge to wrap him up and keep him safe, just as his mother would have wanted her good friend to do. Andy straightened up and saw Nell watching him. He nodded, offered a half smile, and made his way across the room.

"Hey, Nell, like the show?"

"Of course." She tucked her arm in his and asked if he had a minute.

They stepped outside and stood beneath the Lazy Lobster and Soup Café sign hanging above the door. "We cleaned out Tiffany's office today, Andy. Please keep this between us, but we found Harmony's backpack."

"What?" Andy's eyes widened, suddenly alert.

"She was supposed to have an overnight at Tiffany's house the night she died."

"Yeah, I remember. Tiffany told me to come by for doughnuts the next morning. But that would have been the last thing Harmony wanted."

"She left the backpack at Tiffany's, and it seems she kept it."

"From the police?"

"From everyone. Tiffany's sole purpose in life seemed to be protecting you. Maybe she thought there'd be something in it that would look bad for you."

"Bad? Why? Like what? What was in it?"

"It was overnight things, mostly. Harmony's clothes. But there were a couple of other things." Nell pulled out the chain and medallion and showed it to him. She watched his face carefully. At first it seemed as if he'd never seen it before. Then a distant memory flickered in his eyes.

"I saw Harmony with this on just once. It was at school, toward the end of the year. I asked her what it was, and she got mad. Covered it up with her hand, as if it was a secret. And when I saw her later that day, she wasn't wearing it. Weird."

Not so weird. Harmony had secrets—and they were ones even her friend Tiffany knew nothing about. If she were secretly seeing someone, and this came from him, she wouldn't have wanted anyone to see it, Nell suspected.

She slipped it back into her purse. "There's one other thing— something that Harmony wanted Tiffany to hang on to for her. It was a lab report confirming her pregnancy."

Andy's expression didn't change. Nell might as well have told him it might rain. He stuck his hands in the pockets of his jeans and listened for what Nell would say next. With the tip of his boot, he kicked a stone across the pier.

Nell said nothing.

Finally Andy spoke. "Okay. I didn't know Harmony was pregnant until the other night at the Artist's Palate. We had this great secret, Tiff said, that would bond us together for life. I think she thought if the police knew Harmony had been pregnant, maybe they'd reopen the case. Come at me again. So she wouldn't tell them. She'd protect me. But . . ."

"But?"

"There was a kind of threat in her voice. She knew she should have handed everything over to the police after Harmony died, she said. All these years later, her conscience was bothering her. But if we were together, she'd hold on to the secret until she died. It was a subtle kind of blackmail. I'd never have gotten together with her if I'd known how she felt about me, how needy she was. I sure didn't mean to hurt her. I thought it was just a fun thing, someone to be with. But it got heavy and she started suffocating me. When I distanced myself, said we had to cool it, she pulled out the baby secret. She thought it would cement the relationship or something, I guess."

"Did she think you killed Harmony?"

"I've thought a lot about that. From where she stood that night, all she saw was the two of us disappearing between the parked cars. I think she assumed I got in the car with her. That Harmony told me about the baby, and we argued. What would that do to our future? Our scholarships? And somehow during the argument, Harmony accidentally fell into the quarry."

Nell took it all in, heavy with the sadness of Andy's story. If he was right, for fifteen years Tiffany had held on to her own version of what had happened that night. She probably played it over and over in her head. It must have been as real to her as anything in her life. And probably why she never went to see Claire Russell after Harmony died. What could she say to her without revealing what her mind's eye saw?

"And you know what the awful part of that story is? I would have jumped in after her so fast. Harmony couldn't swim. I'd have saved her in an instant, pulled her out. Saved her life."

And she'd have loved you forever. The thoughts in Andy's head were as clear as if he had spoken them aloud. Nell felt his fifteen-year-old sadness ripen right before her. But she went on, needing more answers.

"The other night we assumed the baby Tiffany was talking about was hers, and you let us go on thinking that. Why?"

"Why?" He shifted from one foot to the other. "Because of Harmony's mom, I guess. Tiff said no one knew, not even her mother. Why have Claire suffer all over again, knowing she'd not only lost a daughter but a grandchild? Made no sense to me. And what difference did it make if you thought it was Tiffany's?" He paused and opened the door to the café. "Gotta go. I've some drums that need to go home."

Nell stood, unmoving, on the step. "Andy, just one more thing. About the baby's father . . ."

Andy's face grew hard. His voice was even and his blue eyes pierced directly into Nell's soul.

"No, absolutely not. I didn't get Tiffany or Harmony or anyone else in this town pregnant. Not fifteen years ago or one day ago or one month ago. End of story. Now, shall we?" He opened the door wider.

Nell walked past him and into the restaurant, jostled by a group of diners filing out.

When she looked over their moving heads for Andy, he had disappeared.

Chapter 30

"He was angry," she told Ben the next morning. "I can't blame him."

They sat at the island, an unopened newspaper between them. Ben put down his mug. "I don't blame him, either, though I know why you asked him. You needed to hear him say it. But if Andy's telling the truth, he's been a pawn in this mess. Not only in Tiffany's death, but back when he was a teenager. Imagine having to answer question after question, and never being sure if people believe you? You'd get damn tired of it."

"I believe him," Nell said. "But we need proof, Ben. Without it, how many more years will he have to live under this cloud? Even if they can't charge him with anything, it's still a terrible thing for him to have to live with."

"And Jake, too. But Nell, you're putting yourself out there again, asking questions. How do you know that there wasn't someone right there in the Lazy Lobster, seeing you talking to Andy and wondering what you were asking, where you were going with it? Someone who might be knee-deep in this mess."

Someone who might be the murderer, was what Ben didn't say, at least not out loud. Nell wouldn't admit it to him, but she'd had the same thought. And so had Izzy and Cass. They'd talked about it on the way home from the restaurant and vowed to one another to be cautious. Nell thought of all the marital problems and kids' indiscretions that she'd overheard on Coffee's patio.

"Confirmation of Harmony's pregnancy adds a new twist to this," Ben said. "In a way, it's even worse for Andy. It's another reason he'd have to want her dead."

"But if he's telling the truth, then someone else got her pregnant. Someone else who may have wanted her dead. She had just turned seventeen, Ben. Sixteen, probably, when she got pregnant."

"Rape" was the unspoken word that settled between them.

"From what Claire has told me about Harmony's father, he'd have stopped at nothing if he thought someone had violated his daughter. Harmony was the youngest in her class. It could have been someone over eighteen."

"Was there any talk of Harmony seeing someone else in their class? It's hard to keep things like that secret. Kids see each other in the hall and around town. Where do you go to keep a relationship like that secret? Especially one that ends up in pregnancy." Ben refilled their cups.

"Andy kept his eyes open at school when he suspected something but never saw anything suspicious. Sometimes girls are better at that, but even Tiffany didn't know about it. It was a deep, dark secret."

The ringing of Nell's cell interrupted them. She glanced down.

"It's my sister," she said, looking up.

Ben smiled. "Then I'm out of here." He stood and kissed her on the cheek. "I'll be over at Father Northcutt's place if you need me. I'm reworking his budget for a new homeless shelter. Make sure you close your sunroof—they say it might rain."

Nell kissed her cautious husband back and pressed the TALK button on her phone.

Caroline wanted to go over the to-do list again, and Nell listened patiently, knowing that managing a daughter's wedding from half a country away was difficult. She knew Caroline trusted her to get things done, but having organized her fair share of charity galas in

Kansas City, Caroline had a difficult time completely releasing the reins.

Nell dutifully took notes and realized as Caroline talked that she had, in fact, forgotten one thing. The vases. Laura Danvers had a collection of them that she was loaning them for the reception at Ravenswood-by-the-Sea. She'd pick them up this week, she promised Caroline.

"And the wedding shawl?" Caroline asked.

"Almost finished," Nell assured her. She'd been texting Caroline photos every few days so she could watch it grow. "Like a grandbaby," Nell had teased.

Caroline loved it. And loved the shawl.

"It's . . . it's exquisite, Nell," she said.

Nell could hear the emotion coating her words. Gone was the sometimes rigid, organized Caroline. In her place was the soft, vulnerable mother of the bride.

"And, Sis?" Caroline said, her voice so low now that Nell could barely hear her.

Nell looked at her list to see what else was missing. "Hmm?" she said, mentally ticking off items.

"I love you," her sister said.

"I'll go with you," Birdie said. "I'm teaching my tap class but will stop by right after. Wait for me."

The timing was fine with Nell. It would give her an hour to work on Izzy's shawl. And to think. She carried Birdie's bag out to the deck and spread out a sheet on the table, not taking a chance on what a breeze might whip up.

The sun peeked through the hazy sky and warmed her face and arms. For a minute she could almost forget the shades of gray that hovered over their lives.

Caroline was right. The shawl was exquisite. She touched the lace with her fingertips. It was a true lace design—some of the lace rows being stacked without plain knitting in between.

A labor of love.

Just like a baby was.

Who did Harmony Farrow love, or think she loved? Some seventeen-year-old boy who hadn't begun to live his life but now had a baby on his conscience? What a difficult time. Telling her mother would have been impossible, Nell supposed. How would they keep that silent in a small house? Her father would find out. And then . . . ? What decisions would have been stripped from Harmony? It was beyond Nell's imagining—and her comfort level, she realized. But somehow that pregnancy, planned or unplanned, had triggered events that had touched each one of them. And as irrational a thought as it might be, she didn't want it to be a shadow in the background when her only niece walked down the garden pathway to marry Sam Perry.

Ninety minutes later Harold dropped Birdie off in the big Lincoln. Although he offered to chauffeur them around, they preferred the Endicotts' CRV. "Easier to park," Birdie told Harold, and waved him off.

Nell made sure there was room in the back for the vases, and they set off toward Sea Harbor Point and the Danvers' home.

Laura met them at the door and had iced tea ready, insisting they sit for a minute before loading the vases.

"This is a good time to come—the kids are with a babysitter and I'm actually free for a while." She threw her arms open wide. "A glorious feeling."

They laughed and followed Laura into the family room and a grouping of comfortable chairs.

"So tell me everything," she said. "How are the wedding plans going?"

"Things are fine," Nell said.

"But there's this awful murder investigation going on at the same time," Laura said. "It's horrible. Do you think it's connected to Harmony Farrow's death? It's brought back such awful memories of those times."

"That's right," Nell said. "You were in her class."

Laura nodded. "We had a big class, but I remember her, at least a little bit. Tiffany, too. They were inseparable. We all thought it an odd pair—trio, really, since Andy was usually around."

"Anyone else?"

Laura frowned as she pushed her memory. "No, it was pretty much the three of them. The pretty, slender Harmony, cute Andy, and Tiffany. She was as tall as Andy back then, kind of gawky, but sweet."

"And Andy and Harmony were a couple?" Birdie said.

"Seemed so. They were always together. Even in pictures." She got up and walked over to a cabinet beneath the bookcases. She knelt down and rummaged around in the cabinet. "We had a reunion a few years ago, and I dug up a bunch of photos for it."

The box she pulled out and carried over to the coffee table was bulging. "Here it is, my youth in a cardboard box." She laughed and lifted off the top.

"Your yearbook?" Birdie said, pointing to a cushioned blue book on top of a stack of loose pictures.

"This takes real humility." She took the book out, flipping through the pages. She found the National Honor Society page and handed the book over to Nell and Birdie. "There they are."

Nell scanned the shot. In the back row was Harmony Farrow, beautiful, with full, wavy blond hair falling to her shoulders. And next to her, a younger but unmistakable version of the Fractured Fish drummer, Andy Risso. Both teenagers were smiling, slightly self-conscious. Laura was in the photo, too, in the front row, one of the officers.

Nell turned to the senior section. On the first page were large photos of the class officers, with Laura in the middle.

"President Laura." Nell smiled.

"My fleeting claim to fame," she said.

"Do you remember if there are any other photos of Harmony and Andy? Or maybe of Harmony with another boy?"

"Another boy in our class?"

"Well, we think there might have been another boyfriend. Andy said Harmony had pulled away that last semester."

"These photos were all taken in the fall. Yearbook deadlines, you know. And I think I'd remember if there'd been a photo of her with someone else. I . . . I edited this thing, so I looked at these pictures a zillion times. Also, you know how there are certain people you just assume will always be together? That was Andy and Harmony."

She pulled the box onto her lap. "There are some other loose photos of Harmony—we were on a basketball team together." She rummaged through the box. "My dad took most of these—he never missed a game. I wasn't a very good player, but he refused to believe it."

Nell and Birdie shared a look that said they sincerely doubted Laura Danvers could be mediocre at anything, even basketball.

"Here . . . here we are. The Red Hots in all our glory." She laughed and passed the eight-by-ten photo over to the two women. "These would be more recent than the yearbook photos. We played basketball in the spring. It was a community-center team—the school didn't have a girls' team that year."

Nell slipped on her glasses and scanned the photo, looking for familiar faces. The photo was a little out of focus, but they found Harmony easily. Her blond hair shiny and a bright, glorious smile on her face. Tiffany stood right behind her, and down the row was Laura, her hair pulled back in a ponytail.

Behind the girls was a line of gangly teenage boys in shorts and red T-shirts. "Our cheerleaders," Laura said with a laugh. "We thought it was only fair so made our friends or boyfriends come be our squad. They were awful."

Nell looked at the photo again. She scanned the boys' faces. Andy Risso was definitely not one of them.

"I've got an idea," Laura said suddenly. "I have enough of my father's photos to wallpaper my hallway. Why don't you give these few to Harmony's mother?" She began flipping through the stack, pulling out photos and slipping them into a large envelope. "Dad gave some to my friends, but I bet the Farrows never got any. They weren't usually at the games, I don't think. Maybe these would mean something to Harmony's mom." She handed the envelope to Nell.

Nell thanked her. She suspected Laura was absolutely right. "I think Claire would love these."

They talked about other things then, mostly wedding details that seemed to grow more ominous as the day drew closer. Laura offered to help arrange pickups from the Boston airport when the relatives started to arrive. Their large van would hold nine, she said. And Elliott was a very responsible driver. "It's the banker in him, I guess," she joked.

Finally Birdie pushed a platter of cookies to the opposite side of the table and announced that if she ate one more, she'd never fit into the new dress she'd bought for Izzy and Sam's wedding.

Laura had put the vases in the driveway, wrapped in Bubble Wrap and packed in cardboard boxes. The three women loaded them into Nell's car.

"I'll see you tonight," Laura said, waving them off. "The customers' party for Izzy. Don't forget!"

And they nearly had—another jolting reminder that there were too many things rattling around in their heads. Too many balls to juggle, too many distractions, when there should be only one.

"We have three days left," Birdie said as they drove down the hill.

Nell glanced over at her friend. Birdie always worked better with deadlines. One week, she'd said. That was what they had to bring some closure to the unrest in their town.

They'd already shaved off a couple of days.

"Three days left to put this all to rest. The week is wearing thin."

When Nell pulled into her driveway a while later, she noticed Ben's car wasn't back yet, but several boxes were stacked on the porch.

"More wedding presents," she said to Birdie. "Ben's relatives send them here without thinking."

Birdie laughed. "Saves them from having to look up the address."

She and Birdie had unloaded the vases at the bed-and-breakfast, run a few errands, and finally came back to Nell's to spend some time on the wedding shawl. Nell would sew beads; Birdie would cheerlead. "These fingers just don't like those tiny little needles anymore," she said. "But first, food. I'm starving."

Nell opened the windows and the deck door. She stretched out her arms and threw her head back, soaking in the fresh air. "Ben was wrong about the rain. This would be the perfect day for a wedding."

"It will be a perfect day, no matter what. Even if it storms like crazy, it will be a perfect day. Izzy and Sam's wedding could be nothing else."

Birdie stepped out onto the deck while Nell pulled a container of peach and yogurt soup from the refrigerator. Chilled and spicy. Perfect for a day like today. She filled two mugs and went to the door to find Birdie.

Birdie stood at the long teak table, furrows lining her forehead. It was empty, except for the white sheet draped over its surface. She looked at Nell, a question hanging huge in the air.

In her hand she held the cloth bag in which they'd passed Izzy's wedding shawl back and forth for months.

It was empty, too.

Nell's expression was blank, and then, inch by inch, the blood drained completely from her face. She set the soup mugs on the table. The thick liquid sloshed over the sides. "The wedding shawl . . . It was right there. . . ."

In minutes she and Birdie had scoured the house, upstairs and down.

Nell racked her brain, trying to retrace her movements. She'd been sitting on the porch sewing on beads, she told Birdie slowly, as if each word would bring her closer to where she'd left the shawl. She remembered going inside a couple of times, once to answer the phone and another time to put some clothes in the dryer. She remembered hearing Harold pull into the drive.

But she couldn't remember putting the shawl in the house.

"Could Ben have put it somewhere?"

Ben . . . had he come home? His car was gone. Nell dialed his number, talked just a minute, then hung up and shook her head.

"He hasn't been back home. He's still with Father Larry."

"Who would have been here?"

"I remember locking this door," she said, pointing to the deck door. "It's been blowing open, so I latched it at the last minute so it wouldn't bang in the breeze."

"Did you see the shawl outside when you did that?"

"I didn't see it. But I didn't really look. I heard Harold in the drive, locked the door, grabbed my purse, and came outside."

No one wanted to worry Izzy, so Birdie called Cass, but she wasn't answering, which meant she was out on the *Lady Lobster*, working. She wouldn't have been near the house.

"Let's just sit out here for a minute. Think about this," Birdie said calmly. "No one would come up on your deck and steal Izzy's shawl. It simply wouldn't happen." They sat, their faces grim, sipping the soup and pretending it tasted fine. Pretending it tasted at all.

"There were boxes delivered," Birdie said, then stopped and shook her head. They were grasping at straws. A delivery person wouldn't go around back.

Nell stared out toward the ocean.

"Claire," Birdie said. She stood. "Is she here? Maybe she heard something?"

Without waiting for an answer, the two women were down the steps and across the yard. They crossed the narrow porch in front of the guest cottage and looked in the open window.

Claire Russell stood in the center of the cottage. In front of her, draped over the couch, was the wedding shawl. She was looking down at it, tears streaming down her face.

The movement from outside drew her eyes to the window. Embarrassed, she brushed aside the tears with the back of her hand and rushed to the door.

"I'm so sorry," she said, the expression on Nell's face explaining the fear she'd caused. "Oh, Nell, I've frightened you so. I should have left a note."

Nell and Birdie stepped inside. Nell's hand pressed against the pounding of her heart.

"It's fine now, dear," Birdie said, relieving the tension in the air.

"Your door . . . it was locked. And it looked like rain earlier. So when I saw the shawl out there and both cars were gone, I brought it down here."

Nell breathed deeply and finally managed a smile. "I should never have left it there. Thank you for caring for it. It would have been awful if it had rained." She walked over and touched it, as if making sure it was really there.

"You were crying," Birdie said gently. The word lifted into a question.

Claire tried to brush away their concern. "It's so beautiful." She walked over and pointed to its center. "I was remembering, is all, and remembering often brings tears—both happy and sad, but more often happy these days, thanks to you."

"Did Harmony have a shawl?" Nell asked. And then she remembered the newspaper article that replayed the day Harmony died. It was how they found Harmony's body. A lacy shawl, caught on a branch that jutted out from the quarry's edge.

Claire nodded. "The design was similar to this, only smaller, and I knit it up in grays and deep blue, just like the sea. Harmony loved it." Claire looked over at a side chair. Another shawl was folded on the seat, shimmering in the sunlight. "I kept it. It was torn when they found it at the quarry, but I repaired it and washed it. When I saw Izzy's out there on the deck and the breeze was picking up, I couldn't bear the thought of something happening to it, too. . . ."

"May I look?" Nell asked. She picked it up and gently shook out the folds until the shawl hung loose from her fingertips. Like Izzy's, it was knit in the round—a shell-and-heart motif forming the graceful rows of lace.

"Claire, it's gorgeous. Harmony must have been beautiful in it."

"She was. I finished it the week before graduation. She loved it so much she insisted on wearing it one night. She was just going over to Andy's to study for finals, nothing special, but she absolutely insisted I let her wear it. So of course I did. It's not easy to please a teenager, and I was so thrilled that she liked it."

"I can just see her, in jeans and this gorgeous shawl. I bet she looked like she stepped off a magazine cover. The ultimate study outfit."

Claire smiled, and then she said sheepishly, "I'm not sure that's what they did, though. But I didn't say anything. I just let it be. I was trying hard to pick my battles."

"You don't think they were studying, you mean?" Birdie asked.

Claire looked embarrassed. "Yes, that's what I mean. Unless they were studying in the woods."

Claire noticed Nell's puzzled look and went on.

"I found the shawl the next morning in the kitchen, hanging over the back of a chair. It was covered with thistles. And there were wild berries smashed into some of the folds."

"Did you ask her about it?"

"No. It was so close to graduation, and I saw the look on her face when she came down that morning and saw what she'd done. So I worked on it, repaired a small tear. And the berry stains were minor. The color of the shawl was nearly the same shade of blue. So I plucked off the thistles, one by one, removed the stains as best I could, and it was almost as good as new for graduation."

As good as new.

Birdie and Nell carried the thought up to the house with them a short while later.

As good as new, to be worn again, the night she died.

They walked slowly across the deck to the house, Nell cradling Izzy's shawl in her arms. They hadn't worked on it today as planned, but that was fine. They had the shawl. Finishing could wait.

Besides, they had other things that needed finishing first.

"Birdie, the thistles and berries that Claire found on the shawl that night?"

Birdie nodded.

"The old Markham Quarry was full of them when Andy took me out there. I wonder if that's where she was that night."

"And with someone other than Andy Risso."

Nell nodded.

"So you think the Markham property might have been a meeting place for Harmony and someone? That she'd been there before . . ."

"It was one place the teenage crowd never went, Andy told me. A perfect place to meet if she didn't want anyone to see her."

"Or him."

"Or him. And somehow, if it was a classmate she was meeting, I wouldn't think he'd pick a place that might result in a charge of trespassing."

Perhaps it was just like in the song. Had they been looking in all the wrong places?

And suddenly, the right places seemed ominously close.

Chapter 31

But the right places didn't appear magically with a twitch of the nose. They were the small dots that needed a magnifying glass, a steady hand to hold it, and keen minds to connect them.

But the magnifying glass and minds would have to wait a little bit longer.

Tonight was a festive gathering at the Seaside Knitting Studio— and it didn't matter that the puzzle pieces rattling around in the four knitters' minds had reached painful proportions. The show must go on, as Birdie wisely reminded each of them.

It was Izzy's customers who planned it, and the same customers who talked Mae into reserving the back room. Harriet Brandley and Margaret Garozzo were leading the pack.

And, as Mae told Izzy, "It isn't a wise business decision to alienate customers. Hush up and let them be."

"But Mae," Izzy had pleaded, "enough with the presents already. I'd rather everyone buy yarn to make something they'll enjoy, instead of using their hard-earned money on presents for Sam and me."

"I'll see what we can do about that," Mae said. And then she announced to Harriet Brandley that she had the go-ahead on the gathering. "A bridal shower at the yarn studio would be just fine. Izzy would be thrilled."

In the end, they had all agreed that in lieu of gifts, each guest would knit a square for KasCare, to use in making blankets for children with the AIDS virus, or they'd make hats for Father Northcutt's shelter. The gathering would be to celebrate the upcoming nuptials with food and drink and friendship. And nice, soft wooly hats and squares for charities Izzy loved. A cocktail party at the knitting studio.

"A lovely combination," Nell had said when the e-mail invitation arrived several weeks before.

The night air was cool and crisp, a good thing, Birdie said. At least they'd be able to open the windows. She had suggested they have the party at her home to accommodate the number of people who might want to come, but Harriet had demurred. "This is home to so many of the ladies. They'll be comfortable at Izzy's."

Nell showed up early that evening. The bookstore owner's wife had insisted Nell not do a thing, but she came early anyway. Birdie and Cass were close behind her.

But Harriet had been true to her word. She'd sent Izzy home to change, and with Mae's help, she and Margaret Garozzo had turned the back room into a festive scene, with music playing and a large punch bowl holding something Harriet labeled "wicked." Soft drinks and tea were nearby, and miniature gourmet pizzas that the Garozzos had provided filled several trays. A hand-knit bride and groom atop a carrot cake decorated the table in the middle of Margaret's amazing arrangements of yellow roses.

The group was a punctual one, used to coming in for classes that wouldn't wait for latecomers, and by seven, the room was buzzing with voices, music, and people anxious for the sound of laughter.

"It's been too serious around town," a neighbor of Nell's and an avid knitter said. "We needed a party. And Izzy is the perfect person to celebrate."

When Izzy walked into the room, everyone clapped and broke out in a semblance of "Get Me to the Church on Time." She laughed along with them, clapping her hands to the beat.

Knitting was pulled out, and the stack of eight-by-eight-inch squares quickly grew into a mountain. Small hats appeared, soft and warm, just as Harriet had ordered. Purl was in the middle of it all—a cat in paradise, surrounded by colorful stray strands of yarn that she scampered after with abandon.

"I snuck in," Merry Jackson said. "My knitting is worth squat and I spend little money here, so I'm not much of a customer. But I try, I'm getting better, and mostly I just wanted to come."

Nell hugged her. "That counts. Trying is good." She stood back and looked at Merry again. "Are you all right?"

Merry shrugged off Nell's concern. "I'm fine. Fit as a fiddle, as Birdie says. Working too hard, I guess."

"I'll have to talk to Hank about that."

"Believe me, I have. I told him possession may be nine-tenths of the law, but not of a marriage." Her face grew serious. "Actually, it's Hank who works too hard. But he loves me to be with him. Not working, necessarily. Just with him."

"He loves you."

She shrugged. "How silly can you be to complain about someone hugging you too much? What's wrong with me?" Her smile returned, and she dropped her keys and purse on the table. "Let's party," she said, and did a little dance, her fingers snapping in the air and her body twisting its way over to Izzy.

Laura Danvers slipped in late, in the middle of Harriet's welcoming speech.

"You forgot the photos for Claire," Laura whispered, coming up behind Nell and slipping the envelope into her hand. Nell mouthed a thank-you and pointed to her forgetful head. Then she looked at Laura again, remembering something else in her purse. With a crook of her finger, she asked Laura to follow her back up the step into the shadows of the archway.

"What's up, Nell?" Laura whispered.

Nell pulled the velvet bag from her purse. "You know everyone and everything in this town, and if you don't, your parents do. Do you have any idea what the lines on this medallion mean? A civic group or club maybe? A boys' club?" She slipped it from the bag and held the chain in her fingers, the gold rectangle dangling from it. "It's some lines with a crooked fence at the bottom," she said.

"Strange." Laura looked closer, then lifted the charm into the palm of her hand. She turned it this way and that, and finally her confusion faded away. "Of course. It was sideways; that's why you couldn't read it. It's not a civic club. It belongs to a Pike." She grinned. "Crazy Pikes. Looks like it was taken from a keychain and made into a necklace." She gave it back to Nell and started back to the party.

"Pikes? As in Pikes Peak?"

Laura covered a chuckle with her hand. "No. The fraternity. Pi Kappa Alpha. Those are the Greek letters. See?" She held it sideways and pointed to each one.

Merry stood in the archway and strained to look at the necklace in Nell's hand. Nell handed it to her and she laughed. "Yep, crazy Pikes," she agreed, handing it back. "Was Ben a Pike?"

"No. We found it with Tiffany's things. It belonged to her friend Harmony."

Beatrice Scaglia was talking as they turned their attention back to the party. "This shop is a special little community, all its own," she was saying. "It's our own little therapy haven. Trouble with cranky husbands? Unruly kids? Neighbors who don't cut their grass? Come to Izzy's, pull out your knitting, and your troubles will evaporate in a heartbeat."

"Give me a lifetime membership," Merry Jackson joked, and they all cheered.

The music was turned up and people did as Beatrice ordered, pulling out balls of wool and needles. In minutes the room was filled with needles clicking and the happy chatter of friends and neighbors whipping up soft wool hats and squares, happy to have an excuse to celebrate.

Nell found her purse and slipped the envelope of photos into the back pocket. She looked down at the velvet bag in her hand. *A fraternity. Could Harmony Farrow have been dating a college guy?*

She leaned against the wall between Cass and Birdie, not hearing a word of the tributes to Izzy spinning around the room.

"Your shop is like a womb," Cass was saying to Izzy. They were looking around the room at the crowd of people who had made the Seaside Knitting Studio a part of their lives. "People feel safe and secure here."

"Sometimes too safe. Mae says she could blackmail half the town because of the things she hears in here. She's threatening to write a book."

Birdie laughed. She'd finished her squares and put away her needles for the night. "A knitting exposé. I'd buy it."

The evening moved along quickly, and not until Izzy herself turned the music down a notch did the group consider winding down.

The punch bowl had been drained, leaving nothing but small threads of lime peel on the bottom, the pizza platters were reduced to scraps of spinach and tiny pieces of crust, and Harriet was plugging in the coffeepot.

"A very nice party," Esther Gibson said, gathering up her things.

"I'm glad you could come, Esther. You work too much," Izzy said.

"Nonsense, Izzy. I'm cutting back, but someone has to keep those boys in blue in check."

"Are things busy at the station?" Birdie asked.

"Birdie Favazza, I know you like the back of my hand. What you're asking is, 'What's going on with the Ciccolo investigation?'"

Birdie smiled.

"It's slow moving—they're turning over every stone. But I'm dreadfully afraid it will be shelved. As much as I want that to happen, to just let it all go away, we can't let that happen again." She looked around at all of them. "We simply can't."

The resolve was unspoken, but it was in each of their eyes. An answer to Esther. No, they couldn't let it happen again. Cold cases warmed over were sometimes the worst kinds of all.

. . .

Esther was the first to leave the party, but others followed, and soon Izzy, Birdie, Nell, and Cass stood alone in an empty back room, swept clean and free of crumbs and punch bowls and paper plates.

The party had been a success.

"And now," Birdie said, "we need to unwind."

They sat around the fireplace, weary, needing to talk, but finding comfort in the silence.

"So who?" Cass said finally.

"Who?"

"Who was Harmony hooked up with? Who got her pregnant? It's looming over us like a hot-air balloon, and yet we can't see it."

"It wasn't Andy. If you had seen his eyes the other night, you'd be as sure of that as I am," Nell said.

"And Tiffany's role? It doesn't sound like she knew about the other guy, but she had something that could have opened the case up all over again."

"The lab report, for starters. Harmony had requested it from the lab, which means she anticipated someone might want proof of the pregnancy."

"That's right," Izzy said, jumping into the conversation. "And if a guy demanded proof, he probably didn't want to become a father."

They nodded. Certainly a motive.

"It's also possible that going out to the quarry wasn't a onetime thing." Nell told them about Claire finding Harmony's shawl full of thistles and berries, and the possibility that she was more familiar with the Markham Quarry than anyone had thought.

"She'd tell her mother she was going to Andy's—but wouldn't show up," Cass mused. "She went somewhere. And it seems likely it was to meet a guy."

"Her beautiful shawl, covered with thistles," Izzy murmured, the image vivid in her mind.

"But why there?" Cass asked. "No one ever went out there. The lady who owned it was crazy; at least those were the rumors when we were in high school. She'd come up from her Boston mansion sometimes to stay in a little house out on the property. A story went around that some guys snuck into the quarry one night to skinny-dip, and she took a pellet gun after them. Actually hit one of the guys in the butt. It was off-limits after that."

Birdie laughed. "I heard those rumors, too. Penelope Markham was her name. She was a character. No one really knew her—she was a recluse when she was up here—but there were certainly stories that spun around her."

"So there was a house out there on the land?" Nell asked.

"A small cabin, as I remember," Birdie said. "No one lived in it, except when she came up. The lady could have built something lovely, but for some reason, she never did."

"Have you ever seen it? Was it near the quarry?"

"Could it have been a love nest?" Izzy said, jumping on Nell's thought. "No one ever saw this couple together, at least as far as we know. What better place to meet than a cabin hidden in the woods?"

Birdie was silent, thinking back. "I wish I were better at dates. I remember that the cabin burned down one summer. But I can't remember when that was or when the woman died—or when she stopped coming up here." Birdie pulled her brows together, thinking. "I'll check into that. I agree with Cass that if they were meeting out there, it seems like an odd choice. Penelope Markham wouldn't hesitate to press charges against trespassers."

"Or to shoot them."

Finally Nell brought up the necklace. She repeated her conversation with Laura. "I've been thinking about where she got it," Nell said.

"Someone in college?"

"Maybe. But everyone has noticed how old and worn it is. We could barely read the letters."

"So you're thinking the person could have been older than that? Out of college?" Birdie frowned.

"Yes."

The only sound in the room was the clock above the fireplace. In their minds, each of them was recasting the scenario.

"An older man. Why does that cast an uglier light on all this?" Izzy asked.

A question no one could answer.

"She seemed so protected. How would they have met?"

"That's true—her world seemed small. As far as we know, she went to school, to Andy's, and she played basketball," Birdie said.

"We have these basketball photos," Nell said, reminding herself. She took the envelope out of her purse and pulled out the photos Laura had collected. "Maybe they'll tell us something. The fellows in the background are cheerleaders or assistant coaches."

Cass looked at the top photo. "I recognize a couple of these guys. They would have been college age."

Izzy squinted in an attempt to bring the faces into focus. "I wish it popped a little more. Some of these guys are fading into the background—especially those in the back row."

"It looks like Harmony has something around her neck," Izzy said. She squinted to bring the image into focus. "The necklace, do you think?"

They took turns looking, but the figures were too small.

They flipped through the others quickly. Photos of players running down the court, a blur of movement. Others of the girls sitting on the bench and some candid shots taken at a team picnic.

Nell slipped the photos back into the envelope. "I'll see if Ben can blow these up. Maybe there's someone in the background or something we're missing. That will be my homework."

"Speaking of homework—it's been a long day," Birdie said.

Nell agreed. "And it's late."

There were no objections, and the weary group stood and gathered their bags and knitting supplies. They barely spoke, moving back and forth in slow motion, used to the routine—pulling shades, checking windows, helping Izzy lock doors and turn out lights.

Harbor Road was peaceful when they finally made their way out the front door and across the street to their cars. "We're the quiet end of Harbor Road," Izzy said, nodding toward the sound of music coming from the pier. "That end never sleeps."

They hugged one another good night and climbed into their cars.

From across the street, Purl watched the cars pull out of their parking places and drive on down the street. She circled the window, flicking her tail, then jumped directly onto a pile of cushy green cashmere, right next to the sand castle. Life was good.

Purl settled in—and she would have gone right to sleep, her evening at an end, except for the intriguing shadow that passed in front of the window.

It paused, big and dark, and peered through the window. Purl's back curved, and she stared through the glass, as still as a statue. The figure nodded, as if acknowledging her presence, then slowly began to walk back and forth, a faint sound accompanying its movement. Swish. Swish. Once. Twice. Three times.

And then it was gone.

Quiet fell again, and Purl curled back into a ball, comfortable in the heavenly cloud of yarn. And in minutes—or maybe less—the only sound filling the glass display window was the soft purring of a sleeping cat.

Chapter 32

The call came early the next day from Mae Anderson. Her words were clipped and demanding. "Come down to the shop, Nell. And bring Ben."

"Izzy?" Nell's heart was in her throat.

"She's fine. Everyone's fine. That's the good news. Just come."

Ben had the engine running by the time Nell had grabbed her purse and climbed in beside him. In minutes they pulled up outside the shop. Tommy Porter and Chief Thompson stood on either side of Mae. She was fuming.

But the color in her angry face was no match for the jagged line of red paint sprayed from one corner of Izzy's window to the other.

Tommy had a camera and took some shots, then slipped the camera back into his pocket.

Izzy and Sam pulled up next. Izzy was out of the car in an instant and stood in silence, staring at the window.

"What do you think, Jerry?" Ben said, standing next to the police chief.

"I think someone is desperate."

"And dangerous," Tommy added.

"Maybe," Ben said. "But it's a damn cowardly thing to do. Slashed tires, then spray-paint a window?"

"I've already called a window washer," Mae said. "Got the fellow out of bed."

"It'll be okay," Izzy said. "An easy fix. Thanks, Mae."

"We can't hide Mae's nieces' window display," Nell said, trying to lighten the mood.

"Certainly not." Izzy smiled. "Jillian and Rose did a beautiful job."

Nell was amazed at the calmness in Izzy's voice, but when she stepped closer and wrapped Izzy in her arms, she could feel a shiver pass through her.

"This was meant for all of us, Aunt Nell," Izzy whispered. "Another warning."

Nell nodded.

They gave Tommy the information that he needed, letting him know what time they'd closed up the night before. By the time he had finished his notes, the window washer had arrived with paint-removal equipment, and before they had even moved on inside, the river of red was reduced to a trickle.

"That will show the villain," Mae said through clenched teeth. "He'll get no satisfaction whatsoever from people seeing his handi-work. For all he knows if he walks down this street today, it never happened. It was all a bad nightmare. Maybe it'll drive the fool crazy."

But they all knew it wasn't satisfaction the "fool" wanted; it was cessation. And there was no way that was going to happen. Not now.

When Ben and Nell arrived home a short while later, Birdie was in their kitchen.

"Harold dropped me off. I've put the coffee on."

"Did Izzy call you?" Birdie's sixth sense mystified Nell. Some-times she seemed to know things before they happened.

"Esther called me. She took Mae's call at the police station. I'm going to string this person up by his toes."

"No harm was done, Birdie," Ben said. He walked around the island and gave her a quick hug.

"Not to people, maybe. But think of Izzy's window. And Purl sleeps in that display window, the poor thing."

"If only she could talk," Nell said. "Whoever did this must have been waiting for us to leave last night."

"Somehow, doing something to the knitting shop is doing something to all of us, and I think that was intended. Just like slashing your tires. We were all going to be in that car. We were all in the shop last night."

"He knows entirely too much about you," Ben said. "That *is* dangerous."

Nell had watched the worry lines deepen in Ben's forehead as he talked to Jerry Thompson. But strangely, both men seemed to be calmed down by the vandalism, almost as if, as Ben had said, it made the man seem more cowardly than anything else. She had overheard the chief say something to Tommy to that effect, too—that if the guy wanted to, he could have seriously hurt someone. Even the tire slashing could have been worse—something done to the brakes or steering column, for example, that would actually have hurt the women riding in the car. But these were cowardly scare tactics, not the kind of maliciousness they could have been.

"Did it point to a teenager maybe?" Tommy had asked. But the question had gone unanswered.

What Tommy's question did do was remind Nell of the photos of teenage basketball players that were still in her purse. While Birdie put in some toast, Nell found her purse and pulled them out again.

Ben cleared off the island, and Nell spread them out one after another. Ben stood next to her, looking closely. "Can't wait to talk to Dave Harrison about his exposure settings," he said wryly.

"It was fifteen years ago," Nell retorted. "Besides, Dave was a great dad to Laura, sitting through all those games and taking pictures on top of it."

"The community center didn't have much support back then. I guess Dave stepped in as photographer so they didn't have to pay someone to take an official team photo."

A sudden thought flitted through Nell's head. "Ben, will you be seeing him anytime soon?"

"Him?" he said absently, picking up one of the photographs and looking at it more closely.

"Dave Harrison. Laura Danvers' dad."

Ben set the photo down. "I see him all the time. We joke about who joined which committee first; the curse of retirement, Dave calls it."

"Then there's something I think you should ask him. I think this basketball team might be important. It's the one thing Harmony seemed to enjoy. Something beyond school, beyond home."

"And beyond Andy Risso," Birdie added.

"Exactly. I think there's something here that we're not seeing. Laura said her dad never missed a game. Maybe he saw something that Laura didn't notice. The kind of thing you see from the stands, but maybe not when you're sitting on the bench or running down the court."

Ben chewed on that for a moment, then agreed to do it. In fact, he was seeing Dave later in the day at the yacht club. Maybe there'd be time to talk.

Both Nell and Birdie could see exactly what was going on in Ben's head. The more involved he was with this, the closer watch he could keep on them. Involvement created a protective cloak.

Birdie buttered a piece of toast and slathered it with peach jam. She took a bite, her eyes on Nell.

Nell was still staring at the photographs, her coffee growing cold at her side. Something in the photos was important. But what?

Ben was watching her, too. "Let me scan those into the computer for you before I leave. You can play around with them and maybe see something you don't see now. I'll leave the computer on when I leave."

"Perfect." Nell thanked him, then asked Birdie how they'd go about getting more information on the Markham Quarry. Dates, ownership, that sort of thing.

"I'm ahead of you on this one, Nell. I'm ready when you are. That's why I'm here."

.   .   .

Some of the quarry history Birdie remembered herself. Stories about the eccentric Penelope Markham abounded. A Boston Brahmin spinster, she'd inherited the quarry from her father. For some reason, she liked to visit it at odd times, even though the cabin, built years before, had no plumbing or electricity. In her later years, she came less often, but one was never sure when she'd show up. Birdie couldn't remember when the property was sold to the county or when Penelope died, though she didn't think it was that long ago. In any case, it'd be easy to find out.

The Registrar of Deeds office was in the City Offices Building. Beatrice Scaglia's husband, Sal, had been the registrar for years and greeted the two women warmly.

"It's been a while," he said. "What can I do for you? Please, have a seat." Sal was clearly pleased with the interruption to his day. He was alone in the room with a hefty pile of papers on his desk, but otherwise his only company was still, dusty air. To either side of his desk were filing cabinets and, back against the wall, a row of empty desks, each with a computer, a small pad of paper, and a pen. "It's a slow day." He laughed.

They exchanged niceties, talked briefly about Izzy and Sam's upcoming wedding, and then the women got down to business.

"The Markham Quarry," Birdie said. "We're doing a little research and wondered what kind of deeds you might have on it."

"Well, all of them, Birdie. There's not a plot of land around here that we can't trace. Well, except for the Markham Quarry, because it doesn't exist."

"What do you mean?" Birdie scooted forward on the straight-backed chair. She frowned at him.

Sal laughed at his own attempt at a joke. "What I mean is, it's not the Markham Quarry anymore. In fact, it really doesn't have a name, which may be why everyone still calls it that. In our records it's identified by a number."

"Of course," Nell said patiently. "We should have realized that, Sal."

"That's the place where that young girl died, you know. It was a while ago, almost fifteen years. Awful thing." Sal put on his glasses and tapped some keys on his computer. He looked around the screen. "Yep, you'll find everything you need. He scribbled some numbers on a piece of paper and shoved it across his desk. "Here's the plot number. Help yourself to a computer and let me know if you need anything else."

They pulled over an extra chair and settled in behind the screen. Nell brought up a history of the land, and they read it together, silently, scanning down the rows of type. It was an interesting story. The granite quarry had been an active one for almost fifty years, passing from two Finnish families to the Markham family. Penelope Markham's father, a widower, was killed in a quarry accident while visiting the site, and his only daughter inherited it, eventually closing it down when the granite industry began to diminish.

Nell then brought up the numerous legal deeds that passed the property from one hand to another.

"It looks like the deed went into her estate in the late nineties. That must be when she died."

"Hmm. So all those scared kids were afraid of a ghost with a shotgun," Birdie said.

"Reputations live on."

"Did it go to the county from her estate?"

Nell pulled up another file. "No. The county bought it a few years later."

She pulled up a final file and quickly read through the legalese, then read more slowly. Suddenly she stopped. With her finger she underlined a single sentence on the screen.

Birdie followed the movement of her finger, reading word by word. Penelope Markham had willed the land to a single relative.

She took in a deep breath, then slowly expelled it.

Nell sighed. "It could mean nothing," she said.

They both read it one more time, then jotted down a few notes and closed out of the file. And they knew it meant more than nothing.

The image of someone who knew the Markham land well entered into their thoughts, lurking there, unwanted but refusing to leave. Someone who knew when the small cottage was vacant. Someone who wouldn't have been afraid of Penelope Markham's shotgun.

They were relieved to see that Sal was busy when they slipped out of the office. Neither Birdie nor Nell felt like chitchat.

"We need to check out the dates of that fire," Birdie said as they climbed back in the car. But without actual dates and only a rumor to go on, newspaper reports would take time to find, so instead they made a detour to the fire station.

"So good to have friends in high places," Birdie said as a young fireman directed them to the chief's office. M.J.'s husband, Alex Arcado, was at his desk, only too willing to talk.

"Almost fifteen years go?"

"Somewhere around that time," Nell said. "We think there was a fire at the old Markham Quarry."

Alex turned to his computer and pulled up a page. "Sure. It was shortly after that girl died."

Then he looked again. "Shortly after? That's an understatement. The fire happened right after the girl went missing. The building that burned was in the woods, a short distance from the quarry. They suspected arson because it was contained, didn't spread to the woods or anything. But we never found anything to go on. It wasn't insured for much, so that wasn't the motive—I don't think the owner even claimed anything—so nothing much was made of it. But the place burned to the ground. The thinking was that some kids or vagrants were using it as a hangout and, for whatever reason, burned it down. Maybe an accident, smoking a cigarette, whatever."

"Interesting timing," Birdie said as they headed back to Nell's car.

Izzy was helping someone in the knitting room when they stopped by the yarn studio a few hours later. It was past the lunch hour, but they felt sure she wouldn't have had time to eat, and they asked Mae if they could steal her away.

"Be my guest. And make sure she gets her protein."

"What would we do without you, Mae?" Birdie asked. "You will keep our dear Izzy fit as a fiddle for her wedding day."

Mae laughed, her Ma Kettle laugh, Izzy called it, though Nell suspected Izzy had never seen a single scene of the old-time movie.

"Are you doing okay, Mae?" Nell asked. "Your day didn't exactly get off on the right foot."

"Just got my Irish up. 'Damn fool,' is what I say. Imagine anyone pulling something like this a week before our girl gets married. It's criminal."

Yes, Nell thought. That was exactly what it was.

"The window is fine. Your window washer did a good job," Birdie said. "I may hire him to do my house."

Izzy appeared with Purl in her arms. "I can't seem to let her down. Somehow I know she saw who did this. I want to take her through town and have her point him out."

They laughed at the thought of sweet Purl leading them on a hunt. The cat promptly jumped from Izzy's arms, clearly rejecting the idea.

A table opened up near the back of Harry Garozzo's deli, just as they walked in. With great ceremony, Harry ushered them through the restaurant.

Silently Nell begged him not to break out in a wedding song, but to no avail. Before they were halfway through the restaurant, the plump-faced baker broke out with "Vivo per Lei" in his best Andrea Bocelli imitation.

Izzy sat down, red-faced, and thanked him graciously. A handful of late diners clapped, and Birdie insisted he run off for four glasses of his amazing fruit tea—and BLTs would be fine.

"Now," she said, her hands flat on the table, "where are we?"

The police had no idea who spray-painted the window, Izzy

reported, and probably never would. "But it was an amateurish gesture, they said. Like the person didn't really want to hurt us."

Just scare us off, Nell thought. *Like the tires. A warning.*

"He doesn't want to hurt us," Birdie said out loud.

"But he may have killed Tiffany Ciccolo," Nell reminded them. And the thought was almost unbearable.

Cass arrived just in time to hear Nell detail their trip to the Registrar of Deeds' office.

She drummed her fingers on the table, then came out with some news of her own. "Remember George Hanson?"

"Our delightful schooner captain," Nell said. The amazing day on the boat seemed like years ago instead of less than a week.

"I ran into him this morning at the dock. He's a chatty guy and one of his passengers was late, so we got to talking about things."

"Like where he went to college?" Nell asked.

Cass nodded. "Greek life, all those things. Guess who was in his pledge class?"

Nell sighed. She knew what was coming next, and she wanted to block her ears. Another piece of the puzzle was about to fall to the table with a crash that was almost more than she could bear. And if all their suspicions were right, Harmony's necklace didn't come from Andy or a relative or a flea market.

They wrapped up their sandwiches, much to Harry's dismay, and headed for Nell's home and the photos of Harmony Farrow's basketball team.

Izzy called Sam on the way over.

"Are you supposed to meet him, sweetie?" Nell asked.

"No," Izzy answered. "I just needed to hear his voice.

Ben had left the computer on as he'd promised. He had scanned in all the photos and opened them in a photo-editing program.

Izzy sat down in his chair. "I've used this program before," she said and immediately began pushing keys and dragging duplicates of the photos to the fore.

They were much easier to see on the computer. Most of the

informal shots focused on Laura, sometimes making a face at her dad as she sat on the bench, sometimes making a basket. Izzy flipped through thumbnails. "Here's a couple off-the-court photos. I think it's a picnic. Probably one of those end-of-the-season events."

She enlarged it.

"It's at Stage Fort Park in Gloucester," Nell said, noticing the ocean in the background and a tiny glimpse of playground to the side. The teenagers sat at picnic tables and hung around a grill, and a few stood over near the stone building on the side.

They looked for Harmony among the smiley group at the picnic tables, but she wasn't there.

"What about back there?" Cass said, pointing to several figures in the distance.

Izzy zoomed in, enlarging the figures.

They were standing under an eave, but even with half her face shadowed, the look on Harmony's face was clear. It was glorious. The look of a woman in love. Her head was tilted upward, her eyes focused on the tall, handsome man standing next to her. His dark head was lowered, listening attentively to one of the young coaches.

The team's formal photo told the same story. There was Harmony. A gold chain with a medallion just visible above her uniform top. On one side was Tiffany. And on the other, her body barely touching his, was the man who, if their suppositions were correct, had stolen her heart—and may have walked away as she slipped beneath the quarry waters.

Ben called a short while later. He was with Sam at the police station.

"We had drinks at the club with Laura's father," Ben began.

And the story that unraveled was like pouring mud in the spaces of a flagstone walk. It filled in cracks—and held the path together.

Laura's father had remembered more than they'd expected from those long-ago basketball games, Ben said. He got to know the coaches and assistants pretty well. Nice guys. Great with the girls. He knew the girls, too, especially Laura's friends.

He remembered Harmony Farrow for other reasons. Her striking good looks for one thing. But she was kind of a loner, he said, except for her sidekick, Tiffany. But sometimes he'd watch her from across the gym when she was on the bench. And he'd see the look she'd try to hold back. The look of a young woman brimming with love and trying her darnedest to hide it.

"It was almost as if she'd just become aware of her sexuality," Dave had said. "She was blossoming, basking in it. Not in a promiscuous way, but it was there in the way she walked, the way she moved."

No one imagined that it was ever reciprocated. There was absolutely no sign of that. No favoritism. Dave would have personally jumped off the bench and strangled the guy if there'd been any hint of that. It seemed to be all Harmony, caught up in this raw crush of love. The thing you read about as young girls become women. That was what he thought.

Chief Thompson wanted the photos, Ben told Nell. The necklace and lab report, too. The police had been doing their own investigation for a couple of weeks, Ben said. But they were missing some important pieces. Now they had them.

"One more thing," Ben said before hanging up, "After you talked to Alex Arcado today, he went back to the archives and found a few objects they had found when they put out the fire at the quarry fifteen years ago. Interesting items that at the time didn't mean much. They figured they belonged to Mrs. Markham—some singed underwear, a ring." The ring, it turned out—on more careful examination and using some new cleaning solutions—was a woman's class ring. Sea Harbor High, 1995.

And the police had verified something else—that Penelope Markham had hired her nephew to keep an eye out on the land once she broke her hip the winter of 1994 and became too frail to do it herself.

They piled in Nell's car, leaving before Ben arrived to pick up the photos.

They had a friend who would need them.

Traffic was light, and they drove along the narrow road in silence, shadows falling around them. A lifetime in a day. That was what it felt like. But it was almost over. Finally.

The Artist's Palate was noisy with early Friday night revelers when Nell pulled into the parking lot. People relaxing with one of Hank's incredible beers.

The four women looked around the deck, then walked through the frosted door to the inside bar.

Nell realized with a start that she'd rarely been inside the Palate. The deck was the reason they usually came here.

A mahogany bar, long and polished, ran down one side of the room. Behind it, dozens of imported beers lined a mounted glass shelf. Above the shelf was a line of framed photographs of Boston Celtics players, from Ray Allen to Larry Bird. And high above that, on another shelf, were dozens of heavy mugs that patrons had brought in for display—some with basketball team names, others embossed with fraternity and college names. Harvard, Yale, BU, UMass.

Nell looked for the now-familiar symbols and found them on a large mug right in the middle of the grouping. Pi Kappa Alpha.

Hank's new manager was moving quickly back and forth, taking orders and filling mugs. Birdie asked for directions, and he pointed to the closed door at the end of the bar.

They walked in without knocking and found Hank alone at the desk, writing on a legal pad.

Startled, he looked up. He frowned; then his eyes widened at their expressions. "Merry, is she all right? Is she hurt?"

"She will be fine, eventually," Birdie said.

Hank stared at them. In the next minute a red flush crept up his neck to his face. Dots of sweat covered his forehead and his face registered impending danger and the realization of why they were there.

Several papers flew to the floor as Hank pushed his chair back and stood, his eyes wild and darting around the room. He looked at the high windows lining the office, then the door to the bar.

Nell could feel the quickening of his heartbeat and see in his eyes the frantic need to flee.

To rush out into the day. To escape from the airless room, the shrinking life.

But the sinking realization that there was nowhere to go held him still.

Finally Hank's eyes moved back to the women filling the small space in his office.

For a moment no one spoke, but the silence spoke volumes.

He slumped down in the chair and for an eternity of seconds stared at the surface of his desk. "I'd never have hurt you ladies. I just wanted you to stop, to let things be."

Nell brushed away his words. Slashed tires and a little paint were so trivial in light of what he'd done. "Tell us why, Hank," she asked. "Why did you do it?"

The handsome bar owner seemed to diminish before their eyes, once tall and strapping, now sad and shrunken. His eyes showed a lack of sleep, and his face was pale against a frame of unkempt dark hair.

He tried to get up again, his eyes darting again to the wall of windows, the door, but the life seemed to have drained from his body and he sank back into the chair. "It was an accident. Everything. It was all an accident."

"That Harmony fell in love with you?"

He grimaced painfully at the words, and his eyes focused on the desktop again. "We argued that night. She fell."

"Argued about the baby?"

Hank's voice was dull, unfamiliar. "She wanted to have it. Her father would have crucified us. I'd have been sent to jail. She was . . . she was . . ."

"She was practically a child," Birdie finished.

The words cut through Hank, and he pressed his forehead into his palms as if in pain.

Nell saw him nod. Yes, she was a child.

And he was a fool.

"You took her to your aunt Penelope's cottage. To her quarry. You loved her there, and then you let her drown."

"I couldn't swim." The words were feeble, without meaning or conviction.

Izzy's face was beet red with anger. She stepped toward the desk. "And all these years later, innocent Tiffany Ciccolo went to you for help. Her nice old Red Hots coach who always had a ready ear. He would help her, advise her—so she spilled her secret to you. She told you that Harmony had been pregnant with Andy's baby—as she thought. And she even had the lab report to prove it. But Andy was being foolish, pushing her away."

"She had kept it all from the police—the backpack, the lab report. She'd protected Andy for all these years," Cass said.

Hank tried to regain control. "I warned Tiffany. Told her to forget it. To forget Risso. That's what she should have done. It would all have been fine. But she called me the next night and wanted to talk more. Andy was breaking everything off. And maybe she should turn over what she had to the police and move on with her life. A clean slate. A clean conscience. She asked me to help."

He lifted his head and stared at a large framed photograph on his desk.

A smiling Merry Jackson, her eyes laughing and bright with life, looked out at him. Along the wall were more pictures of Merry— singing with the band, playing her keyboard, driving the convertible he'd given her for her birthday, her hair flying about her face. "She's everything to me. You don't know, you don't understand—she's my whole life. I'd do anything not to lose her."

"Even murder?" Nell found it hard to say the word. Hank looked suddenly helpless. A weak puddle of humanity.

"When I asked her what else she had, she told me about that damn necklace. The medallion. She didn't know what it was, but I knew—the Pike charm. Harmony had wanted something of mine back then, but I'd refused, so she stole it off my key chain one night and made a necklace out of it.

"I tried to get Tiffany to give it to me, the lab report, the backpack. I said I'd take care of everything. I was frantic."

"And then Tiffany figured it out?"

"Yeah. After all those years, she finally put it together. She was so crazy about Andy Risso, she couldn't imagine Harmony ever looking at anyone else. But that night in the salon, she knew. She went crazy. She bit me and screamed that the one last thing she could do for her friend was to go to the police."

He dropped his head. "I was just trying to stop her. To calm her down."

"But if you didn't kill Harmony, if it was an accident, why"—Birdie's voice was shrill—"why this . . . ? Why did you kill innocent Tiffany?"

But they all knew. The scandal. The knowledge that Harmony's father, even all these years later, would likely insist on prosecution for rape. But mostly because he would lose the one person in his life who mattered to him.

A shuffling at the door caused them all to turn.

Merry Jackson stood in the doorframe, a polishing rag in her hand and tears streaming down her face. "You were their basketball coach, for God's sake," she screamed, moving toward the desk. The words were anguished, ripped from her throat and thrown across the room.

In the distance, sirens filled the air.

"Oh, baby," Hank moaned. He started to stand, an agonized look on his face. But before he could move from behind the desk, Merry threw the rag on the floor and turned, directly into the arms of the people who had become as close to her as family could be—and she allowed them to be exactly that.

Chapter 33

Ben made eggs, and Nell mixed the dough for scones. Coffee gurgled in the distance. It was late for breakfast, though they'd been awake for a long time. Moving from the bed took more effort than usual, and cuddling in Ben's arms far outweighed facing a difficult day.

"The worst part is behind us," Ben said, and he was right. The night before had stretched out endlessly as the police recorded page after page of Hank Jackson's life.

They had left the police station and gathered on the Endicott deck, hoping the comfort of one another would later bring sleep.

Hank Jackson had confessed to everything.

Harmony Farrow had woven a spell around him, he said. He never loved her but he loved that she needed him, something his own family never had.

And with his aunt's land at his disposal, he took her there, every chance they got.

Burning down the cabin was a precaution. Harmony wasn't careful and left things around. A fire would take care of anything he might have missed. Like Harmony's class ring.

The only thing Hank hadn't anticipated was Harmony's best friend knowing almost all her secrets and bringing them up fifteen years later as she anguished over a boyfriend to her old basketball coach—the man who always listened, always understood.

Nell pulled her thoughts from the night before to the smell of scones and sounds at the door.

Izzy, Sam, and Birdie came in first, with Cass and Danny Brandley just a few steps behind.

"Scones, please," Cass said, and leaned against the counter.

Ben poured coffee and orange juice. "Quietest I've ever seen this group," he said.

Another voice came from the doorway. Merry Jackson poked her head into the room. "The door was open." Behind her was the rest of the Fractured Fish band.

"Come in, all of you," Nell said. "Ben, put more scones in the oven."

"I came to thank you for being with me last night," Merry said. Her face was drawn, and Nell knew she hadn't slept, but as she had told the police, she would be fine. It might take a while, but she had a bar and grill to run, and a band in which to play, and that was what she'd do.

Nell passed out plates, then stood behind Andy. He hadn't said a word. But Nell knew he would be fine, too. It would take time to process it all, but Andy was strong. He had lost a mother. He would get through this. She touched his shoulder lightly, then moved on to fill orange juice glasses and coffee mugs.

They would all be all right.

Of course they would.

It was Thursday. And in ten short days, they had a wedding to celebrate.

Chapter 34

They gathered in Nell and Ben's bedroom—the wedding party. Izzy was in a small adjacent dressing room with her mother. On the bed, the shawl was laid out in a perfect circle. Sunlight slanted across it, and the silky stitches sparkled like moonlight on water. A perfect circle.

The circle of their friendship.

Cass, Birdie, and Nell were there, dressed in their summery black dresses and strappy sandals, just as Izzy had suggested, though Birdie confessed she had sneakers in her bag.

M.J. herself had taken over the special job of hair and makeup, and true to Tiffany's promise those weeks before, it was a joyous time, with cold drinks or champagne, small sandwiches, and plenty of music.

And now they were ready.

It had rained the day before, enough to freshen Claire's carefully tended plants and turn the pine needles a vibrant deep green. In the morning, the sun came out with a vengeance, drying the grass and the chairs, the deck, and the pathway. Claire was there at dawn.

She had moved into a new apartment with a little patch of garden outside the door, but she had spent hours that week in Izzy's wedding garden—and with Ben and Nell, talking, shedding tears, and beginning to heal. But on Izzy and Sam's special day, she'd be back, sitting proudly in the middle of the wedding yard that had helped bring her back to life.

Nell walked over to the windows, open to the backyard, where guests had begun to gather. A string quartet, sitting in a half circle near the rosebushes, had begun to play. Strains of Beethoven and Bach were magically luring guests to the rows of white chairs that formed a fan across the yard.

Two vases filled with soft blue hydrangeas marked the beginning of the pathway through the middle of the chairs.

Izzy's aisle.

Izzy's aisle. Nell shivered and wrapped her arms around herself.

Birdie came up beside her and smiled. "I have them, too, Nell dear. Shivers of joy."

"Don't forget me." Cass came up on Nell's other side and looped an arm around her waist.

They watched Andy and Pete in the distance, walking toward the pine trees that began the Endicott Woods. Andy carried his drums and Pete his guitar. Merry Jackson was a few steps behind.

"Thank the good lord they have that crazy band," Birdie said. "It will be a tonic no doc could prescribe for our Merry—and Andy, too."

"I thought they were playing at the reception, not the ceremony," Nell said, watching the trio as they arranged their instruments on the grass.

"Don't fret, dear," Birdie said, patting her hand. "Some things are just meant to happen." Her smile told Nell she knew more than she was saying. It also said her lips were sealed and Nell would have to wait to hear what Cass, Birdie, and Izzy had arranged.

Soon enough. Soon enough she'd *hear* their surprise—a single, simple song they had asked Merry, Pete, and Andy to sing during the wedding ceremony. The song that Nell and Ben had danced to nearly forty years before at their own wedding.

"Our Love Is Here to Stay."

"And it is," Izzy would tell her aunt, and then she'd brush away Nell's tears. "Just like yours and Uncle Ben's."

The three women looked out toward the pines again, where the aisle ended and Izzy and Sam's life would begin. Sam stood beside Ben beneath the giant maple tree, a look of total contentment on his face. In minutes, he and Izzy would stand together beneath the tree, facing their family and friends, and tell each other how their lives—and those of all the people sitting there, cheering them on—would be connected forever. How much they loved the way the other smiled, cared for other people, laughed in a goofy way and cried when bad things happened to good people.

Then the officiant would say the final words and present them to their friends.

Sam and Izzy Perry.

Married.

Sam would lift Izzy off the ground, whispering to her that it was a miracle. That he loved her with this life. He'd kiss her soundly as their friends clapped, put her down on the soft mulched ground. And then to her surprise he'd lift her up again, kiss her again, as if he'd never let go.

"He looks almost peaceful," Cass said. "Not anxious or nervous."

Nell nodded. He was smiling easily at friends and family, talking softly to Ben at his side, but his eyes kept returning to the top of the deck, the spot where his partner for life would appear.

"When something's so right, that's how you feel," Birdie said.

They turned away from the window just as the door to the dressing room opened.

Izzy's mother walked out first. She moved to her sister's side and handed Nell a tissue.

They stood with their arms around each other, looking through tears as the young woman who filled both their lives with joy walked into the room.

Izzy stood dry-eyed, composed, and beautiful, a radiant smile filling her face. She looked around at each of them, gathering them into her heart.

Her hair was brushed to a shine and pulled to a knot at her neck.

The watery silk dress fell from spaghetti straps to the floor, flowing over the slender curves of her body in gentle waves. She was elegant.

"Grace Kelly," Birdie murmured.

Izzy laughed, a throaty, slightly too-loud sound that would never have come from the Philadelphia-born princess.

She reached down and took the top off a box on the floor. One by one, she pulled out three silk scarves. They were knit in a graceful loopy pattern, long, narrow, flowing. Late-night homework, Izzy told them.

Each scarf was a different color—deep crimson for Nell, a bright green to match Birdie's eyes, and a brilliant blue scarf for Cass. Brilliant splashes of color against their black dresses.

"From me to you," Izzy said, and handed a scarf to each of them. "The colors of life."

They savored the silky feel and fine stitches, as knitters do, then looped them twice around their necks, the ends trailing gracefully to the bottoms of their dresses.

Cass twirled around the room, the scarf catching the fading sunlight and flowing around her body. "We're beautiful. We will outshine the bride." On the second twirl, she grabbed a tissue from the box on the nightstand and hugged Izzy fiercely.

Izzy laughed and hugged her back. *Her Cass. Her Birdie.*
And her aunt Nell.

Nell and Birdie moved to the bed and picked up Izzy's wedding shawl. They folded it into a half circle and lifted it around her shoulders. Izzy caught it on each side with her arms and it slipped down over her body, a swoosh of exquisite silk and cashmere yarn, of hearts and seashells.

"I'm wrapped in friendship," she said.

They stood in silence, the air filled with the words that they didn't need to say aloud. Nell reached for another tissue. "Just in case," she whispered.

Izzy stood quietly, composed and peaceful and dry-eyed. She looked around the room at the women she loved.

Then she waved her hand like a magic wand.

"Now go, all of you," she said, a slight catch in her voice.

"There's a man out there waiting to marry me."

And so there was.

And so she did.

Izzy's Wedding Shawl

Izzy's shawl was inspired by a shawl designed by the talented Bethany Kok and is reprinted here with her kind permission. Although the Seaside Knitters altered the motifs in the pattern slightly and didn't hand dye their yarn, the feeling of the sea pervades both garments.

For photos of Bethany's shawl, pattern diagrams, bead placement tips, and details on dying the yarn, please visit: www.knitty.com/ISSUEspring09/PATTshipwreck.php

For a printable pattern, please visit my Web site: sallygoldenbaum.com

Size
One

Finished measurement
Diameter: 57 inches after blocking

Materials
Knitpicks bare merino wool, silk sock yarn (The Seaside Knitters used a cashmere silk blend for Izzy's wedding shawl.)

Recommended needle size (all US)
1 set US#4 dp; 1 24- or 32-inch #4 circular; 1 each 40- or 47-inch #4, #5, #8, #9, #10, #10.5, and #11 circular needles (Always use the needle size that gives you the gauge below; each knitter's gauge is unique.)

Gauge

29 stitches/17 rows=4 inches in stockinette stitch on US#4

Approximately 5000 Czech glass seed beads size 8/0; stitch markers, yarn needle, rust-proof pins.

Strawberry Pattern

(Worked in the round over a multiple of 9 sts)

Round 1:	[K2, k2tog, yo, k2tog, yo, k3] to end.
Round 2:	K all sts.
Round 3:	[K1, k2tog, yo, k3, yo, k2tog, k1] to end.
Round 4:	K all sts.
Round 5:	[K3, yo, k3tog, yo, k3] to end.

Bleeding Heart Pattern

(Worked in the round over a multiple of 12 sts)

Round 1:	[Yo, ssk, k7, k2tog, yo, k1] to end.
Round 2:	[Yo, k1, ssk, k5, k2tog, k1, yo, k1] to end.
Round 3:	[Yo, k2, ssk, k3, k2tog, k2, yo, k1] to end.
Round 4:	[Yo, k3, ssk, k1, k2tog, k3, yo, k1] to end.
Round 5:	[Yo, k4, k3tog, k4, yo, k1] to end.
Round 6:	[K3, k2tog, yo, k1, yo, ssk, k4] to end.
Round 7:	[K2, k2tog, k1, yo, k1, yo, k1, ssk, k3] to end.
Round 8:	[K1, k2tog, k2, yo, k1, yo, k2, ssk, k2] to end.
Round 9:	[K2tog, k3, yo, k1, yo, k3, ssk, k1] to end.
Round 10:	[K4, yo, k1, yo, k4, k3tog] to end.
	Before beginning this round, move marker 1 st to the left.

Madeira Pattern

(Worked in the round over a multiple of 10 sts)

Round 1:	[Yo, ssk, k8] to end.
Round 2:	[K1, yo, ssk, k7] to end.
Round 3:	[(Yo, ssk) twice, k6] to end.
Round 4:	[K3, yo, ssk, k5] to end.
Round 5:	[(K1, yo, ssk) twice, k4] to end.
Round 6:	[K5, yo, ssk, k3] to end.
Round 7:	[(K2, yo, ssk) twice, k2] to end.
Round 8:	[K7, yo, ssk, k1] to end.
Round 9:	[K3, yo, ssk] to end.
Round 10:	[K4, yo, ssk, k4] to end.
Round 11:	[K4, yo, ssk, k2, yo, ssk] to end. *Before beginning this round, move marker 1 st to the left.*
Round 12:	[K6, yo, ssk, k2] to end. *Before beginning this round, move marker 1 st to the right.*
Round 13:	[Yo, ssk, k5, yo, ssk, k1] to end.
Round 14:	[K8, yo, ssk] to end.
Round 15:	[yo, ssk, k6, yo, ssk] to end. *Before beginning this round, move marker 1 st to the left.*
Round 16:	[Yo, ssk, k8] to end. *Before beginning this round, move marker 1 st to the right.*
Round 17:	[K1, yo, ssk, k7] to end.
Round 18:	K all sts.
Round 19:	[Yo, ssk] to end.
Round 20:	K all sts.
Round 21:	[K1, k2tog, yo, k7] to end.
Round 22:	[K2, k2tog, yo, k6] to end.
Round 23:	[Yo, k2tog, yo, k6, k2tog] to end. *Before beginning this round, move marker 1 st to the left.*
Round 24:	[K8, k2tog, yo] to end.
Round 25:	[K2tog, yo, k5, k2tog, yo, k1] to end.
Round 26:	[K6, k2tog, yo, k2] to end.
Round 27:	[Yo, k4, k2tog, yo, k2, k2tog] to end. *Before beginning this round, move marker 1 st to the left.*

Round 28:	[K4, k2tog, yo, k4] to end.
Round 29:	[K3, k2tog, yo] to end.
Round 30:	[K2, k2tog, yo, k6] to end.
Round 31:	[K1, k2tog, yo, k3, k2tog, yo, k2] to end.
Round 32:	[K5, k2tog, yo, k3] to end.
Round 33:	[(K1, k2tog, yo) twice, k4] to end.
Round 34:	[K3, k2tog, yo, k5] to end.
Round 35:	[(K2tog, yo) twice, k6] to end.
Round 36:	[K1, k2tog, yo, k7] to end.
Round 37:	[K2tog, yo, k8] to end.

Directions

Using Simple Ring method (see *Pattern Notes*), CO 8 sts. There are 9 sts on needle, including loop formed at beginning of CO. Divide sts between needles and join to begin working in the round. After first few rounds have been worked, pull strand which forms beginning loop to tighten.

As number of sts increases, switch to shorter US #4 circular needle, then to longer US #4 circular needle, as necessary.

Sections 1–3

Round 1:	K9.
Round 2:	[K1, yo] to end. 18 sts.
Rounds 3–5:	K18.
Round 6:	[K1, yo] to end. 36 sts.
Rounds 7–12:	K36.
Round 13:	[K1, yo] to end. 72 sts.

Section 4

Rounds 14–16:	K72.
Rounds 17–21:	Work Rounds 1–5 of Strawberry Pattern.
Rounds 22–25:	K all sts. *Round 26:* [K1, yo] to end. 144 sts.

Section 5

Rounds 27–28:	K144.
Rounds 29–48:	Work Rounds 1–10 of Bleeding Heart Pattern twice.
Round's 49–50:	K144.
Round 51:	[K1, yo] to end. 288 sts.

Section 6

Round 52:	[K144, m1] twice. 290 sts.
Rounds 53–57:	K290.
Rounds 58–94:	Work rounds 1–37 of Madeira Pattern.
Rounds 95–100:	K290.
Round 101:	[K1, yo] to end. 580 sts.

Section 7

Note: While working Section 7, place beads randomly throughout. See *Pattern Notes* online RE: placing beads.

Rounds 102–115:	Using US #8 circular needle, [yo, k2tog] to end.
Rounds 116–129:	Using US #9 circular needle, [yo, k2tog] to end.
Rounds 130–143:	Using US #10 circular needle, [yo, k2tog] to end.
Rounds 144–157:	Using US #10 circular needle, [yo, k2tog] to end.
Round 158:	Using US #11 circular needle, [k1, yo] to end. 1160 sty. Loosely BO all sts.

Finishing

Weave in ends, but do not cut tails. Immerse shawl in lukewarm water until saturated. Block center of shawl (sections 1–6). Block section 7 by gently spreading flat with hands, but do not pin. Border will not lie perfectly flat; edge should curl slightly. Allow to dry completely. Unpin shawl and trim yarn tails.

Pattern © 2009 Bethany Kok

Nell and Ben's Grilled Lobster Tails with Orange Butter Sauce

For the first Friday-night dinner in *The Wedding Shawl*, Ben grills lobster tails for family and friends and bastes them with Nell's special orange butter sauce. It's a hit with all! (Serves 8)

8 6-ounce tails
2–3 sticks unsalted butter
2 tablespoons lemon juice
2 tablespoons orange juice
Grated orange zest from one medium-sized orange
Grated lemon zest from one medium-sized lemon
¼ teaspoon chili powder
1 tablespoon fresh ginger, grated
¼ cup chopped parsley
2 tablespoons capers (optional)
Freshly ground black pepper and salt to taste

Preheat grill to a hot temp. Oil grill racks lightly.

Melt butter in a saucepan over medium heat, and stir in the lemon and orange juice, zest, ginger, chili powder, capers, and parsley. Simmer until butter is melted. Add salt and pepper to taste.

Prepare lobster tails: Cut away the membrane on the underside of each tail, stopping when you reach the fantail at the end. Pull gently apart and insert a metal skewer lengthwise into each one to prevent them from curling up as they cook. Salt and pepper the tails and brush the meat side lightly with the warm butter sauce.

Grill the lobster tails shell side up for 10 minutes, then turn the tails over and spoon the butter sauce over the meat. Continue cooking until the meat is no longer translucent in the middle, about 8–10 minutes more. Ben says to watch the tails carefully so they don't overcook.

Arrange tails on a platter, flesh side up, and serve with small bowls of the remaining butter sauce for dipping.